MALEDICTE

MALEDICTE

Lane Robins

BALLANTINE BOOKS

NEW YORK

A Del Rey Books Trade Paperback Original

Copyright © 2007 by Lane Robins

Published in the United States by Del Rey Books, an imprint of The Random House Publishing Group, a division of Random House, Inc., New York.

DEL REY is a registered trademark and the Del Rey colophon is a trademark of Random House, Inc.

ISBN 978-0-345-49573-0

Library of Congress Cataloging-in-Publication Data
Robins, Lane.
Maledicte / Lane Robins.
p. cm.
"A Del Rey Books trade paperback original"—T.p. verso.
978-0-345-49573-0 (pbk.)
I. Title.
PS3618.O3177M35 2007
813'.6—dc22   2006035571

Printed in the United States of America

www.delreybooks.com

2 4 6 8 9 7 5 3 1

Designed by Stephanie Huntwork

To Jane Gunther for always asking—did you get any writing done?
There wouldn't be a book without you

Why should you love him whom the world hates so?
Because he loves me more than all the world.

—Edward II, Act I, sc. iv
Christopher Marlowe

·ACKNOWLEDGMENTS·

NOTHING IS CREATED in a vacuum. So, thank you to my family, who never once said, You want to do what? To Odyssey Workshop and Jeanne Cavelos for showing me that I not only could write day in day out, but love doing so. To Larry Taylor for endless patience and invaluable critiquing when I needed it most. Thanks also to Caitlin Blasdell and Fleetwood Robbins for their enthusiasm, support, and excellent efforts on my behalf. All of it is deeply appreciated.

The Stirring of Wings

*I*N THE SOUTHERNMOST TIP of the island kingdom of Antyre, a carriage set a rapid pace through the city streets of Murne. The horse-and-four racketed down the broken cobblestone street, shuddering and jolting on the uneven surface. Midmorning sunlight lanced off the blue-lacquered carriage, lighting it like a jewel in a tarnished crown. On either side, narrow houses listed and shed fragments of their façades, littering the streets below with rubble. Once this had been a prosperous merchant neighborhood, the most common thoroughfare between the palace and the sea—before a girl's prayer had been heard by Black-Winged Ani, that treacherous god of love and vengeance.

Once the road had been filled with horse carts and carriages, a throbbing artery pulsing with bustle. Now, corpselike, it rotted; the ground crumbled beneath the ruined buildings and cobbled streets, homes for those desperate enough to live in the merchants' Relicts.

Inside the coach, an elaborately dressed dark man clenched his hands into fists. Kritos stared at the far wall of the coach, ignoring the Relicts outside, his thoughts occupied entirely with his grievances. He cursed himself for an overobedient fool, and he cursed Last and the man's filthy sense of humor.

Kritos levered himself out of the quilted seat, reaching for his stout malacca cane, which had been flung, haphazard, across the coach. Recovering it, he pounded the roof of the carriage. "Slow down, you damned fool. You'll have the wheels off and I'll have your hide."

Slow down, he thought. He was in no hurry to find the boy who meant an end to his comfortable position as Last's heir. He raised the cane, hesitated.

He could order the carriage around now. Tell Last that there was no boy, that the bastard son had died, unwanted, in Antyre's Relicts.

He lowered the cane, indecision and fear warring in his belly. John Coachman would know, damn his eyes, and the boy might surface on his own, seeking his birthright. If the boy lived, Last would find him, no matter what Kritos told him. Last was too well aware of the creditors hounding Kritos to trust his word alone.

His hands knotted around the cane as he pondered more drastic measures. The boy was only a boy, and he was a strong man and armed. Hefting the cane, he swung it in short, brutal strokes, slamming it against the cushioned seat with a satisfying impact. If the boy were dead—

But his hands clenched again in a paroxysm of stifled frustration. Last did not trust him, and Kritos knew well enough that the coachman had undoubtedly been warned to prevent such a thing.

Inevitability slumped his broad shoulders, made him discard his plans with a breath that sounded like a sob. Last was a treacherous bastard, he thought, wholly without irony.

Ahead of the coach, the cobblestones had been worn to a bare edge around what once was a central square, its pits filled in with scavenged rubble, smoothed over with dirt. In it, the Relicts children circled one lad with a stick, watching with an intentness that betrayed that this was no game the children played.

"So you hit 'im onna head, then inna cods, inna belly, and onna head again, 'til they don't never get up no more. Then you cut their purse, innit right?"

"Right, Roach," they chorused. But Roach sought his approval from the two youths standing apart, in a closed circle of their own. He stood, shifting from dusty foot to dusty foot, waiting.

What did they look like, these leaders of children? Children themselves, though not for very much longer. In a year or so, they'd be hunting up a new trade: highwayman, whore, gaolbird, or hangman's bait if they were particularly unlucky. Currently, they appeared much like the others. Rag-clad, barefoot, begrimed, and feral. One was, perhaps, blond under the dust and dirt. The other was as dark as night, with eyes of the same hue, startling and dramatic in a pale, pinched face. No amount of filth could darken hair like that any further.

The might-be-blond had vivid blue eyes and a placid face. He was bigger by a head than his snarl-maned companion. This was Janus, the unknowing object of Kritos's search.

Janus ignored Roach's demand for approval, studying instead his friend's dusty, extended fists. Janus reached out, ready to choose, ready to tap one fist over the other, and paused. Raising his gaze to the smirking silent mouth, to the mocking eyes, Janus touched the brunette's lips, winning the game.

The brunette stuck out a pink tongue, and on it a ring quivered—tarnished, but undeniably gold. The children's eyes lingered on it enviously. A man's ring, it was a little too big for his forefinger, but Janus slid it on, clenching his hand around it. He smiled.

Only then did he turn his attention to the waiting Roach. "You'll never learn, Roach." His voice was roughened with the onset of manhood, and the accent was as different from Roach's as night was from day, elegant, cleanly spoken, not the gutter patois of the other.

"So what'd I forget?" Roach asked.

The brunette, freed from silence, burst into speech. "The same thing you forgot last time and the time before. The shoes. Always remove their shoes. Good shoes sell." Accented like Janus's, an aping of the aristocracy, her voice held a bite to each word that made it utterly distinctive.

"Sorry, Miranda."

"Regret will not put food in your belly when the stolen coin runs out. Then it's back to stealing and whoring again."

The pack tightened, shifting from predators to an assortment of frightened children.

Roach stepped out of the circle. "I'm no whore."

"Not yet," Miranda said, unrelenting.

"Not never," he swore.

"It's his belly, let him learn," Janus said. He fingered the ring and stared at the other children, the fallen houses, the gaping sinkholes, like a young lord surveying the ruin of his empire, holding court one final time.

Carriage wheels clattered, sparking unusual echoes on this forgotten street, and sprayed jagged shards of stone in their wake. At the carriage's approach, the children scattered, only re-forming the pack when it came to a sliding halt. The horses reared in their traces before settling down to heave giant, wet-flanked breaths.

The children perched in empty windows, on piles of broken cobbles. Their thin fingers clenched sticks and loose stone, waiting in silence.

The liveried coachman put one hand on his pistol, one on his whip, daring them to act. Freed of his touch on their reins, the horses danced and bridled until the coachman snapped his whip above their heads.

Kritos stepped from the carriage, sleek in his embroidered finery. Feral eyes grew warily speculative, and Kritos paused, boots still on the carriage rung. He pulled a linen handkerchief from his sleeve, damped with scent, and pressed it to his nose and mouth for a moment.

"Which of you miserable bastards is Janus, son of Celia?"

At this sign of specific interest, Roach and the pack spooked and fled like a burst of hunted doves. Miranda and Janus stayed. Their faces might have been made of the same stone as the houses—blank and still, hiding secrets.

Kritos took the last step down. His mouth twisted as his champagne-shined boots slid in the greasy dirt. "Is one of you Janus?"

Miranda spoke first. "How much to show you where he is?"

Kritos didn't listen to her past his first start of surprise at her accent. His eyes fixed on Janus, on the echoes of Last in Janus's straight jaw and nose, in the gas-flame blue eyes. So this was the prize he was sent to secure. His replacement. The murderous temptation rose again, but Kritos, the strong man, felt distinctly leery of tackling this pair.

While he contemplated, he watched Janus watching Miranda. Signals flowed like water between them, a code learned in faint lifts of eyebrows, of tightened lips and tilted chins, of twitched fingers. No, he had no intention of giving his back to these hellions.

"Pay you," he said, "when I can thrash the information from you?"

"Like to see you try," Miranda said.

"Like to see you catch us," Janus said.

Their lovely aristocratic voices made the words a taunt. Their bodies tensed like strung wire, poised for flight and the shelter of the labyrinthine alleyways. He would have to lull them, let them presume he abided by their rules, all the better to take them by surprise.

Kritos said, "How much?"

"Not so poor as copper. Not so dear as sols," she said.

"Lunas," Janus said.

"Silver? For a gutter-born bastard?" Outrage thickened Kritos's voice and drew Miranda's lips into a cold approximation of a smile.

"Pay what is fair for us. Not for you," she said.

"One luna, then. When you lead me to him." Kritos pressed the scented linen to his mouth.

"Done," Janus said.

Kritos paused, wary. The haggling ended too soon; Kritos had expected them to demand the coin up front, expected them to lose him in the Relict's nooks and alleys. He knew they had no more intention of fulfilling the bargain than he did; for them to agree meant they were not content with the thought of a single luna. They wanted it all.

"We'll lead you." She eeled off, followed by Janus. Neither looked back, the challenge implicit as they entered the narrow, dark alley torn between two houses.

Kritos set his shoulders, judging their span against the gap. The coachman leaned off his perch. "Sir, be careful."

"Do you think me feared of urchins?" Kritos blustered. "Hold the cattle for my return."

Kritos was not afraid, not now when the moment was imminent. Undoubtedly, they planned to trap him, but they had let him take their backs, left themselves at risk.

Caught in his thoughts, squinting in the murky light of the alleyway, Kritos saw the girl brush by the wall, a shadow in the dark; a spill of stones tumbled free, driving at his head. *You'll need more than that, girl,* he thought, leaping aside. The ground gave beneath his feet.

The cascade of stone hadn't been the ambush; the loosely covered pit had. Kritos hit the bottom hard, rolled to his feet, found himself chest-deep in the ground, with damp stone beneath. It was probably the only reason the pit didn't go deep enough to break a man's neck.

He raised his cane just as the girl swung her stick at him, striking the soft tissue beneath his chin. Kritos gagged with pain; his teeth snapped against each other. Slapping her legs with the cane, he made her dance away, but she reversed her grip on the stick, making up the distance, and jabbed the end of it at his face. Kritos jerked and took the blow meant for his temple in his eye instead. Pain flared, and fear. Howling in shock, he flailed with his cane, but couldn't avoid the blow from behind that forced him to his knees.

"His purse, Miranda, hurry," Janus said.

"He's not down yet," Miranda protested.

"Near enough to make no difference, and the coachman might come after him. With the pistol."

Miranda pounced, fingers working on Kritos's purse strings. Janus squeezed beside her to help. Wheezing for breath, tears streaking his face, Kritos fumbled for a weapon and found rough stone at his hand, one of the little avalanche that betrayed him. He swung, felt satisfaction push pain away when the rock made contact.

Miranda screamed, a banshee yelp of rage and shock, and her hands flew to cover the bloody gash along her jaw.

"Bastard!" Janus brought his stick down again, knocking the rock from Kritos's hand, and reaching for the purse himself.

Kritos lunged upward, got a grip on Janus's white throat, and held on. After three stifled breaths, Janus's face started mottling with lack of air. Miranda scrabbled for her dropped stick, and Kritos leaned back against the supporting wall and kicked her in the stomach. She flew backward and stunned herself against the stone.

Janus clawed Kritos's hands, then groped upward, gouging at the man's damaged eye. His thumb slipped along the same rut the girl's stick had made. Kritos screamed and slammed Janus against the earthen and stone wall, dazing him. Kritos kept the boy's slackening form before him, using him as a shield, and struggled to his feet, sobbing with pain and anger. His stranglehold on the boy's throat loosened, and Janus showed signs of recovering.

Miranda crept forward, barely visible against the pit's floor, her hands fisted. She reared back on her haunches; pebbles and dirt stung Kritos's face, and he kicked out again and caught her in the thigh. She tottered and fell at his feet. He kicked her in the face, and she made a small, sighing sound, eyes fluttering shut.

Kritos tightened his grip on Janus's neck, squeezing. The boy choked and spluttered, his nails leaving tracks on Kritos's wrists. Behind him, the girl muttered and swayed to her hands and knees. Kritos swore. If he took the time to kill the boy, she'd be on him again with the tenacity of a weasel.

Kritos pulled Janus after him, dragging him out of the pit, keeping his watering good eye on the dark shape in the dark pit. He backed up, dragging Janus into the uncertain sunlight of the Relicts. The coachman pulled his pistol and swore.

"Put that away," Kritos said. "Get ready to go." Janus had a neck like a young ox, and Kritos's hands were slick with his own blood. Janus muttered and twisted, made every step a battle, digging at Kritos's hands with his own, fumbling at his face, slumping and dragging his weight to slow him. The ring, so newly acquired, slipped and fell into the dirt without a sound.

Kritos resolved his struggle by slamming Janus's head into the edge of the carriage doorframe and dropping the sprawling, limp form onto the floor of the coach. Janus fell half-in, half-out, his bare feet trailing in the gritty dust.

The coachman warned, "Last never said nothing about half-killing nobody."

"Last never had to deal with that hellcat," Kritos said, panting for breath, shuddering all over with belated nerves and denied fear. His hands shook as he bent and forced Janus's slack limbs into the carriage. His face throbbed as the maltreated eye complained and continued its slow weeping of bloody tears.

He clambered into the carriage, uncertain in his balance, and paused, his back to the open door, to kick Janus once, then twice in the ribs, listening for the crack of bone. It was all the vengeance he could allow himself, and it was out of sight of the coachman.

The coachman's cry came nearly too late. Kritos spun, but too slowly, his vision too impaired to see more than a quick dark blur.

The stick caught him in the side, punched through the skin but no further. It was, after all, only a piece of well-worn wood. "Let him go. Pervert. Thief." Even with her voice shrill and panicked, her accent remained unchanged, and for the first time Kritos wondered who the girl was.

From his high perch, the coachman angled his pistol, trying to get a clear shot. He pulled the trigger; the gun exploded, the ball expelled forward, burning powder and shards of metal flying back to scald the coachman's hand. Kritos flung Miranda from him at the same moment, and the ball bypassed Miranda to add yet more stone chips to the earth.

As she lunged at him again, the coachman ripped the air with his whip and wrapped the lash around her chest, spinning her around, leaving her in the dirt, gasping, sniveling, nose running blood.

The sight of her sprawled in the rubble did more to restore Kritos's courage than the coachman coiling his whip for another blow.

"You must want your silver," Kritos said.

He flung his coin purse into her face; the leather pouch burst at the seams and scattered his own trap—the silver lunas that were only painted wood. "What he's worth. Coachman, drive on."

The carriage turned slowly in the open square and headed back the way it had come, faster and faster, as the coachman gave the spooked horses their heads.

LEFT ALONE, Miranda gathered her stick and the tarnished ring with shaking hands. Her head spun and her jaw burned where grit had been ground into the open wound. The whip marks crossing her torso through the thin, ripped shirt seeped. And all of that pain was nothing to her. All she could think of was Kritos, carrying Janus away like a hunter's trophy.

She limped over to the edge of the street and fell, her blood dampening the dirt. She waited for the strength in her legs to come back, and she turned the tarnished ring over and over and over in her hands, peering in to see the words within. *Only each other at the last.* Heart pounding, breath seizing in her chest, refusing to cry, she clenched the ring in fisted hands and curled herself around it.

WHEN HER BREATH RETURNED, she rose and stumbled home—a room with two women, one old bed, a press of mismatched clothing, and some few bits of furniture salvaged out of some refuse bin closer to the civilized parts of the city and hauled back to the Relicts.

Nearest the door, a pale, enervated woman swayed in her seat, her hand loosely caging a bottle of Petal, a potent mixture of Laudable syrup and cheap spirits that turned any grief to a distant dream. She stared into the air as if she could see her past unfolding behind her, her days as the pampered daughter of a lord. Before Janus. Before the stigma of bearing a child, unwed, sent her to the Relicts to find a new life as occasional whore and mother, though she was dismal at both. Her customers only ever visited once, and that for the novelty of fucking an aristocrat. Her sole act of generosity had been to teach the children to read and write, though she leavened that by raining stinging slaps whenever their accents faltered into Relicts cant.

The other woman, Ella, sat on a rough footstool near the fire, coaxing it into life with callused hands. She had been at her peak of attractiveness when she birthed Miranda, fourteen long years ago, and her looks had faded to nonexistence. Her hair, coarse, gray, and unconfined, stood out in rough snarls. But unlike Celia, she could at least manage a gap-toothed smile and a bit of routine coquetry for her progressively more infrequent customers.

Miranda banged the door shut and came in, leaning on her stick. When Miranda moved into the dim glow of the fire, Ella's mouth twisted in dismay. "Not your face. What have you done, child?" Ella cried.

Miranda's rage simmered. Both women were too worn to be successful whores. But Miranda was meant to be a courtesan, meant to pass her earnings on to the older women.

Ella rushed to the clothespress and pulled out a wooden box. In a different world, it might have held a lady's less valuable jewels. Here it held the tricks of a whore's trade: powders and cosmetics, abortifacients, and a scattering of remedies. She dragged Miranda before the footstool, tutting and fretting.

Miranda yanked her arm free. "Celia, they took him."

The pale woman roused herself to a reluctant semblance of life, setting the bottle on the earthen floor. "And who took him from you?"

"A town buck in a blue and gold carriage with a crest." Miranda kept her voice calm, but tears welled with the effort. She was only waiting for the vital information—a name. Without an identity, there was no one to fight.

"Last, it seems," Celia said, picking up her bottle and letting the thick fluid trickle into her open mouth.

"Last?" Miranda said. The name meant nothing, a word in a ring. It should have sounded in her ears like a clarion. But her enemy's name meant nothing. Ella took the opportunity to pull her close, dabbing the long rip along Miranda's jaw with powdered alum before packing it with saved cobweb.

"How do I get him back?" Miranda asked, breaking in that instant years of tradition. She and Janus had learned long ago that their mothers had no answers to the slightest of dilemmas.

"Hush," her mother said. "Don't you talk while I'm cleaning this out."

"Get him back?" Celia repeated. "Why? He only caused us pain and trouble. Let he and Last spite each other and spare us."

" 'Tis a pity about the scarring there'll be," Ella said, finishing her ministrations and turning Miranda's face in her hands, judging the results. "Still— such eyes, such a mouth . . . what a price you'll command and never mind the scar. And with Janus gone, well, you'll get over that stubbornness of yours and do as I say."

Miranda screamed, an animal cry of wordless rejection and rage. She shoved her mother with enough force to send the older woman to the floor. Celia's hooded eyes widened even in her drug-induced haze. Miranda dropped her hand to the rough-edged knife her mother used to shave bits of wood for the fire, knotted her fist around the handle. How dare they simply dismiss him as if he were of no more importance than a customer? She would make them regret their callousness. She stood, hand shaking, body tensed, waiting for release; then, unclenching her fingers, she let the knife fall.

Why kill them? she thought. At this moment, they were dead to her, and she knew that without Janus, without her, the two women would fade away. The rage faded as fast as it came, leaving contempt. She despised their sickening passivity, their languid acceptance of their decaying lives. She would not accept the same.

Miranda paused in the doorway, taking a long last look. She was leaving now. She would never see these women, this room again. She would not rue it.

Night had folded over the Relicts, and the only lights were the small fires set by the desperate, conflagrations of wood and burning cloth. Miranda felt her way down the street with her stick, tapping before her like the blind beggars who worked the boundary between moneyed and poor.

A name was all she had, and it was not enough, but she headed for the border of the Relicts as if she were welcome on the other side. In the worst section, while climbing over fallen masonry, she put her foot through a toppled door, spiderwebbed with rot, and tumbled headlong. She plummeted down the heap, scraping her hands, her shins, and landing with a painful crash against a stone slab. She fought tears, tried to rise, but stumbled and fell to one knee. Her breath labored and the wounds of the day, so long suppressed, made themselves felt with belly-wrenching intensity. Clawing at the stone slab, her fingers caught on rough frescoes, and she drew herself up, found it was a wall. Leaning close, she made out wings and knew what the building was, though she'd never seen it before.

The room was even more damaged than most Relict buildings; the walls had all fallen inward, making a precarious lean-to of stone, but then, this was a temple to Black-Winged Ani, She who had spread ruin through the Relicts. Carved wings created a slanted tunnel, which Miranda crept through. Her destination was the altar. But not to pray for a dead god's aid. Even in this extremity, Miranda was not stirred to begging.

The altar was the sturdiest place in the temple, sheltered deep within the wreckage. Miranda crawled beneath it, let her body relax. In the darkness, the grinning face of Black-Winged Ani stared down at her from every angle. Miranda tucked herself into a ball, wrapping herself around the stick, missing Janus's warmth with an ache greater than the throbbing wounds. She fell asleep to the whispering mutter of prayers, trapped like memories in the stone, fell asleep to Ani's looming scrutiny.

Outside, a cold wind rose.

NESTLING

Maledicte lived and Maledicte died
And only at his birth did anybody cry.
How many people did he kill?
One, two, three . . .

          —Children's skipping song

BARON VORNATTI WAS AN OLD MAN, hunched in his chair, staring at the wonders of his extensive library with a jaded and bleary eye. A sable pelt poured over his wasted legs. Absently, he ruffled the furs while he flipped pages of the book of pornographic woodcuts on his lap. A hedonist and a sensualist, he was much withered by time and pain; on a cold winter's night, he fondled old memories as he once did flesh. But all his precious memories, of women's softly rounded shoulders and mounded breasts, the sweet juncture at their thighs, of young men's ripe buttocks, greedy mouths, and strong square hands, all these could not distract him as they used to do.

His back flared and spasmed. His glassy eyes flew to the old grandfather clock by the door. "Gilly," he roared. "Time!"

Grinding his teeth, Vornatti sagged forward in the chair to ease the strain. The book fell to the floor, splayed on opened pages. He wanted a distraction, something beyond the torment of his bones and illusory remembrances of the flesh. Once, he had found engrossment in the bloody game of court intrigue, but even that had palled with his mastery of it.

In the distant recesses of the library, beyond the firelight, beyond the lamps, glass broke with a sound like cracking ice. Slow, crunching footsteps echoed.

A chill serpent of air wound around Vornatti's ankles, hissing with blown snow.

"My lord?" Gilly said from the doorway. The large silver tray of drug and drink was dwarfed in his hands. His voice put a temporary stop to the footsteps.

"We have an intruder," Vornatti said, straightening with a wince.

"Who's there?" Gilly said, as the footsteps resumed their slow progress, now thudding against the bare wooden floor. He squinted against the glare of the built-up fire, set the tray down on the thick carpeting beside Vornatti.

The footsteps gained the carpet and disappeared in the muffling softness. Gilly lifted a book pole, holding it across his chest, the hook facing the shadows.

"Put it down, damn it, Gilly. Put it down, and give me my Elysia. Let the bastard wait."

Gilly hesitated, but finally set the book pole back against Vornatti's chair.

He bent, turning his back to the shadows, and cradled Vornatti's withered arm against his own. He drew the Elysia into the glass syringe in a cloudy swirl that held something of its origin in it, the elixir left in Naga's serpent-scaled wake. Letting it settle long enough so that the contents stopped their eddying, Gilly pushed the needle into the old man's ropy veins. Vornatti closed his eyes as Gilly worked the plunger, hissed against the bite of it in his blood.

When Gilly looked up, they were no longer alone in the circle of firelight. The intruder shared it with them. It was only a boy, shivering in his thin shirt, blue at the lips. He had shadowed eyes, made darker by a cropped tumble of black curls that seemed to spread shadow out behind him. A thin scar sliced along the left side of his jaw, and he held his right hand behind his back.

Vornatti's eyes opened and he smiled as if a bit of his past had come back in salacious detail.

"What young toothsome have we here?" he murmured, lazy on a release of pain and burgeoning euphoria. "Gilly, only look what the gods have brought me."

"Be silent, old man," the boy said, drawing his arm from behind him. In his hand was a sword.

And such a sword. It was black-bladed, black-hilted. The pommel was a burnished mirrorstone, and the edges were so sharp as to seem blurred in human sight. The cross-hilt was made of stilled, dark wings with wickedly edged feathers more reminiscent of daggers than of flight. Like some remnant from the god-touched times, the sword radiated presence beyond its workmanship.

"Are you Last?" The boy raised the sword, its glitter matched by the wildness in his eyes.

Vornatti wheezed into laughter, slapping Gilly's arm, startling him. "Last."

The boy's face grew red temper lines around the jaw and nose. The scar flared to whiteness. "Don't laugh at me." He pushed the blade forward; Vornatti parried with the book pole, still laughing despite the slice the sword had carved in the wood.

Gilly stepped between Vornatti and the blade, and Vornatti stilled his laughter. "There is more than one noble house in Graston. No, boy, I am not Last. Look here." He thumped the end of the pole on the carpet. "Gilly, get your big feet out of the way and fetch us all drinks."

He stabbed at the floor again. "See that, boy?"

The carpet was burgundy and blue, and in the center a fantastical creature writhed in golden embroidery.

"I am Vornatti, *Baron* Vornatti, since you are not likely to know that. An Itarusine subject, now living in Antyre; Aris's brother-by-law, and accountant. The winged serpent is my crest; Last's crest is a twisted hourglass, and his motto is 'only a Last at the last.' Smug bastard."

"Who's Aris?" the boy said.

"Our king," Gilly said, carrying the tray to the table.

"Oh. Him." The boy studied the elaborate embroidery on the carpet, the slippers Vornatti wore, the crest imprinted on the spine of the long-forgotten book.

"Are you listening, boy?"

The boy didn't answer, but his dark eyes flickered to Vornatti's face, studying the sagging, spotted flesh, the dark rheumy eyes. He let the sword point lower to threaten the floor. "Where do I find Last?"

"What sends you seeking him, blade in hand? Answer me that, first."

The boy frowned, but visibly needed the answer too badly to play coy. "Last took Janus from me, and left me for dead. I will return the favor, reclaim Janus and leave Last dead. Though I will be less careless and see his heart stop before I go."

So much emotion was invested in the reply that it seemed a cantrip or incantation, and as rote as a nightly prayer. It silenced Vornatti, and the only sound was Gilly and the chinking of crystal as he poured the requested drinks.

"I doubt that was Last himself," Vornatti said. "He so rarely soils his hands, and is far more dedicated to a task once undertaken. If it were Last, make no doubts, you would be dead, boy. But who is Janus to warrant such attention?" Vornatti took the goblet Gilly offered him, sipped at the steaming negus. He gestured to Gilly, and Gilly turned the second goblet, the glass meant for him more usually, toward the boy.

Distrust furrowed the boy's features, and he finally said, "The earl of Last's bastard son."

"Last has no living children," Vornatti said.

Gilly pressed the cup into the boy's left hand, spoke to Vornatti. "There were rumors. You remember. Celia Rosamunde, the admiral's daughter."

"Oh. Her." Vornatti mocked the boy's earlier words. "That weak-willed, wanton wench." He laughed at his own wordplay, and to Gilly's surprise, even the boy flickered a bitter smile.

"I thought she died," Vornatti said.

"She was disowned and abandoned when her condition became evident. I heard she made her way to the Relicts and died there."

"Not yet," the boy said. Across the room, the boy's stomach growled audibly. He raised the goblet, and swallowed three great gulps of the sweetened, spiced wine, throat working. Making a face, he dropped the goblet to the carpet.

Vornatti shifted his slippers away from the spreading stain. "If you didn't want it, all you had to do was give it to Gilly," Vornatti said, without heat, his mind occupied. "He reclaimed his bastard son? I had heard that Last's newest wife died of childbed fever and the babe of milksickness."

"This talk means nothing," the boy said. "Tell me where to find Last." He dragged the sword point up to menace Vornatti once more.

"Let's have less of that," Vornatti said. "It grows wearisome. I will tell you what you want to know, for all the good it will do you. Last's estate is yet ten miles from here. Will you walk it in ice and snow?"

The boy's face sagged into momentary despair, and then the determined mask slid back into place. He started for the door.

Vornatti caught his arm with a sudden movement, surprising in a man so seemingly infirm. "Stay the night," Vornatti said. He stroked the boy's scarred cheek.

The boy jerked free, no longer listening, caught up in his own thoughts, bent on following some inner drive that denied obstruction.

"Gilly," Vornatti commanded.

Reluctantly, Gilly roused himself to comply, though had he a choice, he'd be relieved to see the boy's back. Still, obedience was ingrained, and he stepped before the boy, keeping a wary eye on the boy's sword hand. "Come on then. Humor the old bastard and stay."

The boy halted, staring at Gilly. "Get out of my way." Shadows danced in the depths of his eyes, and Gilly stepped out of easy harm's range. Still, he balked the boy at the door.

Gilly was good at anticipating his Lord's requests. From the moment that Vornatti smiled at the intruder, Gilly knew he desired the boy. Other intruders had been summarily and unpleasantly dealt with, the pistol fished out from beneath Vornatti's lap furs, not teased to flushing. With that in the forefront of his thoughts, Gilly had drugged the boy's negus, the Laudable's sticky sweetness masked by the honeyed spice of the heated wine. Gilly was surprised the boy still stood. A single mouthful should have been enough to incapacitate one skinny youth.

Still more surprising was the force of the boy's presence. Gilly found it harder and harder to keep himself blocking the boy's egress. Only Vornatti's expression of cupidity and interest kept Gilly still. Vornatti's mood could shift like the tide; he'd grow bored soon enough with the filthy, bad-tempered lad, but until that moment occurred, Gilly had best obey or suffer Vornatti's own bad temper.

"I'll pay you," Gilly said, inspired. "Enough to rent a hack to Lastrest in the morning."

The boy put out a hand, palm upward, waiting.

"In the morning," Gilly said.

His hand clutched the black hilt. "I should trust you after you've drugged the wine?"

Gilly saw it now, the slackening mouth, the loosening fingers. The signs he had expected long minutes ago—but the boy was fighting the effects of the drug with the considerable force of his will. Gilly wondered how much longer the boy could stay standing.

"I'm tired, Gilly. Show our guest to a room and be done with it." Vornatti leaned forward, creaked out of his chair, and reached for his fallen book. "The painted room, mind you."

Gilly nodded. He bowed to the young savage as if he were truly a guest, and said, "Follow me."

His back was tense with his concern that the boy was not following, and tense with the cat-feeling that the boy *was* following, albeit on footsteps too silent to hear. Gilly turned and found the boy paused in the long stone-paved hall.

The boy stared into the great, clouded mirror that hung on the gilded and flocked walls, a spot of uncertain shadow in the midst of rich colors and elaborate hangings. Touching the rippled glass, the boy leaned close, fingered his reflection.

"You are comely enough," Gilly said, wondering if the boy had ever seen his face in a looking glass before. Despite the jarring notes of sword and accent, Gilly knew the boy was no more of the aristocracy than he himself was. "But it's no assignation we head to, only rest."

"There is nothing before me but a rendezvous," the boy said, his thickening tongue slurring his words. The boy pressed his face against the cool glass, closing his eyes.

Gilly took the boy's arm, and the boy leaned against him, looked up at him with enormously pupiled eyes. "Have you seen Janus?"

"I have not. Is he fair like Last?"

"Fair," he agreed on a sigh. He tugged Gilly's blond tail of hair; his dark-fringed eyes closed, then flickered open in sudden awareness. "Bastard. I'd better get my lunas in the morning." He shoved Gilly away.

Gilly led the boy away from the mirror, and looked back over his shoulder, expecting to see the boy's reflection lingering behind, as stubborn as the boy himself.

At the painted room, Gilly unlocked the door, went inside, and lit the gas lamps. The boy stared at the furnishings in a near stupor.

The room was shadowed. The gaslight illumined only a circle the size of a man's outstretched arms, and the chamber was easily thrice that, if not more. The bed itself was a small room, walled of swagged draperies, embroidered with gilded serpents. Even to Gilly's eyes, they seemed to undulate in the wavering light; how must they appear to the drugged boy? Thick carpeting underfoot stifled sound, turning each movement into a secretive whisper. Heavy, dense curtains draped the distant walls, though Gilly knew there were no windows behind them, only the murals that gave the room its name. One drape, drawn back, revealed nothing but the image of rushing water, full of movement without progress. This room was a well-appointed prison.

The boy shivered as if he had sensed Gilly's thought, but headed for the swaddled bed as if for a long-sought rest. Gilly watched the boy clamber up the bed steps and lie down. Only then did the boy release the sword from his grip. It sprawled over the counterpane beside him like a living thing.

Gilly closed the door, drew out the key, and locked it, sealing away the boy and his sword.

The click of the bolt sliding home sounded as final as a headman's ax in the silent hall. Gilly winced, expecting the boy to rouse, sputtering curses and making futile strikes against the heft of the oaken door, but the moment passed in peace. Tucking the key into his vest pocket, Gilly returned to the library.

Vornatti waited, slumped down in his chair, too worn tonight to make the walk to his chambers without aid.

"The boy?" Vornatti said, without raising his rough-whiskered chin from his chest.

"Caged. Asleep," Gilly said.

"Good. I'm not inclined to conduct business at this hour." Vornatti pressed his hands into the arms of the chair, trying to raise himself. Though his face grayed with effort and his hands whitened, his body stayed motionless. Gilly forestalled further effort, slipping the rug from Vornatti's lap, setting the pistol aside, and, his hands beneath Vornatti's shoulders, hefted the diminished weight of what had once been a big man. Vornatti fell against Gilly's side, muttering. "Too much Elysia," he said.

"Too much winter," Gilly said. "I measure your dose most carefully." He lifted the old man into his arms like a child, chary of his grip on brittle limbs, and carried him down the hall to his quarters.

Despite the prevailing fashion for the master's quarters to be housed higher than the common riffraff of ground dwellers, Vornatti's rooms were on the main floor, dictated by his long illness, and guarded from intruders by Gilly. Gilly's footsteps grew muffled as he set foot to the thickly piled carpets of Vornatti's room.

A barbarian's bedroom, Gilly remembered thinking, when he first came to stand wide-eyed and tentative on the sill. An oddity in the kingdom of Antyre—Vornatti's bedroom had been furnished in Itarusine fashion, a carved, curved bed with high sloping sides, covered not only with Antyrrian linens, wools, and velvets, but the heavy pelts of winter snowbears, imported from Itarus at exorbitant cost.

Afraid of falling in his later years, of exacerbating the swelling in his back, Vornatti kept adding carpets, until the floor had risen high enough to make Gilly step up into the room. The fireplace along the exterior wall glowed darkly, muted by ash and spent coal. Gilly frowned at it, at the ghost of his breath in the air. He set Vornatti down on the bed, and helped him remove his dressing gown, draping it over the bedstead. He knelt and removed the slippers from his feet. Despite the homely wool stockings, Vornatti's feet were white and cold to the touch. Gilly chafed them until Vornatti drew away. "Enough, Gilly, leave me my skin."

"You're the one who complains that cold feet keep you from your rest," Gilly said, and Vornatti settled his feet back into Gilly's hands.

Vornatti tangled his fingers in Gilly's hair, pulled the tie loose, and combed his locks with gnarled motions. "My Gilly," Vornatti said, and Gilly, still kneeling, assessed the tone. Amorous? He hoped not, thought not.

He straightened, took himself away from Vornatti's caress, and drew back the linens to the scent of hot earth. The heated bricks were still warm to the touch when he tugged them out, and helped Vornatti into their place.

Vornatti stroked the skin at Gilly's throat, the soft cotton of his shirt over his chest, but the caresses were cursory. Again he stepped away from Vornatti's touch where normally he would have allowed it, or even prolonged it, making such small contact the opening move in their barter of desire and favor. He didn't need anything tonight but information, and Vornatti had always been free with that.

"Are you going to send for the magistrate? Turn the boy over to him and his workhouse?" Gilly's belly clenched with anxiety. He was worried by Vornatti's interest, by his own conviction that the boy's presence could alter the fragile balance of his life with the baron.

"That boy's too delicate for the workhouse," Vornatti said, wincing as Gilly folded back the bedding and his bones took the weight of the furs, linens, and quilts.

"You think him delicate?" Gilly asked, remembering the boy's grip on the sword, the willful refusal to give in to the drugged wine. The boy and his sword raised the fine hairs on his neck. Vornatti would not find this boy as pliable as the city whores he used to collect.

Vornatti laughed, a harsh, quick bray. "Perhaps not. But still, I intend to keep him."

"He's not a dog," Gilly said. "You can't keep people."

"Kept you, didn't I?" Vornatti said. "Found you, liked you, took you home, and here you stay."

"You bought me," Gilly said, watching the red coals of the fire dim further, the room grow more chill.

"And what's keeping me from buying him? Who knows what he'd do for food, for warmth?" Vornatti stroked the fur coverlet in a speculative fashion.

"What would you do with him?" Gilly asked.

"You saw his face and form and need ask? But don't fuss yourself; he won't replace you," Vornatti said, splitting his lips into a malevolent grin. "I've trained you to a nicety."

"Another pet then?" Gilly said, flushing.

Vornatti sighed and closed his eyes. "You know my sentiments regarding Last. Do you think I would turn that boy away? When his desires so mirror my own?"

Gilly paused in his restless tidying to sit on the bed, shaken. "You plot treason. . . ." Gilly was hushed by Vornatti's fingers tightening on his thigh, by the malevolence in his dark eyes, unwinking.

"Plotting? I do no such thing. If I aid a starveling boy, that's charity. If I give him information, that's education. All I am doing is putting the piece in play."

*F*ULL DAYLIGHT SEEPED beneath the heavy, pooled draperies in Gilly's room, waking him from a familiar dream turned nightmare. He clawed free from the winding cloths his linens had become, shuddering at their clammy touch, reminded irresistibly of the catafalques. As was not uncommon, Gilly had dreamed deep and dark, and found himself alone among the tombs of the five dead gods. Familiar, the sight of the white-shrouded coffins, the vast room around them smelling of ancient dust and decaying opulence. The carvings beneath the restless shrouds peeked through as the linens shifted with his approach, revealing the aspects and symbols he understood only while dreaming, shaping the great names: Baxit, Ani, Naga, Espit, Haith. The dead gods.

Familiar and yet— Some tremor lingered in the silent mausoleum, as if something had run through, leaving stirred air in its wake, as if something stood in the shadows of the tombs, holding an indrawn breath, preparing to speak. A single sudden thought took life in his skin, as chilling as ice water: What if the sound had been the gods Themselves, the echoes of Their final words?

The threat had been enough to wake Gilly into gasping awareness. To dream of the dead gods was a chancy thing at best; to hear Their words was a burden few mortals could bear. Gilly's mother had once lamented the timing of Gilly's birth, assuring him that such dreams should have seen him an intercessor. But the gods were gone, and Gilly's path had led him not to the contemplative life, but to a life as Vornatti's companion.

A groan shivered into the day-lit silence; the sobbing of tortured wood, and Gilly's breath seized while he tried the sound against the one he hadn't heard. The echo of forced wood, a coffin shifting. . . . Sense reasserted itself. His room was next to the prisoned boy's. That was all he heard, the boy hunting a way out of his cage. Ignoring the bed steps, he dropped to the floor and hastened to pull back the curtains.

The old woman who acted as their housekeeper had been about her rounds. The fire was newly laid, but unlit; the morning tray of tea and toast was chill to the touch. Gilly sighed. The old woman had her way of making her disapproval felt. Baron Vornatti kept city hours—late nights and later mornings. Chrisanthe might work for Vornatti's coin, but she would not compromise. The tray had been deposited with the dawn, many hours ago. Gilly hadn't seen dawn light since the time he attended court with Vornatti and they returned home with the paling grayness. The last time he woke with the dawn was before Vornatti, back on the farm, when he had dreamed in torn sheets, shared with the two brothers closest in age.

Gilly drank down the tea in a gulp; cold and overbrewed, it did nothing to soothe his nerves. Not for the first time, he considered dismissing Chrisanthe. He would do so in a heartbeat, were it not that Vornatti's reputation precluded a household of competent servants. The country servants were afraid of Vornatti; reputations were all servants had, and scandals lingered. A lad or girl who worked for Vornatti would find no other position after. The thought made Gilly shiver. Vornatti was an old man, after all, and Gilly still young. What would happen to him when Vornatti gave in to mortality?

But scandals, though they discommoded their household, also kept it a power in the king's court. One of Gilly's chores, when Vornatti could bear to part from him, was to ferret out the latest gossip, faint whispers of things not yet known. Vornatti used such information to keep himself a player in the game of politics. Bartered information and his considerable fortune kept Vornatti a welcomed presence in the Antyrrian court, rather than a shunned creature, the hated Itarusine warden.

A longer, more shuddering moan drew Gilly's thoughts back to what he had been avoiding. The boy.

Vornatti would still be sleeping, unconscious with Elysia and drink; it fell on Gilly to care for this strange guest. Gilly poured another cup of tea, lifted the tray. Hunger had been the boy's downfall last night. He would still be hungry.

Inside the room, the activity had stopped. Gilly set the tray down and listened. Silence. Gilly fished out the key, slipped it into the lock. The latch drew back with a protest. Gilly pushed the door but it refused to budge.

Shoving, Gilly pitted his not-inconsiderable strength against it. The door yielded a scant inch, and yielded it with the shuddering groan of shifting furniture. Gilly peered through the crack into the dimness beyond, jerking back as the blade slid toward him with a slow shine.

"You've barricaded the door," Gilly said.

"A prison can also repel," the boy said, his voice fierce and quiet.

Gilly sighed with enough force that his shoulders rose and fell. "And here I've brought you tea and toast." Exasperation laced his words. Overnight, he had forgotten the boy's bloody-mindedness, his irritability. Had he really expected to find the boy meekly waiting, grateful to be let out, and willing to help entertain Vornatti over a long winter? Gilly chastised himself because he had. Had thought only of the boy's hunger and obvious poverty, and not of his pride.

"You can't stay in there forever," Gilly said. He slid down and sat on the exquisitely tiled floor of the hall, tracing the leafy patterns, green and gold, with a forefinger, listening for a reply. Patience, he thought, would be the only way. As patient as he must be during Vornatti's worst megrims. But cautious, too; he took care to sit beyond the reach of the sword.

He heard a faint sound, the wild-animal complaint of a starving body, and said, "You'll get hungrier if you don't come out. And you're too thin to miss meals."

"I can live at least a week on the mice you let infest this place. Crack their heads, drink their blood, chew their flesh. Gnaw their tails, their feet when there's no meat left elsewhere. I'd last at least a week, maybe a fortnight without any aid from you."

Gilly fought a reluctant smile, a little charmed by the boy's manifest obstinance. "You'll waste that blade's edge on mice? Don't do that. Come on out," Gilly said. "Have tea, have toast; we'll see what old Chrisanthe has left for us in the chafing dishes. There is no need to barricade yourself away."

"I don't know who you are or what you want," the boy said.

"I'm just a servant," Gilly said. The usual burn touched his throat at the admittance. "I don't want anything, except for you to come out. And you have not been forthcoming yourself. Have you no name, no history?"

"None to share with a servant," the boy said.

Gilly flinched, flicked on the raw, and peered through the crack in the door again. The boy sat, wedged in between the wardrobe and bed steps that barricaded the door. He had added strength by ripping down the drapes and tying them around the blockade. He sat now in a dim cavern of cloth and wood, just barely big enough to fit him, and shivered with cold and hunger in the thin bar of light that streamed in over Gilly's shoulder.

Silently, Gilly passed a piece of toast through the crack, felt the boy take it, and waited for the complaint about the coldness of it. But either the boy's bravado was lacking, or his knowledge didn't go so far as to encompass toast and heat. He ate it in three silent bites.

"You owe me silver."

"Do I," Gilly said. "Will you trust a servant's word then?"

"You promised," the boy said.

"I did," Gilly said. "Lunas enough to get you to Lastrest, but they won't help you."

"Why?"

"It's winter, and Last will be abroad, in the Itarusine court. It is his habit. Supposedly, he loves the ice and snows, but it's an open secret that he visits only to keep abreast of the Itarusine king's schemes. Last will have emptied his house of all but a few servants, taken the rest with him. He will not be there." Gilly smiled, getting a little pleasure in the boy's body curling tighter on itself; the lad wasn't the only one who could wound with words. "You've chosen the wrong season for your hunt."

"Lies." A faint breath of air.

"I just hate to see lunas go to waste. When you could use them to buy food."

"Stop talking about food," the boy said, his voice cracking.

Repenting, Gilly passed him the rest of the toast. "I will take you to Lastrest if you must go, but you will see that I am telling the truth."

There was nothing but silence from the boy's side. Pity flared in him suddenly, seeing the boy's unwelcome choices: starvation or servitude. Was it any wonder he was uncivil?

"Stay with us," Gilly said. "The old bastard's not so bad to work for. Feeds me well, and I sleep on warmed sheets."

"Not a whore," the boy whispered, going quieter, his words fading into a bare susurration. A hissed name? Janus.

"I'll call for Vornatti's coach. It will take you to Lastrest, faster than the stagecoach, faster than a hack, and you can see that I am only telling you the truth. Then it will bring you back here."

"No," the boy said.

"Where else will you go?" Gilly said. "Even if I gave you silver, it wouldn't last you the winter."

"A ship," the boy said.

"Go abroad? After Last?" Gilly said. "I don't have enough lunas for that. And even if you did get there, it's colder there, snow all year round, and they'd kill you for your sword. Listen, boy. Listen. Vornatti would see Last ruined. Vornatti sees his vengeance in you."

Furniture stuttered into reluctant movement, and after a time, the boy eeled out the widened crack. His face was dusty and blanched beneath, his hands shaking with the effort of moving the furniture again. Gilly swallowed. Another thing he had forgotten—the uncanny effect of those dark eyes against the pallor of his skin. Vornatti would devour him entire. The sword, unsheathed at his side, twitched as if it had read Gilly's thought. The boy leaned against the wall, raised his head, and said, "You owe me lunas, still."

"How do you figure that?" Gilly said, grateful for the distraction. "I am loaning you Vornatti's coach."

"Your promise was enough lunas for a hack, without reliance on whether I took one or not."

Gilly paused a moment, surprised to find that even after what must be a severe setback to his hopes, the boy could haggle like a merchant and reason like a solicitor. Then he laughed, pleased at such an agile wit; he fished into his pocket and passed three lunas to the grimy hand.

The boy smiled, not the faint flicker from last night, but a slow thing that bloomed into a mockery of pleasure. "How enlightening. To know what my price is. Some silver, the offer of food, and nebulous mention of vengeance. I just hope the food is good."

Gilly caught his breath at the self-loathing in the boy's voice, sought for words, and finally said, "There's usually venison steaks, fresh-made bread, milk, and eggs."

He reached for the boy's elbow to escort him to the breakfast room, but the boy jerked away. Gilly gestured him down the hallway.

The boy's eyes widened in the breakfast room as Gilly handed him a loaded plate. "Here. If you want more, look on the sideboard. I'll be back presently."

It was a gamble leaving the boy alone, but Gilly thought that the food, in such quantity, would occupy the boy long enough. After all, on that first morning in Vornatti's house, Gilly himself hadn't fled. And Vornatti offered the boy more than he had ever offered Gilly—his vengeance.

Baron Vornatti was only now rousing to querulous waking. He gave Gilly no time to speak, but began issuing complaints and commands. "My hands are numb, Gilly. Rub them, get me warmed water, and some damned hot tea—that raddled bitch left the trays too early again. I want my gold dressing gown today, and it's near time for . . ." His voice trailed away and the dissatisfaction dragging his tone sharpened to anticipation. "The boy, Gilly. The boy."

"The boy is eating, and will be doing so, I judge, for some time. He is starving." Gilly yanked the bell cord, and when Chrisanthe appeared, demanded hot tea and warmed water for the washbasin. Vornatti's fire was burning low, and Gilly stoked it to life again.

Gilly poured the tea, washed the old bastard's hands with the rest of the warm water, watched the knotted fingers uncurl. He helped him into the quilted robe, found slippers for his feet, and added yet another log to the fire until it blazed. When he would have aided Vornatti to his bath, the old man shrugged him off. "I want to see the boy. See if he's worth the trouble I mean to expend on him."

In the breakfast room, the boy had finished his sampling of the chafing dishes, and paced the length of the room, pausing to stare out the windows at the blustering wind and snow. He spun at their entrance, poised to flee.

"Ah, come here, boy," Vornatti said, from the depths of the wheeled chair. "Come and let me look at you."

Catlike, the boy approached. He took his time, pausing to look at a portrait blurred with age, the ice-silvered windows, the pattern on the parquet, the engraved dishes still heating on the sideboard, making it clear that he was obeying only his own whim and that if he ended up before Vornatti, well, that was only happenstance. But he stood before Vornatti docilely enough, the sword hanging loose in his hand, waiting for the man's eyes to stop tracing his features.

"How old are you, boy?"

"Near fifteen."

"Small for your age. And slight. Do you know how to use that weapon of yours?" Vornatti said.

"Well enough to strike from behind," the boy said.

Vornatti laughed, delighted by this boy's audacity, by his blunt scheming. At least, Gilly thought, delighted by audacity in such a pleasant form.

"Don't laugh at me," the boy ground out.

"You've a lot of Itarusine blood in you, right enough," Vornatti said. "More than just your looks—it's in your very manner, that touchy pride. I don't suppose your heritage is anything more than the usual Relicts tangle of sailor and whore?"

"If my mother thought my father Quality instead of a conscripted sailor, she'd have battened on him like a lamprey. One useless woman feeding off a useless kind. Aristocrats." He spat on the floor.

"Such an insolent tongue. Once, I would have challenged you for such incivility, and you would have trembled. I was held a master of the blade in my youth," Vornatti said.

In the first act of courtesy Gilly had seen, the boy did not laugh, though Gilly saw the retort quivering on those curling lips. But perhaps it was not courtesy, only belated calculation. Gilly had invoked the specter of Vornatti's aid against Last, offered a coach to Last's estate. Would the boy jeopardize that for a retort better swallowed?

"What is your name?"

The boy ignored the question, paced back to the windows, looked over his shoulder, a black shadow against the daylight. "Will the coach travel in this snow?"

"The open coach, in this weather?" Vornatti asked. "No. Gilly, go with him, take the carriage. Take hot bricks, and wine, and furs to keep warm. It's near a day's journey in this muck." He clutched his robe tighter about him as if he could feel the bite of the wind, the snow flung from the horses' hooves.

"I can't leave you," Gilly said, though the chance of a day free from Vornatti's demands tempted him. Even if it were spent nursemaiding an entirely too irritable boy.

"Give me my Elysia and I'll doze the day with wine and books," Vornatti said.

Gilly kept his eyes lowered as he nodded, but a quick series of thoughts had crossed his mind. The boy wanted coin and a trip to Lastrest. Gilly could provide both as payment to see the problematic boy gone, without Vornatti there to object.

"Gilly, I expect you to bring our lad back safe and sound," Vornatti said, and Gilly nodded again, mutiny fading. Vornatti always knew.

He called for the carriage to be brought around, the coachman rousted from his warm rooms in the stable. Vornatti insisted that they take every precaution against the cold, and Gilly set the housekeeper to heating bricks in her oven, to filling flasks with spiced tea and a basket with food. Gilly watched the boy's face, hoping to see some hint of appreciation that all this was done for him. But the boy's face stayed blank, as sublimely arrogant as the Quality he claimed to despise.

At Vornatti's instruction, Gilly brought Vornatti's best greatcoat out from the wardrobe, a supple thing of leather and fur. Throughout all this, the boy stared out the window, his breath clouding the glass, his hand knotted around the sword.

"May I see that?" Gilly asked, his hand outstretched.

The boy twitched, his reverie shattered, the blade swinging up in startled reaction. Gilly caught it in his gloved hand, and the thick glove parted beneath the blade. A thin stripe of blood crossed his palm. "Well, it's sharp enough," Gilly said, "But you cannot continue carrying it like that. You need a sheath, or better still, leave it behind."

"And if Last is there, then what will I do? Pelt him with stones and snowballs?"

"Last will not be there," Gilly said.

"So you say. I will keep the sword by my side." But he accepted the sheath Gilly found, even suffered him to strap the belt around his narrow hips. The boy shrugged into the heavy coat Vornatti offered, allowed the man to fumble the fastenings shut.

Vornatti stood on careful legs, his fingers at the top button, soft fur touching his hands, the boy's dark hair mixed with sable. He stooped, caught the boy's tense mouth with his own, and fell back into his chair. "Travel well."

Vornatti had calculated well. The boy's face flushed red, but the sword was safely sheathed and buckled beneath the greatcoat, essentially unreachable. The boy scrubbed at his mouth with a gloved hand, stormed out of the room. Gilly followed, and despite the inherent unfairness of Vornatti, rich and powerful, controlling the boy, found himself suppressing a laugh at Vornatti's incorrigible nature, and at the would-be murderer's indignation. Perhaps they deserved each other.

· 3 ·

GILLY REGAINED HIS CUSTOMARY PLACIDITY by the time he joined the boy inside the carriage. The boy sulked in the corner, face nearly buried in the fur collar, eyes shuttered by dark lashes.

"Drive on," Gilly called. "The sooner there, the sooner back."

The coach lurched to motion. A strange, silent ride it would be, too, Gilly thought, traveling through the snowfall with a shadow for a companion. When the hiss of snow and silence numbed Gilly's ears, he determined to coax the boy out of his megrims. "Are you warm enough?" Gilly asked.

The boy turned his head to meet Gilly's eyes but made no answer, his face scornful. The boy, wrapped in fur, a hot brick at his feet, full-bellied, was probably warm for the first winter of his life.

Basic civilities having failed, Gilly tried bluntness. "Tell me about this Janus of yours."

The boy looked out at the falling snow.

"You intend to rescue him, so there must be some fondness there. Is Janus your protector? Your friend? Your brother? Lover?"

"Stop saying his name like you have a right to it," the boy said, a frantic edge to his voice. His chest heaved, visible even beneath the bulky coat, and Gilly sighed.

"You are a nervy creature. I only thought to pass the time by getting better acquainted. Since I don't know you, I asked questions, but you may ask them of me, if you prefer."

Drifting snow and the muffled rhythm of hoofbeats were the only response he got. Gilly shrugged, sank down into the seat, and composed himself for a nap.

"Are you his whore?" The question jerked him out of his doze, made heat scald his face and ears.

"All servants are such," Gilly said, taking shelter in philosophy. "We do as we're told for money, whether we want to or not. The most we can do is choose our masters."

"I'm my own master," the boy said. "And semantics aside, you're a whore."

Gilly flinched at the weary contempt in the boy's voice, reminded of the only time he went home. His father had spoken to him in just that tone. Unfair, Gilly had thought then. They'd sold him to Vornatti; what had they expected? "I—Vornatti—I obey his whims and accept his advances. Why shouldn't I? He took me from a farm that couldn't feed me, and gave me a library, good food, a room to myself, and free license when in the city." By the end of his speech, Gilly had nearly convinced himself once more of the wisdom of his bargain. "He will grant you similar gifts."

"If I please him," the boy muttered. "Make myself a toy for his whims and desires. Make myself a thing rather than a person. A possession easily replaced when he tires of it. How long have you been with him?" When Gilly choked on his answer, the boy smiled before staring out the window; his breath frosted on the cloudy glass.

Quiet minutes passed with the only sound being that of the wet impact of snow spattering the carriage like sea spume.

"How uncivil you are," Gilly said. "Vornatti's offered to aid you—"

"Catch me believing anything that an aristocrat says," the boy bit out. "They all cleave together."

"And you know so much of their ways," Gilly said, gently mocking. "Do you think you're the only one to hate Last? I promise you, Vornatti's distaste for the man runs to the bone."

At the boy's skeptical expression, Gilly said, "It's true. They met more than thirty years ago in the Itarusine court. It's a dangerous place, rife with assassin princes and poisonous noblewomen. A frozen land of coldhearted people who pride themselves on their courage, their aggression, and their willingness to do anything to see their desires met. It makes our court seem milkwater in comparison.

"For Last, only a fourth son even if of royal blood, a season in the Itarusine court was his opportunity to marry well, to gain a fortune he would not inherit on his own, perhaps make an alliance between the two courts. But Last proved too stiff-necked, too conservative in his views to thrive there, and when he met Vornatti—well, I believe they arranged a duel before they finished making their first bows to each other."

The boy gazed out the clouded glass again, seemingly uninterested, but his fingers sketched brittle shapes in the fog his breath left. Tiny crosses that could be daggers, could be swords. Gilly said, "By the time the duel became fact, Last had absorbed enough of Itarusine ways that he paid Vornatti's whore to render him insensible. When Vornatti missed the duel, Last declared him a craven. It wasn't done out of fear; Last is an admirable swordsman. Rather, it was done out of spite. It ruined Vornatti, far more effectively than even a lost duel could. It took until Xipos for him to regain his reputation."

"One thwarted duel and you think Vornatti can hate Last as I do?"

"There's more, there's always more. And far too much to explain now." It wasn't time so much that stilled Gilly's tongue as consideration. Vornatti had few weaknesses, but the reminder of his sister was one of them. Aurora Vornatti had been the old bastard's heart, the only person he loved purely. When Aris Ixion had chosen to wed her, Last had spread slander wide and far trying to dissuade him. Whispers of wantonness, of inbreeding, even of flesh turned poisonous. Aris had earned Vornatti's friendship by denying the rumors. But when the long-awaited heir proved damaged, when Aurora died of his birth, the slander rose again and followed her to the grave.

Sometimes, it seemed to Gilly that Antyre itself was trailing after her into the grave. Xipos the first blow, and Aurora a deadly second thrust. Aris seemed unable to recover from either.

Gilly frowned. If the boy hadn't known Aris, their king— "You understand about Xipos?"

After a blank, black look, during which Gilly recalled the utter self-absorption of his audience and the lack of education, he explained the Xipos War. As much as that prolonged and bloody decade could be explained. The cause was simple enough: Itarus attempted to seize Xipos and its winter ports from Antyre's grip. But the battling grew so protracted and vicious that even the gods grew sick of it, the cause of their vanishment.

The poisonous offshoot of battle, assassination, claimed the king and crown prince; the second son died on the front; and the third son, the quiet scholar, Aris Ixion, inherited a kingdom at war. Aris, who valued life more than land, acted decisively. He surrendered, no matter that the terms of concession were ruinous: tithes, taxes, forced exports to Itarus that were sold back to Antyre at a hefty profit. If it weren't for Antyre's colonies in the Explorations, Itarus would have conquered Antyre one coin at a time.

"Grigor, the Itarusine king, sent Vornatti to be Antyre's auditor and warden, which places him ideally to aid you." The boy raised his head from where he had been resting it against the cushions. "I thought that might wake you," Gilly said, smiling.

"I don't need his aid," the boy said.

"You'd be frozen back at the first hedgerow without it," Gilly countered.

The carriage came to a halt, rocking gently on its wheels in the wind and snow. The coachman leaned his snow-crowned head in, pulled the ice-crusted muffler from his mouth. His breath plumed in the still air. "Gates are closed to Lastrest, Gilly."

"Open them and drive on."

A rush of cold air greeted Gilly's words. The boy had clambered out and was floundering through the deeper snow beside the road. Gilly framed himself in the door and called out, "It's still a mile or more. Too far to walk, boy."

The boy stepped between the bars of the gate while the coachman shoved at them, trying to free the gate from the clutch of the snowdrifts. Gilly cursed and went to help. On the other side, the boy tripped over the long skirt of the coat, and sprawled, frosting the sable fur, then got up again, heading for the trackless white of the drive.

Once the gates were ajar, Gilly's longer legs allowed him to catch the boy. He grabbed the boy's shoulder and shoved him back toward the coach. "Get in. You'll freeze and Vornatti will be angry with me."

The boy's face was white, blanched by strong emotion, and he shivered under Gilly's rough grasp. "There will be no one there. Don't fuss yourself so." The boy sat with deceptive patience as the coach furrowed its way through the snow.

At the manor, the coachman pointed out the shuttered windows, the door knocker taken off the latch. "No one's here, Gilly."

"We'll ask the servants, to be sure. At the least, they might offer us some hospitality from the cold," Gilly said. He pounded on the door. Snow crusted his shoulders, and his gloved fingers had gone numb before an old man answered.

"Last has gone abroad to join his son. He will not return until the spring." The old man spoke it all in one breath, as inanimate as a puppet, and as disinterested. He started to shut the door, but Gilly leaned against it.

"Join his son?"

"Yes, the boy has been educated abroad these sixteen years, and the earl wishes to see how his lessoning has gone before he introduces him to the court." More puppetry speech, but irritation surfaced in the old man's eyes as the wind stung his exposed face.

"His *bastard* son, Janus?" Gilly said.

The butler's mouth primmed. "It is my understanding that Janus is the son of a prior, unreported marriage."

"Of course," Gilly agreed. "My mistake." *An unrecorded marriage, and a new heir for the earl of Last, a new member of the royal family?* The immensity of the news left him stunned. *A bastard—heir to the earldom, to the throne?* Gilly turned to see what the boy was making of all this, and found him gone. The door slammed at his back. "Where is he?" Gilly asked the coachman.

"Went round 'longside, like he knew what he was doing."

"You didn't stop him?"

The coachman shrugged.

Faintly, Gilly heard the chime of glass breaking. Exasperated, he hurried after the boy, stumbling in the deep footprints of his path.

The coat had been discarded, a dark blotch in the snow beside an ivy-covered wall. The ivy was brown and sere, withered by the cold, but up above a window flashed, and something weightier than ice fell to the drift beside him. Gilly stooped, picked up the shard of glass, and swore. He backtracked, pounded on the door until his hands stung with impact, but this time no one answered.

"Drive down to the gate, blanket the horses, and wait for us. I'd rather them not grow suspicious of our continued presence."

He returned to the wall of ivy and stared upward. Gilly estimated that he had at least eighty pounds over the boy, but the ivy showed no breakages from the boy's ascent. Maybe it would hold his weight, he thought. Or maybe he would plummet to the snow beneath and break a leg or his neck.

Gilly took off his coat, dropped it over the boy's, firmed his gloves around his fingers, and began to climb. Ivy leaves crumbled beneath his hands; the vines stayed firm, until, within an armspan of the window, they started to peel away from the mortar. Gilly lunged upward, hooked his hands over the sill, and pulled himself inward, landing on the dusty floor of an unused bedchamber. He wrinkled his nose, repressed a sneeze and a sneer that Last couldn't get good servants either, and set off tracking the boy's damp footprints.

He found the boy standing in the shadowed alcove of a long hallway. "What are you—"

The boy put an icy hand over Gilly's mouth, drew him into the alcove. "There's someone coming." His whisper warmed Gilly's ear.

They watched the maid carrying the bundles of whites pass them and head down distant, uncarpeted stairs.

"What are you doing?" Gilly repeated.

"Learning my enemy."

Gilly sighed. "I can tell you about him. And in the comfort of Vornatti's library. Or at his dining table if you're hungry again."

The boy wandered into the hallway, looked down the stairs into a dim long room, near bare of furnishings. "What is that?"

Gilly peered over the boy's shoulder. "Portrait gallery. Pictures of his ancestors."

"He knows what they all look like?" The boy was impressed by that, by the simple fact that the earl of Last knew who fathered him, who fathered his father, and so on, and more, could trace images of himself in their features. "I want to see." He descended the stairs and Gilly hastened after him.

The nearest panel was blank. The boy turned to Gilly, his face demanding explanation. Gilly, keeping a nervous eye and ear out, said, "That's for the next earl, the current earl's son. The portraits go by birth order."

"So this is Last?" The boy walked on to the next portrait, heading farther into the house, farther from the window and escape.

Gilly caught him up. "Yes. This is Michel Ixion, the fourteenth earl of Last."

The boy's eyes narrowed. "Is it like him?"

"Enough," Gilly said. The boy touched the painting, put his palm flat against the canvas, then drew his hand into a claw as if he might start tearing at it, as if he could slake his bloodlust on a picture. Gilly tugged the boy away, memories of rural superstition making his skin crawl, thinking of pins stuck in dolls and left on altars for godly intercession, never mind that the gods could not answer.

The boy's wrist trembled against Gilly's hand, the fine bones taut under Gilly's fingers, but he didn't resist. His eyes fell on the blank panel again and his breath caught. "This is for Janus?"

"It's unlikely. He is a bastard, no matter the story they intend to put out. It's far more likely that Last means to use Janus as a bargaining chip in his next marriage—a tangible, albeit scandalous, counter to the rumors of tainted blood."

Even as Gilly said it, he wondered, *Why legitimize the bastard at all?* It wasn't like Last, a stalwart traditionalist, to fly in the face of custom, to not only recognize his bastard son, but to legitimize him. But maybe someone had commanded him. . . . Gilly collected rumors for Vornatti, and at the heart of them was the king, that melancholy scholar who'd been saddled with the burden of the throne—a burden he could set down only for an heir. Last was no solution—only a year's difference lay between the two—and Kritos, though younger, was a wastrel, a gambler, and a fool. Perhaps Aris, trapped on his throne, dreamed of Janus.

But the three counselors would be hard to convince. Like Last, the duke of Love was a traditionalist, and would condemn Janus for the irregularity of his birth. But perhaps he could be bought; he had a marriageable daughter. DeGuerre was a believer in blood and a military man; he might accept the bloodline, and ignore the lack of marriage papers. After all, Celia was an admiral's daughter. And Westfall, despite his trappings of egalitarianism, had a young man's awe of the royal blood, even watered down. *A bastard king?*

The boy murmured at his side, waking him from his political reverie. "This could be his?"

"It is impossible to allow him the earldom and not put him in line for the throne," Gilly said. "So it's unlikely, but I suppose, if Last died suddenly—"

"He will." The boy touched the sword hilt, smiled a little, then stared at the empty spot again. "The throne. This house?" Incredulity laced the boy's voice at the idea of the house more than of the throne. Gilly understood that. The throne was so far distant from his experience it might as well be a dream, but the possibility that Janus could live in a house like this—

"The king has but one child, and that one born simple. He whiles his time away in padded nurseries, playing with dolls. There are few members left in the house of Last. The king, the earl, and their nephew, Kritos."

"Kritos," the boy said, a bare whisper.

Footsteps echoed down the hallway; Gilly snatched at the boy to drag him back up the stairs, but the boy eluded him, passed through another door. "What's this room?"

"Last's study," Gilly said. He closed the door behind them, turning the key in the lock.

The boy skimmed around the room, pocketing trinkets: an enameled snuff box, a gold-handled letter opener, a quill pen and an ink bottle, a silver paperweight, and a crystal carving of Baxit, the cat-headed god of indolence and reason. He unearthed a gilt-edged porcelain dish of old toffees and, after a quick sniff, put two in his mouth, closed his eyes, and chewed. Then he tilted the rest into his shirt. As a visible afterthought, he dropped the delicate dish into his sleeve as well. Gilly bit back a laugh. "We must go. The horses—"

The boy investigated the books on the shelves, touching brightly colored leather bindings and tracing his finger over the gilded titles. Sitting at the desk, the boy used the letter opener to pry open the locked drawer. Sheaves of paper curled out.

"Let me see," Gilly said, reading. "Creditors, debts, and bills from Kritos. Such a wastrel. Won't please Last, that's for certain." A smile quirked his lips. "Perhaps Kritos will drive Last to apoplexy and spare you the trouble."

The boy's eyes sharpened, went black with rage, and Gilly felt the smile vanish from his lips as if it never existed.

"I dream of killing him," the boy said, "his blood painting my blade, his cry in my ears as I touch his heart. . . ." His fist tightened around the hilt, fingers whitening as if he meant to withdraw it.

"Because of Janus," Gilly said, stepping back out of reach of the boy's sword, edgy again. He had almost forgotten this boy's vendetta in a strange enjoyment of this leisurely housebreaking.

"Janus," the boy echoed. Something softer warmed the bleak fury in his eyes, and his grip lessened. His face grew still and troubled; Gilly wondered what the boy was thinking on—his bloody plans for Last, or the butler's unwelcome confirmation that his prey had slipped his grasp. In this quiet state, the boy was malleable, allowing Gilly to usher him out of the study.

After a brief consideration of the state of the ivy, Gilly dragged the boy down another flight of stairs to find a ground-floor window. Gilly dropped out into the deep snow, and then held up his hands. "Come on."

"I don't want your help," the boy said, flinging himself into the snow and frost.

"At least put on your coat," Gilly said, reclaiming them from the snowbank, and flinging the boy's at him.

The boy snarled and Gilly walked on, leaving the boy to flounder his way through the drifts, hampered by the heavy coat. Gilly reached the coach long before the boy, climbed into it, and sat, sipping hot, whiskey-laced tea from the flask. The boy staggered up, white from head to toe with blown snow, and shuddering with chill. His eyelashes were frosted and his face showed signs of suspicious dampness. Gilly wondered if the boy had been crying as he fought his way down the drive.

The boy clung to the edge of the coach, panting, shaking, soaked through. Again, Gilly offered a hand. The boy flinched, put his hands over his face, and then let out a sigh. He reached out and Gilly tugged him into the coach, rapped on the roof to let the coachman know to start.

"What'd you do? Swim your way through the drifts?" Gilly asked, peeling the sodden coat from the boy's arms and back. "I've heard that in Itarus there are sports like that, where bored lordlings drag themselves behind sleighs, but I don't think even they manage to get so much snow packed into their skin." He pulled a woolen blanket from their basket, draped it around the boy, then passed him the flask. "Drink this. It'll warm you."

The boy's teeth chattered on the edge of the flask, but a faint tinge of color seeped into his cheeks after the first few gulps. He looked up at Gilly with a cringing wariness. "Can I get to Itarus?"

"If you sell everything you stole from Last's house and that sword, you might have enough. But then what? You'd be alone, hunting Last, hunting Janus in a country where you didn't speak the language. In a country of poisoners and duelists who'd make mincemeat of you before you ever reached your goal."

The boy turned his face, drew in a breath and held it. In his lap, his hands clawed at each other. "If I stay—"

"If you stay, you'll wait out the year in comfort, in warmth, fed well, with a man who can explain the ways of the court and the aristocracy—who might even aid you." Gilly took the flask away from the boy, drank another draft, more for the whiskey in it than for the warmth. He felt like a procurer.

The boy wrapped the blanket tighter and tucked his head into it, like a bird ducking its head beneath its wing.

This time, Gilly found no need to break the silence of the ride and the ever-darkening sky.

Chrisanthe greeted them at the door with a sour "He's been waiting for you. Having fits, thinking you was tipped into a ditch."

Gilly went straight into the library, shrugging off the lashings of snow that adhered to his sleeves and hair. The boy's footsteps followed, but Gilly didn't look back. The boy had to make his own decision.

He knelt down. "How was your day, old bastard? Did Chrisanthe give you your Elysia?"

"Near broke the needle off in my arm, stupid cow. But you've come back and you've brought the boy with you." He patted Gilly's cheek. "We'll feast. Stir up Cook."

Gilly returned, the cook's grumbling ringing in his ears, to hear Vornatti speaking. "Well, boy, did you find we were telling you true?"

The boy didn't reply in words; instead, he opened his pockets and showed Vornatti the small valuables he had pilfered, laying them out like offerings. Vornatti reached forward and picked up the little crystal figure. "Baxit. Not surprising. Some men are too stubborn to give up on the past."

"You can have it," the boy said. "The other things too. For my board."

Gilly raised a brow, waited for Vornatti's response, to see if he would let the boy buy himself a position as guest.

"I don't take renters. And I have trinkets enough," Vornatti said. "Keep these trifles to decorate your room."

The boy sucked in his breath, moved to the fireplace, stared out at the snow. Finally, moving as stiffly as a wounded man, he walked back toward Vornatti, hand on sword hilt. Gilly tensed, but the boy only scooped up the fallen toffees, the little dish, and took a step back.

"You're staying then?" Vornatti said, reaching out to fold his fingers in the boy's hair, caressing the dark, snow-damp locks.

The boy remained still with a small but visible effort; his eyes flickered again to the fireplace, to the fur coat shedding its icy rills of melted snow, to Chrisanthe grumbling in under the weight of a laden tray, and said, "Until spring."

4

I won't do it," the boy said, taking a step back, away from Gilly, closer to the door and escape.

Gilly, sweating with effort, emptied another iron kettle full of near-boiling water into Vornatti's bath. Pushing the steam-damp hair from his face, Gilly assessed the boy, standing as rigid as a nervy horse, looking at the sloping marble tub with every evidence of horror.

"You will," Gilly said. "You stink. And you likely have lice. Two things Vornatti doesn't much care for. You're lucky he's been as patient as he has. He had me scrubbed the very first moment he brought me home, and I was far cleaner than you."

"You die if you wash in winter," the boy said, taking another step back at the next gush of water added.

"That's ridiculous," Gilly said. "My mother scrubbed us all once a week, no matter the season. Vornatti insists on a bath daily, and you've seen his advanced age."

"I don't want a bath," the boy said, withdrawing like a repulsed cat. "If my stink keeps him away, so much the better."

Gilly grunted as he hefted another of the water-heavy kettles. "You'll have one. The only choice you have in the matter is whether you want to be held down and scrubbed—" He ignored the boy snarling and drawing the sword, and continued, "or whether I leave you here with the soap and your dignity. Think, boy—at best you'd avoid the waters tonight—but you'd find yourself drugged again, and bathed all unwitting. The baron may be an old man, but his sense of smell is keen."

Letting the last kettle fall with a clang, Gilly wiped his hands on his breeches, then opened an armoire. "There are dressing gowns here. Put one on while you dry off and you'll catch no chill. We'll find you clothes later." The boy's eyes were still wild, and Gilly sighed, let the vexation in his tone ease. He supposed, to a boy like this, brought up city-poor, immersion in water might be frightening.

"I'll leave you the key to the door. You know, boy, some people, myself included, enjoy a bath after a cold day. The water is very pleasant—as long as you don't let it grow chill." He laid the key beside the bath and left the boy, sword still drawn, staring at the steaming water.

THE CLOSING DOOR woke the boy from his stillness. Reaching forward, he closed the key in his fist, then turned to the door. He turned the key in the lock, tested the latch, then set the sword down on a wide bench. *Vornatti must sit there,* he thought, *before his bath, drawing off his clothes. No,* he thought, his mouth twisting, *Vornatti sits there and* Gilly *draws off his clothes.*

The boy touched the steaming water with cautious fingers, setting off small ripples. He put his fingers to his mouth, then sat in Vornatti's chair. Toeing off his boots, he hesitated, looking at the locked door once again. He leaned his head against the door, listening; the dense wood gave back only silence.

Gingerly, the boy rose and unfastened the rough strip of canvas that made his belt. His breeches sagged past his knees and he stepped out of them. His stained linen shirt cloaked him from neck to thigh, and after another wary moment, he pulled that off as well with the air of a conjurer.

And with a conjurer's touch, the moment changed. One moment a grubby, skinny stripling boy stood before the bath—the next, a young woman, unbinding another strip of dirty canvas from across her budding chest. Her side was mottled dark with old blood, spilled from a wound that had healed long since. She touched the flaking residue, touched the pale pink weal of the whip mark, frowning.

Taking up the soap, she held her breath, then stepped into the bath. After her first shuddering moment, when the heat of the water and the chill of the air warred over her, she calmed, sank down into the water.

Nerving herself, she took a breath and ducked her head; she came up to a sudden draft in the room. Spinning, water slopping over the edge, she clawed at the rim of the bath. Vornatti laughed, closed the door behind him. "Looking for this?" he said, taking cautious steps forward, holding her blade. His eyes glittered.

"Get out," she said, clutching the soap with shaking fingers.

"You have so much to learn," he said, voice full of amusement. "You've learned two things now already. One—a door that is locked can be unlocked. Guard your secrets accordingly. Two—keep your sword by your side. A blade's no good, no matter how sharp, if it's out of reach."

He settled stiffly onto the bench, and leaned forward, his eyes lingering on her skin. "A girl, then." He smiled. "It's been too long since I've had a girl."

She threw the soap at him; he raised her blade and bisected the soap, then winced. "Elysia only takes the pain away, my girl, it doesn't restore youth. This sword is a young man's weapon."

"It's mine," she said, surging out of the water, snatching it from his hand.

"Forgive me," Vornatti said. "But tell me then—was it chance or choice that made us take you for a lad?"

She pulled on a dressing gown, sank into a sulky heap near the fire. "I am not a fool. A girl with a sword is asking only for someone to take it from her."

"You intend to face Last as a boy."

"Would he face a girl? I think he would not. I think he'd call forth his coachman to beat me down again, and ride on." As she spoke, she tapped the tip of the blade on the hearth, chipping bits of brick loose like old blood.

Vornatti leaned forward and laid his hand on her shoulder. "What's your name, girl? After all, we're to be intimates. I'd like to know what to call you, what *Janus* called you—" He broke off, the sword pressing up against the crepey skin of his neck.

"What he called me is of no matter. That girl is dead. And you don't need my name, don't need it to call me to heel. After all, I'm rarely to be out of your reach. Unless—" The sword shifted a tiny, meaningful increment.

"Will you kill me? Then what? Flee my home back into the snows, as desperate as you came?"

"I'll rob this place blind," she said, rising, the blade steady, depositing a line of brick dust against his pale skin.

"And what about Gilly? All I need do is call out—then your secret would be shared with one more."

"He'd probably thank me for killing you," she said.

"Would he? If he had to go back to the farm where he came from, bury his wit in the soil? Till the fields alone, next to the graves of his family, dead of the plague? He has no one, no one but myself, and nothing but what I provide. I own him as surely as I own my horses, which would suffer if set free." Vornatti pushed the blade aside, touched her face, her neck. "It's not so much I want from you. A name."

She shivered as his fingers spidered into the vee of the dressing gown, cupped her breast, touched the curling scar beside it. "I will not give it."

"You're too thin," he said, withdrawing. "Get Gilly to feed you more. If I wanted to stroke drawn skin and bones, I'd find my pleasure in myself and spare myself troublesome chits and lads."

He slumped back on the bench; she took advantage of the space to move away.

"So tell me, girl," he said, voice growing weaker. "Shall I have Gilly find you breeches or a skirt?"

"Breeches," she said.

Vornatti dozed, jerked awake. "Well, I own I'm glad not to share your secret with Gilly. He's a devil with the maids. Thinks I don't know he spends his allowance on willing barmaids in Graston village." He coughed, breathed heavily for a moment, studied the heap of her fallen clothing.

"You bind your breasts? The scant handfuls that they are? Well, I can help you there. One of my—friends was an actress who specialized in male roles. Her corset should fit you and be more secure than any length of linen. Come now, girl, aren't you going to thank me? It's not every man who'd help a girl find vengeance. . . ."

He patted his cheek, his mouth. Clutching the robe closer about her, she leaned forward, touched his cheek, his lips with her own. Vornatti smiled.

"Let me tell you one thing more, if boy you'll be: To play the part, you must believe the part—forget who you were. Rumor and gossip are everywhere in this country, even when it involves insignificant little chits like yourself."

"That was the mistake Kritos made, thinking me insignificant enough to leave me alive," she said, *he* said, the suppressed savagery in his voice enough to stifle Vornatti's smile.

GILLY, WAITING OUTSIDE the baron's quarters, went in at the sound of the slamming door. Vornatti staggered over to his wheeled chair, panting. Gilly took the handles and drew him over to the bed. Vornatti laughed. "Such a lovely surprise under the filth, Gilly, you've no idea. . . ."

The door to the bath slammed open; the boy stalked out, clad in Gilly's old breeches and shirt, long ago outgrown. He shot Vornatti a look composed of equal parts anger and wariness, but the black look Gilly earned was all rage. Gilly stepped back under the weight of it.

"I'm tired, Gilly," Vornatti said, holding up his arms. "I won't want dinner."

Gilly put him to bed and went after the boy. He hadn't gone far; Gilly stepped out, and found himself skipping back against the door, the sword at his chest.

"There were two keys," the boy said. "You let me believe—"

"Enough," Gilly said, too tired to be wary. He ducked the sword and, cat-quick, seized the boy's thin wrists in his hands. The boy kicked his shins, and Gilly, remembering squabbles with his hot-tempered little brother, twisted the boy's wrists sharply, making him drop the sword. When the boy still fought, twisting and biting, Gilly lifted him by his wrists, dangled him in the air. "Enough," he repeated. It had always worked on his brother, on fighting dogs, and feral cats. It worked now. The boy sagged in his grip, wiggling only a little.

Gilly released him. The boy fell to the floor. Gilly winced as the boy turned a wary face up to him.

"Sorry," Gilly said. He picked up the sword; the curling hilt scraped his knuckles, and the whole thing seemed to whisper against his palm. "Here," he said, "take it." He thrust it out at the boy, regretted touching it at all. It hadn't felt quite like steel, felt born, not forged, and malign by nature. Perhaps it *had* been god-created, but such artifacts were few and jealously hoarded. Gilly fisted his hand, ridding himself of the sensation it left behind. With growing concern, he watched the boy sheathe it: Where had the boy found such a blade? He knew better than to expect an answer were he to ask.

"Are you hungry? There's dinner waiting. It's venison again. It's mostly venison all winter. You'll be sick of it come spring."

The boy stood. "I'm not hungry," he said.

"You're skin and bones," Gilly said, wondering if he was always doomed to argue with the boy.

"So he said. But why I should gain flesh simply to please his lecherous—" The boy's jaw snapped shut; his eyes blazed.

Gilly took the boy's elbow in his hand, walked him toward the library, wanting to be, if not friends, at least amicable, if the boy's temper could allow such a thing. To that end, Gilly said, "I know something that might make you feel better." He drew the boy past the books to the frosted doors. They stepped outside into the winter night; their breaths fled from them like ghosts.

Gilly bent, pulled up a handful of broken marble, snow-dusted. "It's the old facing from the house. I like to get my anger out this way." He hefted the fragments, tested the weight, and pivoted, hurling the missiles at the orchard. The rocks hit the nearest tree, scattering icicles.

Gilly collected another handful, thinking of Vornatti giving him precise instructions regarding keys and bathing rooms. He sent another tree-load of ice to the ground, letting the sound drown out his guilt.

He handed the boy the next stone, cold and damp with snow. "Imagine you're throwing your anger, your frustration out." Another game he'd played with his brother, who could only be distracted from his tempers, rarely soothed.

The boy closed his eyes, his jaw clenched, the scar flared red, and then he threw. The stone sailed forward, effortlessly hitting the tree. Icicles cascaded, but before Gilly could hand him another stone, the next tree shed its icy teeth. Then the next and the next, until the entire orchard was crashing and shattering with one thrown stone. Gilly caught a shuddering breath at the glittering wreckage the boy had made.

VORNATTI RUSTLED PAPER in his lap, unfolding the envelope. Gilly watched, intrigued. Usually the old bastard tossed Gilly his post, trusting Gilly to file away the gossip, the bills, Aris's reports on profits sent to Itarus, and to act on the few business letters he received. But this letter lacked the creamy color of Antyrrian vellum, was tinted slightly blue, nearly translucent. The thick lines of script shone through the paper.

"What think you of this?" Vornatti said, passing the letter to Gilly.

Across the library, the boy looked up from his contemplation of Vornatti's book.

"Read it aloud, Gilly, since it concerns our young friend."

The boy shut the book, not bothering to mark his page. And why would he, Gilly thought, when he could only be looking at the pictures, and not the text?

"Gilly," Vornatti warned.

"Sir," Gilly said, began. "It's from Itarus," he said, surprised. "How did you—"

"I have my ways, Gilly. You'd do well to remember that." Vornatti closed his eyes. "Read."

"It's a copy of a letter from Kritos to Last," Gilly said. The boy stiffened, silent. Gilly angled the letter to get the most of the firelight on the crossed words.

"Michel, cousin, while I acknowledge that you have come to Itarus as I requested, I did not intend for you to dally within the foreign court, and leave me with your ill-begotten, ill-tempered bastard son. He is unmanageable. A feral dog would have more gratitude. A rabid animal would have shown less rage. We've had to lock him in the turret, to keep him from escape attempts. If we were not on Ice Island, he would have succeeded. I can not even enter his room without his attack.

"It's all very well to suggest threatening him, to derive obedience through fear, but he's not so blind as that. He knows you want him alive, and what else have I to threaten him with? He cares not for hunger nor cold nor beatings, though at least those serve to weaken his outbursts.

"No, cousin, if you have any hopes of firing him off among the Itarusine court, and then among our own, you will have to take a hand. As it is, I have the severest doubts he can ever learn our ways. I wash my hands of his education. I will be his jailer only. If you would have me do otherwise, you must take a hand yourself.

"Kritos."

The boy stood, his hands shaking. "Kritos." The loathing in his voice darkened the atmosphere of the room, bringing winter darkness to the fire-lit circle.

"How did you get this?" Gilly asked, turning the letter over in his hands, looking for some hint of the sender.

"A matter of enmity," Vornatti said. "Last hates me. As does my heir, Dantalion. As such, they are acquaintances, at least during the days of the Winter Court. It's a small matter to pay one of Dantalion's servants to copy any interesting letters."

"Is there anything else?" the boy asked. "Did Last go to aid Kritos?"

Gilly watched the tremor move from the boy's hands through his spine and disappear, leaving him as still as a crouching cat.

"So greedy," Vornatti said. "Here I've worked one prodigious collection of information, from my chair, mind you, and you only ask for more. Will you thank me?"

"You derive too much pleasure from your intrigues to need my thanks," the boy said. "Tell me."

"I did receive word that Last has retired to Ice Island," Vornatti said.

The boy's face shuttered, locking away emotion, but Gilly had seen a quick wash of perplexity cross his face, as if he didn't know whether to take Last's involvement as a good thing or bad.

"Come then, thank me," Vornatti said. "Or are you as unmannered as Last's whelp?"

"I'm worse," the boy said.

Vornatti laughed. "How do you figure that, boy? You've been brought to heel, domesticated by food and a little frost. The only independence you have left is your stubborn refusal to grant us your name."

The boy looked to the barren trees in the orchard outside. This winter, they had not gathered icicles for more than a night without rocks being hurled at them. The black rage in the boy's eyes sank back; he dutifully crawled into Vornatti's lap and kissed him. Vornatti stroked the black curls, but the moment Vornatti's lips left his to draw breath, the boy was across the room, never mind that he left strands of his hair in Vornatti's clutching fingers.

"Gilly," Vornatti said, smiling. "I'm tired."

Obediently, Gilly rose, folded the letter in neat quarters, and set it on the desk.

When he returned an hour later, flushed and straightening his clothes, he found the boy still in the library. Gilly hastily tucked his shirt back into his breeches, embarrassed anew under the boy's dark eyes.

Seeking distraction, he discovered it in the boy sprawled beside the fireplace, in the book spread open before him. Gilly remembered the frustration he had felt once, touching the incomprehensible secrets of letters and words.

"I'll teach you to read if you like. And write," Gilly offered.

The boy propped himself on his elbows. "Do you think I come to look at the pictures?" He passed the book to Gilly.

The book was not one of Vornatti's pornographic woodcuts. It was instead Sofia Grigorian's text-dense treatise on exotic poisons used in the Itarusine court.

"Are you suggesting you can read?"

"I am telling you I can. And write." The boy's lips curled in a smirk that Gilly was beginning to recognize. It betokened the boy's worst tempers. The news from Itarus was not to his liking, Gilly thought. Despite everything, the boy had hoped for Janus's return this year.

"So you see how little I need you," the boy continued. "I can read my own damn letters. And I don't need Vornatti's lecherous aid, either."

Gilly's own temper quickened as the boy's words woke the caresses Vornatti had pressed to his skin.

He yanked the boy to his feet. Gilly handed him a quill and the Itarusine envelope. "Prove it. Write something for me then."

"Anything," the boy said, defiant.

"Anything?" Gilly grinned. "Promise?"

The boy hesitated in the face of that smile. But then he raised his chin. The smirk deepened. "Anything."

"Your name."

The boy's face froze and he whispered, "Bastard. And you'll run off to tell him, won't you?"

"If you are incapable . . ." Gilly said, goading him.

The boy dipped the quill into the inkwell, shook the excess off, and bent over the paper with a faint awkwardness that spoke of inexperience. But the scrolling ink spread over the silky parchment smoothly and quickly, stirring Gilly's breath while he read the letters as they formed.

The boy stepped back, bowed, tossed the quill onto the desk with a spattering of inky drops, and left the room, all so smoothly done that he was gone before Gilly's eyes rose from the paper and the single word that the boy claimed as his name.

Maledicte.

GILLY WOKE TO THE ROUGH sound of Vornatti's labored breathing in his ear and, from farther down the hall, the distant protest of moving furniture. Gilly wondered drowsily if something new had distressed the boy and he had built barricades in his room last night, or if he was thieving furniture from the other rooms. A settee had already disappeared into the boy's quarters, and once, Gilly had found the boy preparing to move an enameled table down the wide, slippery stairs. Gilly had carried it down himself, but the boy, as suspicious as a mother cat, had maneuvered it inside without Gilly's help. The boy—*Maledicte*, Gilly thought, jerking awake all at once, unnerved again. The name rang in his ears like the voices of mad intercessors and witches, ill-omened.

Vornatti's gnarled hand sought Gilly's thigh. "Who would have thought," Vornatti rasped, "the boy would find such tame pursuits to amuse him through the cold season."

Gilly smiled, but when Vornatti's hands stroked higher, he pulled away, freed himself from the smothering weight of eiderdown and fur. "I'll start the fire," he said.

"Linger yet," Vornatti commanded. "It's rare enough I wake with you in my bed these days. It makes me wonder what sent you fleeing into my arms last night."

Gilly shrugged, fed the spills into the redly burning coals, grew a little flamelet, and fed the first log in.

"That's not an answer, Gilly," Vornatti said, mood souring along with his voice. He gasped, and Gilly knew the old man's pains had caught up with him once again.

Gilly stirred a spoonful of Laudable into the leftovers of last night's wine. "Drink this."

Vornatti gulped it. "Tell me why, Gilly. Do you want something out of the ordinary way?"

"I'm not a whore," Gilly said, stoppering the lid so hard the seal cracked in his hands.

"Well, not *just* a whore," Vornatti said, mocking. "There are endless supplies of reasonably intelligent young men. There are endless supplies of reasonably willing young men. But there are few who are both. And gentle—" Vornatti touched the rough stubble on Gilly's cheeks, his tone losing its petulance. "What was it that frightened you? The boy?"

"I suppose," Gilly said. "I didn't want to be alone in the dark, with only the boy in my head for company."

"But such fascinating company," Vornatti said, gloating.

Gilly knelt beside the bed, found Vornatti's slippers, and slid them onto his feet. Head still lowered, he said. "Sir, have you never thought that this might be a dangerous thing? This boy—sometimes he seems merely a youth with a temper; at other times, he seems uncanny, his rage unnatural, that sword with raven wings like Black-Winged Ani. . . ."

"Black Ani," Vornatti said. In his voice, Gilly heard old remembrances, and wondered what it had been like, to live under the eyes of the gods.

"The sword, the hunger for vengeance. His will. His determination. Even his name. Ani could—"

"The gods are dead, Gilly. Any man who fought at Xipos in the endgame knows that. Xipos proved it; men made offerings grim and great, and men died, churned into mud and blood, screaming for Haith's mercy and hearing *nothing*. That *sword* is nothing—stolen from some incautious aristocrat, nothing more. The boy has a magpie heart, we've seen that." Vornatti tugged his dressing gown closer across his shoulders; it sagged where his flesh had once filled it, revealing the great, pitted scars over his spine and hip, the source of his pains and problems, the place where a warhorse had danced across his back with rough iron shoes.

"But—" Gilly started, remembering the feel of the sword beneath his hand and shivering.

"The gods are gone," Vornatti said. "Baxit Himself gave us that gift. Though some swear it was His curse. To live at our own behest. To answer our own prayers."

Gilly nodded, obediently.

"My superstitious Gilly, I am an old man," Vornatti said. "I grew up in the god times. And I saw one god-possessed. . . . If this boy were Ani's, he would have slaughtered us both rather than falter in his forward steps. There is an old book of such histories in the library, should you doubt me. I think you merely mazed with nightmares. Haven't I heard you call out in your sleep while you dream of dead things?"

Gilly nodded, this time with more belief. Maledicte was likely nothing but a clever actor, skilled in evoking dread. It would serve him well, should he ever come to grips with Last, Gilly thought. He refused to think on the sword and the feeling it left in his skin.

"But you learned his name?" Vornatti said. "Tell me."

"Maledicte," Gilly said.

Vornatti threw back his head and laughed.

A SHADOW CROSSED GILLY'S LINE of sight as he crouched beside the shelves, pulling out the books rarely read. His hand closed on the spine of one old enough to have grown foxed and spotted, the leather cracking. *The Book of Vengeances.*

Vornatti, Gilly thought, had never succumbed to the worst affliction of old age, that of a faulty memory. The book opened in Gilly's hands to an illustrated page black with ink and a raven's eyes, to a man battling, though knives pierced his flesh. The shadow moved over him again, and he twitched, closing the book reflexively.

The boy stood behind him, eyes calculating. "You don't guard your back very well."

"I'm only a servant," Gilly said. "I don't need to."

"I suppose that's true. And you don't have to fight for your food, your clothes, or your hair as Relicts children do."

"Is that—"

"Where I come from? Of course. You've known that all along," Maledicte said. "Or did you think Ani birthed me from an egg?" His lips curled in amusement.

Gilly sighed in embarrassment. "Vornatti told you."

"Vornatti found it funny; you, fearing me." Maledicte's face darkened. "I could take you, though."

Gilly said, "I shook you once, and I can do it again." He kept his tone matter-of-fact, and the boy slid away from the confrontation.

"Your hair's all over cobwebs," he said. "No one would buy it in that state, not even for pillow stuffing." The boy set the sword down, reached out, and tugged the ribbon from Gilly's hair with agile fingers. "Turn around."

Hesitantly, Gilly did. Maledicte moved behind him, unfastened his hair, and stroked cool fingers through to Gilly's nape. Gilly tensed; the boy's gentler moods all too often presaged a sting so delicate that only later did it smart and bleed. "What do you want?"

Maledicte backed away, spread his arms wide, and said, "Tell me what you see."

Gingerly, uncertain of Maledicte's mood, Gilly said, "A boy pretty enough to attract attention, disconcerting enough to repel, and very young."

Maledicte's brows snapped down. "Not dangerous? And why so young? I am near a man's age."

"You are not wearing the sword," Gilly said. "And your slightness, coupled with your light voice, will always strike men as youthful."

Maledicte sank onto the library stool, ran his hands through his hair, first pushing the curls back, then raking them forward to leave only his dark eyes visible. "I would not want Last to laugh at me," Maledicte whispered. "Tell me how to be feared, Gilly. You who know so much."

Gilly sat beside Maledicte, flattered that the boy sought his advice, a sign that perhaps he might think Gilly something more than just Vornatti's pet. "You have time."

"The trees are budding, the songbirds sing, and daylight grows. It is almost spring. Last will return, though not Janus. . . ." Maledicte's breath flowed out and with it, seemingly his strength. He slumped against the bookshelf, restless hands knotting Gilly's ribbon, shaping the cloth as he could not shape the future. "If I kill Last, what will it avail me with Janus still caged in Itarus? Last sent him there, and only Last will bring him back."

"Kritos would kill him if he could," Gilly agreed, "rather than spend one copper on him. But perhaps Vornatti could be relied upon."

"Vornatti, least of all." Maledicte rose to pace the room. "Vornatti has his own agenda for me, his own desires. I am but a reflection of what he wants me to be. He shelters me, indulges me, and whispers sweet vengeful fancies in my ears, but they are his fancies, his vengeance. Not mine.

"My schemes are . . . far from complete. And I know of no way to make them more so. I will not have Last mock me, a boy with a blade. I cannot face him at all; my skills are too uneven, and there is no satisfaction in being cut down by Last's men.

"So you see my dilemma, Gilly?" The boy held his hands out in calculated supplication. "You have all the answers for Vornatti; have you none for me?"

Gilly's eyes fell before Maledicte's steady ones, startled at the boy's candor and need. The boy waited silently for Gilly's advice, seemingly patient, though Gilly could see the boy's hands twisting into fists.

Gilly hastened into speech. "Wait. Learn to use the sword. Last is a swordsman of some skill. And you—"

"Vornatti has tried to instruct me, but he is too old, his directions meaningless."

"Vornatti will hire a master if you ask," Gilly said, fighting a sudden sense of disloyalty. It was more than advice Maledicte needed; he needed an ally. "In the right way." He grabbed Maledicte's hands, pulled him near. "Listen, and let me tell you how to manage him."

He bent his blond head to Maledicte's dark one and began to speak, voicing things he had never consciously plotted, small details of pleasure and drugs and wine, and when to ask, and how. The lecture made him cringe, made him realize he worked Vornatti like any paid companion. If Maledicte said anything scathing now, he'd never be able to speak so again, but the boy stayed attentive and blessedly silent. When Maledicte left, Gilly turned, scalded in his own skin, to distract himself with *The Book of Vengeances*. But it was gone in the boy's light-fingered wake.

VORNATTI SAT IN HIS CHAIR in the library. The fire burned low, and a sure sign of encroaching spring was that Vornatti did not demand that it be built up at once. Gilly dusted the books; their butler had quit after entering Maledicte's room without knocking and finding his cravat ruined by a black blade and his own blood.

Maledicte sat on the floor beside Vornatti's chair, reading aloud from the pages spread over his lap, pausing every other page to sip from the goblet beside him.

Vornatti's right hand rested in the boy's dark hair, fingers lost in the tumbled curls, moving in lazy increments.

Gilly looked back to his dusting and smiled a little sourly. So tranquil, so falsely domestic—Maledicte had been heeding his advice.

Maledicte paused in his reading. It was an account of a young girl's first visit to the court, supposedly true, but from the detailed and violent debaucheries awaiting her on the successive pages, hopefully false. Vornatti chose it this evening, saying, "This is why one always wants a protector in the court, Maledicte. Of course, you have the sword, and you're no girl, so you'll find this tale more amusing than cautionary."

"Is the court really so decadent?" Maledicte asked.

"Quite so. It's a hard time, this, though the nobles refuse to acknowledge it. And with the gods gone, there is little men fear. But for all of that, the court is beautiful: there is no time so lovely as twilight, after all.

"The courtiers meet in gilded ballrooms; they compete with each other to be the most beautiful, the most noticed." Vornatti smiled down at the boy and continued.

"Everything is gilt or silver; you'd want to thieve it all. The rooms, the furniture, the clothing—their clothing is something to see. Every shade under the sun and moon, every stone under the earth and sea is there, burnished and made perfect.

"The courtiers' tongues seem gilded as well, their manners stiffened by the same embroidery that clings to their gowns and jackets. The men carry swords they may not draw in the ballrooms, to show fierceness many of them lack. And they whisper, like dry leaves in autumn, all the things they dare not say aloud."

Vornatti looked down and said, "A savage, unrestrained tongue like yours, my boy, would scandalize them, raise their whispering into sounds of the surf rushing at your back."

Maledicte smiled. "They do love a good scandal. You've told me so yourself." He brushed his fingers over Vornatti's mouth, allowed the old man to press a kiss to his palm.

"Good night," Maledicte said, withdrawing his hand, his smiles. He left the room; Vornatti stared hungrily after his slim, retreating back.

Gilly joined Vornatti, levered himself down to the floor, and picked up Maledicte's near-empty goblet. He swirled the wine within, ruby against crystal, heart's blood on ice.

"He means you to take him to court. To wait for Janus's return there," Gilly said.

"I believe he does."

"Is he mad? It is one thing to aid him in his quest, to loose him like a falcon in the field, another altogether to set him in the king's court." Gilly chose his goad as carefully as Maledicte had chosen his.

"Why shouldn't I provide entree? It'll give me something new to draw his affections. And why not? It's been too long since I was there in the midst of it all."

"He's not even an aristocrat. He's . . . common." The word choked Gilly even as he forced it over his tongue.

Vornatti chuckled. "There's nothing common about our boy, and well you know it, Gilly." He contemplated aloud, "Still, he will need training in swordplay, dance, dress, and manners, of course, though you have rubbed off the worst excesses already, and some new clothes. His accent is already acceptable." He was as pleased with this idea as if he had thought of it himself.

"Best of all," Vornatti said, touching his lips as if he could still feel Maledicte's caress. "Best of all, none of this can be accomplished overnight. Even should he prove an excellent student, it'll be next spring at the earliest. For some small outlay of lessons and wardrobe, I'll have him twice as long. And you doubted he could be tamed so easily."

Gilly swallowed the lees from Maledicte's cup, tasting their bitterness. Vornatti grinned, malevolent glee touching his eyes, livening his old face. "Can't you see it? Their faces as he enters the court—elegant, wicked, and entirely too beautiful."

"Perhaps," Gilly said. Beyond the opened door, Maledicte lingered in the hall, listening. Maledicte touched two fingers to his mouth, and inclined them toward Gilly.

"He'll have to have some rank, some right to be there among them," Gilly said. "And his antecedents do not bear scrutiny, no matter his appearance." Another soft guide.

"He'll be my ward, of course. Last thought Aurora base-born when she was not, thought me foisting an impostor on the court when I was not. I wonder what he'll make of Maledicte."

5

Of all the myriad choices open to a clever poisoner, perhaps none is more versatile than the commonly scorned stonethroat. An aspyhxiant and paralytic, it is most often employed to rid one's home of rats, and oneself of enemies.

However, there are more subtle uses. . . .

—A Lady's Treatise, attributed to Sofia Grigorian

MALEDICTE STOOD, MUTE AND REBELLIOUS, while Vornatti raged at him. "You are impossible," Vornatti shouted. "Bad enough you went through four dance instructors in two years, wounding two of them seriously, and scarring another, so that I ended up paying *Gilly* to teach you. Now, you attempt the same on your newest swordmaster, which shows both disrespect and a serious lack of judgment. You may have learned more than your last master could teach, but Thorn has much still to show you. Do you know what it cost me to keep him here?"

"He called me little *girl,* mocking me," Maledicte said, voice shrill with outrage.

"And why shouldn't he?" Vornatti snapped. "I was a fool to think this could work. You've not learned anything, not dared anything. I think your vaunted vengeance is nothing more than an excuse to allow yourself to linger here, fed and pampered, indulged and petted."

"I will kill Last," Maledicte said.

"Master Thorn sent you sprawling. Last would skewer you without a moment's thought."

Maledicte paced the floor, breath coming fast, regretting the sword left in his room, and hating the fact that he feared Vornatti would be rid of him.

"You've not learned anything so far as I can tell—though I've paid dearly for the lessons."

"You've taken it out on my hide," Maledicte spat. "Your hands on me—"

"You rate your charms too highly," Vornatti said. "I could find the same in any brothel, and sweeter-tempered."

Maledicte fisted his hands, strangled by emotion again, fear and rage warring in him.

"Show me you've mastered one lesson," Vornatti said. "Make me believe your disguise can hold. A dance, a duel, or even the delicate uses of poison that I've taught you. Show me you've learned anything at all, or I'll send you back to the Relicts."

Maledicte slammed the door behind himself and fled to the gardens, rage scorching his belly; he couldn't turn his ire on Vornatti, not without retribution he was unwilling to court, but the swordmaster—*little girl*— Rage reddened his gaze and he sought out the poison chest Vornatti had given him.

Now he sat, coolheaded and cold-palmed in the grotto at the far edge of Vornatti's estate, watching the tenth cat lick up fish paste, oblivious of its nine dead predecessors. His temper had chilled, leaving the path clear. Master Thorn was no fool; he would not take food or drink from Maledicte's hand. Vornatti's proof would have to be found elsewhere. *Little girl.* Corsets and clothing could only take him so far.

Maledicte watched the cat, hands chilled, white-knuckled around the crystal vial; he would sate the snake-eye glitter in Vornatti's face, would prove his worth. Hadn't risked anything? Maledicte would risk everything. . . .

The cat staggered, mouth working in silent, pained outrage, and finally slunk, spitting, beneath the bench.

Maledicte raised the vial, crystal warmed by his death grip on it, and tapped the last dose onto his tongue. The clay taste of cold graves filled his mouth, and he nearly gagged before swallowing. His breath fled; his throat seized; tears scalded his eyes as he choked. The sound, the pain reminded him of the Relicts battle, gasping for air, and Janus gone. . . .

He clutched the pain tight, fought for breath. Miranda had lived through that battle, that pain: Maledicte would live through this one. Spots danced before his eyes, his need for breath frenzied now. "Janus," he moaned, a bare thread of sound. "Janus."

GILLY TAPPED the door once more, listening to the sound of an empty room. Wherever Maledicte had hidden himself away, it wasn't in the painted room, that combination prison and shelter. Gilly turned the knob, the brass cold under his nervous fingers, and went in.

This was the first time in two years that he had been inside, the first time since the room had become Maledicte's, and he half expected it to be filled with remnants of the boy's bloody dreams of vengeance. Too many nights, woken from his own recurring nightmares, Gilly had walked the hall and heard the boy muttering behind the closed door. He always moved on quickly, imagining Maledicte within, wild-eyed and raving, a madman with a feathered sword. Some mornings it was a shock to see that the boy was not the savage of his imagination, but a youngster quick to tease, and equally quick to help Gilly defy Vornatti's more objectionable whims.

Still, Gilly found himself thinking more of Maledicte as the would-be killer, as he encroached into his room. All the drapes had been drawn, baring contradictory murals of snowfall and spring, of velvet night and golden days. Gilly found the effect oddly unsettling, flinched at the unveiled image of a lurking wolf, eyes gleaming through a snowscape. Not for the first time, Gilly thought that Vornatti had uncomfortable tastes. No matter the luxury, the predator lurked beneath.

Looking away from the walls, Gilly tallied furniture, thinking, *Oh, so that's what's become of the divan, the chinoiserie table, the best candlesticks. A magpie heart.* Gilly smiled, but lost his amusement as he looked closer at the low table near the high, four-postered bed. The sword lay there, mute testimony that Maledicte had returned after his lesson's abrupt cessation. Beside it, a lady's embroidery box rested, an elaborate thing of interlocking wood and small, carved flowers. Old, Gilly thought, and odd; he doubted Maledicte soothed his nerves sewing primroses onto linen.

Closer, Gilly saw that it was a puzzle box. There had been a rage for the elaborate toys some years back. Gilly had always liked them, the reward of a sealed box blossoming beneath his fingers. He sat down on the edge of the bed, picked the box up; the lid gaped, left open, as if Maledicte, having agreed to wait, having bided not one but three winters, had no patience left to spare for small things.

Inside, where there should have been skeins of silk on ivory bobbins, there was a dazzling gloss of crystal vials, miniature works of glass-blowing art, each sealed. One space yawned, empty. Gilly pulled a vial free, turned it up to the light, peering into the smoky glass. Something that looked like coarse salt, grayed with ash. It sparked memories of rat poison and traps his father had set on the farm. *Arsenixa.*

Gilly's fingers shook and he set the vial back. Vornatti had taught Gilly to read and to write, but Maledicte already knew both. And Vornatti liked to give lessons. Looking at the demure little chest again, Gilly's stomach roiled.

Slumping onto the bed in distress, Gilly found something thicker than linens pressed against his palm. He pulled the coverlet back, then the ticking itself. The leather-bound book had lost some of its faded gilding: *of Vengeances,* Gilly read. The long-missing book, squirreled away. Gilly collected the book and fled the room.

"THERE YOU ARE," GILLY SAID. The early-evening light blued the air, and made of Maledicte a hunched darkness crouched in the stony outcropping. Around his feet lay rigid shadows with stiffened tails and legs, opened mouths, and black tongues. The smell of must and murdered cats lingered in the enclosure.

Maledicte rose unhurriedly, cradling a cat in his arms. In the pale, filtered sunlight, its color seemed the dusty gray of old cobwebs; its soulless amber eyes winked and gleamed.

Its mouth gaped and its tongue curled back, its ears flattened, but no sullen complaint reached Gilly's ears. Maledicte touched his lips to its head, set it down on the stone and earthen floor. His hands slid into a sunbeam, showed forearms red with bloody gouges. For all that, Maledicte looked smug as the cat slunk from sight.

Gilly stepped closer to Maledicte; his boot struck glass and sent it scattering over the floor to splinter against a wall.

"So clumsy," Maledicte said. His eyes burned with wicked amusement when Gilly's head whipped back to him. The boy's light voice was changed, made furred, raspy, as if he had traded with the cat. Remembering the cat's silence, Gilly amended himself. Stolen.

The half-seen memory of curving crystal spurting away from him flickered back into his mind, and he said, "Poison?," thinking of the empty space in the embroidery box.

Maledicte said, "Stonethroat."

"You tested dosages on the cook's cats? To see what would change but not kill?"

"I would have used hounds, being more man-sized, but Vornatti doesn't keep kennels."

"Why do this?"

Maledicte coughed, hand flying to his neck. He dropped his hands to his side. "I will not be mocked, not by Thorn, nor by Vornatti."

"You poisoned yourself to lower your voice?" Gilly said. "You couldn't wait for nature?"

"I've done nothing but wait," Maledicte said, his face flushing. "While Vornatti snarls and paws at me and time passes. A third winter approaches and Janus is as far from me as he has ever been."

Gilly folded himself onto the grotto bench, shivering at the clamminess of damp stone seeping through his breeches. "Maybe his lessons go no more smoothly than yours."

Maledicte shrugged, eyes still worried.

"Do you fear he will forget you?" Gilly asked.

Maledicte turned his face up, startled and horrified. Gilly shuddered. Had the boy never thought that time passed for Janus also?

"If he has forgotten . . ." Maledicte said, his ruined voice as devastated as his eyes.

Gilly winced away from the raw pain, and Maledicte levered himself onto the bench with a cough and a sigh. Gilly smelled blood, sweat, and a pungency to both that reminded him of the poisonous trial Maledicte had inflicted upon himself.

Maledicte turned a curved fragment of glass about in his fingers, stilled them, and looked at the glass. "Am I forgettable?"

"No," Gilly whispered. Maddening. Mercurial. Charming. Never forgettable.

Maledicte coughed again, a series of quick outward breaths like a man puffing to liven a fire.

"Are you well?" Gilly asked. His fingers trembled as he took Maledicte's damp wrist in his grip. Maledicte's pulse hammered steadily, more so than Gilly's. Gilly was all too aware of the boy's ashy pallor, the warm stickiness of blood on his hands.

"Well enough," Maledicte said. He freed his wrist, slid down to lean his head back on the bench. He kicked a dead cat from under his boot with a moue of disgust.

"Except the months speed by and I am no more forward."

Daring, Gilly stroked the damp, dark hair. Maledicte sighed, rolled his head, settled it in Gilly's lap. Gilly froze, as startled as if a wild creature had unaccountably failed to bite. He twitched his fingers into life again, slid them over Maledicte's nape.

"Maledicte," Gilly whispered, the word an invocation. "Dark words, dark paths, a heart laden with secrets, and no one to rely on."

"There's always you," Maledicte said, so softly, so muffled by damaged throat, by the sweep of Gilly's sleeves curtaining his face, that Gilly felt that his trust was no more than a distant rumor, fragile and easily disproved. His fingers worked loose a tangle from the dark head.

It was with some reluctance that Gilly roughed his voice to speech, pointing out Maledicte's slow-bleeding arms, the bodies that needed to be disposed of before they lost a cook, and the lateness of the hour for sitting in a damp grotto.

Gilly would not allow Maledicte to help with the dead cats, concerned that some taint of death would sift free and unbalance Maledicte's fragile control over the stonethroat. So Maledicte watched, his arms bound in wide strips torn from Gilly's shirt, his eyes as flat and opaque as the stones Gilly cleaned. Still, Gilly thought he heard the soft falling weight of blood on earth. Maybe it was only ghostly steps from the dead creatures Gilly shoveled into a sack, or maybe—maybe it was the faint ticking of an unseen clock, counting down the moments until Maledicte must act.

6

Maledicte snooped and Maledicte pried.
No one escaped from Maledicte's spy.
How many secrets did he find?
One . . . two . . . three . . .

VORNATTI PUSHED BACK HIS DINNER PLATE, the roast hen only pulled apart, not eaten, and turned on Maledicte. "Your appetite seems well enough."

"Shouldn't it be?" Maledicte said, licking his fingers, his voice the mutter of a feral cat.

Vornatti slapped him. "Manners!" Maledicte surged out of his seat as if he meant to return the blow.

Gilly said, "Mal," quietly in a warning. It seemed to him that in the cold months since the self-inflicted poisoning, Maledicte's temper had grown apace. Or perhaps it was only the uncanny rasp, a menace bred purely by sound. Gilly thought that Last would have little desire to laugh now, if he encountered the boy and his sword.

"To think I thought you could act as a courtier," Vornatti continued. "Dogs lick themselves. People do not."

"But I am your dog, am I not?" Maledicte said, visibly warring with his own temper. "You've trained me to heel."

Before Vornatti could retort, Gilly knelt beside Vornatti's chair. "Tell me, my lord, what have we done to displease you?" There was something, some balance that had changed; ever since Maledicte had poisoned himself, Vornatti had veered between pride in Maledicte's lessons and rage at the smallest infraction. Gilly thought perhaps Vornatti had also been spooked by Maledicte's success with the stonethroat. He sighed. *Fanciful.* Vornatti's moods were, as ever, dictated by pain, Elysia, and events, not by superstition.

Vornatti's face, drawn into tight lines, eased at Gilly's conciliatory tone. He stroked the line of his jaw, his neck. Maledicte leaned up against the wall; the silent weight of his watchful presence heated Gilly's skin with embarrassment.

"I've heard from Aris," Vornatti said finally. "I have his permission to present my ward to the court without the usual petty testing of manner and dress. Aris," Vornatti said, "grants a favor for a favor."

At Maledicte's questioning gaze, Gilly said, "On occasion, Vornatti . . . pads Aris's financial reports to Itarus and to Antyre's benefit."

"Still, it seems Aris's approval matters little," Vornatti said. "I also received the broadsheets today. Look you at them, and tell me what you see." He fished the folded sheets out from his chair, passed them to Gilly. Gilly spread them over the tablecloth, smoothing the crumpled lines. His breath caught. The infamous artist Poole had turned his attention to the court.

The caricature claimed most of the front page, a myopically drawn king, a book in one hand, a trailing leash in the other. The hounds, named for members of the court and for political entities like Itarus and the antimachinists, ran freely around him, fighting, fornicating, and fouling the palace. It was titled "The Learned King."

"Is Poole mad?" Gilly asked. "Was he arrested?"

"No," Vornatti said. "Aris couldn't be bothered. The disrespect of the court and papers is ingrained."

Gilly sucked in his breath, but it was Maledicte who said it for him, paying more attention than Gilly had thought. "So the king's welcome does not insure my acceptance? Without such acceptance, I have no way to reach Last."

"Not only your vengeance is at stake, but my position. If they spurn my ward— I have been shunned before, and I will not suffer it again. Gilly! We need to be assured of our acceptance. You will go to town and find such assurance. I want one of the counselors—Lovesy, DeGuerre, or Westfall—to greet us with open arms. Do what you must. Dig up what you must."

"Leave here?"

"Maledicte can care for me, can he not?" Vornatti traded a long look with Maledicte; after a time, Maledicte dropped his eyes and nodded. Vornatti smiled and gestured to his side. Maledicte came silently over, and nestled down, leaning against Vornatti's thigh. "Good dog," Vornatti said. "You can growl all you want, but you know better than to bite."

Gilly, watching the redness rise and fall in Maledicte's cheek, wondered if that was entirely true.

"Gilly, start with the betting books," Vornatti said. "There's always scandal there, if you know how to look."

He nodded understanding and obedience, and left the room, glancing back once to see Vornatti leaning over Maledicte, biting at the marble curve of his neck.

In MURNE, Gilly found his duty more tedious than taxing, the obstacles many but responsive to his handling. While his target was apparent from the first study of the betting books at the Horned Bull, that rough tavern where the most disreputable bets were laid, the evidence proved more difficult to gather. Still, several weeks later, Gilly held proof of a scandal in his hand, not regarding a counselor himself, but a counselor's close kin—more than potent enough for their needs. Vornatti, notified by letter, had agreed, and sent Gilly a bonus, as well as further instructions.

A bonus Gilly felt well earned. Gilly left the meeting with their chosen victim feeling that only luck and good planning had kept him alive. The Marquis DeGuerre was a very angry young man; Gilly was glad to immerse himself in the less dangerous details of preparing Vornatti's town house after his long absence, taking care in the meantime to stay safely away from DeGuerre's reach. With such determination and little distraction, he was able to send word to Vornatti that the house was readied ahead of schedule.

"Welcome to Murne, my lord," Gilly said, greeting Vornatti at the door of the Dove Street residence. Vornatti, white with the strain of two days' travel, nevertheless walked across the threshhold, leaning on a stout cane. Maledicte pushed the wheeled chair behind and came in, dressed in city finery—delicate lawn shirt, leather breeches, a satin vest, all the opalescent black of a raven's wing. Gilly helped Vornatti into his chair, and turned back, drawn like a magnet to the elegance of the boy.

"You look the part now," Gilly said.

Maledicte dropped into a bow, smiled up at him. "Gilly." His voice held distinct pleasure, a purr beneath the rasp, and Gilly hoped it wasn't merely for his success. He hoped that the month apart hadn't undone their tenuous friendship, that a month alone with Vornatti hadn't raised Maledicte's temper to a razor edge.

"You're rather elegant yourself," Maledicte said, tugging Gilly's blond queue, eyeing his embroidered livery. "But what's all this?" He gestured to the collection of flowers and wrapped packages.

Gilly cast a cautious look around at the other staff, waiting along the wall for Vornatti's acknowledgment, and spoke quietly. "Once DeGuerre folded, other courtiers remembered Vornatti's ways and sent tribute, an urging to look elsewhere."

Maledicte laughed. "Afraid of you and your watchful eyes. And they've not even met me yet."

"Gilly," Vornatti said, interrupting their chatter. "I'm tired. Show me to my room, and supervise the unpacking. I don't trust the maids; they look a shifty lot," Vornatti said, then grinned. "Especially that saucy one." His cane swung out, jabbed at her ankle-high skirts.

"What's your name?" he asked.

"Livia, sir," she said, dropping a curtsy. Vornatti's cane stirred her skirts, revealing her calf. He patted her wrist. "You weren't hired by the housekeeper, I'm sure. Not with those legs. I'll wager Gilly hired you personally. He has a weakness for red-haired maids."

Livia nodded, dimpling.

Vornatti dismissed them all, letting his eyes linger on Livia's retreating skirts, and when Gilly moved to carry the baron's personal luggage, Vornatti put his cane in his path, slapping Gilly's shins with that always-deceptive turn of speed the old man had. Like his crest, the serpent, which struck at speed and without mercy, Gilly thought, wincing.

"Gilly," Vornatti said. "Your dalliances stop the moment you fail to please me."

"Yes," Gilly said, flushing.

"You've had free run for a month now. Don't forget who pays—"

"Leave off, old bastard," Maledicte said, stepping between the two, touching Gilly's hand in passing. "You don't need to crack the whip."

"And you, youngling, need to recall that we're in town now, and the rules are different. Gilly, help me to my room."

Obedient and silent, Gilly did, guiding Vornatti's chair down the hallway to a room that had once been the second parlor, before Gilly's frantic redecoration. The last time Vornatti had lived in town, he could manage the wide, polished stairs to the upper floors.

Maledicte, as ward to Vornatti, had been given the room Vornatti would no longer occupy, the master chamber on the second floor. Thinking of Maledicte's quick defense, Gilly was pleased that he'd taken the time and some of his bonus to fill a bedside dish with toffees of the kind Maledicte had pilfered from Last.

Gilly's room was also on the floor for family and guests, showing his position for what it was, neither fish nor fowl. The maids served him, Cook chivied him like a mischievous lordling, the butler grudgingly conferred with him. Yet his room overlooked the mews and the trash bins; the furnishings were pieces not good enough for the baron or his guests.

But late in the night, Gilly didn't dwell on arbitrary inequalities, though his eyes lingered on the scarred dresser opposite his bed. Instead, he listened to the peaceful silence of the sleeping house, wishing he could rejoin it. Sweat glistened at the neck of his nightshirt, damped his back and arms, catching the light of his bedside candle. A handful of spent matches attested to his failed attempts to light the candle with trembling hands. He had not dreamed this past month, and yet, the very day Maledicte set foot under the Dove Street roof, the nightmare returned.

He shook himself like a wet dog, shrugging off tendrils of nervousness and fear as if they were droplets of water. Settling himself into the sheets again, he reached to snuff his hard-earned flame. Then, instead, he rolled his back to the light, pulling the linens over his shoulders.

The nightmare returned as if he had never managed to wake from it. The catafalques again, and one tomb split asunder, the crushing, underground darkness, lightless save for the sullen bloody glow around Her. She perched, talons dug into a dead man's chest, Her beaked face stabbing into the soft, opened belly. Clotted gore blurred Her features. All Gilly could see were Her starving eyes and a few strands of pale hair gleaming in the offal smearing Her face. Gilly took hesitant steps, wanting to name

Her victim, but She had been there already and the eyes were gone, the face ruined.

The unlight that showed him Black-Winged Ani coiled, shifted, and revealed Maledicte, down on one knee, leaning on the sword. He looked at Gilly with eyes as hungry as Ani's and said, "Is this my vengeance completed? This is not how I expected it to be."

Ani rose up behind him, Her wings shutting out even that bloody light, a taloned foot reaching for Maledicte's shoulder. Maledicte's hand ghosted up, a pale spider in the darkness, and rested atop Her clawed foot; in protest or acceptance, Gilly couldn't tell. She bent Her face to Maledicte's, Her beak hovering closer and closer to Maledicte's eyes.

"Mine" was all She said, but Her voice was as merciless as floodwaters.

Gilly woke for the second time with a racing heart and nausea stirring his belly. His ears rang with the aftermath of Her voice. The candle flame danced with the rushing wind of his breath and Gilly reached for it. As he moved, he saw someone standing in the doorway, a shadow blooming against the small flame.

The maid Livia? Gilly thought, hoping to lose his fear in the game of pleasure. But she wouldn't have come to his room, risking her position, not now that Vornatti had taken residence.

"Awake, finally?" The rasp identified the speaker beyond any doubt. Maledicte strolled over to the bed, stopping a few feet from the edge.

Still fully dressed in his fanciful black, the candlelight coiling around him, he woke some of the dream dread in Gilly. But instead of despair, Maledicte's current expression hovered toward offense.

"What were you dreaming, Gilly?" he asked. "You tossed and turned so, and you—" His voice, brittle, broke and faded.

"It was a nightmare. A most unpleasant one."

"You said my name in it. I thought you'd seen me come in, but you were sleeping. What were you dreaming?" It was more than interest. It was an angry demand.

Gilly pushed his sweaty hair back, feeling worn beyond his measure, and not in any mood to decipher the why of Maledicte's anger.

"You have no right to dream of me," Maledicte said.

Gilly sighed. "Dreaming is a magic beyond reason, Mal. I am sorry that your presence in my dream offended you. It doesn't mean anything." Except that Ani, supposedly dead and gone, lived well in his dreams.

"Are you trying to burn the house down?" Maledicte said, changing the subject. "Or have you taken to tippling the old bastard's opiates?"

"Did you come in to cut up at me?" Gilly asked. "If so, please go away. I'm tired. While you explored your new territory, I worked."

As changeable as mercury, Maledicte said, "My poor Gilly. I'll let you sleep, but I do recommend that you put out the candle. I can think of more pleasant deaths than burning in your bed."

"What do you need?" Gilly said. "I am quite awake and intend to stay so." To prove his point, he propped himself up into a sitting position against the mounded pillows.

Maledicte drifted to the side of the bed, settled himself. The feather mattress shifted under his weight. "I want to know what magic you worked to gain our entrance. Whose secrets were so interesting. . . ?"

Gilly mistrusted the dark humor in Maledicte's eyes and tried to delay. "I met a boy who knew your Janus."

Maledicte's face shuttered into blankness. "Did you."

"A boy called Roach? Was working in the Bull and robbing their customers, given the chance."

"Roach," Maledicte said, recognition evident in the wariness of his voice. "What had he to say?"

Gilly shrugged. "Our paths crossed only briefly." Roach, skulking in the alley, had tried to rob Gilly of his hard-won letter and the scandalous information within. Gilly, pleased with his success, had merely shaken Roach silly, and told him he was a fool to try to steal something he couldn't even read. "He said Janus taught him to read. Said that Janus killed his girl."

"Roach is a fool," Maledicte said. "Best forget him and his words, Gilly." Maledicte rose, and lit another candle from the first. But instead of warming the room, the second flame only added more shadows to lurk in the corners.

Gilly tore his apprehensive gaze from them, focused on Maledicte's acid voice. "Didn't you have better things to do than listen to a Relicts rat?"

"I had what I needed by then," Gilly said. He took the candle back from Maledicte and settled it firmly beside him once more, wondering what kept the dream still so close. His own fear? Or Maledicte's presence?

"Which was—?" Maledicte drawled. "So far I've not learned what secret was so powerful."

"An indiscreet letter from the Marquis DeGuerre to his sister," Gilly said. "Not a counselor himself, but a counselor's nephew. It sufficed."

"You played housebreaker?" Maledicte asked. "I cannot imagine you doing so. You're rather too big."

"I hired Livia away from DeGuerre," Gilly admitted. "She pilfered the letter as she left his employ."

"Very clever," Maledicte said, his tone mocking. "But Gilly, don't you think Vornatti's household is rather full of riffraff by now? The old profligate himself, his pet blackmailer, a thieving maidservant—"

"And a stripling killer," Gilly said. He had meant the words to be a gentle tease, but with Ani's presence lingering in his mind, the words came out like a taunt.

Maledicte frowned, temper risen. "We'll see whether Last finds me as amusing as you do. Go back to your dreams, Gilly." He snuffed the candle with quick, angry fingers, and Gilly caught his arm.

"Mal, don't," he said.

"Frighted of the dark?" Maledicte said, freeing himself, stumbling over a book beside the bed. "No wonder, if this is the nonsense you read." He tossed *The Book of Vengeances* onto Gilly's lap and started for the door.

"Don't be so touchy," Gilly said. "I meant no offense." But after three years of feeding and training, the boy hadn't grown much in truth.

Maledicte slumped into a chair, put his feet up on Gilly's bed. "Last cannot come too soon to suit me. This waiting palls." His eyes grew as dark as the shadows, and Gilly's mouth dried, imagining Ani reaching out to claim Maledicte from the gloom encircling him. Even once Maledicte left, Gilly watched the flame and found tenuous solace in its light until it burned down with sunrise.

7

MALEDICTE STOOD, limned in the sulfurous candlelight that was de rigueur for formal occasions, flattering to the aged roués and dames, adding glamour to insipid youths. The nobles' ballroom was a half-moon bordered with elaborate gardens on the curving side, shuttered with gilded doors along the straight edge. For special nights, the king threw open the doors, folding them in on themselves, making a full moon of the ballroom. But the nobles' ballroom was there for their delectation; it was full from spring to fall and, if boredom weighed too heavily, through the winter as well.

In the antechamber behind Maledicte, Vornatti penned his signature in the guest book. Maledicte had already signed, and Gilly added his under the line of servant-attendant.

Vornatti snapped the book shut, to the irritation of those trying to read the name of the new attendee over his shoulder. "Haven't the discretion to wait 'til we're in?"

Maledicte heard all this faintly, watching the ballroom. One or two dancers paused in their steps, their eyes slewing to the doorway. A cluster of young gentlemen began an endless night of betting and gambling. Jewels flashed like captured sunlight fed back to the sky. The inlaid marble flooring was patterned like broken seashells, and the drift of dresses and seafoam lace made the room sway like ocean waves. Blue-gray drapes fluttered and whispered at alcoves, at exits, at every furtive movement.

Maledicte stood in the door, neither in nor out. If he stepped forward, the game became inevitable, even if the result remained uncertain. If he stepped back, he forfeited the prize he so dearly craved. He was wrong, he thought; the floor didn't resemble the sea, but shadowy wings rising in a twilight sky. At his side, the sword hilt brushed his shaking fingers; a shudder rippled across his nape, traveled down his rigid spine in a convulsive bout of nerve storms, and was done. He stepped forward.

Maledicte wore dove gray tonight, a demure color, and yet all eyes moved toward him. He bowed to those who followed their gazes and came to meet him. One nobleman, fox-haired, broad-shouldered, and lean, glanced up, his eyes registering hatred. But he moved across the floor, made a clipped bow to their party, and said, "Baron Vornatti."

"Ah, Marquis, I don't think you know my ward, Maledicte."

The marquis nodded. "Maledicte. I bid you—welcome."

"So formal," Maledicte said. He heard Gilly suck breath in beside him, and stifled a smile. "When it seems we know you so well. Tell me, sir, how is your sweet sister?"

DeGuerre's face stiffened; he turned on his heel, walking away. Vornatti laughed.

Gilly rushed into speech. "Be careful, Mal, he is a very angry man. And angry men are hard to hold by secrets. I do not know how long it will be before he strikes at you. If I'd known you would speak so, I would never have told you the contents of that letter."

"Don't fret, Gilly," Maledicte said. "I only said it to amuse."

"Amuse?" Gilly said. "Amuse who?"

"Myself," Maledicte said. "Don't lecture. Tell me instead who these people are."

Vornatti smiled again, and said, "Yes, Gilly. Show me how well you remember your faces."

"The gentleman in the corner is Dominick Isley, Lord Echo, Mal, and perhaps even you've heard of him. He heads Echo's Particulars, his private band of thief takers, bill collectors, and gallowsmen."

"I know them," Maledicte said, thinking of frantic scrambles in the Relicts, dodging the sound of Echo's bells.

"Our scrutiny has drawn his attention," Gilly warned.

Echo strolled over, nodded curtly to Vornatti. "Still alive, old reprobate?"

"Solely to spite you, I've found myself an heir," Vornatti said.

Echo surveyed Maledicte, nostrils flaring as if he scented the Relicts lingering on Maledicte's skin. "Your kin?"

Maledicte said, "In temperament, perhaps."

"Your parentage?" Echo demanded. "If not kin to Vornatti, then who? Who was your sire?"

Maledicte raised his brows at Echo's interrogation but drawled, "A bit of a scandal there." Vornatti set his hand on Maledicte's arm, hand closing tightly, gloved fingers pinching the long nerve. "And one my kind guardian would prefer I not discuss."

Maledicte sighed; Vornatti wanted to cloak him in rumor and speculation, and had set Gilly to plant lies, slandering various dead noblemen. Maledicte wanted to spit the truth in their face, show them that a Relict rat was human, regardless of blood. He knew, though, that even had he done so, brought Ella cringing and fawning forward, the nobles would deny it, and turn their belief back to more-palatable rumor.

Echo blinked, unused to being denied. "Your mother, then?"

Maledicte tugged his arm free from Vornatti's painful grip, and leaned closer to Echo. "I'll give you a hint. They called her Lady Night, and she collected men's tithes with a smile, a moan, and a curse," Maledicte said.

Nearby, a woman in a bronze-green gown laughed, her eyes meeting Maledicte's with wicked amusement. "Such a scandal." She mimicked his earlier words.

Maledicte smiled at her before turning to Echo once more. "You seem perplexed. I will let you ponder her identity on your own."

Echo flushed at the dismissal in Maledicte's voice, cast him a fulminating glance, and left.

"Be careful, Mal," Gilly said. "He's more clever than he appears."

"He'd have to be," Maledicte said, frowning. "That's twice tonight you've told me to be careful, Gilly. I think you don't want me to enjoy myself at all."

"Aris likes him," Vornatti said. "That's reason enough to be cautious. Aris would have him head of the Kingsguard would Echo only agree. But Echo enjoys his thief-taking ways too well to change his prey from rats to aristocrats."

"Unless they're *poor* aristocrats," Gilly said. "He has jailed several of those, and so pretends to evenhandedness."

"Is that so," Maledicte said, watching Echo make his way across the room, inclining his head to some, and fetching up near a young man sipping moodily from his goblet. "Who stands beside him?"

"Can't you guess?" Gilly said.

"Limp cravat, mud on his boots, hair disordered and yet—people smile at him, bow to him. Lord Westfall."

"The same," Gilly said. "The third of Aris's advisers and the only one here tonight. A financier of Echo's Particulars, and Aris's gesture toward the future. Westfall is machine-mad, his mind occupied with gears and levers that will miraculously insure Antyre's prosperity—if he can keep the anti-machinists from destroying his factories as he builds them. So far, they're winning."

"Why isn't Last one of Aris's counselors?" Maledicte asked.

Vornatti answered, leaning back in his chair to take the wine Gilly offered him. "He's a traditionalist past the point of sense. Had he ascended the throne, Itarus and Antyre would war openly yet. It's the gods, though, that did him in. His refusal to admit Their absence. Aris is a modern king, uninterested in the ways of dead gods."

"And of course, there *are* whispers that Last attempted to wrest the throne from Aris in the first moments of his ascension. A hard thing to forgive, even for a kindly king." The new voice belonged to the noble lady in the bronze-green gown that burnished her auburn hair to a flame. "You are new come to the court," she accused.

"I am," Maledicte said.

"Tell me then, is it gaucherie or insouciance that allows you to stare so scornfully?"

"Insouciance, of course," Maledicte said, with the first pure enjoyment he'd had. "What cavalier ever admits to gaucherie? But, Lady, a question in return. I thought it not the thing for a lady to approach a strange courtier. Is it lack of manners or audacity that drives you?"

The lady laughed, a delicate trill of sound. "Neither in my case, though what lady would ever declare herself mannerless? I am quite well acquainted with your guardian." She curtsied toward Vornatti, her skirts pooling outward in elegant sweeps. "Will you introduce us then, sir? Or have you been so long from the court that you forget our friendship?"

Vornatti kissed her pale hand a breath too long, and said, "Only a madman or fool would allow himself to forget the charming Lady Mirabile. May I make my ward known to you?"

"I think not," she said, her lips curling with amusement. "His tongue is perhaps too rough, unless—" She paused to flash a dimpled cheek at Maledicte. "Unless you've had him schooled in dancing."

"Expensively schooled," Vornatti said, glaring briefly at Maledicte.

"Then," Mirabile said, "you may present me. And you may take my hand for the after-dinner dance set." She curtsied again, and departed.

"Gilly, I've been upstaged," Maledicte whispered, half smiling, half offended. "Who is she?"

"A woman, wicked and wild-natured enough to seduce a onetime intercessor. Darian Chancel's widow and murderess. As well as Vornatti's onetime paramour."

"Watch your tongue, Gilly," Vornatti cautioned. "What courtiers prattle about could see a servant whipped."

"Echo jailed her," Gilly lowered his voice. "But evidence was hard to come by. There was a matter of another man who she accused of the crime. It cost her everything to buy her freedom—her estate, her fortune, her reputation. Now she leeches off friends and hunts a husband again."

Vornatti said, "You see what wonders civility affords, Maledicte? Mirabile's dearest friend is Brierly Westfall, and so she lives on Westfall's estate, where Echo visits daily. I hear they often sit to tea together." He laughed. "And I wager Echo is more uncomfortable than she. Mirabile is a most dangerous woman."

GILLY RETURNED TO THE BALLROOM after ferrying a weary Vornatti to the Dove Street house, wondering if Maledicte's training had held without Vornatti to insure discipline, without Gilly to gesture disapproval. Peering around the room, he ignored the thump and rattle of a dowager tapping her cane on the tile. "Servant," she said. "Servant!"

"Lady," Gilly turned, bowing hastily, recognizing the temperamental and inquisitive baroness they called Lady Secret for her inability to keep one.

"You're Vornatti's, are you not?" The diamonds piled in her falsely dark hair winked in emphasis as she nodded in answer to her own question. "His ward is Itarusine, is he not? Has the look of one, all dark eyes and bones. Like Vornatti in his youth. Like the queen."

Like a lowly Itarusine sailor, Gilly thought, marveling again at the strange magic of flesh that created Maledicte. A creature fey and beautiful from blood as common as seawater. "He is Antyrrian," Gilly said. "He makes his bows to Aris, not Grigor."

She snorted, irritated at being corrected. Gilly bowed and escaped. Mulling what it meant for Maledicte's success that the baroness had taken an interest, it took him more time than it should have to notice the change in the air. A silent current ran the room, carried on whisper and scandal, as dangerous as a snake at twilight. Gilly tracked the source through widened eyes and bent heads, a trail of murmuring. At its center, of course, was Maledicte. Hastily, Gilly headed toward his charge, overcome with irritation. Not even a solitary hour; Maledicte was dangerously hard work.

Even now, Maledicte leaned close enough to the Lady Mirabile to warm her marble flesh with his breath as he spoke. Her eyes widened and gleamed; her teeth flashed in a small, practiced smile.

Gilly, close enough to overhear Maledicte's words, took Maledicte's sleeve in white-gloved hands and tugged like a demanding child. Maledicte paused, his mouth hovering by the spider-shaped patch on Mirabile's cheek.

"Is something wrong, Gilly?" Maledicte asked.

Lady Mirabile twined her arm around Maledicte's, forcing Gilly to move his hands or touch her skin. He let go his grip and met the wicked, jaded eyes of Lady Mirabile and, worse, the astonished gray gaze of Brierly Westfall. A servant interrupting his master? Mirabile laughed musically at his discomfiture.

Across the ballroom, DeGuerre heard Mirabile's triumphant voice, turned to look, and, espying Maledicte, turned his back.

The blackness of that brief glance restored Gilly's courage. "Outside, please?"

Either the "please" mollified Maledicte or Mirabile had begun to bore him; Maledicte took Gilly's gloved hand in his own. "Ladies. Forgive me." He sketched a bow; his hair, worn loose, fell curling over his shoulders. Mirabile's fingers twitched as if she would like to tangle those dark locks in her bloodless hands. She tossed her head in mechanical, charming disappointment, but Gilly knew her irritation and chagrin were real.

Gilly ushered Maledicte through the ballroom, toward the gilded antechamber, where heaps of discarded floral tributes perfumed the air and dusted the floor with bright, fallen petals.

"Have I been errant, Gilly? Mirabile seemed to admire my audacious tongue. Of course, I think she expects me to spend some time later with her, where my audacious tongue would be only for her enjoyment."

Gilly yanked Maledicte into the blue-curtained alcove that served as the cloakroom. Maledicte stumbled against Gilly and snarled, "Surely my sins, whatever they are, do not merit manhandling."

"Shh," Gilly said. "Be silent."

Maledicte's lips thinned, his eyes blackened, but the rage never surfaced. "You're angry at me."

Gilly shoved Maledicte toward a seat near the curtain.

"Temper, temper," Maledicte teased. His mouth opened; his tongue touched his teeth. He scented trouble and was pleased at the prospect. He folded himself down on a woman's fur-lined cloak, smoothing the pelt against his face. "Tell me why you're angry?"

"DeGuerre." Gilly tore the cloak from Mal's hands, hurled it over another hook.

"Everything is going quite well," Maledicte said.

"Well?" Gilly said. "Blackmail requires one person to hold a secret over another, and to keep that secret in exchange for goods, money, or services."

"I am passing familiar with the concept." Maledicte reached past the curtains to capture a goblet from a startled waiter, heading out toward the balconies and a rendezvous. He sipped, curled his lips in appreciation.

"Maledicte," Gilly said. A single word containing three years of exasperation. He raked his hands through his hair, catching his fingers in the queue and leaving it in tufty disarray. "You told Lady Mirabile and Brierly Westfall, the biggest gossips in the court, about Lilia DeGuerre."

"I hinted, Gilly."

"Every whisper you spread loosens our grip on DeGuerre. We need DeGuerre."

"No, we don't." Maledicte stood, pushed the goblet into Gilly's startled hands, the wine sloshing. "Sit."

Gilly did, his anger draining away, fear leaving him weak. DeGuerre was a powerful man with a bad temper. A counselor's nephew. A man not to be taunted. Maledicte smiled, slow and smug, and Gilly's concern grew. "If this is not some vicious whimsy, what is it?"

"DeGuerre gained us admittance to the court. Lady Westfall will keep us here to please her friend Mirabile."

"That frees you to mock a dangerous man, to spill his secrets to his peers? Mirabile is undoubtedly at DeGuerre's side even now, whispering your oh-so-audacious words into his ears, saying of course there's no truth in the matter, is there, but she thought he should know what is being said."

"If she's not, I've been most misled as to her character."

Gilly drank the excellent wine in one long draft. Maledicte moved behind him, unfastened the drooping laces in Gilly's hair. He smoothed the wheaten strands, refastened the ties. "There. All better. But really, Gilly, you should have more care for your appearance."

"DeGuerre will try to disprove your words with steel."

Maledicte touched the frown lines etching themselves between Gilly's brows as if he could remove Gilly's fears by the smoothing of his flesh. "I welcome it," Maledicte said. "I have been trained to fight, Gilly, but have not yet dueled. How can I face Last without knowing how my skills, belatedly learned, stack up against one trained from birth?"

"It's a foolish risk," Gilly said.

"But mine to take," Maledicte said, touching the hilt of his sword with contemplative fingers. "Come, Gilly, I haven't much time if I'm to goad DeGuerre to a duel. Aris is coming, and I've heard he frowns on such activities."

"I told you that, if you'll remember," Gilly said.

"Ah, that might explain why I believe it." Maledicte slid past the heavy drapes. "Wait a moment or two before returning to the ballroom. To be circumspect."

Gilly sighed. "I am your servant, Maledicte. I am beneath notice." He set the goblet on the floor of the cloakroom, followed Maledicte.

In the ballroom's wide doorway, DeGuerre stood, an arm outstretched as if he would bar Maledicte's reentry; his other hand hovered near the sword hilt on his hip.

Maledicte stood before him, smaller, slighter, and smiling. "Leaving the field of battle early?" He slipped past the man's locked arm like a shadow, and looked back over his shoulder. "My regards to Lilia. You have no idea how fondly I think of her."

DeGuerre spun, snatched Maledicte's sleeve; the seam gave in a slow syncopation of popping thread. "You're nothing. You're nothing at all. A common little catamite."

Maledicte stepped closer to the angry, bull-like figure. "Do you suppose that's what Lilia says—writhing, moaning, under her husband's thrusting? He was nothing to me, my darling, nothing at all. . . ." Maledicte forced his ruined voice into a parody of a woman's high tones. The rasp lent an air of gasping breathiness to the words, the sound of a woman in the throes of ecstasy or torment.

DeGuerre's face blanched. His eyes shone.

Maledicte said, "How it must gnaw at you. Loving her as you do, knowing she's lying with another, unable to protest. Knowing that there is one person for you, loving them through all hardships, and then, the sudden shock when it's all ripped away, like an unexpected gut wound that stinks and festers. Love rules you, Leonides DeGuerre, and torments you. We are not so different after all."

Gilly let out his breath, relaxing, but the sympathetic tone did what no taunt had. DeGuerre clenched his fist.

It was no openhanded slap that he landed, a gentleman's response to an affront, but a boxer's blow. Maledicte stumbled, head snapping to the side. The stiff cicatrix along his jaw cracked; a thin, red-beaded line welled up, touching the high edges of his lace collar. The violence rippled outward, quieting the court. Only the musicians continued, sawing out tunes for people no longer dancing.

"Not mannerly," Maledicte said. "And worse, it leaves your intentions in doubt. Are you inviting me to duel? I warn you, I have a bad temper in the mornings."

"Duel over filthy lies that no one believes," DeGuerre said, raising his voice for the court's listening ears. "I think not."

"You've killed to stifle those whispers before. Are you afraid of me?" Maledicte smiled.

Gilly bit his lip; if Maledicte's words stung too harshly, DeGuerre wouldn't wait until dawn, but would strike now, heedless of the court's traditions.

"One doesn't duel with vermin," DeGuerre said. "Or acknowledge their lies."

"You could sue me for slander," Maledicte said. "If you could prove my words false."

DeGuerre struck him again, backhanding him from the other direction.

Maledicte raised his head. Blood rouged his mouth. "If you intend to beat me to death, don't expect me to abstain from steel. Otherwise, declare the duel."

"Never with you. Relict rat." DeGuerre's breath came as fast and as hard as if he had been running; his hands shook. He took a stilling breath, then said. "Everyone knows commoners lack the moral sense to understand honor."

Before him, Maledicte seemed composed and faintly amused. He lowered his voice, luring DeGuerre closer. "But at least we don't fuck our siblings. It takes a nobleman to think of that." DeGuerre's face reddened in patches over his cheekbones, as if Maledicte's vulgarity had been an actual blow.

DeGuerre drew his sword in one flash of economic motion. The metallic rasp of the drawn blade spread, and the whispers rose. Blade drawn in the court. Lady Westfall, the highest-ranking hostess present, stepped forward, but said nothing; Mirabile's nails dug into her friend's hand, her eyes avid.

The two men circled each other like angry cats, DeGuerre's grip steady under the long weight of his blade, Maledicte's arms held out to his side, flaunting his still-empty hands. "Are you wronged or am I, DeGuerre? Do you claim affront? Or do I?"

"Draw your blade," DeGuerre said, "and stop your mouth."

"I will not draw until you admit I am your equal," Maledicte said.

Damn fool, Gilly thought. Anxiety rose in him like pain. *Draw your sword and have done with it. How will you take your vengeance from the grave?*

"You cower behind words. Draw your blade," DeGuerre repeated. He thrust his sword forward.

Maledicte leaped back, as quick and precise as an insect. The second thrust he ducked under, his curls ruffled by the blade's passage. Gilly could hear his panting, and the sound of whickering horses from outside.

DeGuerre's third thrust met steel. Maledicte rose from his half crouch, the black blade held before him.

This was the first time anyone within the court had seen the blade, the reality of it below the elaborate hilt. The sword might as well have flamed for all the horrified attention it claimed. It woke hungry shadows in the room, and changed Maledicte from merely another asp-tongued courtier to something much more, something dangerous.

8

OW THAT I HAVE YOUR REGARD," Maledicte said, "shall we agree to continue this at a more civilized time?"

"I would rather see if you've earned that fancy blade," DeGuerre said. He stepped forward, silver flashing from his blade, from the argent lace on Maledicte's quick-moving sleeves. The bell-ring of steel against steel tolled once, twice, growing louder, more resonant. Maledicte evaded another slash with boneless grace, dancing six steps back, out of range.

"Tradition demands we fight in the dawn."

"I'll trade tradition to see you die," DeGuerre said, rushing forward. Maledicte pivoted, regained his distance.

"You aren't good enough," Maledicte said, smiling.

They closed again, the shuff of their boots over the polished tiles a whisper beneath the chiming rasp of metal.

Small flickers of triumph darted over Maledicte's pale features, small moments where a touch could have been made. Instead, Maledicte bypassed openings; he prolonged the duel, playing with DeGuerre, testing himself.

"A natural gift," Master Thorn had said grudgingly as he left Vornatti's employ, bandages wound the length of his arm, a white swath around his neck. "His timing, his footwork, his extension, and his balance—" He touched his throat and said, "deadly." Watching now, Gilly shivered. Didn't a gift imply a giver?

A new sound entered the room—hoarse panting, the clicking of nails on the marble tiles. Gilly blanched; the duel had gone on too long, and whether DeGuerre improved or not, Maledicte had lost. Only one man brought his hound to the ballroom.

He raised his head. The king stood in the wide doorway, his hand resting on the brindle mastiff's withers, face layered with weariness and surprise. Beside him, the Kingsguard, clad in lapis and gold, hastily spread out, encircling him, pistols drawn. A sandy-bearded man pushed past them, cheeks flushing. "Who dares this?"

"Isn't that my question, brother?" Aris asked, releasing the hound. The mastiff pushed through the two front guards, and Aris followed him through the space.

Gilly caught a wheeling glimpse of the room, the interest in jaded eyes, the ashen dismay on Lady Westfall's face, the two men wagering at the most distant point of the room, the musicians' silence.

Maledicte, his back to the door, sucked in a breath as if Gilly's alarm had been transmitted, wordlessly, to him. He cast down his sword, though it seemed to writhe in his hand, and fell to his knees, lowering his head before the king's approach. Scarlet with rage, DeGuerre finished his extension, and his blade sliced the edge of Maledicte's shoulder. Maledicte hissed; his jaw clenched. Gilly's hands tore at his own sleeve, watching the wound's red tide rise.

"Sire," Maledicte said.

DeGuerre dropped his sword. Blood spattered the pale marble. "Sire." He knelt, as stiffly as an old man.

"To bare blades in the king's presence is treason," Last spoke, his eyes lingering on Maledicte, the stranger in the court's midst.

"Who drew first blade?" Aris asked, through lips compressed and pale.

"I did, sire," DeGuerre confessed, at the same moment Lady Westfall, pinched by Mirabile, said, "DeGuerre."

"Dueling in the ballroom is forbidden. As well you know, DeGuerre." Once more, the earl of Last spoke before Aris could. The earl's disapproval was marked in the downward sweeps of his brows, adding more rigid lines to his austere features.

"What matters where they duel, in the park or the courts? Blood shed is blood lost, be it on marble or dirt," Aris said, raking the assembled nobles with scorn in his face and voice. "But to stab a man as he kneels in fealty, DeGuerre . . ."

"How came you to do such a thing," Last said, "you with the best of our blood in your lines? Your uncle a king's counselor? Were you mad?" Last cast a wary glance at Maledicte's slender form. "Or witched?"

"Michel, search for your demons elsewhere. The court is mine, the offense mine. And the sentence *mine*," Aris said. His brows drew down, so like his brother's, and Gilly felt a spurt of hope. If Last pushed, Aris would pull.

"Leonides DeGuerre, of late I have heard distressing things about you. I think perhaps you would be better off for several years abroad, away from the . . . temptations and miseries you find so readily here. Seek the Explorations or Kyrda and make your fortune elsewhere. You may rise and go."

"As for the lad—" The king swept his eyes over the dark, bent head, the slim form. "Get the lad a physician and send him back to the schoolroom," he said, turning on his heel and tapping his thigh for the hound to follow.

Gilly, freed from his obeisance, darted to Maledicte's side, touched him with gentle hands, the red stain darkening the pale sleeve.

"Aris, the lad is guilty of more than—" Last trailed off as, beneath Aris's tensing hand, the mastiff growled.

"*My* court, brother," Aris said, and then, with a spurt of open irritation, "Oh, do get up, lad." He reached for Maledicte's shoulder, and paused as Maledicte raised his eyes to meet Aris's.

The king startled at Maledicte's blackly lashed eyes, at his curling hair, at his mouth, at the pale skin. He came closer, pushing the hound out of his way.

"You—you are Vornatti's ward?" Aris said, voice low.

"I am," Maledicte said.

The king's face grew shuttered. The silence in the room strained in Gilly's ears. Maledicte swayed, jerked himself to rigidity again. A few new drops of blood spattered on the marble.

"You seem guilty of nothing but impetuosity," Aris said, the words a bare breath, his eyes locked on Maledicte's dark ones. He cleared his throat, spoke again. "You may return to this court as you will."

Maledicte bent his head, hiding his strained face. "You are kind."

The king's eyes never left the bowed, dark head. "Get to a physician. Lad."

"Some lessons in manners would be more to the point, Aris," Last said.

"Or are we to have yet another foreign decadent making hash of our tradition? Is the court not tired of such?"

"The court, Michel," Aris said wearily, "is entranced at the wonderful entertainment we've had this night."

Last stiffened, a marionette instead of a man. He bent at the waist, and left.

The king watched him go, and then said, "And yet he is correct. Will you swear, lad, that you will never draw a blade again in my presence?"

"I so swear, my liege." When the king proffered his hand, Maledicte kissed the crested ring.

The king turned and left, his guards following and half the court. The remaining nobles clustered in little knots of bright fabric, to discuss and whisper. Gilly heard a scrap of conversation as he drew Maledicte to his feet, moved toward the door.

"Last was right. DeGuerre must have been witched to so lose his senses."

Gilly turned, seeking the dangerous speaker. Witchcraft was not a word to be spread lightly, not when he'd seen Aris's face go so still and empty for that one moment, as if the page of his thoughts had been erased and rewritten. Not when witchcraft was the only force left that the nobles feared.

"Hardly a sign of bewitchment," Mirabile's elegant voice said. "To be so goaded by an agile tongue and mind."

"But that sword, Mirabile, and if not witchcraft then what else can it be?" Lady Secret asked, her voice pitched to carry while at the same time still pretending to a whisper. "Your Chancel was a theologian, surely you must—"

"Oh la, Secret, what makes you think I ever had any interest in his prosing on about dead things?" Mirabile laughed, but her eyes on Maledicte held speculation and a faint hint of surprise. Gilly dragged Maledicte toward the door, away from that too-intent gaze.

Maledicte clutched Gilly's arm, halting their steps. "The sword, Gilly. Let me go. I cannot leave it."

Its blade had sunk into the marble floor nearly a finger's length; Maledicte yanked it free with an impatient grace that made the court widen the clearing around him.

Outside, in the cool, damp air, their boots crunched unevenly over the oyster-shell drive as Gilly supported Maledicte. Gilly called out as they reached the entrance to the stables; their hired coachman rose from the grouping of his fellows and their game of dice. He lit the lanterns inside the coach and held the door for them.

Gilly ripped off his servant's cravat, only loosely starched, and pressed it over Maledicte's bloody sleeve. "Hold this," he said.

Maledicte's white fingers pressed the cloth tight. "I know what to do. It's not much of a wound."

"Enough to make you stagger and faint," Gilly said. He fumbled for his handkerchief to pad the wound.

"Last came in with Aris. Within reach of my sword," Maledicte whispered through white lips. "And I did nothing."

Gilly, securing the rough bandage of cravat and handkerchief with his hair ribbon, paused. "Yes," Gilly said, taken aback, realizing that Maledicte's sudden weakness came from that rather than blood loss—that pain was less to him than vengeance. Gilly's hands trembled; he stilled them.

"What if I've missed my moment?" Maledicte said, his color fading further.

"Don't be ridiculous," Gilly said roughly, frowning as he saw a bloody line forming over Maledicte's ribs also. "The summer-solstice ball comes in a month. And the moment will repeat itself: you can still run Last through in a crowd full of witnesses and get shot by the Kingsguard for your pains. That is what would have happened tonight, had you not held your—" Gilly jerked his hand from Maledicte's shirt buttons when Maledicte slapped at him.

"Leave it," Maledicte snapped. "I've told you it's not much; it only stings and burns."

As the coach lurched to motion, Maledicte leaned back into the seat cushions with a wince, and no thought for his blood painting the embroidered fabric.

"You are fortunate," Gilly said.

"DeGuerre could never have touched me had I not thrown down my blade. I should have finished him first," Maledicte muttered.

"Not the duel," Gilly said. "Fortunate that Aris forgave you. He could have banished you as easily as he did DeGuerre."

"He forgave me for Vornatti's sake," Maledicte said. "Their paths are linked after all, kin by marriage, bound by money." He shifted in the seat. A small sound that might have been a groan stifled itself behind clenched teeth.

"We'll be home in moments." Gilly put his head out the carriage window and demanded the coachman's flask, passed it to Maledicte.

Maledicte tilted the flask; his anticipatory wince gave way to startlement and a smile. "He has raided Vornatti's good spirits, Gilly."

Gilly paid little attention beyond noting color seeping back into Maledicte's lips, thinking instead about the expression frozen on the king's face—the interest heating the cool eyes. "For Vornatti's sake only? I think there is more to it."

"What does it matter? He forgave me and that's enough. Aris is of no interest to me, save that he seems to hold Last in dislike. Still, not so much as I do. . . ." His lips compressed, his hand clenched on the hilt of the naked blade resting beside him. "I should have struck instead of knelt."

Shivering a little at the hunger in Maledicte's voice, wondering if that hunger would be so intense if Maledicte were not touching the blade, his vengeful instrument, Gilly said, "I thought you intended to wait on Janus?"

"Janus," Maledicte said, his hand unknotting. "I must see what they've made of him before I know how best to act. If he loves me not—" Maledicte's voice caught. "If he loves me not, I will kill him, and Last for taking him from me.

"If he loves me, I will still murder Last for taking him from me. Either way it means blood." Maledicte sat forward, hunched himself over his knees, a restless savor in his eyes, clasping the sword hilt again.

Gilly's skin crawled, the hair raising along his arms. Surreptitiously, he made a little X of his forefingers, invoking the old country charm against the god-touched. He had not had time to peruse *The Book of Vengeances* as he would have liked, but the little he had translated, slowly changing the Itarusine words for Antyrrian, had chilled him.

History claimed that a compact, irreversible, could be entered into, binding Ani and Her devotee to a single task, but that the compact became active only after the first kill. Were Gilly's fears real, his dreams more than dreams, were Ani not so dead as She once was, those implications would distress him beyond measure—that Maledicte, who hunted Last, would build strength in shed blood.

Gilly's mouth dried; he snagged the flask back and sipped. He was a fool, dreading the impossible. The gods were gone, and Maledicte—Maledicte was merely a man. The dreams were not evidence, the sword's presence inconclusive, his dueling skills purchased—if Maledicte survived poison, it owed only to caution; if he never sickened, it owed only to luck. All of it was sea-fire proof, prone to disappearing when Gilly sought answers, leaving him only with a knot in his belly and the taste of copper in his mouth where he had bitten his tongue.

The pleasure in Maledicte's eyes while dueling came back to him, that gloating joy as he danced around DeGuerre's strikes. Even while Gilly dwelled on nightmare possibilities, Maledicte smiled, stroking the feathered hilt, eyes black and clouded.

9

*I*T WAS A FINE DAY, just past the cusp of noon, and Gilly chose to walk to the baker's, escaping the cluster of noble-women who had come to gossip again with the most scandalous courtier in several seasons. The first day the crush had arrived, Maledicte had found it amusing to parade himself. But a week into the season, Maledicte's temper sharpened as his interest waned; today he'd abandoned his guests to Vornatti's care.

Gilly, summoned to the formal parlor, found the room more crowded than before; the very walls, the spinet, even the small stage, seemed overlaid with women. Mirabile had seized the position of hostess and sat entirely too close to Vornatti, distributing tea and spite with an equal hand. When Gilly presented himself, careful not to tread on any trailing hems, Vornatti had dispatched him to roust Maledicte from wherever he had hidden himself.

A lucky word with the cook had sent Gilly out-of-doors, hunting tea cakes as well as Maledicte. He stretched under the sunlight and found himself smiling. Of late, he'd been too much in stuffy, overcrowded rooms. The brisk wind and the faint smell of the sea were balm to his senses. He passed the Dove Square speakers, the men standing on rough-made pulpits, preaching egalitarianism, sedition, economics. In the midst of this, one man, dressed in country best, dared to speak for the absent gods, and was booed to silence.

Gilly dropped a few coppers into the intercessor's cast-off coat. The intercessor stroked the symbol of Baxit, the god of indolence and reason, above Gilly's head. *Let it stop the dreams*, Gilly thought, nodding his head in thanks before moving on toward the shops.

His business done with the baker, Gilly paused, unwilling to go back. He had not found Maledicte and had no desire to be scolded by Vornatti or thrown into polite confines with women he could not touch. Sifting ideas and excuses, he kept walking, heading toward the quay. He would bring back fresh fish and crab for Vornatti, and some of the succulent oysters that Maledicte and Gilly shared an unfashionable taste for. He took the winding way, through the alleys behind the shops, the way the cart horses went.

The alleys were intermittently crowded; Gilly stepped aside for a cart bearing sacks of sugar and fine spices from the Explorations. The stamp on the bags, a blue moon, told Gilly that this was the best of the imports, destined not to be sold to Itarus and Dainand, but to be made into elaborate sweets for the Antyrrian court. The redolence of cinnamon and raw cocoa lingered.

The soughing of the waves, the spluttering suck of water around the pier and ship hulls, announced the docks before he saw them. The last twist of the alley dropped and provided a cobblestoned view that ran, illusory, into the gray waters.

Gilly went down, intending to watch the ships and sailors at dock, perhaps find his friend Reg's ship at berth, when a flutter of delicate cloth caught his eye. A sprig of the nobility stood on the quay, his pale shirt gold-shot in the sunlight, his hair black and wind-tossed. Gilly stopped. Not just any young noble, but his.

Maledicte stared at the water, the ships coming in, the new ships being built, his body rocking slightly with the movement of the sea as if he were imagining himself on it.

"Planning on catching a ship abroad?" Gilly asked.

Maledicte shifted his gaze to a ship with a red and gold-spotted prow and a figurehead like a dolphin. "Why should I make all the effort? Besides, I have Vornatti's assurance he'll return. I can trust that, can't I?"

The bitterness in his voice slowed Gilly's approach. "Of course," Gilly said. "What's got you so cross so early?" Gilly sat down on the pier, dangled his legs over the eddying water. This close to shore, the waves carried refuse: draggled gull feathers, floating fish, silver bellies up, and ropes of seaweed torn loose from their beds by rough anchors.

"Mirabile," Maledicte said. "She shadows my every move, clinging to my arm, matching my clothes—it's uncanny."

Gilly laughed. "Mal, we broker in information, sift through servants' tales for our benefit, why not Mirabile? She must pay someone in the house."

"You?" Maledicte said. Gilly looked up into sun dazzle and Maledicte's shadowed face.

"Livia, likely," Gilly said. "She likes coin. It's harmless enough."

"Well, tell Livia to stop, or to feed Mirabile lies, that I'm wearing rose when I'm wearing blue. She's too vain to cling if she clashes." Maledicte kicked a small strip of tar-daubed wood into the water.

"If she learned you had misled her deliberately, she'd be offended, and she's not one to take offense lightly," Gilly said. "She's courting you, Mal."

Maledicte snarled. "Why me? No, her reason doesn't matter. Stop her."

"All right," Gilly said, and Maledicte ceased his fidgeting.

"Just like that?"

Gilly grinned; for once he had surprised Maledicte. "I know what to say. It's only a matter of feeding the information to her."

Maledicte let out a long sigh, his shoulders loosening. "No one taught me how to repel the nobles. All my lessons were to fit in. It was easier before I learned proper etiquette."

Gilly stifled a laugh. "How would you have rid yourself of her before you became such a pattern card of propriety?"

Maledicte shrugged. "With a stick."

Gilly let the laugh free. But when the first wash of amusement had faded, he knew it was the truth. He'd seen the boy Roach and his rude weaponry, knew the damage a savage hand and a stick could inflict. And Maledicte wasn't just any Relict rat; a glossy dark feather washed by, and Gilly's good humor died with resurgence of his fears, waking something in its stead.

Gilly didn't understand it—why that one drifting feather should spur him to the point that he had avoided for a week, for far longer, were he honest with himself. A dream of Ani. A boy with a feather-hilt sword and a thirst for vengeance. The words rose in his throat, the question, the need for an answer. Knowledge had to be preferable to this gnawing uncertainty. But Maledicte's moods were tricky, and Gilly swallowed the first simple question for a more cautious approach, attempting to creep up on truth. He cleared his throat of nervousness.

"You came from the Relicts," Gilly said. "Have you ever heard the story of how they came to be?"

"Of course I have. The noble girl, spurned by her merchant lover, prayed to Ani. Ani answered *her* prayer by destroying the merchant, the shops, the streets, everything he ever loved." Maledicte sank down to sit beside Gilly, sheltering in the lee of Gilly's broader body. "Just proves the power of the nobles, even over the gods."

Gilly shrugged, kept it casual with an effort. "I know a different version. Should I tell you?"

Maledicte aped Gilly's shrug. "If you must."

"The noble girl's name was Liana, the merchant was no merchant at all, being even more common than that. A delivery man named Edward. She loved him beyond all reason. She gave him everything—her body, her heart, the jewelry she stole from her home. And when she had nothing more to give, he left her for another. The rage and pain she felt were too much to bear and she cried out to Ani to avenge her hurt, to deny that he could love someone else, that the other woman could exist."

"So the Relicts—" Maledicte said.

"*No.* Nothing happened. Ani didn't act Herself, but She crept into Liana's dreams, bartering love for vengeance, rage for power. Liana drowned her rival in a swan pond. Edward found his new love there, soaked in black feathers though all the swans were gray, and knew Liana had asked Ani for intervention."

Gilly fisted his hand; even in *tales* the proof of Ani's touch seemed ephemeral at best, until it was far too late for any doubt. The rook feather eddied below them, riding the waves, and Gilly looked from it to Maledicte, wondering if Ani might be listening behind those black eyes.

"Go on then," Maledicte said.

"Once the deed was done, Liana found nothing left in her heart but grief. Ani muttered, reminding her that she had cried out against her lover also and their compact must be completed. But there was no hatred left for Ani to fuel; though Liana sought Edward, it was only to beg forgiveness.

"It was then that Ani roared to life, Her wingbeats leveling the Relicts. Liana and Edward disappeared beneath the rubble, entombed together in the city. Vengeance, once begun, cannot be stopped. Black-Winged Ani has no pity in Her, and Her wings are carrion wings."

Maledicte watched the wavelets foam and fade against the pilings, wordless. Gilly tilted his chin up, peered into the dark eyes, his fingers trembling as he finally braved the question. "Where did you get the sword, Maledicte? Why do I dream of Ani when you're near? Did you call out to Her? Did She answer?" His fingers tightened as Maledicte's silence continued.

Maledicte's eyes stayed enigmatic behind barring lashes. He tugged his chin free from Gilly's fingers, dropped a piece of shell into the water, watching the ripples overtake the waves and fade before answering. "I never called Her." He flicked a quick glance at Gilly, cooling Gilly's burgeoning relief, and continued, voice low. "Yet, while I was dreaming, She woke in me, whispered such things— When I slept, it was summer. I woke to winter, the feel of feathers in my skull and skin, and a black sword at my side."

In that moment, Gilly knew he had expected Maledicte to laugh at him, to shelve his doubts behind a wall of scorn for his gullible nature. Gilly had expected to laugh at himself, and to compliment Maledicte's talents for acting. This impossible admission woke shock in his belly, set his blood to racing, and rendered him mute. The gods not gone. Maledicte bound to Black-Winged Ani. He shuddered, wanting to surge to his feet and flee, heedless that he might offend Mal—or Ani!—mortally. His breath seized in his chest.

The thing that balked him, cooled him, kept him from panic, however, was a memory of another quiet moment, and how lovely it had felt to hold Maledicte's trust, to be the one who could tease truth out from semblance.

Maledicte shivered as if he would unsay his words, remove Her looming presence. Gilly dropped a wary arm over his shoulders, seeking something to take the chill from between them, to chase the nearly solid mass of fear from his belly.

"That ship, you see it?" He pointed to a massive square-rigged ship entering the cove, setting up a frenzy of motion on a far pier. Its figurehead shone molten in the sunlight, a curled cat with a fish's flukes.

"It looks like gold," Maledicte said, ignoring the quiver in Gilly's voice, focusing on the ship with an avidity that suggested that he also hunted an escape from his confession.

"It is." Gilly found a shaky smile at Maledicte's astonishment. As always the ships soothed him as nothing else could. The fear unclenched; his voice evened out. "That's the *Virga*. She sails to the Explorations and comes back with treasures—spices, wood for our shipbuilders, and strange pets, birds, and small scampering monkeys that look nearly human. Someday I'll be on that ship. Headed for the new world, where people build ascending temples of dirt and stone to speak to their sky gods, see what they have to teach me. Though, according to most accounts, they're only savages."

"Why do we call them savages if they have temples and religion? That's more than we have," Maledicte said, his hair whipping in the sea breeze, his booted feet swinging off the pier, his frozen stillness broken.

Gilly laughed, drew closer to Maledicte, inclined his head in the studied manner of a professional gossip. He raised his brows, and exclaimed in falsely arch tones, "Oh, my dear, haven't you *heard,* don't you *know*—?"

Maledicte's ease faded. He cast a slantwise glance at Gilly, testing for unexpected mockery.

Laying his hand on Maledicte's arm, careful of the bandages beneath the full sleeve, Gilly dropped his voice to a penetrating whisper. "My dear, they wear *feathers* where we wear *leathers.*"

Maledicte's eyes widened and he laughed, a stuttering, raw thing in his ruined throat.

Gilly grinned, pleased with the result of his teasing. He had wanted Maledicte to laugh earlier; he shook back the shiver that wanted free, concentrating instead on their innocuous conversation.

"For breeches? Are the feathers ticklish?"

"I suppose there's a hide backing. But they wear feathers all over. On their feet, in their hair, all shades of red, gold, blue, and green. They have birds down there bigger than our owls, and more brightly patterned than our pheasants."

"What else, Gilly?"

Maledicte seemed honestly interested, completely at ease, and Gilly wondered if perhaps he had only been teasing. But—*I woke, a black sword in my hand,* Maledicte said, his voice drowned in memory. Gilly shuddered. He fell into the security of speech, nearly babbling. "They find gold on the ground, in the waters, and they make soft, hand-malleable jewelry from it. Wide necklaces, armbands, earrings, rings. They even press gold between their teeth so that their smiles are as bright as their feathered clothing. They have dark eyes, like yours, but their skin is the color of strong tea, and they draw pictures on it with clays and dyes. They drink chocolate with every meal under warm blue skies." Gilly spoke mostly for himself, remembering the tales his sailor friend, Reg, told. Maledicte, rapt, watched the *Virga*, resting his chin on his drawn-up knees, setting Gilly to wondering where Maledicte's interests lay: The gold? The tropical warmth? The images of strange cities and stranger men?

Maledicte shivered and said, "I'm hungry." The complaint was blessedly familiar, and Gilly relaxed into it.

"Cook said you missed breakfast, and I know you missed tea. Let's go get you an ice." Gilly stood, offered his hand.

Maledicte took it, shook the dust from the pier off, and said. "I have no money. Vornatti was angry this morning and wouldn't make me my allowance."

"A true aristocrat doesn't even think about money. He assumes all shops offer credit and are pleased to do so."

Maledicte merely nodded, his face pale, his lips drawn.

"Your side? Your arm?" Gilly asked, stopping in his tracks. Since Maledicte's injuries, Gilly had feared infection. The boy had not let him see to the wounds, instead had trusted his skin to Vornatti's suturing.

"Sore," Maledicte admitted.

"You'll be lucky if the wounds don't fester. Vornatti is no physician."

"It heals, regardless," Maledicte said.

Yes, Gilly thought, the knowledge assailing him again, a slap of frigid seawater, scouring and impossible to digest. Wasn't healing one of Ani's gifts? Something good turned to malign purpose; it was hard to stop a man immune to violence. But Maledicte had bled enough—

"Stop staring," Maledicte said. "You promised me food."

Gilly found them a table in the public rooms of the Glorious, the ice shop popular among the maidservants and merchants, secretaries, sailors, and laborers. It had once been a temple to Naga, the serpentine god of health and avarice, and the rooms still boasted elaborate murals of undulating waves and scale; the columns were Naga rising from the sea depths, fanged mouths gaping and holding coats.

In the midst of this they sat, eating tart lime ices and sugar pastries, drinking bitter coffee with sweet sludge at the bottom. Maledicte's lips reddened with the cold kiss of the confection, his cheeks flushed by the steaming drink.

"Vornatti must have grown bored with his company," Gilly said, looking at the carriage drawing up to a discreet storefront, marked only by three silver balls on a cord.

Following Gilly's gaze, Maledicte turned his head. They watched Mirabile step out of the carriage, her dress loosely cloaked for anonymity, carrying a parcel. She disappeared into the dark recesses of the shop.

"A pawnshop?" Maledicte said, shifting to shelter behind Gilly, out of sight.

Gilly said, "She's popping her valuables. Or more likely Westfall's. I doubt she has anything left of value. But if she wed someone wealthy . . ."

Maledicte pushed his plate away. "She can't think of anything else?"

"There's nothing else for her to do," Gilly said. "She's an aristocrat, not trained to do anything. Or allowed to. Women in this society are ruined so easily."

"You sound sorry for her."

"No," Gilly said. "She had a rich husband and killed him. You might keep that in mind when you speak with her."

"I don't have to," Maledicte said, recovering his appetite, stealing the rest of Gilly's pastry. "My tasks require swords. This one doesn't. This task is yours."

10

Throughout time, men have been driven by outraged pride or loss to commit terrible acts of vengeance, demonstrating how dangerous, how vile man can be when he chooses to turn intellect to malign purpose. But nothing man can do is so dreadful as one aided by Black-Winged Ani, the god of love and vengeance. Under Her aegis, a single man's vengeance can consume not only families, but cities.

—Darian Chancel, "On Theology"

MIRABILE GLIMMERED in shades of orange and flame that brought warmth to her icy perfection, and echoed the fire and gilt of Maledicte's coat. At his entrance into the ballroom, she joined him as neatly as if they had planned it. Unusually, there was a faint tint of color in her cheeks; Maledicte, having heard the gossip, didn't wonder at it.

A trill of laughter touched his ears. "No, really my dear, Westfall had to pay for his own silver-backed brushes. Can you imagine—" Lady Secret and her listeners fell silent as Maledicte and Mirabile passed, stifling their smiles.

Outside, Maledicte had heard much of the same, that Adam Westfall tired of his unwanted guest, and pressured his wife to be rid of her. Maledicte only wished the man would do it soon and spare him yet another series of encounters with her delicately acid tongue.

"Tell me, Maledicte, how fares Vornatti, that you missed the Lovesys' ball? I thought you had meant to attend."

"That's the difficulty with bribing servant girls," Maledicte said. "They cost you coin and are unreliable."

Mirabile laughed. "You do say such terrible things." She leaned closer, offering a tantalizing glimpse of perfumed, powdered skin. "But you haven't excused your absence, and to spurn a counselor's ball requires an apology at least."

"I, too, noted your absence. You sent no word." The pleasant voice dropped Mirabile into a curtsy, Maledicte into a bow, as Aris joined them.

"Sire," Maledicte said. "Vornatti was ailing and I felt my place was beside him." It was as close as he would come to the truth, that after Gilly's and his disobedience that day by the sea, they had been punished. Gilly had been sent to sleep in the stables for a week, and Maledicte—Vornatti had kept him so close he might have been wearing a leash.

Mirabile murmured, "Yes, I believe I've seen what Vornatti considers your place." Maledicte felt a sudden crest of hatred for her tongue, for the fact that Mirabile, a favored visitor, had witnessed Vornatti's dominance with laughing eyes.

"You're pale tonight, lad. Do not let the idleness of town life cheat you of your health. You should dance more," Aris said, frown easing. "Put color in those fair cheeks."

"As I have been urging him to do," Mirabile said, tapping Maledicte's shoulder with her fan. "But will he dance? No, he will not." She held out her hand with expectant grace as the musicians began opening measures to a country dance, as if all the days of watching Maledicte obey Vornatti's whims made her wishes inviolate also.

Maledicte stepped out of reach without thinking. Mirabile's perfect features etched a quick frown and smoothed again. "You see, sire?"

"Ill-done of you, lad," Aris said. "We noblemen must never disappoint a charming and beautiful lady."

Mirabile claimed Maledicte's hand with a possessiveness that made his skin itch. "Yet you do not dance," Maledicte said, irritation bleeding into his voice. Belatedly, he tried to mask it with flattery, as he would for Vornatti. "And to be bold, my king, you are far more a maiden's dream than I."

Aris laughed, flushing a little. He reached for Mirabile's hand. "We will assay the floor together, Mirabile, and teach this pup some manners."

Mirabile curtsied again, topazes winking in her ruddy hair. "You honor me, sire."

"Come lad, find a partner," Aris said, smiling. He held up a gloved hand; the musicians paused.

In the silence, Maledicte's eyes slewed around. For a bare moment, they lit on Gilly, near hidden in the shadows of the balcony, before falling on a tiny, porcelain doll of a debutante whose chaperone had her head bent away in gossip. Maledicte took quick strides to her side. "Lady?"

The musicians surged into the involved patterns of the Labyrinthine. Maledicte and his partner moved neatly, with careful grace and the physical wariness of two people unacquainted. When Maledicte raised his eyes from the girl's downturned face, he found Aris's intelligent blue eyes fixed on him, and Maledicte stumbled.

Maledicte dropped into the final bow, brushed his lips over his partner's hand. She faded away, rejoining her frowning chaperone.

Aris bent over Mirabile's hand, and Maledicte took the moment to escape toward the balcony's evening shadows. Gilly saw him coming, raised the flask from his coat pocket.

A hand on his arm halted Maledicte. He spun and swallowed his bile. "Sire."

"Maledicte, come with me." The king released his hold on Maledicte's silk-covered arm, walked on, sure that Maledicte would follow. The scalloped balconies and quiet alcoves were popular enough that Aris had to search several doorways until he found a vacant one.

Aris sank down onto one of the carved marble benches that ran the perimeter of the balcony. On either side, tree roses shielded them from view. Below, the gardens smelled of damp moss and night flowers opening. Maledicte stood before him, hesitant and worried. He knew his temper was foul tonight, knew also that it led him into incautious behavior.

"You are new to my court and with Vornatti as your only guide, perhaps less informed than you should be of the social niceties."

"I apologize for my reluctance to dance, sire. I will make amends and dance every set left this evening. If you will it," Maledicte said, despite his aversion for such things. He did not care to stand so close to the other men, to hold women his height, fearing that it would only point out his slightness, risking his mask. Was that all—such a small thing to incur a king's displeasure. Maledicte bit his lips, closed his eyes, wishing again that he could simply reclaim Janus without all this mummery.

"You may do as you please, but Mal—" Aris's voice shifted as he assumed the intimacy of a friend. "Mal, a word of caution. While it is understood that certain young men find the company of other men preferable to the ladies, I would not have the lines of the dance ruined by such a pair. It requires discretion. Can you be discreet?"

"Do you find me so gauche as to expect such from me?" His tone was more insulted than concerned, but he was irritated out of reason that the king's interest extended so far into his life.

"I find you—" Aris hesitated, pulling a rose from the tree beside him and breathing in its scent. Its petals were near blown and browning at the edge; they shed at the touch of his breath. "I find you hard to predict. A creature of impulse in a rigid court, and I would not see my brother set against you. He has more power than I would like. . . ."

Maledicte paused, listening to the silence of what Aris had not mentioned—the effort it took Aris to tread the path between pleasing Vornatti, who held the purse strings of Antyre, and satisfying his ambitious brother.

Before Maledicte could speak, strains of music drifted outward, and Aris smiled. "The Labyrinthine again." He rose.

"Shall I dance it?" Maledicte asked.

"Not until you rectify your steps," Aris said.

Maledicte flushed, annoyed that Aris had seen him stumble.

"It's not so hard," Aris said, "But it takes some thought for one not brought up on it." He held out his hand.

MIRABILE, THWARTED IN HER PURSUIT by Aris's easy theft of her partner, stalked toward a balcony. She faltered when she saw it occupied, but then, with a sudden smile, came forward. "Such a moody creature, your master," Mirabile said, joining Gilly in the shadowed alcove.

"Lady?" Gilly said, his eyes on Maledicte vanishing after the king.

"Don't look so foolish," Mirabile said. "Sweet Livia tells me you're the man behind the scenes. Gilly, is it? Tell me about Maledicte."

"What do you want to know that Livia can't tell you?" Gilly said absently. Maledicte had seemed ordinary enough tonight, or as ordinary as he could be. Ani's presence seemed more dreamlike now than in his nightmares.

"I want to know what all women want to know. How much he dotes on me."

Gilly's attention sharpened. "Shouldn't you ask instead about his prospects? Or do you seek a marriage purely for love?"

"Purely for love?" Mirabile said, eyes flattening with wariness. "Maledicte has more to offer than love alone."

"Not money," Gilly said, leaning against a pillar. "Vornatti grants him an allowance, that's all." Her pleasant expression changed to one of slit-eyed anger. "You lie. Livia says Maledicte has coin of his own."

"Livia," Gilly said, with a rush of anger, "is a *servant*. She thinks ten sols is a fortune. Instead of the overlace on your dress."

Mirabile twitched, hands clawing at her long skirts as if she'd recoup the money spent on them. "But his future prospects . . . Vornatti will settle a yearly allowance on him, surely."

"He prefers to keep Maledicte under his own roof. Should Maledicte wed, Vornatti will cease funding him, he's that possessive." Gilly's tone soured, the very bitterness in it adding weight to his words. But a week spent ostracized from the house, spent worrying about his own position, left him a pessimist. Alone in the stable with only the dreams for company—dreams of Ani's laughter, waking to find the horses kicking and thrashing as if they, too, felt Her.

"You know nothing," Mirabile said, nearly spitting in her anger. "You're just a servant."

"The one behind the scenes," Gilly retorted.

"Between the bedsheets. You're nothing but Vornatti's toy."

Gilly flinched. "Nonetheless, what I tell you is true. Though Vornatti may be wealthy, he has no obligation to Maledicte. Indeed, he cut back his allowance a week ago."

Mirabile's face blanched, her green eyes closing. Her hands still twisted around each other. "Good night, Mirabile," Gilly said.

She slapped him, curving her nails inward. He jerked back, saved himself from the worst of their sting, though his cheek burned.

"*Lady* Mirabile. If I have nothing else, I have that, and you are only a servant."

Pushing past him, she hesitated in the ballroom doors, then, raising her head, returned to the court.

"LIKE SO," ARIS SAID, as the tune came around, his hand clasping Maledicte's. Maledicte took a breath, made the delicate feint inward, the retreat, then the elaborate pivot and bow, all the time aware of the king's hand on his. He tripped, and Aris, patiently, said, "Again."

"You're quite the teacher," Maledicte said.

Aris smiled. "I've always been thorough in my studies."

"And I, apparently, shirked mine," Maledicte said.

"You waltz splendidly," the king said. "Your teacher should be commended."

Maledicte hid a smile, remembering spinning Gilly in the waltz until he pled dizziness and shortness of breath.

In the ballroom, the measure came round again, and Aris held out his hand. "Once more?"

"Aris!" Last said, looming behind Aris, body blocking the glow of the ballroom.

"My brother, the hound," Aris muttered.

Maledicte stepped away from Aris, and Last's mouth, outlined by his pale beard, turned downward.

"Remember discretion," Aris said, stepping aside to let Maledicte return to the ballroom.

Maledicte touched his sword hilt, stroked the feathers, considering Last's presence, anger eating through his veins. The earl had taken Janus, had sent Kritos to recover him as if he were nothing more than a strayed possession— Wings fluttered in his chest, a heartbeat of rage and pain. To strike *now* and be done with it . . .

"Maledicte?" Aris's brows drew downward as Maledicte stood, his hand locked on the sword hilt.

Maledicte's hand flew from the sword. He was badly startled. How long had he gaped at Last like a rabid dog? He sketched a hasty bow, gave it an elaborate fillip to make Aris smile, and fled into the ballroom. Ani shrieked within him. A second time, to be so close, and not to strike . . . "Not yet," he said, speaking to that heat in his blood.

Coming onto the floor, he saw Gilly peering through a doorway and detoured again. This time he reached the safety of Gilly's side. "I need a drink."

Gilly paused in his search for his pocket flask. "What did the king want?"

Maledicte shrugged, slung himself down onto a bench, laid his legs along the length of it, precluding Gilly's joining him. "To teach me to dance. To lecture me on my behavior. Between him and Mirabile, my card is full." Maledicte sulked, studying the toes of his polished boots.

"I've put a stop to Mirabile," Gilly said. "And apparently she picked my pockets while I did so. No flask, Mal, I'm sorry."

"Gilly!" Maledicte said. "What matters a flask when you've removed the huntress from my trail? Dare I ask how?"

"Simple truth made you unsuitable," Gilly said, still touching his coat pockets with a faint frown on his face, as if trying to recall the exact moment the flask disappeared.

"Truth?" Maledicte said, coldness shifting in his belly like a snake. "What truth is that?"

"That Vornatti's fortune is not your own."

"To think a lack of a fortune could ever be beneficial." His grim amusement faltered. He stepped closer, touched Gilly's cheek. "What's this?"

Gilly touched the scratch at the cheekbone. "She wasn't best pleased with what I had to say."

"Should I repay her for that?" Maledicte asked, his tamped-down rage resurfacing, redirecting. "Spill the fact that I won't have her? If the duns are after her—"

"No," Gilly said. "Leave her alone. She's rat-vicious, best not cornered."

Maledicte sighed. "Take me home. I'm bored with the wonders of the court, sick of the people in it; I can't kill the ones I want to, so why stay?" He tugged Gilly's hair, touched the red mark once more, wiping away a quick smear of blood from the thin scratch, and headed back into the ballroom and the main doors.

THE CROWD PARTED FOR THEM QUICKLY, and Gilly, unable to push his way through for fear of damaging noble flesh and feelings, watched Maledicte slip away.

"Going home to your master like a faithful dog?" Mirabile said, appearing next to him. Gilly said nothing. On the balcony, unseen, he had been able to speak his mind. Here, a wrong word could see him whipped.

She circled him, radiating anger and danger, like a predatory beast. She stroked the length of his spine, and whispered, "Do you wag your tail for anyone? Or just Vornatti?"

Gilly bit his lip and tasted blood.

"He listens to me. I could spin him such tales—he'd have you cast out. . . ."

"Mirabile," Maledicte said, returning, his face white, his eyes hot. "Watch yourself. Gossip is a knife, and it's at your throat. Would you like me to push it closer still?"

Gilly shuddered at the quiet rage in Maledicte's voice, at the surprise in Mirabile's eyes, the reassessment of Gilly's status in the Vornatti household.

"Come, Gilly," Maledicte said, seizing Gilly's hand and tugging him along, heedless of the nobles in their path.

"The main door's back that way," Gilly said when he could speak. "Mal, you shouldn't have defended me."

"We'll go through the gardens and avoid any more display of noble manners. My temper is as sharp as my blade and eager to be loosed." He dropped from the rail of the curving balcony to the earth four feet below. Gilly followed, landing soundlessly in the soft moss.

Near the entrance to the garden maze that lay between them and the road, Maledicte put his hand out to halt Gilly. Gilly stepped back until they were both in the deep shadow of statuary and hedge, looking up at a dark balcony on the king's side of the ballroom. Two men stood in the shadows, and at their feet a great dog raised its head, sniffing the night air.

". . . eager to meet this boy of yours, Michel, no matter the irregularities of his birth. Bring him at once when he arrives. We need more young men in the court, men not spoiled as we are, with old secrets and schemes, soured by battles fought decades ago."

Last said, "Youth is no great thing, Aris. It masks threat and schemes as well as any old face."

The king said, "You mean Vornatti's ward. Maledicte."

"I do."

"He's but a young man with his own pleasures to seek, his own wants."

"He carries hate and hunger with him. His eyes burn with it." Last swung his cane, clipped roses from the hedge before him.

"Mmm," the king murmured. "I see no such thing in his eyes. Yours though—"

"You're a fool, Aris. Shall I tell you what I hear, whispered in the air of the court? One word, blown like leaves: 'witch.' They know him for what he is, an accursed creature."

"You sound like a country intercessor, seeing the old gods in every shadow. But you forget, as the gods are dead, so are your witches. Without the gods' power to scavenge, a witch is nothing but caged spite. Maledicte seems a pleasant boy, albeit one with an unfortunate mentor."

Last snarled. "Fool, twice over. To have loved that Vornatti woman who brought neither healthy child nor power, and to defend his creature, now. Black-Winged Ani has touched him, made him Her lover—"

Beneath them, Gilly shuddered and Maledicte moved closer, a gesture of support, or perhaps for shelter.

"Michel, superstition is the mark of a fool," the king said; Last drew his lips closed over set teeth and jaw. He stalked back through the doorway, setting the hound to growling after him. Aris brushed back his hair, displacing his circlet, and resettled it. "Eavesdropping is a standard of the court. I see you're practicing noble manners." He looked into the shadows, pinning Maledicte and Gilly with his amused gaze. His eyes flickered downward. "But remember discretion."

Maledicte's hand, resting on Gilly's hip, recoiled. Gilly dropped into a hasty bow.

The king grinned like a young man and sauntered into the darkness, the hound rumbling to its feet with a sigh.

"Come on," Maledicte said, and they plunged into the green moonstruck darkness of ivy-covered stone and thick hedges. Tiny white flowers coiled around animal statues like a spattering of stars.

Gilly pointed to a small carving within a mortared niche. "As long as we follow the mouse we should come to the center and then the exit."

"Do you know every secret, Gilly?" Maledicte asked, taking that first turning, disappearing into shadows, leaving only his voice behind. The breeze painted each shaking leaf with moonlight and dappled the pathway so that it seemed silvered with frost.

Gilly trailed after him, on smooth grassy paths designed to be strolled in the night. Moonflowers spotlighted a lover's bench; a stone mouse leaped on its side and directed their next turn.

The trail opened into a garden, ringed with pathways like the spokes of a wheel, its shape an echo of the city itself. Night-blooming jasmine laced the air with heady fumes. Maledicte spun in the center of it, staring at the starry sky. "Can you see Her, Gilly?"

Gilly saw nothing, but heard the rasp and rush of feathers. Hoarse calls and rattles came from all around them, and the leafy walls of the maze gave birth to dozens of rooks. The air filled with the drumbeat sound of their wings, and the stars above flickered. When he could speak, his heartbeat slowing back to a normal pace, Gilly said, "We must have disturbed their nesting."

"You don't think She's watching me?" Maledicte said.

"They're just rooks, startled to find intruders in the maze." The maze, which had seemed peaceful and secluded, now closed about him like a net. Was this how it would be? His eyes opened now? Not for the first time since the pier, Gilly wished for blindness, for his question to have died unspoken.

"This way, Gilly." Maledicte moved on, and Gilly followed. But somewhere in the maze of trails and turns, shaken by the soaring rooks and led astray by moonlight, they lost the correct path and found themselves in a cul-de-sac of whispering leaves. Frowning, Gilly headed back for the last turn, but Maledicte's stillness halted him.

Paused, his feet no longer stirring the grass, Gilly heard it: the clipped, echoing sounds of hooves drawing closer on cobbled streets. He parted the ivy, revealing the training wires beneath, and peered through. "It's a carriage," he said. "A rented hack." Around them, the rooks settled like blight on the trees that lined the drive.

Maledicte's face was bleached of color in the night. He drew his sword, slashed the ivy. It parted like paper, and Maledicte stepped out of the maze, though he kept to the shadows. A man stepped down from the hack, dark and well dressed, far too well dressed to require the services of a rental driver. A large man with glossy dark hair, and an elaborate malacca cane. Maledicte tensed like a dog on point. Faint chords of familiarity woke in Gilly, but it wasn't until the noble turned his head, exposing an eye filmed and scarred, that Gilly knew him.

KRITOS MET THEIR GAZES and his face grew disquieted, as if there were some danger to seeing a tall blond and a slight brunette coming out of the shadows. He was slow to put his back to them, slow to climb the steps toward the court, though perhaps some of his deliberate pace was due to the heavy aroma of spirits that lingered around him like a cloud.

Maledicte stood like marble, only his rocketing heart betraying him, sending a bloody flush to his cheek. The rooks' wings, shifting, whispered partite beats: Kritos. Hissing the name. Tolling the name. Maledicte had not thought he would feel anything but hate for this man, but a wild wash of joy made his mouth quiver. And why not? Kritos's return heralded Janus's. Janus was within reach at long last— Maledicte clenched his hands, took steady breaths, and watched Kritos belabor the great doors. This drunkard had been a threat to him once?

The doors slammed back, the footmen scrambling to shield the delicate inlays from contact with the stone. Kritos stepped forward as if the doors had flung themselves wide for him, and was immediately distracted. "Last, there you are," Kritos said. "What do you mean, denying me your house? I am your blood."

"Where is Janus?" the earl asked.

"At Lastrest. Recuperating from the sea voyage. Answer me. Why was I denied entrance to your house?" Kritos's voice rasped with desperation.

"I am weary of your debts. I warned you that I would stand for no more of it. Yet, not returned a full day, and I hear you've lost your coach and its team to the tables. I will not have you as an anchor on my purse any longer. I have let the moneylenders know this." Last brushed past Kritos and was stopped by Kritos's grip on his arm.

"Aris won't stand for it. I'm blood kin," Kritos said.

"Oddly enough," Last said, "this is the only action Aris and I have agreed on in years. But he thinks responsibility will make a better man of you, while I . . . doubt it.

"So were I you, nephew, I would not waste my limited time arguing. You had best find yourself an heiress to take on your debts." The earl shook off Kritos's clutching fingers, cast an inimical glance at Gilly and Maledicte, and lowered his voice.

Maledicte closed his eyes, the better to hear words that were balm to his senses. *Let Kritos suffer*, he thought. *Let him face the streets, the rats, the poverty.*

Last's voice, clipped with anger, slid into his ears, jolting him with one name. "... Janus is more clever at card playing than you are at card sharping. I do have some family feeling. Consider those debts cleared." Ignoring Kritos's choleric flush, the earl proceeded down the stairs, signaling for his own coachman to pull up behind Kritos's waiting hack.

Behind him, Kritos lashed out with his cane, the heavy wood meant to crush Last's fair head. Maledicte froze, imagining his chance at vengeance gone, but Last pivoted as smoothly as a serpent; the cane cracked into his gloved palm and he yanked it from Kritos's hands. Overbalanced and overwrought, Kritos tumbled down the wide stairs, landing in the oyster-shell gravel to the detriment of his skin and clothes. He moaned as he staggered to his feet.

"Take my nephew someplace to sober up," Last said, speaking to the coachman. The man shook his head, mute, unwilling, until Last tossed him a luna.

Last looked on Kritos's limping form dispassionately. "As always, you make poor gambles, Kritos. Attack the man who can and will disinherit you without further qualm? And to do so before Vornatti's catamite and his spy. How fast the word will spread of your straits, and you with no one to blame but yourself."

Maledicte sketched the briefest of bows when Kritos turned a furious face toward them and said, "Such delicious gossip it is, too. The family loyalty of the House of Last." He shivered in small spurts along his spine, the only outlet he afforded his rage. So close, and yet, Janus still eluded his grasp. Killing Last now when he could be caught before he reached Janus was— unthinkable. He could not move; the urge to kill and the need to wait warred in him, keeping him frozen as Last paced forward.

"What is your game, boy?" Last looked down his narrow nose; he was close enough that Maledicte had to look up to see those pale, icy eyes.

"Is this a game? I never thought it one. As for my conduct, I do as I see fit." His voice, raspy, covered the shiver in it.

"Were you not Vornatti's ward, you'd find out how little that arrogance would avail you," Last said. "But tell me, boy, what do you want with my brother?"

Maledicte forced a smile, despite the ache in his guts that pointed out how close Last was, how sharp the black blade was, how quickly the deed could be done. A pastel froth of dresses spilled down the stairs as the youngest debutantes and their chaperones came outside, looking for their coaches. They stopped; one lady giggled uncertainly, sensing the charged atmosphere, the muttering rooks flanking the drive.

"I want nothing from Aris that he has not already given me, but what I want from you—" Maledicte said.

"I have done nothing to you, and yet I could swear to your enmity."

"Have you something on your conscience? Some wrong done? Shall I remind you? You gave me a gift once before you learned its value and took it back," Maledicte said, breath catching in anger. Careless, he thought. If Last understood, raised his mind from petty offenses to himself, from the confusion over Aris's support, would he not whisk Janus away once again?

He tempered the ragged edge from his voice and said, "Your coach is waiting, your grace, and I have nothing more to say to you tonight." The cool dismissal whitened the skin around Last's nose even as it flushed his thick neck.

Last reached out as if he would shake or strangle Maledicte, but his hands dropped to his side at a gasp from the throng of women. "I will see you gone from the court," he said, as he stepped up into his coach. "Revealed for what you are."

"What am I?" Maledicte whispered as Last closed the coach's door. "I wish you would tell me."

Last gave the coachman a signal and the horses drew him away. Maledicte stood trembling, until Gilly took his hand and led him home.

11

VORNATTI'S DOVE STREET RESIDENCE was lit against the silky fogs creeping inward from the sea, making itself a welcoming beacon in the twilight. Inside, that echo of hospitality continued as maids laid silver out, as the cook prepared her courses, as Vornatti waited for his dinner guests.

In his bedchamber, Maledicte paced, irritated that Vornatti staged this party now, when he wanted to flee the city and hunt Janus down at Lastrest. But Vornatti had insisted on the party; more, he had disabled the coach and disallowed Maledicte any coin. Once, Maledicte thought, such obstacles would have only slowed him, not stopped him. But now, he had grown soft—or practical—and knew there was no point attempting the forty-mile journey afoot. Not when Janus was destined to attend the solstice ball; not when morning might see Vornatti more agreeable.

Still, his temper was bad, and at the sight of a carriage come unfashionably early, he slammed his window shut, cracking the glass.

Since his bloodless confrontation of Last, Ani had gnawed at him, muttering and seething, until his entire body ached with fluttering wings and razor beaks. His mind, like feathers in an eddy, kept coming round and round, always returning to blood-drenched dreams. His hand cramped on the sword hilt, seized yet again to no purpose. Ani, restless, threatened to withdraw Her support, the compact annulled by his dilatoriness. *Coward,* Ani jeered, Her message in his clenching fist on the hilt: *Last must die.*

"He will," Maledicte muttered. "I swore it. I swore."

Behind him, the door, left ajar for Gilly, whispered open. Maledicte tensed his shoulders, pulled the drapes across the blank-eyed glass. "Not yet," he said.

"Are you practicing your lines?" The voice wasn't Gilly's low voice, husked with the indelible country accent, but a woman's, delicately arch. "I thought your wit more ready than that."

Rage muted Maledicte's response. He turned. Mirabile lingered in the doorway, and as he met her eyes, she took a step inward, her hands trailing across the jambs, emphasizing her invasion of his room. Like the night sky, she swept inward, all in dark satin and fog-gray trim.

"Apparently, I was mistaken," she said. "A flaw in your nature. You should correct it. Those who practice their thoughts are often caught flat-footed."

"Get out—" Maledicte whispered, then with effort removed his hand from the sword hilt again, and assayed a reasonable façade of courtly speech. "I have a care for my reputation, even if you do not. A man's bedchamber is no place for a lady."

"What *has* the baron been teaching you?" Mirabile said, her lips curving. "Shall I show you otherwise? Prove that a lady indeed has a place in a man's bedchamber?" She glided toward him, her dark skirts creeping ahead of her.

Maledicte stepped back, bumped the wall. She laughed and settled herself on his bed, rested her cheek against the canopy post, stroked its length. "As nervous as a virgin. How unflattering," she said. "And feared for your reputation? Let me teach you this, Maledicte, that scandalous creatures such as myself, such as you"—she nodded toward him with a regal incline of her head—"need not fear the strictures of propriety. The peerage expects misbehavior from us. We are free in ways they will never be, granted license by their hunger for scandalous gossip."

"They don't need our actions to feed their gossip. I believe they make it out of whole cloth."

"Strong words from a man who owes much of his place to the collection and manipulation of rumor," Mirabile said, laughing. "If you claim such disinterest, I will stifle a whisper I meant to share—a gift of sorts, to mend this awkward dislike you bear for me." She rose, crossed the room, her presence as warm beside him as an animal's.

Maledicte leaned against the window, wishing he were back in the ballroom with a low balcony and velvet grass behind him instead of a steep drop to a thorny garden. "Dislike?" he said. "Is that what you term my feelings to be?"

"Hush," she said, putting her hand to his mouth. Perfume rose from her skin, the dizzying, cloying attar of imported jasmine. She tipped her mouth toward his. He turned his head, and she, determined, followed, brought her lips to his. Again, he reached for the sword, but Mirabile caught his hand and brought it to her bodice, the scented intersection of flesh and satin.

Snarling, Maledicte shoved her away, drew the sword in a long hiss. Evading its blade, Mirabile fell over her long skirts. Her eyes darkened; her face stiffened in insult. But her voice stayed sweet. "So very gauche. If you were not so lovely, I wonder if I'd bother with you. Still, you might at least pretend to civility. Were I to report your behavior to Vornatti—"

"If you report this, Vornatti would see me cast out, which would gain you neither husband nor the wealth you crave." Maledicte sheathed the sword again, fighting the urge to see blood wet its blade. Any blood.

Mirabile rose, brushing at a creased panel on her skirt. "But would gain me the satisfaction of seeing you so discommoded. Still, you're quite correct, that's not the result I wish." She shook out her skirts, then settled herself at his dressing table, sorting the discarded jumble of stickpins and fobs, leafing through *The Book of Vengeances*, and smiling at the illustrations. "So I'll return to my first purpose. Shall I tell you the gossip?"

"I'll hear it from a dozen mouths by morning," Maledicte said, watching her hands, thinking of Westfall's stolen belongings, of Gilly's missing flask, but, unwilling to get closer, allowed her to set the book aside for his embroidery box.

"How you wrong me," she said. "My gossip is never the ordinary. I am as clever as your baron when it comes to ferreting secrets." Her agile fingers sought the catch.

"Tell me if you must," Maledicte said.

Her fingers stilled as she smiled at him. "Last dislikes you very much; you return the sentiment," she said.

"Old news," Maledicte interrupted.

"But Kritos dislikes him beyond that. You'll not suffer Last for long. Kritos means to kill him before Last has a chance to disinherit him in favor of Janus. It is his only way to salvage his debts. So he raises coin, even now, to hire an assassin."

Outrage scoured him, all unexpected. His vengeance—stolen? And by the man who had done him such wrong before?

Mirabile's fingers found the catch; the lid opened. Her painted mouth made a delicate "oh" of surprise, and then her lips curled. "Not what I expected," she said. "But perhaps you and I can understand each other. Shall I make myself clear?"

"I wish you would," Maledicte said, the rage fading slowly as he wrestled for control. He watched her select the vial of arsenixa, admiring it in the lamplight as if it were a gemstone.

"I need funds desperately," she said, "thus a husband. But my reputation is such that the moneyed men, who can afford to be selective, will not be caught. And time grows short.

"My lord Westfall is a most impatient host, and Brierly has had the poor judgment to allow herself to become with child. Her vanity is so great that she will not be seen while she is increasing, and so we must rusticate with her. And I will not stomach a country clod for a husband." She ran her nails along the crystalline vials until they hummed.

Maledicte reminded her, "My fortunes are as negligible as yours."

"So your dog said, barking most convincingly. I see only one option left me," she said.

Maledicte stiffened. "Surely—"

"Hmm—" she said, interrupting him, tugging out a soft roll of cloth-bound powders. "You are not so indifferent to the female sex as you pretend. Not and keep Harlot's Friend in such ready supply. I own I am glad to see it here."

"Potions be damned," Maledicte said. "Make your point and be gone, Lady."

Her hands clenched, then eased as she mastered her temper. "Shall I be blunt? Even Vornatti must grow bored in his bed. He has his rough servant and he has your elegance—don't try to deny it," she said. "I know what they call you in the court when your back is to them—Vornatti's catamite. And I must believe them, since you so nobly defended your fellow, Gilly—you're both whores, one simply better dressed than the other."

"I am not a whore," he said, reflexively. His anger leaped but fell back beneath caution. She wanted something of him, more than the obvious. Her entire visit felt a sortie, its purpose cloaked in layers. She wanted his alliance in her schemes; he believed that. But his acceptance or denial was not the answer to quench the burning question in her eyes. Maledicte wanted badly to know what she truly sought; he would deny her everything he could.

"Whore or not, it doesn't signify," she said, "except that lovely as you both are—surely he's surfeited with male flesh. He's willing to pay and pay well for his desires. My price isn't so dear, a simple ceremony and ring."

"You think he'd wed you? He can find other women without wedding them," Maledicte said.

"He will wed me," she said, the fury so long missing from her face flaring to life. "Be careful, Maledicte. I would like to have you at my side, in my bed, a partner in this, but I will not tolerate your disrespect."

"Respect you? When my contempt grows apace?" Maledicte said.

Mirabile's hand curled inward, her forearm tensed; that warning was enough for Maledicte. As her hand rose, fingers clawed, he freed the sword, using the blade like a shield.

Her sharp nails sang along its length; her hand closed over his on the hilt. She shuddered as the steel feathers bit into her skin, raising blood on her white hands. The rage faded from her eyes, her face; her jaw slackened, lips quivered. "What—" she gasped. "I hear . . . whispers, a question—" For a moment, her face went slack, as her own driving question was answered with another.

Maledicte jerked the sword away, her fingers welling blood. She brought her hand to her mouth, licked the wounds, her eyes never leaving his. "It's true. Chancel, blight him, was right. All true," she said breathlessly. "You *are* Ani's creature—the gods are no more gone than the sun at sundown. . . . Tell me how you did it," she said, her voice feverish, the white flesh of her breasts flushing. "Tell me! Is it true? All true? Are you immune to poison, to injury? Such power you must have, perhaps enough to share?" She leaned toward him, all fervor and white teeth bared in wild rejoicing.

"You're mad," he said. "And long past your welcome." He pushed past her and fled, hating to leave her loose in his chamber, but equally loath to stay with Ani stirring to an interest beyond Maledicte's vengeance. Coldness grew in his belly, coiling, twisting; what if Ani, grown sick of his slow scheming, left him?

What of Kritos? Though Maledicte had little respect for the man's ability, what if Kritos succeeded? What would Ani do then?

Polite laughter rose from the floor below and he checked in his stairward movement, thinking the laughter directed at him, at his allowing Mirabile to cozen the truth from him that he had never meant to reveal. He growled, retraced his steps, and slipped down the servants' stairs, stroking his fingers for balance along the ill-lit walls.

GILLY LOOKED UP from the household books. This, too, was his task, the endless daily budgeting and balancing of accounts. Of late, he found the minutiae soothing. So he sat now, lamp wicking down on the desk, one long leg curled back beneath the chair rungs. When Maledicte drifted into the study, a vision in dark silks, he found his first response not pleasure but dismay.

"Shouldn't you be with your dinner guests?" he asked.

"Absolutely not," Maledicte said, sulking into the deep, plush chair that Vornatti usually claimed. "What did you say to her, Gilly?"

"Her?" Gilly echoed.

"Mirabile," Maledicte said, kicking at the carved legs of the chair in bad temper.

"She's not still hunting you?" Gilly said, surprised.

"No. Yes," Maledicte said. "She's decided to wed Vornatti and make me her paramour."

Gilly scoffed, unconcerned with the black look Maledicte turned on him. "And you deciphered this how?"

"No effort at all," Maledicte said, rising smoothly, stalking the room. "She told me so herself in my chambers." He growled wordlessly and for the first time, Gilly saw the knife edge beneath the familiar petulance and temper.

Gilly said, "She was in your room?"

"I left her there," Maledicte said.

"Mal—" Gilly trailed off, thinking of Mirabile in Maledicte's room, snooping, finding more than she could have imagined. "Go roust her out. You cannot withstand her scrutiny. Her husband believed in the gods' survival—"

"Gilly, don't be foolish," Maledicte said, "The damage is most thoroughly done. She is now quite introduced to Ani." He settled down on the desk, careful of the ink bottle and the fallen pen, as if Gilly's outburst soothed his own.

"She knows?" Gilly said.

"She cornered me until she provoked the response she wanted. And while I despise her, I must admire her boldness. It's quite inspired me."

"To what end?" Gilly asked, closing the ledger over his fingertip. He misliked the angry precision of Maledicte's words, the fey light in his dark eyes.

"I thought to dedicate my night to gambling," he said, taking the ledger from Gilly and flipping through it.

"Your entire existence seems one gamble after another. You have a dinner party to attend and the old bastard to soothe—what do you seek at the gambling tables?" Gilly took the ledger back, set it in the drawer, and shut it.

"Kritos."

Ritos?" Gilly repeated. "You are a gambler, then. Vornatti will be furious if you slight him again."

"I am well aware that Vornatti will not support me in this. Of late, he counsels temperance. So it must be done quickly. You'll have to raid the house box for me, Gilly."

"I thought you meant to kill Kritos. Not game with him," Gilly said.

"I want to beat him first." A brief, ugly light flared and smoldered in Maledicte's eyes; Gilly looked away, fed more of the wick into the lamp, chasing the clustering shadows from the desk, fearing more than simple temper in Maledicte's eyes.

"Do you even know how to play?" Gilly asked.

"Well enough to win," Maledicte said.

Gilly's breath snagged in his chest, not only at the resurgence of the smothering rage in Maledicte's eyes, but at his own realization that this was the moment he had been dreading, the moment when Ani's compact would be sealed with blood, no matter that it came cloaked in ridiculous questions of card games. Gilly sought something to dissuade Maledicte. "You believe you can win at will?"

"Of course. It's called card-sharping, Gilly; have you never heard of it? I assure you, it's all the rage in some circles." Maledicte smiled, sharp-toothed, as if he or Ani understood Gilly's attempts at delay.

"Why am I not surprised?" Gilly sat back in the chair, tilted the seat for a less-shadowed view. "Are you good enough, Mal? This will be different than rooking sotted sailors at the pier, or wherever you gained your experience. Kritos belongs to the worst hells in the city. Where getting caught sharping will see far more than a reputation ruined."

"Don't fret, Gilly," Maledicte said. "I do excellently well. Shall I prove it to you?"

"Go to Vornatti's dinner, Mal."

"No more delay," Maledicte said.

Gilly clenched his hands. "Mal—"

"It will be done, with or without your aid," Maledicte said. "Kritos has decided to deprive us of our prey. To kill Last for his own selfish desires. Did you expect me to grow bored of my enemies? My hatred? I am not Vornatti, content to nurture a grudge for years with no satiation in sight. Janus has returned. I could go to Lastrest this moment and slaughter Last; we could live like royalty until the Kingsguard or Echo's Particulars managed to bring us down. Be thankful I'm content with Kritos tonight."

"I'll call for a hack," Gilly said, his mouth dry.

Maledicte bowed and left, claiming he needed to change into something more suitable, with all the airy insouciance of a man going out for a night's pleasure instead of a murder. Left alone, Gilly laid his head down on the desk, tangled his fingers in his hair, thinking. Short of drugging Maledicte, he saw no way to avert this. And Maledicte, though he trusted Gilly, would be unlikely to take food or drink from Gilly's hand tonight. The solution was as distant as ever by the time the hack arrived, and Gilly found himself following Maledicte into it in a brooding silence of his own.

THEY PAID THE HACK TO take them as far as it would, the driver loath to travel Jove Street at night.

"I do believe you, you know," Gilly said, watching Maledicte palm another card with a demonstrative flourish, and wishing he'd never expressed his doubts. Maledicte had made him play and lose hand after hand in the swaying carriage, until his head pounded. Gilly focused and caught the cheat this time, tapped Maledicte's wrist. "Be careful, Mal. Sleight of hand relies on vision driven by expectation. Some men see more clearly than you think. The Fiery Hell is no place to be caught cheating."

"You'll be at my back," Maledicte said, smiling in a way that did nothing to soothe Gilly's nerves.

The hack rattled to a stop, the horses blowing out steam in the foggy dark. The last of the twilight was making way for the darkness seeping down from the sky. On other streets, the young boys employed as lamplighters would be running from post to post with their long tapers, making small, defiant blazes against the invading night.

But on Jove Street, light was unwelcomed. Only a small torch affixed to the jamb gave enough of a glow to allow a visitor to decipher the address: Fire 3 Jove Street—known as the Fiery Hell to its regulars.

There were other gambling houses, more genteel in their façades, more tempting to the dallying aristocracy, where women and men, lords and ladies went to be gently daring, frivolous, and above all, seen. But the Fiery Hell took its games seriously, unleavened with court manners or excess speech. No waiters circled, offering sweetened wines or spirits. No music played, and no whores waited for a lucky gambler. There were only the tables and the players, including impoverished aristocrats so desperate to recoup fortunes they would risk a knife in the ribs. The Fiery Hell was Kritos's best chance.

Gilly hefted the brass knocker in his hand, dropped it down on the faceplate. The sharp rapping left muffled cracks echoing down the cooling, darkening street.

The door opened; Gilly looked up, surprised at having to do so, but the man filled the doorframe as effectively as the oak door itself. Gilly nudged Maledicte. "Stormy Jack," he whispered. "The boxer."

Maledicte looked at Gilly blankly and shrugged. Gilly sighed. "Just don't irritate him."

Pausing in the foyer, Maledicte and Gilly studied the tables, while Jack latched the door behind them. The Fiery Hell had been stripped of any pretension of being a domicile. In every available space the tables dominated the house, each one surrounded by close-packed men, some muttering, some gray and silent.

Maledicte headed toward the darkest corner as if he could sense his quarry. Gilly went after him, seeing not the crowds, but the pistols in coat pockets, the knives and swords hung on chairs or slung onto tables as prizes. All around the walls lurked employees as big as the doorman.

Maledicte intended to cheat here? Gilly had known it was a foolish idea; now he found it a suicidal one.

In the corner of the room, at a small table, Kritos sat alone, his back to the wall and its peeling flocking. Maledicte slung himself into the chair opposite.

"What do you want?" Kritos asked, his good eye bleared with drink and bitterness. Maledicte touched the table before him, as if feeling the games that had gone before.

"To gamble with you, of course," he said.

Gilly pressed in close behind Maledicte, listening, watching that slim, rigid spine.

"When Vornatti keeps you as short of coin as Last keeps me? I know who you are and I'll not waste my time," Kritos said, starting to rise. Maledicte shoved the table across the broken parquet and pushed Kritos back into his seat.

"You listen to too much gossip. That's the mark of a fool," Maledicte said.

"Watch your tongue," Kritos said, but wearily, as if he lacked the energy to take offense. Gilly, watching his face, thought that Kritos intended to parlay his entrance fees into a night's lodging.

"Surely you can come up with some small stake, or you wouldn't be here," Maledicte said, leaning across the table. "I'm not as particular as these gentlemen. I'll wager for things other than coin."

Kritos laughed, hoarse and unamused. "Why should I? What have I to win?"

Maledicte tipped a handful of coins out on the table. They gleamed with the moon's cool frost in the dark room. "Not so poor as coppers," Maledicte said. "Not so dangerous as sols. Lunas."

Kritos licked his lips. "I've no coin."

"When has that ever balked an aristocrat?" Maledicte asked.

Kritos hesitated a minute longer, looking at Maledicte. Gilly saw the moment when Kritos made his decision, saw the quick flash of scorn on Kritos's face as he relegated Maledicte to fool and fop. "If you're that eager to play . . ." He waved over one of the Hell's attendants, one with a curved scar through his mouth. "A house stake for me, Smiles."

"Your hide," Smiles said, and dropped a roll of mixed coins to the table.

"House takes thirty percent of your winnings, plus the stake back." Kritos waved him off, though his lips tightened at the reminder.

Two hours later, Kritos was richer a tidy pile of coins, as well as the random miscellany Maledicte had allowed to represent coins when Kritos upped the stakes beyond his current coin: a palm-sized miniature meant for Aris, a sailor's compass, the jadestone buttons from his vest, and the Itarusine-made lace from his cuffs. Two of the room's guards, drawn by the scent of unusual play, prowled around the table.

Gilly thought Maledicte had let it run too long, had allowed Kritos to win too often and risked losing him from his net. As if in unity with his thoughts, Kritos made to rise.

Maledicte sighed. "One more?" He eyed the table with an inexplicable avarice until Gilly realized that his attention focused on the miniature, and who the subject must be. The newest member of the House of Last, Janus Ixion.

"I think not," Kritos said, scooping the pile toward himself.

Wordlessly, Maledicte tipped the last contents of his purse out. Sols, this time, and Kritos halted where he stood.

"Very well," Kritos said. "But I'll want a new deck. Just to be sure, you understand."

"Of course," Maledicte said.

HANDS LATER, Maledicte had lost sols to gain lunas and was frowning over his cards. Kritos smiled. "My game again, I think," he said, laying out the elements. "Land, sea, sky, fire, all mine," he said. "Kings all."

Gilly peered into Maledicte's hands and stifled a wince. While he had a representation of all the suits, Maledicte lacked high cards enough to beat Kritos, but it was close. He had three queens to trump three kings, but the last suit, that of air, had only a scattering of seven seabirds as his high card. Not enough.

Maledicte shifted in his seat, and the guards leaned closer, watching his hands; Kritos's eye narrowed. Maledicte smiled at them all, and set the cards down. "Your fortune has waned. My hand." He laid down the fire cards and queen, the earth cards and queen, sea and sea queen. He set out the air cards one by one: butterflies and clouds and starry nights. The suspicion in Kritos's eye deepened. The seven-gulls card lingered in Maledicte's hand last, and Gilly shivered, wondering if Maledicte was going to try to cheat now, under all these eyes, but Maledicte merely smiled and set it down.

The queen of air, Black-Winged Ani, Her dark feathers filling the card. Kritos lunged to his feet. "Impossible."

Behind him, a pasteboard fluttered to the floor, unseen by the others—a dark card. The queen of air, palmed to prevent Maledicte's win. But even as it fell, Gilly watched the color leach from it, the dark pinions traded for the sun-speckled backs of seven gulls.

Maledicte shoved the table again, harder, knocking Kritos back against the wall, winding him. "Are you calling me a cheat? I'm sure these gentlemen will tell you they saw no such thing."

Rising unhurriedly, Maledicte swept the coins and trinkets into his purse, and handed it to Gilly. The miniature went into his own pocket. "Good night."

"Another game," Kritos demanded.

"No," Maledicte said, heading for the door. Gilly stumbled after, still waiting for the protest to go up. His back burned with the heat of it. Looking back over his shoulder, he saw Kritos watching them, his face furious, even as the house guards closed in to reclaim their stake.

He hurried Maledicte outside, and started casting for a hack, looking down the dark streets, listening for approaching hoofbeats, but heard only Maledicte's stuttering laughter.

"I thought you meant to kill him," Gilly said, giving up the futile hunt.

"I do," Maledicte said, "and I will, but Gilly, wasn't it wonderful? Such a foolish thing to please me so, and yet the games went so well."

"With Ani's aid," Gilly said. "Or dare you say that the transformation of the queen was a cheat learned in the Relicts?"

"Transformation?" Maledicte said. At the pure incomprehension in his tone, Gilly's stomach clenched.

"Never mind," he said. "Let's go home."

"Did you see his face, Gilly? Wasn't it perfect?"

"Yes," Gilly said, casting cautious glances back over his shoulder at the near-empty street, at the disreputable building they had just left. He *had* seen Kritos's expression; fury and barely cloaked desperation. It made him leery of the distance they must travel afoot to find a hire carriage. This late, no carriage would appear on Jove Street, in the shadow world of narrow, winding alleys and blinded gas lamps, no matter how he wished it. No god listened to his will. "We need to be gone, before he manages to convince the Fiery Hell he can best regain their money by hunting you."

Maledicte merely shrugged, his steps still slow.

Gilly turned his head again. Was that a man following in their wake, sidling along the dark walls? Was that the tap of booted heels trying for silence, or the drip of water condensing against stone walls and sliding to the street? Gilly was certain of one thing only: On this street, at this hour, no one they met would be a friend. He picked up his pace, hooking his arm through Maledicte's. "Let's not dally. We're some ways yet from Sybarite Street, and there'll be no carriages closer than that."

"There's an alley through the houses," Maledicte said. "It'll save us the entire walk up this street and then the walk back down to the carriage stand on Sybarite. Somewhere. Ah, here it is."

Gilly pictured the streets of the city, spread out like a spiderweb, the long sweep of the seven main streets, and the nameless curling crossings that linked them all. Maledicte was right. But only the change of sound, the lack of reverberation, told Gilly that the shadow Maledicte faced was more than a recessed door. The darkness swallowed his words and fed nothing back.

"This should bring us out near Clara's, and there are always hacks there, waiting for the men to stagger away. If you're nervous of the night air, the dark . . ."

Maledicte turned; the quick flash of teeth told Gilly Maledicte was mocking his fears. "Not the night, the people in it." Gilly peered into the alley, saw the wall curve away into velvety darkness, and yet, as he studied it, a lambent glow traveled back, carrying the flushed color and acrid scent of the additives used in Syb Street gas lamps. "Let me go first," he said, and stepped into the alley.

"Why didn't I think of that?" Maledicte asked. "It makes so much sense to let the unarmed man go first into danger. Are you sure you're as clever as you think?" The rasp of his voice was leavened by a breathy amusement. They headed into the alley, their boots sliding on fog-slick cobbles and unseen effluvia.

"You're going to lose that tongue of yours yet," Gilly warned. The light ahead grew marginally brighter, coated the dark walls with blushed contours.

Maledicte opened his mouth, and Gilly said, "I think you want us to be attacked. Just hush now, I can't hear if we're being followed if you keep talking."

"Someone *is* following you," Maledicte said, in a carrying mutter. "Me. How you expect to hear anything but my boots stumbling around in this muck . . ."

Gilly turned in laughing exasperation, ready to put Maledicte before him, just to shut his mouth, and the startled inhalation of breath was all the warning he could manage to give.

IT WAS ALL MALEDICTE HAD been waiting for. He stepped aside, pivoted, drew the sword. There was barely room for its length in the narrow alley; the tip scraped, unseen, against the opposite wall, and Kritos's cane impacted on the sheltering steel of the blade rather than on Maledicte's vulnerable nape.

"Not very good with that thing," Maledicte said. "You couldn't hit old man Last; what makes you think you can touch me?"

The cane slid along the flat of the blade. Beyond words, Kritos continued to grind his cane against the unseen blade. In the shadows, the blade was only an extension of darkness; frustration knotted Kritos's jaw, bared his teeth as he fought what must have seemed like invisible forces bent on his failure.

Maledicte's wrist trembled with effort, but he succeeded in turning his hand, and with it, the angle of the blade. The wooden cane gave against the sword edge, splitting, and Kritos stumbled forward, roaring.

Maledicte skipped back, nearly falling over Gilly as he attempted to get between the combatants. "Don't be a fool," Maledicte spared the breath to say.

Concentrating on the weight at the end of his wrist, Maledicte thrust at Kritos, backing him away, cursing because he, too, was hampered by this dim light. Kritos avoided a lunge with a desperate effort. Maledicte, overextended, felt the rush of warm air on his throat, saw Kritos stretching one hand out for his neck. It ghosted toward him, pale and indistinct, then clear, the fingers clenching as if Maledicte's neck were already within their grip.

"Mal, watch out," Gilly cried.

"Hush, hush," Maledicte said, recovering his balance, raising the sword and batting Kritos's outreaching arm into the wall. Quickly, Maledicte threw his weight onto the blade, the wall, and the arm pinned between.

A solid slap of flash against flesh exploded by his head. Gilly had reached over Maledicte's shoulder and caught Kritos's other fist in his own.

"I can do this without your help," Maledicte gritted out, though a small part of him sang at the comfort of Gilly's help, reminding him of days long gone. Thinking of them, Maledicte stepped forward and brought his knee up with brutal force into the man's belly; when Kritos curled forward, Maledicte slammed his left fist into his throat.

Gagging, Kritos folded to his hands and knees, blood splashing where the blade had ripped at his escaping arm. He scrabbled back and Maledicte thrust the blade at the pale target of his good eye. Kritos cried out, hurling himself backward, overbalancing, landing on his back, still struggling for air. Maledicte grinned, raised the sword, heard Ani moaning Her pleasure inside him, and drove it downward. Beside him, Gilly flinched.

But Maledicte only used the sword to pin the man to the cobbles and the earth below, through one ornate and now-ruined sleeve. "I suppose I should let you up, fight you like a gentleman. But then, the first gentleman I ever met didn't fight fair either."

"Mal," Gilly said, reaching outward.

Maledicte evaded his grip, dropping to put both his knees into Kritos's belly. He fumbled in his pocket, pulled out a small purse.

Kritos's struggle increased. He shoved at Maledicte with his free arm, ripping at Maledicte's hair, reddening his jawline. "You—" Kritos said, on a stifled breath.

"None of that," Maledicte said, dodging another blow, clamping his hand over Kritos's mouth lest anything secret slip out. But he had wanted Kritos to know him, and that the man did, at the last, when it was too late, made both him and Ani purr with delight. The loose hand tore at his face again, scrabbling. "Gilly, get that arm, would you?"

The feeble blows stopped. Maledicte upended the purse of wooden coins over Kritos's heaving chest. Faint glimmers of silvering still lingered on them. "I saved them for you," Maledicte said.

"No—" Kritos said, true fear reaching his face, past the outrage, the bluster, and the desperation. He tried to surge upward, and Maledicte ground his weight downward, stabilizing himself by gripping the sword's hilt.

Done with words, Maledicte yanked at the sword hilt, not bothering to pull the tip of the blade from its earthen sheath, but rather slanting the entire blade sideways like the closing blade of a scissors. Kritos yelled but the blade silenced him in a rush of wheezy air and blood. Maledicte put his thinly gloved hand down on the blade edge and pushed, in a step that should have seen him lose fingers, but only made the sword edge sink deeper until it ground against bone.

Kritos convulsed; his hands, freed by Gilly's repulsed recoil, clutched at Maledicte's forearms. Maledicte rode the spasms until they ceased, until Kritos's grip fell slack. Blood ran down the sword, pooling in the feathered hilt. Maledicte pulled his gloves off, ran his finger down the same path, chasing the blood. The dim alleyway robbed some of his satisfaction; in the darkness, the blood looked black rather than crimson, but the tang of it in the air . . . He stood, feeling as unsteady on his feet as a newborn creature.

Gilly bent and picked his gloves up when Maledicte turned away from the corpse. "Careless," he said. His voice cracked.

Maledicte recovered his sword and wiped it off with the muddy remains of Kritos's cloak, humming tunelessly. He broke off to laugh, giddy with satisfaction. "That will teach him to interfere in my life. Or would, if he weren't past any lessoning now."

Gilly's face whitened until he seemed a ghost in the dark alley; he bent over the cobbles, retching. Maledicte rose hastily, took him down the alley away from the body. "What is it, Gilly? What's the matter?"

"I've never killed anyone before," Gilly said, swallowing audibly.

"You haven't yet. Don't get greedy. Kritos was all mine, and I could have done it without you," Maledicte said.

"You'd have had your brains dashed out on the alley wall without me," Gilly said.

"No," Maledicte said, "But your aid was timely all the same." He reached up to touch Gilly's face. Gilly flinched, and Maledicte let his hand drop, scowling. "Wallow in your conscience if you will. But remember, I told you when we set out that I meant to see him dead tonight. I am a man of my word and will after all—"

GILLY CLOSED HIS EYES and ears to Maledicte's contented ramblings; he felt as if he had strayed into one of his nightmares. Behind his closed eyes, the alley felt overfull of presences and scents: the acid smell of his own sickness, the smell of turned earth and blood that lingered, and something else, something out of place in this dark world of cobbles and stone—the scent of musty feathers. Opening his eyes, he saw Maledicte had returned to the body, admiring his work, saw the doubled shadow clinging to him in the low, fevered light, rough-edged like wings.

Gilly rubbed his face, the bridge of his nose between his eyes, and pulled his hand away, repelled. His fingers were damp and sticky, splashed with Kritos's blood. Ani's compact sealed in blood. He leaned against the wall and retched in dry miserable heaves.

Maledicte came back and took Gilly's sleeve. Gilly shuddered, imagining something new within Maledicte, something hungry. But Maledicte's voice, raspy and cool, was his own. "There's a rain barrel up ahead. Come on."

The shock of the cold water cleared Gilly's senses, and he washed his hands with steady fingers. Maledicte splashed happily about in it, rinsing his hands, the blade.

Gilly found a smile himself, a brittle thing, but Maledicte, delighted, was a charming companion, and Kritos— Gilly managed to lose the iron weight that had settled in his chest, at least until the hack they found disgorged them into Dove Street Square.

Gilly felt the eyes on him as soon as he stepped out of the carriage. Looking around, he saw no one at first, then made out the dusty gray coat of the homeless intercessor, huddled up against the central fountain. The man nodded his head in greeting, but when Maledicte stepped out onto the cobbles, smiling, the intercessor's eyes widened and he sketched a symbol in the air.

With sudden dismay, Gilly recognized it, the inverted blessing of Baxit, the *avert* against the god-possessed. As Maledicte passed the fountain, the intercessor disappeared into the deeper shadows with an alacrity that spoke of fear.

· 13 ·

GILLY WOKE WITH VORNATTI'S BELL ringing in his ears, and the nagging sense that there had been earlier bells still, not only Vornatti's summoning bell, but deep, resonating tones. Perhaps it was only guilt; Kritos's body could not have been found soon enough for the palace bells to bemoan the loss of one of their own. The sunlight, though, streamed dark gold across the floor, the color of midmorning. Swearing, Gilly staggered to his feet, cursing himself for staying up past the time of their return, brooding over the murder, the intercessor's fear, and dulling those thoughts with drinking. A glance at the clock in the hall warned him it was nearer noon than morning, and again he was late with Vornatti's shot.

Vornatti hunched, still abed, sleep-bleared and roaring at Livia. She held the loaded syringe in trembling hands.

"Give it here," Gilly said, taking it from her. She passed it over with a gasp of relief, and Gilly bent to find an unbruised vein in Vornatti's arm. His guilt, malleable, shifted from Kritos to a miserable wondering of how dreadful it must be for Vornatti to wake to pain while Gilly slept, babying an aching head.

Vornatti's teeth gritted as the Elysia slid into his vein, and then, slowly, his body started to relax.

"Late again, Gilly—" Vornatti growled, seizing Gilly's collar as if to shake him.

Livia, busying herself near the door, returned with a cup of tea, hot and steaming. "Here, sir."

Vornatti wrapped his knotted hands around the teacup, distracted by Livia's skirts, inches shorter than propriety suggested, and damped besides, Gilly thought. Livia shot a quick conspiratorial smile at him as he backed away.

"Did you hear the news, sir? Such goings-on as the milkman brought us this morning. Kritos found stripped and gutted in the alleys near the wharves."

Vornatti set his tea down, untouched. "Last night?"

"Yes, sir."

In the distant recesses of the house, the butler could be heard opening the door, and a clear, cool voice rising upward. "Livia," Vornatti said. "Go downstairs and bring the Lady Mirabile to my chamber."

"Here, sir?" she repeated.

"Give me time to get him dressed," Gilly added.

He bent over Vornatti, undid the sash of the man's robe. "Do you want the—"

Vornatti slapped him. "I should give your job to Livia. Do you forget who pays you?"

"No," Gilly said, kneeling beside the bed, head throbbing.

Vornatti put his hand into Gilly's hair, turned his face upward to meet his. "Worse for drink, Gilly? My drink? While I held my dinner party, my faithful servant and my ward were where? Where was Maledicte?"

"Lady Mirabile is impatient," Gilly said, slipping Vornatti's robe off. "You wouldn't want her to find you still in bedclothes."

"Did he do it, Gilly?" Vornatti said, voice low, maddened. "Did he kill Kritos?"

Gilly found a loose vest and coat that could cover Vornatti's nightshirt and settled him in his wheeled chair, hoping that the Elysia would erase Vornatti's temper, his inquisitiveness. His hands trembled as he continued dressing Vornatti, imagining what Vornatti might do to punish them.

Livia scratched once on the door and ushered Mirabile in; Vornatti caught Gilly's hand and muttered, "I'll have words for you, later."

Gilly bowed his head to Mirabile, avoiding the eager, wild light in her eyes, and fled.

Her voice carried into the hallway. "—dead and by such vile means as one can scarcely comprehend—"

Gilly leaned against the wall, felt the silk wallpaper smooth and slick under his hot cheek, remembered the blood on his hands, and Kritos's death throes. But he also remembered Kritos coming after them, in the dark and from behind.

Livia put a hand on his arm, startling him with her presence. "He's in a right mood today, isn't he? And his party went so well last night, I'd've thought he'd be sleeping all the day."

Gilly shrugged, still irritated at the gossip she had chosen to bring. "He's contrary. Have you seen Maledicte?"

Livia made a face at the abruptness of his tone, but answered readily enough. "He's in the parlor with Lord Echo. Is it true Maledicte gamed with Kritos last night?"

"Go back to your duties," Gilly said. He wouldn't be responsible for any more information slipping from Livia's tongue to Mirabile's ear. Livia sighed, but disappeared obediently.

Gilly hurried toward the parlor. Echo was not a foolish man, and Maledicte's temperament led too often to incautious words for him to feel sanguine about the two of them closeted away together. A sudden wash of guilt stopped him as he reached for the door, and he slumped against the wall instead, weakened by a pounding heart, and a face that he knew would betray him instantly.

Through the door, he heard Echo speaking. ". . . realized you were acquainted enough with Kritos to play cards with him."

"How acquainted must one be to take another's coin?" Maledicte said, in full court archness.

"True enough," Echo said, "Still, to gamble with Kritos showed a distinct lack of caution. The man was a well-known scoundrel."

"You came to lecture me? Or did you have a higher purpose?" Maledicte said.

After a silent second where Gilly imagined Echo biting back his temper, he heard him say, "Did you see anyone who might have wished Kritos ill?"

"Have you been to the Fiery Hell?" Maledicte asked. "Even *I* found it a veritable snake pit."

"You have nothing more useful to say?"

"I so rarely do," Maledicte agreed, and Echo's quick-moving footsteps were the only warning Gilly had to back away from being an obvious eavesdropper. Still, the quickness of it insured that the guilt he felt written on his skin was overlaid with startlement. Echo's own temper did the rest for him; he left without further word.

Gilly tapped at the door and went in. Maledicte looked up from his seat, his boots propped on the hearthstone, and smiled. He set something small down on the chair arm beside him.

"Did you hear the bells this morning?" Maledicte asked. "A lovely way to wake."

"I missed them," Gilly said. "Mal—"

"Vornatti?" Maledicte asked.

"He knows now, whether he heard the bells or not. Livia brought the news, and Mirabile has brought the gossip. He's furious." Gilly paced, unable to settle, and picked up the miniature from beside Maledicte, holding it up toward the lamplight. "He wants to see you immediately."

"And interrupt Mirabile's visit?" Maledicte said, rising and claiming the portrait, tucking it away in his vest. "Or worse, give her the pleasure of seeing me dressed down before her? No, Gilly. Vornatti can wait."

"They found Kritos in the Relicts," Gilly said. He lowered himself into Maledicte's vacated seat.

"Not surprising," Maledicte said. He picked up the blade and began stalking shadows with impatient stabs and thrusts. "You don't think Kritos walked the streets unnoticed, do you? The scavengers would have started to work with their little knives, making sure they found all he had to hide. After the scavengers had at him, they would have discarded him as far from their territory as they could, unwilling to find Echo on their doorsteps. Probably the Relicts. The rats would have finished the job then, taking his laces and boots and hair, the pieces the scavengers left. If he'd near rotted before he was found, perhaps one of your rough sailor friends would have seen him chopped for chum—"

"Shut up," Gilly said, the nausea swirling in his belly, churning, mingling with his dread of Vornatti's punishment.

Maledicte paused, blade inscribing an uplift in the air, a stroke like a wingbeat. "That is where I was born, Gilly."

They were sitting in near silence when footsteps paused in the hall outside. Maledicte rose to drop the latch on the door, but it opened before he could do so. Mirabile came in, smiling.

"Maledicte—" she said, holding her hands out. Gilly, making himself unobtrusive, watched Maledicte's muscles shift, as if he couldn't decide between flight or fight.

"Lady," he said, his voice neutral.

"So formal?" she asked, her tone arch. "When we are to be family soon?"

Maledicte stiffened like an affronted cat.

Mirabile trilled laughter, and held out her wrist again, showing the bright band of gemstones circling it. Emeralds, Gilly thought numbly. The old bastard's given her emeralds to match her eyes.

"From your so-generous guardian," Mirabile said. She leaned closer to let Maledicte admire the bracelet. "I expect the rest of the set when I return from the country. The necklace, the earrings, the ring . . ."

"You're deluded," Maledicte said, "a woman who cannot discern the difference between a bridal gift and a whore's trinket."

Mirabile's green eyes darkened, but before she could speak, Maledicte continued, his voice as delicately acid as it had been the night he faced DeGuerre. "Or are you telling me he offered for your hand? That Vornatti propelled himself from his chair and to his knees before you? I think not."

Her smile held with effort. "You had best watch yourself, Maledicte. He is most displeased with you, and I am as elegant and as lovely as you."

"But so much older," Maledicte murmured, and Gilly winced.

"I see you're in no civil mood," she said. "Perhaps your guardian's lecture will teach you to mind your manners." She dropped a tiny curtsy toward Maledicte and turned, flirting her skirts as she left.

Looking after her, Gilly missed Maledicte's first words, but the sullen rage in them reclaimed his attention. "Did you buy that bracelet for Vornatti and not tell me?"

"No," Gilly said, hastily. "No, Mal." At the black anger in Maledicte's eyes, Gilly stifled his next words—that likely Livia had done it, and pocketed herself a few coppers as well.

"Think you that he favors her enough for marriage?" Despite the rage cording his throat, tightening the silken lines of his cravat, Maledicte's voice was quiet.

"You said it yourself—it's a whore's gift, a trinket he can use to keep her dancing to his tune. And a small price to pay for raising your doubts, I'd lay wager. He's angry, Maledicte. Not an idiot."

"If he wanted to wed Mirabile, he'd have to be, wouldn't he?" Maledicte said, the flush leaving his cheeks, the tension slackening from his hands. "A woman who's murdered one husband already and who plots to cuckold her second before the marriage lines are even written."

"Still," Gilly said, "Best go to him now, and take your punishment. Soothe him if you can."

"Soothe him?" Maledicte said. "He gave her jewelry."

"He's so angry, Mal, please. Last time, I ended in the stables, while you only had to serve him as I do. He's angrier this time, and I always pay for it. . . ." He trailed off, unsure where the bitterness in his voice had come from.

Maledicte's eyes widened and then he said, "I'll go to him at once."

VORNATTI'S CHAMBER SEEMED SUBDUED, AS if the death bells had shocked it to stillness. Maledicte looked at the room with new eyes, eyes that were looking into the uncertain future. Vornatti was a scarecrow of a man, hunched in a wing chair, drawn up before an unlit fire, dozing, but Maledicte knew better than to presume helplessness. Maledicte looked at the bed, plush heaps of featherdown and velvet and linen, followed the line of the posts up to the ceiling and its obscene fresco of fornicating cupids.

He found himself amused at Vornatti's unflagging concupiscence, at the determination that filled the man's hours. The smile was fragile, though. Though Maledicte flouted Vornatti's strictures, gave in to his own whims, still he dreaded displeasing Vornatti too greatly, wary of the man's vindictiveness and temper.

Vornatti woke, coughed, then said, "Boy, come here."

Maledicte turned. Surely he had done this already, the slender youth, the sword, an old man's lures. He dropped the sword on the cluttered bed chest, beside the potions and formulas, the shaving soap and scent. A bottle tipped with a crystalline ring, but kept its stopper. Maledicte crouched beside Vornatti. "What do you want, Vornatti?"

The baron's dark eyes fixed on Maledicte's upturned face. "You killed Kritos."

"I did," Maledicte said. A denial would only feed Vornatti's anger. *Soothe him*, Gilly had pled.

To that end, Maledicte stood, slipping off his coat, his boots, the stiff, brocaded vest, undressing piece by piece.

The baron's eyes softened a little, anger tempered by a more familiar appreciation.

Maledicte settled gently in Vornatti's lap, resting his head against his shoulder, as falsely obedient as a young wife, allowing Vornatti's hand to slip along his thigh. "Echo seems unsuspecting."

"Kritos was a fool and a bad gambler; such men come to bad ends routinely," Vornatti said, absently. His knotted fingers slid upward, traced circles over Maledicte's hipbones.

"See there, no harm done. Don't begrudge me Kritos's death. In turn, I'll—"

Vornatti put a gnarled hand to Maledicte's lips. "A bargain, my boy."

"We struck one already. In the library of your country home."

"I am not doddering, Maledicte. I remember our agreement." Vornatti laid his hand on Maledicte's head, holding it to his shoulder. "I was wrong."

Maledicte waited, heart pounding, wondering whether Vornatti intended to be rid of him. Despite Gilly's words, Vornatti didn't seem angry, and that raised nervous hackles on Maledicte's neck. The old man plotted.

"You can only lose in this quest of yours. You will always be the outsider, always an object of suspicion, and they will turn on you without hesitation. Better I had let you stab Last in the back than teach you to think of honor and nobility. Antyre is not Itarus to admire the cunning of those trained like assassin princes."

Maledicte nipped the fingers so near his mouth, and Vornatti pulled his hand away. "Is that what you have taught me? And here I called your lessons vice."

Vornatti chuckled. "Ah lad, your wicked, disrespectful tongue." The humor faded from his face, draining to melancholy. "I am an old man, Maledicte, and I find myself prey to an old man's most insidious and foolish disease. I would keep you, your wicked mouth, your liquid eyes, your tempers and tempests, only for myself. Keep you mine alone."

Disgust flared in him, twisting his lips. Stay here? Limit his touches to

Vornatti's withered flesh when Janus awaited? Maledicte started to rise, patience gone, blood drumming in his veins; Vornatti tangled a fist in Maledicte's hair, sent him to his knees by his chair. "Listen to me, boy. Bide your time. Last will keep until you are better established, or until I am gone and cannot watch you fall. My name grants you some safety but not enough for a direct attack. Such can only end in death or prison. Stay with me. Continue as we have been, and I'll make it worth your while. You know you can trust me to keep my word. Haven't I kept your other secrets safe, my *girl*? Stay and I'll reward you. Make you my ward in truth. My heir."

"Do you think I can be bought?" Maledicte asked, fisting his hands in his lap. The sword slid from the chest with a protesting scrape and fell to the rugs below.

"Haven't I bought you once already? Now, all I'm buying is your time. You're a young . . . man. Last, curse him, is a healthy man. And I, Maledicte, am an old man. My blood fails beneath my skin, but even dying men have favors to bestow. Wait and you'll have money enough to escape from Antyre when they turn on you, teeth bared and bloody."

Maledicte said, "You swore you hated Last."

"And I am content to know you will destroy him. I have no need to see it. Perhaps my vengeance should have been taken when my blood first burned. However it occurs, that fire is cold now and I'd exchange chill for warmth. Yours would be preferable. If you persist on your impatient course, I will make do with Mirabile, and set you back to the streets."

"You speak to me of vengeance fading, yet you would have me balk and delay? I have not that luxury. You had not the spur to act that I have." Maledicte escaped from Vornatti's anchoring hand, seized up his shirt, and shrugged it on.

"Janus," Vornatti growled.

"Ani," Maledicte countered to Vornatti's scoffing laugh. He had woken, newly aware of Her, Her contentment that he had sealed their compact, satisfaction that more blood would be forthcoming. Vornatti's prattling of delay made Her shift like a snake coiling to strike.

Vornatti leaned forward in his chair, hands clutching the padded leather armrests. "Forget the boy; he has surely forgotten you. What can he offer you? He's only a bastard nephew to a dreaming king. He'll never be earl, never inherit. Last will see to that, count on it. And he has never attempted to find you. Your desire is one-sided, boy. Stay your hand."

Maledicte took refuge in the inane persiflage of Vornatti's favorite literature. "Why sir, this is all so sudden." The acid snarl to his voice removed all humor from the words.

Vornatti's eyes squinched, peering at him. Maledicte stepped back farther into the shadows, out of Vornatti's sight, given over to an uncontrollable shaking. He trembled like a spooked horse, from head to toe, while he thought. It was too soon to dispense with Vornatti's patronage—and inciting his wrath so near the solstice ball—

"Is that a refusal?" Vornatti asked. "Casting you back to the streets not enough? I could expose you first, girl. Or cast Gilly out alongside you. He's begun to bore me anyhow, and I know others who seek his services, though they would not treat him as kindly."

Maledicte's shivering ceased as quickly as it had come, his composure restored. "Won't you even grant me the time to think on it? The heroines in your novels always have time to think on it."

"You're no heroine," Vornatti said.

"And you're no gentleman."

Vornatti laughed. "Stay or go. Yes or no, Maledicte."

"Damn you," Maledicte said, plunged away from Vornatti as if he would flee, but then returned. "Yes, damn you."

"As greedy and as fickle as I thought. After all, Janus is nothing but a boy you no longer know." Vornatti leaned forward, took Maledicte's hands. "Thank me, boy. You've learned something it has taken me years to learn: We all outgrow our pasts. Now kiss me and cry friends."

Maledicte kissed his dry cheek, amazed that the choked rage within him wasn't enough to scald Vornatti's skin. "Shall I send for Gilly, let him dress you for court?"

Vornatti said, "Call Gilly by all means. We'll let him know you're staying. But first—" He drew Maledicte to his lap again, slipped the shirt away.

MALEDICTE SEETHED QUIETLY while Vornatti tugged at the bell rope, his face carefully controlled while Gilly heard the news. He raised his eyes to see the expression on Gilly's face: pure, unadulterated alarm. But then, Gilly believed in Ani's presence, and Vornatti, fool several times over, did not. There was no future but vengeance for him.

Maledicte ascended the stairs, turning the gas lamps down as he went, leaving a smothering trail of darkness behind him, hoping to balk Gilly in pursuit. Though it had been his choice to stay, the easy temper in his blood also blamed Gilly.

But Gilly, with longer legs, caught him at the first landing, seized his shoulder. "What are you planning?"

"Don't," Maledicte said, Ani already an angry presence in his blood. To be manhandled was more than he could stand. Heedless, Gilly shook him. "Tell me why you agreed to put off your vengeance."

Maledicte put his hand on Gilly's chest, shoved him away without effort, watched Gilly fly back and hit the far wall. Maledicte's hands shook, a resurgence of the eager trembling that had beset him in Vornatti's room, spreading over his entire body.

"Maledicte?" Gilly said, rising, caution on his face.

Maledicte slid down the wall, crouched in the shadows, ashamed of himself. "Who else would I be?"

The name hung in the air between them. Gilly hesitated, then dropped to his knees beside Maledicte. "Lean on me. I'll help you upstairs. I'll bring you up some milk, warmed and scented with vanilla and almonds."

"As if Ani can be cured like a cold, or Vornatti's caresses made sweet," Maledicte said, acid in his voice, then in a different tone. "Thank you, Gilly, my gentle Gilly. . . ." He lapsed into silence as they made their way up the dark stairs, Gilly looking back over their shoulders, as if he expected to see Ani sweeping after them.

· 14 ·

ON THE EVENING OF THE SOLSTICE BALL, Gilly and Maledicte found themselves part of a line of coaches, wending their way through the city streets to the palace at so slow a pace that noblemen sauntered from coach to coach, visiting, chatting, flirting, admiring costumes. From his perch on the driver's bench, Gilly watched it all, and couldn't help but contrast the general giddiness with his passenger's stillness. Costumed forlornly as the Heartsore Chevalier, that tragic figure of legend, Maledicte drew the coach curtains whenever nobles drew near, sulking into silence.

Gilly hated the costume, the sleek white wrappings of vest and coat and pants, hated the crimson touches at wrist and neck; most of all he hated the expression in Maledicte's eyes, as if this moment might be too much to bear.

Gilly's nerves were strung tight enough as it was; hadn't they left Vornatti home, lost in a drugged sleep when he had meant to attend? Maledicte's doing, of course, and done so swiftly that Gilly had not understood until he tried to rouse Vornatti. His remonstrance had died when Maledicte turned on him, raging. "Do you think I could have borne it? Hunting Janus with Vornatti draped over my skin? Touching me as if he had my welcome?"

At the ballroom, Gilly tossed the reins to a waiting stableboy, and opened the carriage door. Maledicte stepped out like a ghost, one hand on the sword.

Maledicte started up the stairs with Gilly behind, and paused at the great Book of Names. On the last page, recently scribed, his goal was marked.

Janus Ixion, Lord Last: the name was scrawled with such black finality that Gilly was not surprised to see the next names rough and surrounded by splatters. Janus had destroyed the nib.

Maledicte touched the ink with his gloved fingers. The ink sank in, still wet, black staining into the red silk gloves. Maledicte wiped his hand against his mouth, shoved past Gilly, and escaped into the night air, past the cloying sweetness of heaped violets and jasmine, lilies and heliotrope, and the slow-burning haze of beeswax candles. Gilly found Maledicte outside, pacing beside the ivy maze.

"Mal—"

"It stinks in there, like rot. Do you think anyone has ever told Aris that crushed flowers smell like a grave?"

Gilly held out a gentling hand.

Maledicte turned, retched into the leaves. Gilly stepped back when Maledicte looked up. His eyes were wild. His hands shook like those of a man with fever, and his voice trembled. "Comes the moment when everything changes. This idyll dies, and it has been an idyll, hasn't it? Even with Vornatti's tempers and demands and threats? I'm feared to see it end." He stretched up and pressed his lips against the drawn corner of Gilly's mouth.

Gilly could smell Maledicte's skin, scenting faintly of lilac, could feel the smoothness of Maledicte's cheek against the stubble rising on his own. "Feared of Last? Of Janus? I won't believe either with the course you've set."

"Not them. Last is a dead man, and Janus is neither alive nor dead 'til he speaks. I fear myself, Gilly, the brush of feathers in my mind. If Janus spurns me— Her feathers urge me to darker hungers, and Her wings smell of death and bloody iron." He hid his face in Gilly's neck, but shied away when Gilly reached up a comforting hand.

"If Janus spurns me, or remembers me not, there will be nothing left of me. Only Ani's puppet. But still, there is no going back."

"Would you go back, if you could?" Gilly asked, voice rough.

"No," Maledicte answered immediately, without the need for thought, his eyes black and very cold. "Why are we standing in the dark, Gilly, when the ball awaits? I've killed one Last already. Let's see how many this night holds."

Gilly followed him inside, where the nobles' ballroom had been doubled with the drawing back of the barriers between the king's ballroom and theirs. While the nobles' ballroom was painted in washes of blue and dust, Aris's ballroom was all rose and gold, and so the dancers whirled from twilight to sunrise. Maledicte walked on, unaware, his eyes flicking from one bare face to the next. The Bright Solstice required costumes but not masks; those were saved for winter's Dark Solstice, where one wore masks to shield identity from the hungry dead.

Gilly paced beside him, looking for a man he'd never seen, but felt sure he would recognize. As the moments passed, and Maledicte's expression grew fixed, Gilly whispered, "Follow the gossip, the bent heads. A newcomer leaves such in his tracks. It will lead you to him."

Maledicte granted Gilly a shaky smile, then stiffened like a hound on scent. Gilly followed his gaze.

The young man entering from the balconies could only be Janus Ixion; he was the butter stamp of Last, pale-eyed, gilt-haired, tall, and broad-shouldered. The brief impression Gilly had gleaned from the miniature had been of a vapid nobleman, but he had assumed it due to an artist overeager to please Last.

But the reality was no better; Gilly felt disappointment turn his stomach. This was the face that had driven Maledicte so far? This was Janus, this elegantly draped figure in blue velveteen and gold? His face was as empty as that of any longtime court roué. Where Maledicte still carried a rat's wariness, Janus seemed pampered from birth, the perfect son of an aging aristocrat, with an expression as devoid of intelligence as it was of interest. Here, in the glittering heart of Antyre, Janus conveyed only boredom.

Gilly felt a shiver in the air, turned. Maledicte was no longer at his side, but had disappeared while Gilly gaped. He caught a glimpse of him, moving along the perimeter of the room, following in Janus's idle path like his shadow.

Gilly hissed, watching the game begin. Cat catch mouse, with both men playing. Janus was aware of his shadow, acted the complicit mouse, limited himself to small turns of his neck and head, trying not to catch sight of his pursuer. If he spotted the shadow too soon, too obviously, the game would end, and interest and amusement sparked in those incandescent blue eyes, livening the mask of his face.

The court grew progressively more silent, watching in avid delight.

"Must we continue with this roundaboutation?" Janus spoke aloud, his voice laced with amusement, though he had yet to acknowledge his pursuer with even a glance. In his voice, Gilly heard the same careless arrogance that drove Maledicte's speech, but layered in tones like sculpted velvet. "I'm but new come to this court, and fail to see how I have erred in your opinion. If I have offended your sister, mother, lover, I apologize. If it's other than that, let it wait. We have affrighted the musicians to silence."

"They sounded like cats strangling anyway, and I should know," Maledicte said. His raspy voice was shocking after Janus's polished one.

Janus, startled, turned to confront his shadow, and the amused smoothness of his face shifted. Even Gilly, standing so near, could not name the sentiment, the emotion fleeing too quickly to identify, like a ripple over deep water and gone.

Janus took a step toward Maledicte; the courtiers, the maidens caught between slipped away, and the whispering court found their eyes drawn not to either man but to the emptiness between them, the nexus of space that slowly closed.

Maledicte took another step. His face was as pale as his shirt.

"Have we danced enough?" Janus said. "So come, then, declare yourself and have at me." His lips stayed parted after his words; his face tightened as Maledicte took the space between them and made it an illusion, not the impenetrable barrier it seemed.

"Janus Ixion—" Maledicte said, at the heart of the circle. His voice caressed the syllables, and again that flicker of emotion swept Janus's face.

"Lord Last," Janus said, dropping into a bow, his golden hair sliding, gleaming over sky-blue shoulders.

The sweeping arc of the black blade stopped his descent. He tilted his head up, pale throat like marble. "Not in the mood, hmmm?" Janus stood straight, spread his arms. "Have at me then; I will not fight you."

Maledicte wavered, visibly unable to move forward or back. Janus's arms closed; he caught Maledicte's wrist, his other hand caught the shoulder of Maledicte's embroidered coat and drew him closer. Then he released Maledicte's sword hand, all as smoothly done as if it were only the steps of a dance and not a potential duel.

"Will you strike me?" Janus asked. His voice, which so far had been pitched for the horrified, fascinated, scandalized audience, dropped to a husk. There was the faintest sound of despairing entreaty in his words, as if Maledicte's enmity was too heavy a weight to shoulder.

The black blade shivered in the light, a shadow chased by candle flames, moving. Falling. It clattered to the marble floor and Janus smiled. He slid his hand over Maledicte's shoulder, into the dark hair, and bending close, put his kiss first on Maledicte's mouth, then on the silk-covered throat. Maledicte threw his head back, in a movement as voluptuous as any woman's.

Janus murmured something too low for the riveted crowd. Gilly strained, but even his clever ears missed the word. A name? A prayer?

What Janus said, of course, in his crushed-velvet voice, was *Miranda*.

The silence faltered as whispers broke over the court like the tide. Janus stepped apart from Maledicte, dropped into a bow again, elegant and courtly. Maledicte returned it after a moment, and where Janus's bow was all Antyrrian languor, Maledicte's carried the stiff perfection of Vornatti's teaching. Maledicte spoke a few quiet words, drowned in the hiss of the court, and turned away.

The courtiers flooded inward, erasing the stage Janus and Maledicte had created with their presence; scandalmongers sailed from one side of the room to another, tongues preparing to wag. Trying to follow who might have the most dangerous words to spill, Gilly lost sight of Maledicte in the mass. A faint whisper in his ear, a quick scent of lilac, and Maledicte slipped by him and disappeared with an eerie grace. Gilly turned, trying to track him, and instead caught sight of Mirabile standing, frozen, her face a mere mask. Shock, Gilly thought, and worse—*betrayal*. Janus fit nowhere in her plans for Maledicte.

Still near the epicenter of the storm, Janus accepted a glass from Westfall's hand, smiled his thanks, and headed toward the balcony doors.

His cue, Gilly knew. Maledicte's command ghosted through his mind. *Show Janus to the carriage. We're stealing him away.*

Except Gilly could think of nothing he would like less than to take Janus through the romantic tangles of the king's maze where he had walked with Maledicte. He told himself it was relief that Maledicte was not launched on his erasure of self, his bloody vendetta without care for his own life.

A quick movement, checked, drew his attention to the dais, to Aris staying the Kingsguard in their search for Maledicte, and wearing a fine, high flush on his cheekbones. Anger, Gilly feared. The king's eyes shifted to meet his. Gilly dropped his gaze immediately, caught staring at the king like a country fool. But more disturbing to his composure was the unwilling recognition of their shared emotion, the bite of unreasoning jealousy.

The voices of the court were roaring now, the musicians fighting to be heard, belaboring their instruments to make up for their earlier silences. Gilly, making his way out, collected comments like tiles from a mosaic. "Sword in the court. Again. And yet Aris does nothing—"

"Last will not be amused that his son set us such a scene."

"It's enchantment, I tell you." Mirabile's face was livening finally to well-controlled rage, taking Maledicte's actions as an affront to her own charms. "First he claims Aris's approval and now his nephew's. But *how*, is the question. I have seen things he would not like me to tell, an altar, books of spells . . ."

"A devotee of the dead gods?" her hearer, Micah Chalefont, sneered. "Only fools believe in them."

"Fools deny the evidence of their own senses. I am not so witless," Mirabile said, snapping her fan closed. The certainty in her voice stifled Chalefont and made Gilly hasten his steps.

He found Janus waiting silently in the dimness; when Gilly approached, those blank blue eyes showed only disinterest. "This way," Gilly said, gesturing into the maze, and Janus's eyes burned with eagerness.

MALEDICTE PULLED HIMSELF from Janus's embrace, settled on the opposite side of the carriage, leaned forward and knotted Janus's hands in his own. He laughed soundlessly, his constricted throat unable to voice the emotion. "I dreaded this moment, feared I'd never see you again. That you wouldn't know me if I did . . . What a fool to forget how we fit together."

"I'd know you anywhere, Miranda—"

"No," Maledicte frowned, a fleeting thing, displaced by joy. "Miranda's dead. Murdered in the Relicts like the rat she was."

"That's as Roach told me. That you were dead, and at my hand. Absurd. As if I could ever harm you. . . ."

Maledicte was glad of the dimness of the carriage, the swaying that shadowed their faces and granted them a sweet intimacy, all too aware of the flush on his cheeks, the rush of pleasure at Janus's careless words. "You went back?"

"Soon as the *Kiss* docked. Soon as I could convince Kritos that the voyage had made me ill. The only familiar face I found was Roach." Janus laughed and kissed Maledicte with a greedy mouth. "And here we are."

Their noses bumped, their foreheads jarred each other's when the carriage bumped over rough stones. Janus, distracted, peered out the window at Dove Street passing by with its line of tall, trim houses and sculpted lawns. "Where are we going?"

"My town house." Maledicte slid on the seat, pushing his back into the plush warmth of the cushions, his fingers slipping from Janus's grip, then leaning forward again, unwilling to let go.

"This isn't just some raid on the nobles' court then?"

"I told you. Miranda's dead. Despite the masquerade, I am much as you see me. I am Maledicte, ward to Baron Vornatti, a courtier and not a lady." Maledicte gave a little half bow, constrained by the seat. "I warn you now. I am a known entity in the court, and you've undoubtedly blacked your reputation tonight."

"You always were the clever one, Mir—Maledicte, was it? Quite a mouthful, love. But tell me, do you know that Kritos is dead now? Do you know that?" Janus said, settling back. "Struck down by an unseen hand, left for rat food." A smile played about his lips, the same secret communication in his eyes that Maledicte had missed so sorely.

"He took you from me. Should I have let that go unrevenged?" Maledicte said. Ani grumbled beneath the joy in his blood, and he said, "But let's not talk of vengeance now." He put himself into Janus's lap and kissed him again and again.

MALEDICTE SECURED HIS BEDCHAMBER DOOR while Janus's teeth teased his nape. Janus raised his head, looked around at the sumptuous room, at the fireplace, still faintly red with burning coals, the wide chair beside it, the tall windows with their heavy crimson drapes, the plush, high bed. "Your baron treats you well." The question lurked in his tone.

"For a price," Maledicte admitted, then skirted the pointed truth for a few lesser ones. "The keeper of my secrets, and my own personal blackmailer. If I displease him, he threatens me with exposure in the court."

"Would that be such a dreadful thing?"

"I would be ruined. A woman in Vornatti's house, unchaperoned? A woman with a sword? Not even Vornatti's novels tell such audacious tales. Besides," Maledicte said, "I'm rather attached to my persona and the freedom it brings." It was all the explanation he could give on the matter, and he shivered, wondering what Janus thought, to find Miranda in a circumstance she had always sworn she would never be in.

Janus kissed the silk cravat on Maledicte's throat once more, then loosed the knot with careful fingers. "They truly believe you a man? With your sleek skin and smooth throat—" He traced the bared lines of chin and neck and collarbone. "I expected a scar to match your voice. It is not an affectation."

"No," Maledicte said, "stonethroat."

Janus kissed the pale skin at the base of Maledicte's throat, touched his tongue to the hollow there, a tiny flicker of warmth that sparked likewise in his veins. "Such a gamble."

"Risks are necessary when one seeks a prize of inimitable value," Maledicte said, opening Janus's shirt, finishing the job begun in the carriage, easing the stiff, formal vest off, then the silken lawn. In the low-lit room, Janus's skin gleamed like gold, and heated Maledicte's blood like fine brandy. Maledicte shoved him toward the wing chair, and once Janus was seated, pulled off his boots, glad beyond measure that Vornatti seemed to have faded from Janus's thoughts. Maledicte looked again at Janus, at the lazy, hungry expression in those familiar eyes, and gave himself to the moment—more, to their future, for the first time feeling he had more than a tentative grasp on it. He found himself smiling again.

Janus tugged him into his lap, unbuttoned Maledicte's shirt, slipped the silk away, and paused, amused. "A corset?"

"Padded," Maledicte said, touching his sides, his belly, his back. "Throughout here, to bulk up my waist, flatten my breasts. This masquerade would be less successful otherwise. Unhook me." He presented the elaborate back to Janus's waiting hands.

"How do you manage to lace this by yourself?" Janus laughed. "Every lady I've met needed a maid or a man."

Maledicte moaned as the hooks parted with faint pops and the corset fell free. "Practice. Necessity. And it needn't be as tight as the ladies' corsets. It needs only to disguise," Maledicte said into Janus's hair, nipping at his earlobes.

Janus slid his hands around the exposed narrow waist, the curve of spine and hip, the small, soft breasts. Maledicte sighed, and leaned into his hands, arching back as Janus kissed each tender tip. Things did change, he thought a little deliriously. Janus had changed, grown taller, broader, stronger, harder. Maledicte basked against him, the scent of his skin rising over the court colognes, and smiled hungrily.

He stroked his hands down Janus's ribs, the sleek, muscle-padded heat of them, trailing light fingertips down Janus's belly. Janus's breath grew a little more rapid, and Maledicte chose to slide away from a more intimate touch, even as Janus shifted his hips toward his hands. A delightful thought occurred: This time, they had all the time in the world—no stolen moment made fragile by Ella's importunate callers, by Celia's drunken rages, by Roach's jealous dogging of their heels. This time was theirs alone, and he intended to savor every moment, to relearn the feel of Janus's skin against his own.

"What's this?" Janus asked, stopping his caresses to touch the red lines on Maledicte's left arm and side.

"Sword strike from the Marquis DeGuerre." Maledicte studied it again, briefly bewildered by a history not shared.

"And this one?" Janus traced the long, serpentine scar that wrapped her left hipbone, veered around her back, and licked the base of her right breast.

"Whip," Maledicte said. "Kritos, in the Relicts."

"Bastard," Janus muttered, bending to kiss the upward curl of the weal, a wash of breath and heat that made Maledicte gasp, draw him closer.

"Just another dead aristocrat now," Maledicte said, clutching Janus's shoulders as his lips left the scar and moved down the pale, soft skin of Maledicte's belly.

Janus untied the laces in Maledicte's hair, setting it tumbling free, framing Maledicte's face and shoulders in whispery tendrils that made him shudder with sensation. "None so blind . . ." Janus murmured. "You look like no man I've ever seen."

Maledicte preened. "Gilly calls it vision driven by expectation."

"Gilly knows?" Janus asked. His lips paused in their brushing over Maledicte's skin, tightened in a frown.

"No," Maledicte said, flushing at the very thought. "The fewer to know this secret, the fewer to tell it."

"Are you so sure he is unaware?" Janus asked. "If he has mentioned—"

"He was referring to cheating at cards, and simple sleight of hand. He has not thought to apply his rule to me, I assure you." Maledicte ran trembling fingers through Janus's hair, admiring the sparks of sunlight captured in the golden strands.

"He's aided you, acted your partner," Janus said. He slipped away from Maledicte, paced across the room to poke at the coals, sending sparks upward in swirls of angry heat.

"My partner on my path to retrieving you," Maledicte said. "You must be my partner now as well."

"Like secrets, partners are often best kept to two," Janus said. "Vornatti knows—"

"Janus," Maledicte said, impatient with the subject, only aware of the flickering firelight over Janus's skin, and the answering heat in his own. "Come here and free me of these boots and breeches, unless you fancy taking me as if we were gentlemen in the stables, fumbling and baring only what we must."

Janus grinned, mood sweetened. "Another time, perhaps." He knelt, and tugged Maledicte's boots off; he ran his hands up the thin leather of Maledicte's breeches, began sliding them down, lingering to kiss the inside of his bared thighs. "Very nice legs . . . for a gentleman of the court." The words tickled against his skin, made him shiver, made him writhe.

"I admit the court finds me a rather girlish young man in appearance." But his good spirits chilled. First Vornatti, now this. He felt that every moment exposed pitfalls he hadn't imagined, every moment revealing a threat to this fragile joy. He touched Janus's mouth, halting further banter, and stepped out of the entangling leather. "But Janus, they do believe me a man, and while it is understood, so says Aris, that some men have appetites only for their own, it is not a fashionable thing. And I will not give up this role. I am Maledicte now, and so I think myself male, all evidence to the contrary aside." Maledicte gestured, encompassing bared flesh. "Your reputation may suffer if you are seen in my company overmuch."

The last words were pained; only now did Maledicte realize the trap he had laid for himself. To become female again was unthinkable, and yet his guise could cost him Janus.

He turned, studied himself in the mirror, distracted from worrying in the shock of self-exploration. It had been so long since he had taken the risk of loitering unclothed, or even thought of himself as Miranda; though he had all her desires, her dreams, he spoke truly to Janus when he declared her dead. Maledicte could not put himself back in her position, could not remake time, unable to remember how it felt to not carry this secret.

"I suppose I should be grateful I don't resemble Ella," Maledicte said, "or this rebirth would have been impossible. My lines are more male than female."

Janus laughed, snaked an arm over her shoulders; she shivered in relief and want at the sight of his form alongside her in the glass. "You are blind yourself. You are barely taller than most women of the court. Your voice is your most believable attribute, but this—" He cupped one breast, then the other, stroked his fingers over her nipples, making them stiffen. "This is purely female."

Maledicte's heart raced; he leaned back against Janus's chest, playing now, directing his attention. "My hips are not broad enough."

Janus slid his hand downward, splaying his fingers down Maledicte's belly, lingering, teasing, his voice furred by desire. "The women of the court wear corsets, boning, bustle, and padding to make them shapes different from their own."

His fingers slipped into the warm cleft of her thighs, moving in gentle patterns, growing warm, her skin growing slick against his touch, and Maledicte trembled. "Do you still think yourself male?" Janus whispered. "Do you fear I will leave you at the say-so of the court? What care I for their approval when I have you in my arms again?"

Again Maledicte flushed, the pale skin staining pink over cheeks and throat. Maledicte turned in Janus's arms, kissed him as if to devour the taste of him. Maledicte guided Janus's steps until he tumbled backward onto the bed, a golden expanse over rich crimson. Maledicte crept up Janus's body, touching, kissing, tasting, with the same greedy, gloating hunger a starving man mustered for a sudden feast.

Janus arched his body into a bow, let Maledicte slide his breeches off and to the floor. Maledicte nestled warmly between his legs and allowed himself a leisurely reacquaintance with Janus's body. Measuring tongue tip by tongue tip how Janus had grown, how he continued to do so, until Janus gasped and strained against Maledicte's teasing kisses. Janus drew him up, and they tangled, each trying to map the other in touches and kisses and the shiver of skin against skin. Janus licked the shell of Maledicte's ear, stirred gentle fingers through her heat. In return, Maledicte lapped at Janus's throat, tasted their mingled salt, and chased the taste up to his jaw. Janus obliged him, tilting his head back, and then erupted into choking laughter. Maledicte raised his head.

"There are some quite perverse cupids watching," Janus said.

"Vornatti's obscenely fond of them. He had them commissioned for every private room of the house," Maledicte said, flinching even as Vornatti's name slipped his lips.

"Vornatti," Janus breathed, catching Maledicte's hands, stilling the caresses. "What are we to do with him? I gather he will not be pleased to share you. Come to think on it, neither am I." Though the words were indifferent, the tone was not.

Again, Maledicte hovered on the brink of explanation. Again, he slid away—what could he say? That to regain Janus, Miranda would have done far worse than forswear oft-stated avowals and barter her body? Surely Janus knew that already. So instead of an explanation of how this came to be, he found himself murmuring an explanation of why it would continue, sweetening the sting of it with a meandering touch that teased nipples, traced ribs, delved into his navel, and wrapped warmly around his shaft.

"I have no name of my own, no funds that he has not granted. To leave him would be to leave with nothing save what we could carry."

Janus laid his hands over Maledicte's, slowing the pleasure so he could find words. "I have no funds either, save for what I won from Kritos. And we can't risk your exposure, so you say—still, something must be done. You killed Kritos. . . ." Janus lay back, rested his head on his hands, silently urging Maledicte's caresses to resume.

"A gambler with a multitude of foes," Maledicte said, frowning. He traced swords and feathers across Janus's skin.

"One old man should prove little challenge. Especially one who grants you such access to his person." Janus's jaw tightened; Maledicte licked; the tension in Janus's face traded anger for pleasure.

"True enough," Maledicte said slowly, letting his thoughts turn dark, his movements still, sifting memories of Vornatti's demands, his threats, comparing rewards and chastisements, against the lure of money to hand. He shuddered a little and climbed up to nestle into Janus's strength, soaking in his surety, the pleasure of scheming with him once again.

"Is there any reason to wait?" Janus asked. "If not—"

Maledicte kissed him again, stopping his words. "He's promised me an inheritance. I'm minded to collect it."

"Then I'll not stop you. Not when you look so fierce. So mercenary," Janus said, toying with the black curls that lay over Maledicte's shoulder. He raised the lock to his mouth, kissed it. "So bewitching. I've missed you. . . ." He rolled them both over, pinned Maledicte between his arms, under his thighs. "But inherit soonest, Mal."

Maledicte drew Janus's head down to kiss him. "Anything for you." He gasped, parted his thighs, and lost his hold on his courtier's mask. This physical definition was so much more real than the shadowy grasp of personality and will.

With Janus sliding in, possessing her, there was nothing left but Miranda, clawing Janus still closer. "Janus—" she breathed, her voice caught by the damage in her throat, muted.

"Shh," Janus said, "my love, my courtier, my dark cavalier . . ."

Maledicte's fingers tensed and dug into Janus's back, scraping the sleek indentation of the spine between muscle, the gas lights streaming and filtering through the pale gold mesh of Janus's hair, the cherubs watching, coaxing, laughing. Maledicte closed her lashes against the incandescent blue flame of Janus's eyes, lost in this blissful heat of touch and friction, of scent and sound. Janus's panting was in her ear, and for a brief moment it sounded like the rasp of feathery wings, and Maledicte's eyes flew open, trading quick startlement for rushing pleasure in the wash of blue and gold and velvet voice that was Janus in ecstasy.

Janus's moan gave way to a breathless laugh, his blond hair drifting like spiderwebs. "And they think you a man. . . ."

Maledicte ran speechless fingers up Janus's chest, tugged him down to lie beside her, and slowly reassembled the guise she lived within.

Janus continued, "You always were good at misdirection, though. Remember when you bullied all the rats into pretending to be street players at the market? While we muddled along, shouting our lines, jeered at by everyone within earshot, you and Roach stole a feast for us all."

Maledicte turned his face in the pillow; his lips quirked. "Small potatoes only. I have a larger scheme now."

"How can that be? Am I not your end-all and be-all? Are you not completed now that I am here?" Janus said, looking at Maledicte with apparent sincerity. "Are we not bound together from childhood to death?"

Maledicte broke into a rasping laugh. "False sentimentality from you? I'd say you were disguised, and yet I know you are sober."

"Drunk on you," Janus said. The archness that underlaid his last set of pretty words was missing, though his expression never changed.

Maledicte touched Janus's pale lips, slid from the bed in a sleek line of white flesh. He pulled the drapes back from one wall.

The curtain pull revealed not the outside world, glazed through silvery glass, but a small alcove with a tall, narrow table. After Mirabile's visit, Maledicte had stored the poisons chest out of easy sight. Maledicte dug through the bottles, and retrieved a small bit of bright gold.

Maledicte approached, hands held out, fisted before him, to play their long-gone guessing game. At the last second, as Janus reached forward, he opened his right hand to reveal the ring. He could not bear to have Janus misguess.

"I saved it; Kritos let it fall. It's not much now, but it's still for you." Maledicte looked at it once more, remembering it through Relict eyes, the treasure that had fallen into his hands. Gilly said such rings were common during the war—bits of jewelry melted down, reshaped, and engraved with some false trumpery, extolling the glories of battle and the hearts left at home. Knowing now the gold was of questionable quality, and the sentiment looted from a dead man's hand, Maledicte still found it apt.

Janus took the ring, rolled it in his hands, chasing the chill of the metal away, measuring its width against his forefinger. Once, it had been too big. Now it was almost too small; it required some effort to slide it down to sit above his signet ring. He took it off again, tilted it so he could see the inscription. "I remember this. *Only each other at the last.*" He turned the ring around in his hands. "It was warm where you had kept it in your mouth and when I put it on, it felt like a kiss. My signet reads: *Only a Last at the Last.*" His mouth twisted, and he tugged his crested signet off, trading it to his left hand. "I like this motto better," he said, sliding the plainer ring on in its place.

He reached for Maledicte, drew him back into the nest of linens, stroked the dark head resting on his chest. "It's been so long, I don't want to loose my grip for fear you'll slip away. All this because I wanted to rob Kritos before he was properly out, steal his gold for you. And still, I haven't any gold to give you, nor jewelry." He grinned lazily. "Probably for the best. I would never have thought of stickpins, watches, and cuff links."

"Can you get jewelry?" Maledicte asked.

Janus laughed again. "Some, I suppose. Greedy?"

Maledicte leaned close, listening to Janus's heartbeat, a steady sound, a companion from long ago, listening to the quiet sound of Ani's wings answering. "It's only that I mean to kill him, you understand. And if Vornatti's promises are lies, we'll be penniless."

"Last," Janus said, his voice flattening.

"The jewels I own will be needed for our flight. If we're careful, we could stay in Antyre," Maledicte said, voicing plans he had barely allowed himself to think through, too afraid to plan beyond this reunion. "We could live in the country, away from this rat-hunted city. But if the murder goes badly, we'll have to flee Antyre completely and that takes funds."

Janus's supple mouth frowned, his pale eyes narrowing.

"What is it?" Maledicte said, frightened. For one moment everything had been as planned, but in the wolf-pale eyes of his lover, something forced changes. "Never tell me you love him," Maledicte said. "I've sworn to kill him. I must kill him."

"You need not scruple otherwise on my account," Janus said, pushing himself up against the pillows, propping his chin on his knee. "I bear him no fondness, but his title, his land—" Janus's tone dropped to an intimate whisper. "It's a tricky business being a nobleman's bastard, especially if one has ambition. To allow me access to the courts, Last pretended the past had happened otherwise, that Celia and he had wed, that I am legitimate. No one believes him, of course. Whoever heard of an earl not searching for an infant heir stolen away? But Aris supports me, and if I can gain the support of the counselors, then—"

"Then what?" Maledicte interrupted. "How will this see Last dead?"

"It won't, you'll have to do that," Janus said, "but it will give me his title if done at the right moment. You crave Vornatti's money. I want the title."

Maledicte said, "It's only a word—"

Janus shook his head. "A title is power. Listen, Mir—Mal, listen. This position of ours, of *yours*, is precarious."

"I'll kill Last; we can rob his coffers and flee."

"And then what?" Janus said. "Money runs out. You used to teach that to those rats of yours. What happens then? Stealing? Starving? Whoring? Hasn't Vornatti been enough for you? I suppose we could take up a profession, but what are we suited for?"

Maledicte trembled; Janus stroked her belly, soothing.

"You used to cry," Janus said, sliding back down to lie beside Maledicte. "In the cold, when the hunger was so bad. I'd bleed myself just so you could have something warm in your mouth. I swore every year it would be better and it never was. I never want to feel so desperate again."

Turning, Maledicte kissed Janus's throat and whispered, "I must kill him." As if in counterpoint, the sword, resting against the bed, fell with a hiss of scraped velvet.

"With your pretty little blade?" Janus asked. "Last is a brute but a damn good swordsman. And I mistrust the steel in painted blades." Janus reached out a long arm, picked up the sheathed sword, and drew it. "Too often the paint dulls the edge."

Janus fell silent, studying the blade, his fingers caged in the feather hilt. He raised a hand, curled it around the thin edges of the blade, and flinched. Blood beaded up along his fingertips and thumb and dripped to the sheets. "Where did you get this?"

When Maledicte hesitated, afraid to wake Ani from Her cautious slumber by invoking Her name, Janus shrugged. "Vornatti? Generous of him." He attempted to sheathe the sword; the feather hilt clung and bloodied his knuckles. He dropped the blade.

"Ani gave it to me," Maledicte said, the first time he had acknowledged Her gift aloud, a small act of worship. But far better to wake Her attention than to let Janus think Vornatti's touch reached so far into his life. Another frisson licked his nerves—would Janus share this, the specter of a vengeful god?

"Black-Winged Ani is a myth meant to frighten superstitious bastards like my father. The dead gods returned? They never existed at all."

Maledicte clambered over Janus, recovering sheath and sword and mating them with a practiced motion, albeit with a tinge of temper. "Ani exists. I swore I would kill Last. I swore it to Her."

"All I ask for is delay," Janus said. "Time to insure myself the earldom. After that it doesn't matter what happens—we'd be as safe as we never were before."

Maledicte trembled again, not in half-remembered dread of the Relicts, but at Ani listening to Janus's casual blasphemy, at the thought of staying his hand when She yearned for the kill.

"So you'll wait?" Janus said, lying back, licking the tiny cuts on his fingers closed.

"Ani willing," Maledicte whispered, too low for Janus to hear.

"I think I'd make a splendid earl," Janus said, smiling. He snuffed out the last low-burning lamp and dropped them into darkness.

*I*T WAS EARLY AFTERNOON BEFORE Janus and Maledicte bestirred themselves. Maledicte, hunting Gilly, found him reading in the parlor. He leaned over Gilly's shoulder, eliciting a start, a flush, and a guilty twitch. Tweaking the book from Gilly's unresisting hand, Maledicte sighed. "*The Book of Vengeances* again? You spend more time thinking on Ani than I do." He flipped the book into the ashy fireplace, avoiding the snatch Gilly made, and shifted to stand before the hearth.

"Come, we're going to Whitspur Street. Janus wants to explore the city. We'll stop at Rosany's Booksellers and you can buy something less inclined to bring nightmares."

"Mal—" Gilly started, but Maledicte, hearing footsteps in the hall, turned, his skin warming as Janus approached. Janus met his eyes and smiled, leaning in and kissing his temple. Maledicte wove his fingers in Janus's hands, content, Gilly's dark dreams and Ani's rage insignificant.

"Ready, Mal?"

"We both are," Maledicte said, releasing Janus to pull Gilly to his feet.

"Without luncheon? What kind of host would I be if I allowed my unexpected guest to leave hungry?" Vornatti rasped, drawing three heads to where he rested against the doorjamb. Maledicte stepped away from Janus, unnerved by the intensity of Vornatti's gaze, by the simple fact that, though Vornatti's morning dose of Elysia would have worn off, the man confronted them on his feet. He should have been a pitiable sight, all grayed age and aches; instead, he radiated the wary strength of a veteran soldier.

Maledicte's thoughts raced. He had assured Janus that Vornatti would be still abed, had played up the baron's poor flesh and feebleness to soothe Janus's jealousy, and more, to keep Janus from slipping out at dawn. He had believed it himself; this moment found him flat-footed. Janus was more sanguine than he. A bare flicker of distaste crossed his lips before he smiled at Vornatti. "Too gracious of you, sir. I hope my presence hasn't troubled you overmuch."

"Visitors are always a pleasure. Trouble only comes from allowing them to stay past their welcome," Vornatti said. He limped heavily into the room, and said, "I do warn you it is only bachelor fare. I have no hostess, though this is a lack I mean to remedy."

Maledicte said, "If it's Mirabile you mean, she leaves today with the West-falls to the countryside. You'll have to be quick, old man, or chase after her like a hound on a scent." He tried for insouciance though his lips were cold with dread and his body crackling with nervous energy. Vornatti had the power to throw him to the streets, to throw Gilly out; did he have the power to finish the blow and see Janus sent away also, when it was Aris who wanted him in Murne? But Aris preferred lives to land once; he might put the king-dom's fortunes above his own this time, if Vornatti made it too costly to do otherwise. . . .

"A message will suffice to bring her to my side," Vornatti said.

"Messengers are often unreliable," Maledicte said.

Vornatti grimaced at him, then glared at Gilly, who lowered his gaze in wordless agreement. Janus studied the bookshelves with polite courtesy.

"Perhaps you could spare me the trouble," Vornatti said, "of hunting a re-liable messenger, and play hostess yourself. I could find you a dress—" He crooked an arm; Maledicte saw no alternative other than an immediate un-masking, so with a quick look at Gilly, he took Vornatti's arm in his own.

Vornatti leaned on him, wrapping a possessive arm about his waist, and pressed his lips to Maledicte's cheek.

In silence, Maledicte led Vornatti into the dining room, all too aware of Janus's watchful eyes on his back, on Vornatti's stroking fingers. Maledicte settled Vornatti into his seat and attempted to slip free of his grasp. Vornatti only shifted his grip, tugging. Face scalding, Maledicte sat before him, pressed tightly against Vornatti's chest and wandering hands. Janus sank into the seat opposite and Maledicte shivered at the placidity in Janus's face, wondering what the mask hid. Rage at Vornatti's manhandling? Or, worse, kindling disgust at Maledicte's obedience?

Vornatti bent him back, hand in his hair, and tasted the hollow beneath Maledicte's ear, overlaying the bruise Janus's kiss had made. Maledicte jerked free, rocking the chair, and winding Vornatti. "Our bargain," Vornatti warned.

"Still holds," Maledicte said, biting back rage, trading it for calculation. "But surely your generosity will allow me one day with my old friend. . . . Like a bride-to-be bidding her old life farewell."

Vornatti chuffed with disgust, but let Maledicte claim an empty seat, out of his reach. Janus drank tea as if their conversation were only the usual pleasantries. Once served, the three dined in silence, Vornatti pushing his food around the plate, his eyes never leaving Maledicte; Janus eating steadily and with appetite. Maledicte removed bones from the fish without eating anything, finding solace in the steady ruination of flesh before him.

" 'Tis a pity I had no way of knowing I would be at your table," Janus said. "Your cousin Dantalion asked if I could relay a message, but having heard that you were rarely in Murne, I denied him. I do apologize."

"Dantalion has nothing to say of interest to me," Vornatti snapped. "His only interest lies in knowing how near I am to dying, and how close he is to his presumed inheritance." Vornatti grinned malevolently at Maledicte. "But that is my business, and none of his."

Maledicte smiled vaguely in response, all the while feeling the sharp bite of anxiety in his belly as he twisted his long-held scheme into new configurations. To kill Last, to do so in a way that enabled Janus to inherit, to do so from a position of power—it all rested on Vornatti's whim. One wrong word, and Vornatti might change his mind on the importance of kin, might recognize the truth Maledicte felt naked in his eyes: He would never relinquish Janus. Time was short. With Janus's kiss so recent on his skin, his warmth still lingering between his thighs, Maledicte could not imagine accepting a caress from Vornatti, never mind feigning welcome.

Janus mopped his roll over his plate in the Itarusine fashion, chasing savory juices from the smoked fish. "I suppose I should have expected that. After all, my father and Dantalion are rather cronies. And I've heard of the enmity between my father and yourself. He swears you a craven, running from a duel."

Vornatti slapped the table beside his plate, making his glass jerk and teeter. "He dares—"

"But then," Janus added hastily, "the nobles of two courts can attest to Last's easily offended nature. I am quite prepared to find you unobjectionable."

"How very kind of you," Vornatti said. "Mal, isn't it wonderful—such condescension from Last's bastard?" Maledicte felt the blood rush to his face, his tongue leap to defend Janus; instead he fisted his hands beneath the sheltering cloth. Vornatti had to believe that Maledicte was his. The scheme aborning in Maledicte's mind demanded such.

"Don't," Vornatti said abruptly, turning his gaze from Maledicte to Janus, "labor under the impression that you're fooling me with your agreeable manners, Ixion. I, too, was taught in the Itarusine court. I, too, know how to smile and spit poison. But having lived so long, I've found I much prefer bluntness. So I tell you—you are not as clever as you think, and this is the last time an Ixion will run tame beneath my roof."

Janus dabbed at his mouth and rose. "So manners yield to candor and temper; I'm vanquished, sir. I will quit your house and never bother you more. Mal? I'll see you on the promenade." Without waiting for a response, he kissed Maledicte leisurely and left.

Maledicte licked his lips, savoring the taste left behind like a promise, like absolution. He opened his eyes to find Vornatti glaring. "That smacked of later, not farewell. Did you dismiss him or no?"

"A day only," Maledicte said, facing Vornatti and turning to his meal with more appetite. "You were correct, after all. Janus is not as I remember him." That was even true, Maledicte thought complacently, at least in the details. The Janus he had known was an impulsive, temperamental boy; this Janus—Maledicte's lips curved against his will—this Janus was subtle, and infinitely more dangerous. "I will see him out," Maledicte said. "Given your obvious disdain, you'll want me to make sure he hasn't lifted any of the silver. . . ." He escaped before Vornatti could laugh or protest.

Janus caught him up as Maledicte reached the hall, leaned him against the wall and kissed him. Maledicte twined his arms around Janus's neck, keeping a wary eye on the closed door of the dining room.

"You must kill him," Janus whispered. "It's intolerable." He took Maledicte's wrists in his hand and caged them against the wall above Maledicte's head. Closing his eyes, Maledicte shivered, gave himself over to Janus's confident touch. Let Vornatti come out; if he complained, Maledicte would spit him on the sword without another thought. Janus nipped at his throat, and murmured against his pulse, "Do it soon."

LINGERING IN THE KITCHEN, Gilly heard the front door open and close, and wondered who had left, and who had won. Whether Janus had gone with Maledicte by his side, or whether Maledicte was closeted with Vornatti, spitting useless anger. Gilly bit his lip; Vornatti was willfully blind if he thought Maledicte would tolerate his ownership much longer. No matter Vornatti's influence and strength of will, Maledicte was every inch the savage creature Vornatti liked to call him. And Vornatti was old now.

Gilly remembered the first time he'd met Vornatti—the tall, elegant man complimenting Gilly's parents on their fine crop. Even then Gilly had been aware of undercurrents. While his father preened at Vornatti's praise for his fields, Gilly had seen the dark eyes assessing them all, and knew the crop Vornatti meant was himself and his brothers.

The bell rang fiercely in the kitchen, jangling on the board, barely stilling before it rang again.

Maledicte the victor, Gilly thought, and Vornatti left alone and angry. He shuddered. While Janus and Maledicte had been here, Vornatti's attention and outrage had centered on them. Now the man's violent whims would turn to him.

"Best go to him before he has the bell from the board," Cook said, turning from her assessment of the pantry, looking at him with pity. "He'll only get worse."

"I know," Gilly said, knowing he'd be kneeling before him, choking in the close scent of age and Elysia, all in the name of soothing the man's outraged pride. For a moment, he envied Maledicte and his bloody approach to life, the certainty that Vornatti was only a temporary affliction.

"Why do you put up with his ways? My boys wouldn't stand for it. You should find a new place, though I'd miss you sorely, Gilly lad."

"No one will have me, knowing the uses I've been put to. At least, no one who won't expect the same," Gilly said.

Cook turned back to her inventory, her silence only confirmation of his fear. She made a note or two, and finally said, "Kettle's on. Take some tea afore you go."

The bell rang again, and Gilly shook a handful of tea leaves into a mug of steaming water before leaving.

But knowing Vornatti, knowing his moods, Gilly detoured first to the library, searching for something to distract him. He gulped the tea while skimming the shelves for something Vornatti hadn't read recently, or for new purchases not read at all. Grimacing at the acrid cling of tea leaves on his tongue, Gilly dribbled them back into the cup.

Like the nobles he dined with, Gilly rarely had his tea unstrained, and the damp leaves woke lingering superstitions. He swirled the dregs around once, twice, then once again. Mindful of the varnish on the shelves, he found a sheet of blotting paper, and with an almost forgotten motion, upended the mug. Raising it, he stared at the blurred heaps of leaves, trying to read the pattern. But there was no symbol he recognized in the L-shaped spread, no chair, no hourglass, no raised hand.

Superstitious foolery, he chastised himself. What had he expected? He picked up the book he had laid aside; when he looked back, his breath caught—not a symbol, but the thing itself. The leaves made a perfect gallows tree.

WHITSPUR STREET WAS A FRANTIC cluster of millinery shops and tailors, divertissements, and gossip. Janus studied the broadsheets pinned above the boy hawking them, the images of courtiers at play, and incendiary articles urging Aris to shun the most recent trade delegates from Dainand. "Don't buy that," Maledicte said. "It's only gossip, and days-old gossip at that."

Janus tossed the boy a copper anyway, and folded the sheet under his arm. "I'm more interested in the news. Westfall mentioned a potential treaty with Kyrda, one that might offset some of the damage done by Aris's Xipos surrender. The broadsheets run several pages—surely there must be some substance to it."

Maledicte laughed. "You'll be disappointed." He took Janus's elbow in his hand, and they strolled the raised walkway along the shop entries, while carriages clattered by on the cobbles below. From the distant green paths of Jackal Park, faint shouting came across the still air, the chanting of angry citizens protesting Aris's new ban on Itarusine imports. Janus listened to them for a minute and sighed. "Shortsighted." Whether he meant Aris or the protesting men, Maledicte didn't know or care, simply pleased to have Janus at his side.

Janus's clothes, still the fine wear of the evening before, spoke quiet scandal and drew several glances from passing nobles. Maledicte teased, "A good thing you didn't go in costume."

Janus leaned close as if to leave a kiss, but whispered instead, "I did. I went as Last's dutiful, obedient son." His words warmed more than Maledicte's nape, set Black-Winged Ani to heated delight.

Lord Edgebrooke and his wife stepped from the walkway and threaded the crowded street rather than be forced to acknowledge them. For the open scandal of it, or for something less tangible? Maledicte shrugged. Let Gilly worry about that; he would filter the rumors and feed back all Maledicte needed to know.

Maledicte paused in Rosany's doorway, at the display in the windows, looking at books. "I should select something for poor Gilly, left to Vornatti's mercies."

"He's a servant. You needn't reward him for doing his duty," Janus said.

Maledicte laid a hand on his arm. "Gilly's my friend."

Janus sighed, the temper fading from his eyes. "I apologize. It's only that he's had your companionship while I've been deprived of it. I find myself envious of all the moments I've missed, of all the moments he had with you."

Maledicte's lips curved. "Pretty words. You've been trained well in courtly ways." His smile faltered. "I suppose you had occasion to practice such things with the Itarusine ladies."

"As if I could ever care for vapid noblewomen who think of nothing but gossip."

As they dallied, a shadow fell across them, an approaching nobleman who chose not to step from the path. Maledicte looked up and his face stiffened to feral stillness. "Last."

Janus smiled, lips curling to malicious amusement. "This should prove entertaining," he said, voice low in Maledicte's ear. "But do restrain yourself, hmm?"

Any response Maledicte would have made was stymied by Last's nearness. "Father," Janus said, tipping his head. "Have you met Maledicte?"

"To my chagrin," Last said, his face darkening above his high collar. "Is this the kind of companion you seek? A scandalous courtier?"

"I am not the only scandalous one, surely," Maledicte said. "Or is my presence so overwhelming that the court can think of nothing but me?" Maledicte felt a vicious triumph when Last's color intensified. Janus might force him to postpone the kill, but he would not give up baiting the man for anything. Janus's hand closed on his nape in warning, and Maledicte realized that Aris approached.

"Surely, Michel, you will not add to scandal by enacting a scene on Whitspur Street. After all, what happens in the court can only be reported secondhand in the scandal sheets, implausible hearsay. But lose your temper here, and there are a dozen witnesses who work for the broadsheets. Do try to leash your temper. For once." Aris joined them, two of the Kingsguard idling at his back and the brindled hound pacing beside him.

Last turned. "Aris?"

"Am I unrecognizable without my crown, brother?"

"You will acknowledge this creature on the streets? In front of the same audience you warn me of?"

"I will," Aris said, turning his faded eyes on Maledicte. "Though, my impetuous courtier, I remind you that I urged discretion; instead you create the season's greatest scandal," Aris said. "How come you to know my nephew?"

"Last's spurning of Celia Rosamunde sent Janus to me," Maledicte said, with a little bow in the earl's direction. "I thank him for it. As for scandal, sire—though I am loath to say it, your court thrives on scandal and spite. Mirabile, and others like her, sell tales to the scandal sheets purely so they can see their gossip in print and picture."

Last spluttered, and Janus laid a warning hand on Maledicte's sleeve. Maledicte shook him off, aware of Aris's gaze on them both.

"Scandal and spite, perhaps. But it also thrives on decorum and rules. My rules, Maledicte. Do you realize they wait to see me banish you? You have put me in a difficult position. To flout my own rules or to displease your guardian when I need his goodwill—"

"Banish me?" Maledicte echoed, his heart skipping for the first time since their conversation began. Banished. Away from Janus? He clutched Janus's sleeve.

At Aris's side, Last smiled, savoring the moment. It sparked such bloodlust in Maledicte that he felt his eyes must be reddened with it. The sword could have Last before anyone could pull him back. The world narrowed to red simplicity.

"Did you not swear me an oath that you would never draw your blade in court again? After I stayed your punishment once before?" Aris's words came from a distance.

Maledicte looked away from Last, his thoughts calming, turning. He rested his hand on the hilt. "I swore . . . I would never draw it in your presence, sire."

"You would sidestep my strictures so carefully? Laws are more than the words composing them, Maledicte."

"I did not think at all, acted the impetuous youth you called me," Maledicte said, trying to shape words fast enough to soothe Aris. At his back, Janus's steady breathing brushed his nape, and the sound, the sensation staved off his growing alarm.

"That is no excuse, nor even an acknowledgment of wrongdoing," Last said.

"Father," Janus said, his respectful courtesy never faltering. "It is King Aris's offense, his decision. But should you be allowed a say, so should I."

Last purpled again at the unexpected insolence.

Aris's face relaxed at his brother's discomposure; the tightness left his voice. "What would you say in Maledicte's defense?"

"Only that deeds are misunderstood all too often. Only that if I took no offense, saw no wrong, and had the blade at my throat, perhaps there was no wrong meant."

Maledicte would have smiled were he not afraid it would be misinterpreted. But he was pleased and surprised; not at Janus's defense—he expected nothing less—but at the sweep and subtlety of the words. Janus had changed, had learned the discretion Maledicte forgot when his temper was raised.

"You are presumptuous, Janus. You set your wrongs above the king's," Last said. "Perhaps you are not as ready for the court as I assumed, and require another year's training." Maledicte went cold. He could not allow Last to take Janus from him again.

"Leave him be, Michel," Aris said. "I, for one, am pleased to find someone so loyal to a companion. Tell me, Janus, would you be resentful if I removed Maledicte from the court?"

"Saddened, say instead. You are my king, my uncle, my kin, and as such, incapable of wrongdoing."

Maledicte wanted badly to applaud. Janus had mastered what he could not—the art of cynical humor without the edge that offended.

"Have his words won me a reprieve?" Maledicte asked, unable to keep silent longer.

Last started to speak, but Aris overrode him: "If you swear, without reservation, without duplicitous intent, that your blade stays sheathed within my court. And the gods alone know what the papers will have to say." Aris lowered his voice, stepped closer. "But Mal, remember discretion."

"I swear," Maledicte said, bending his head. He felt the king's hand hover above it, barely touching his dark curls. He heard Last's chuff of disgust, watched him stalk off without further word, and raised his eyes to Aris's. The pale eyes flickered from his to Janus, standing so close, and a quick frown crossed his mouth. He reached out and pulled Maledicte a pace away.

"I accept your oath for a second time, and yet I await an apology," Aris said.

Maledicte felt his temper stirring and stifled it. Too much was at risk and yet . . . he could not be other than he was, and his words came out edged. "Shall I kneel before you, here and now, begging you to show mercy, sire? Speak the word and I will prostrate myself before you. My future is in your hands."

Aris tilted Maledicte's face up to his own. "Michel would have your tongue removed for speaking so—" He released Maledicte's chin. "But I am not my brother; I do not seek insult in every speech. I will forgive you, but as penalty, I will steal your companion from you. Janus and I have had little chance yet to speak."

Aris gestured ahead of him. "Nephew."

Using the king's body to shield them from most of the watchers, Janus pressed his lips to Maledicte's palm before following his uncle. Maledicte shivered, chilled by Janus's absence, his mood plummeting. He wanted to run after them, refuse to let Janus from his sight. "Restraint," Janus had whispered, his breath warm in the shell of his ear. "Discretion," Aris had demanded. Maledicte watched Janus board the king's carriage and did nothing. When the carriage was gone, he thought of home, the delight gone from the day with Janus. But at the thought of Dove Street, of Vornatti, his plan shifted. He had other tasks to complete before he could return home.

*W*ILL YOU TAKE WINE?" ARIS asked, waving away the young page who brought a sheaf of papers toward him, and closing Janus and himself into his sitting room.

"Please," Janus said, accepting the crystal goblet with graceful hands. Aris studied the lad, liking what he saw—the unmistakable stamp of family blood, the confident manner. He found it hard to believe that the young man had spent most of his life in the worst slum Antyre had.

"Did Celia teach you the ways of the court?" Aris asked, sitting down in a dark, velvet-upholstered chair. The mastiff settled on his boots with a groan, and Aris groaned back. "Off my feet, dammit, Bane."

"Celia?" Janus said, lowering his goblet and swirling the claret; a ruby whirlpool formed and faded. "She taught me to speak properly, when she remembered my existence," Janus said. "Her world is bounded by her supply of the old Laudable."

"I am sorry to hear it. Perhaps that explains her absence. I rather expected her to return once your name appeared in the broadsheets, claiming her bloodright, or sols for her part in keeping your past quiet," Aris said. "You have not seen her since your return?"

Blue eyes met Aris's, and he was aware that he had startled Janus; yet Aris himself found surprise in Janus's reaction. Had the boy no family feeling at all?

"I went back," Janus said, finally. "They were gone."

"They?"

"Her compatriot," Janus said. "Another whore. I presume they found a patron, or died of rat fever."

Janus's words were empty of emotion, and Aris was bothered by this;
surely it was natural for a boy to mourn his mother. But then, whores and
addicts did not make for comfortable family.

"How do you and Michel get on?" The door swung open as another mastiff sought out its master, pushing the door with its heavy head. Bane raised
his lip, rumbled, and the newcomer settled down near the fireplace.

Janus smiled. "I like his dogs immensely."

"Only his dogs?" Aris laughed. "My poor brother. But have you no other
response to his care?"

Standing, Janus paced the room. "I do not love him. His reclamation of
me was too clumsy for that. Yet I am grateful to him for this new life. Should
I tell you how I feel for my uncle?" He sat on the floor beside the fireplace
and stroked the fine stripes in the bitch's fur. "Or will you tell me something
instead—what you would say that requires such privacy? While I am honored to bear you company, I sense a motive beyond socializing."

"Of course you're right. But can you not think of anything you've done
that might require discreet discussion?"

Janus bent his head over the hound, rubbed her soft ears. Her tail
thumped against the granite hearth. "Maledicte," he said.

"Maledicte," Aris agreed. "Your father would have me command you
cease relations with the lad. Make it a matter for law, not family."

"Will you?" Janus asked, as if it were only a matter of small importance.

Aris didn't answer right away; he watched his placid nephew and found
himself wondering what Maledicte admired in him, what fire, what source
of desire. Aris thought Janus a pleasant addition to their dwindling family,
but milk-watered for his taste, and, he would think, for Maledicte's. A tiny
thread of suspicion arose; perhaps Janus played a part. Earnestness and honesty were not common traits for men trained in either royal court, nor, he
would think, for the Relicts. But then, he recalled Janus's arguments with
Last and sighed. A man playing the part of utter amiability would work not
to offend anyone.

"Uncle?" Janus said.

"Do you love Maledicte?" Aris asked.

"Beyond all reason," Janus said.

"Rumor declares you bewitched."

"Only by the oldest magic, that of lover and loved."

Aris could not help but smile at the romantic simplicity of the declaration. He remembered arguing with Michel in the great ivy bower of Lastrest, arguing his reasons for marrying Aurora Vornatti, an Itarusine noble, and moreover, kin to a man his brother despised. "With Kritos gone, you are Last's heir," Aris pointed out.

"I am not heir as yet," Janus said. "Father feels my progress incomplete."

"You could aid him," Aris said.

"By giving up Mal?" Janus said. "Please do not ask that of me."

"I will not," Aris said, surprising himself. "You will not be the first nobleman to keep company with a courtier. But you must convince Michel that you mean to honor our line. Do you understand?" Aris leaned forward, resting his hands on the great dog's back as if it were a lectern, he the tutor and Janus the student.

"I must marry," Janus said. "Produce an heir. A healthy one."

"Marry *well*. A girl of impeccable lineage to offset the irregularity of yours," Aris said. "I have heard of your exploits in Itarus. If there is any accuracy to them, you should have no difficulty with a wife."

"With the bedding, you mean," Janus said. His mouth, so long sober, slid into a grin. "No difficulties. But choosing a wife—"

"I could name one for you," Aris said.

Diffidently, Janus said, "Grant me some time to choose my own?"

Aris set his goblet down. "If you select a bride by the close of the year and present her for approval, you may find your own. If you do not, I will choose for you, and you may be thankful it will be my task and not Michel's." The dogs, at Aris's subtle signal, rose and stretched, their tongues lolling.

Janus stood and waited for dismissal.

"Have you—" Aris paused. "Have you met your cousin yet?"

"I have not," Janus said.

"Come then, he likes visitors."

Aris opened the door, releasing the dogs, and the page, slumped against the wall, hastily stood. "Sire, Captain Jasper says will you—"

"Not at the moment, Marcus."

Janus said, "If there's something that demands your attention, Uncle . . . I understand there are some accords to be made."

Aris strode down the hall, talking over his shoulder, his words clipped. "The Dainanders seek to renew our trade agreement, but like Itarus, they want it all to their benefit and none to ours. They think to take advantage of my ban on Itarusine imports. But they discount the Explorations, which are beginning to bear fruit—the nobles may exclaim all they like over exotic fripperies and sideshow spectacles of savages, but the last six ships from the Explorations brought us corn, rice, and wheat, far dearer to my heart. So, I see no need to cede to Dainand's unreasonable demands. Let them wait and rethink their avarice."

"And the Kyrdic delegation?" Janus said.

Before him, Aris stopped, and looked back. "You seem to be well informed."

"I am Last's son," Janus said. "Am I not supposed to take an interest in Antyre's affairs?"

Aris smiled. "I'm pleased you are. But the Kyrdics may wait also—to be blunt, I am not so sure that they are not a stalking horse for Itarus, with Grigor grown weary of our failure to be annexed. I see no other reason for Kyrda's interest in our shipbuilding."

The dogs loped up the stairs ahead of them, rushing down the long hallway. Aris smiled at the sight, his good humor restoring itself in fondness for the brutes. "They're Adi's hounds really, and grudge the hours I keep them beside me."

The nursery guard had let the dogs in and Aris could hear their wagging tails thumping the carpet. The guard opened the door, bowing.

"Papa," the boy said, rolling on the thick carpet with the hounds. He rose to his knees, saw Janus, and went silent.

Aris tried to see his son from different eyes, and yet the tragedy was still there—the good-looking lad of twelve, who could not be made to think, learn, or even clean himself as a two-year-old might. Thin-boned for his age, he lacked the gawkiness that preceded adolescence. For Adiran, there would be no adulthood, only this fairy-child existence in a boundless present.

The boy darted to Aris, clung to his side, and stared at Janus. Janus bowed. "Your highness?"

"Blue." The prince advanced, hand outstretched. At the last moment, Janus caught his hand gently.

"Yes, my eyes are as blue as yours." Janus's nostrils flared slightly, as if he could smell it as an animal could, the wrongness in his boy.

"Adiran, this is your cousin, Janus," Aris said. "Will you greet him?"

Ten years of training, ten years of repetition, ten years of concentrated effort on the part of Aris, and Adiran responded to the cue with a clumsy bow.

Then he whirled and claimed his boiled sweet from Aris's pockets. Aris pulled his son into his lap. The boy tucked his head under Aris's chin and worked on the candy, taking it out to look at it, putting it back in. "He has a sweet nature," Aris said, "which makes it easier for us and for him. But sometimes I wonder if he's not aware, imprisoned within his own mind. . . ."

Janus raised his hands, dropped them; his words died away and Aris liked him the better for it.

"My poor son will be king, at least in name," Aris said. "Itarus will devour him entire." He shuttered his heart against the pain of that. On the fireplace mantel, the icon of Espit, god of creation and despair, mocked him from Her tangled web, Her laughing mouth at war with Her veiled, teary eyes. Aris, who had removed all other traces of the gods from his quarters, had let this one remain, perhaps simply because it was the loveliest version of Weeping Espit he had seen. It had something of his wife in it, in the way tears caught on Her smile.

Janus lowered his eyes, then said tentatively, "Uncle, you are not an old man. Will you not marry again?"

Aris rocked the child, hearing in Janus's words the echo of Michel. "I will not risk prisoning another child in a broken mind. You must take that risk for me, Janus. Do not deny me that." He stood, shifted Adiran's weight to more even distribution along his hip and side. The boy tangled his thin arms around his father like spiderwebbing, fragile and yet binding. "Can you find your way out, Janus, or shall I have Marcus guide you?"

"Please," Janus said.

The door opened again and Jasper, the head of his Kingsguard, entered with a cursory bow. "Sire, the antimachinists have burned Westfall's newest engine, and he expects the Kingsguard to act. We need your command—" Aris sighed at the frustration pinking Jasper's fair face, and sighed again at Marcus peering around Jasper's solid form, papers still clasped close. "Of course," he said, letting Adiran down to play.

Dismissed, Janus bowed, and followed Marcus out, retracing their steps down quiet corridors, stone overlaid with wood and plaster, and was let out into the courtyard, illuminated with hung lamps and candles. From his vantage point in the nursery over the yard, from behind barred windows, Aris watched him go.

It was late evening before Maledicte returned, and Gilly, hearing his footsteps in the hall, crept away from a dozing Vornatti. He found the hall deserted, Maledicte's coat abandoned over the stair railing. He finally ran Maledicte to earth in the formal parlor when he heard the sound of quiet laughter.

To his nameless relief, he found Maledicte alone, kneeling before the stage; he had expected Maledicte to return in Janus's company, braving Vornatti's wrath.

On the little stage, a toy puppet theater rested. Without looking back, Maledicte said, "See what Janus has sent me?" Maledicte dragged the tiny crow-god across the false world, laughing. Within Ani's beak dangled the threads of a smaller puppet, jerking as Ani twitched, strings within strings within strings. Gilly raised his eyes, saw the strings extending beyond the theater, saw them stretching beyond Maledicte and himself and Vornatti, stretching to encompass the far reaches of the city.

"Only a fool plays puppets with gods," Gilly snapped. The day had been one well-devised torment after another; Vornatti still kept his Itarusine inventiveness as well as his temper.

Maledicte only said, "Then many people are fools. These theaters are apparently quite popular."

"They were meant to tell the gods' tale," Gilly said, remembering his mother telling the story.

"Tell it to me," Maledicte said.

"No," Gilly said. "You know it already—our demands and dreams drove the gods first to quarreling, then to fighting, and finally, on Baxit's command, to Their own oblivion. The only way They could escape us."

"If you think Ani dead, then I wonder that you fear Her at all," Maledicte said, taking the figure from Gilly's hand. "Still, I suppose it stands to reason. Baxit seems much like Aris, trying to guide those who, while crying for help, disregard his words."

Gilly hesitated, a frisson touching his spine. "Baxit? You've encountered—"

"Do you think Ani shares?" Maledicte said. "Don't be a fool. I was merely speculating."

In the distance, they could hear the bell shrilling as Vornatti, woken, yanked the bell rope.

"Come soothe him," Gilly said, taking Maledicte's arm. "And don't mention Janus."

Maledicte laughed. "Don't fret so, Gilly. I brought him gifts. Won't he be pleased to know I thought of him?"

Gilly hesitated, alerted by something off in Maledicte's tone. He seemed entirely too blithe, a child with a gleeful secret. "Mal?" Gilly asked.

"I brought something for you too," Maledicte said, selecting a small parcel layered in translucent cloth.

"For me?"

Maledicte passed him the flat package. "I bought it off your sailor friend, Reg. He swore you would like it, as if I had any doubts." He took the remaining packages and went toward Vornatti's room.

Gilly peeled back the gilt-edged organza until the object came clear. It was an etched piece of whale ivory, the lines filled in with ink and gold leaf, detailing an elaborate scene. A feather-clad man climbed stairs toward the clouds, a streak of golden sunlight leading the way.

Gilly smiled, touched out of all proportion. He placed the engraving in his room, amid his small collection of treasures: an elaborate puzzle box Vornatti gave him that held his meager savings, his four books, edges fuzzed with repeated readings, a curved piece of sea glass cradling a twisted seashell, gold on the outside, luscious pink within. He touched the whale ivory at the pinnacle of sun and sky, the gilt warming beneath his fingers.

Then, recalling Maledicte's strange cheer, he hastened to Vornatti's chamber. Vornatti was still echoing variants of Gilly's own unvoiced question. "But where have you been?"

Maledicte shrugged. "I've told you and told you." He dropped a nosegay of lilies and evening primroses on the bedside table. "I even brought you flowers, since you spent all day closeted inside, and missed the gardens in bloom. Though, I admit, they're nothing like as lovely as the bracelet you gave Mirabile."

Vornatti said, "So she showed you my gift."

"Yes, and a foolish thing it was," Maledicte said. "Like any beggar, she'll come back for more."

"What makes you think I'll disappoint her?" Vornatti asked, leaning back against his pillows, smirking. "Perhaps there will be a wedding upon her return to the city. Didn't I say as much earlier, or were your senses too taken up with Last's whelp?"

Maledicte's eyes darkened, then he shrugged. "You're far too wily to be caught by the kind who'd see you cuckolded on your wedding night. Besides, we have our bargain, and as I abstain from Janus, so you must abstain from Mirabile." He seized Vornatti's grayed head in his hands, kissed his forehead and lips. "Don't be irascible, you'll spoil my good temper."

"You are done with Janus?" Vornatti asked, skeptically. "Your grand passion burnt out in a day?"

"I solemnly swear," Maledicte said, "to any god you care to claim, that you will never see me dealing with an Ixion again. Not Janus, not Last. Do you know, Janus has no interest in gossip at all? It's all news and trade agreements, and the plight of ex-soldiers. He has as many dreary opinions as Westfall. He asked my opinion of Aris's ban on Itarusine imports. I ask you—"

Vornatti smiled and Maledicte brought up the remaining packages. The first one, lumpen under lashings of gauze, revealed a statuette in the best brothel art tradition, which Maledicte danced along Vornatti's bedsheets. "I thought of you at once when I saw it."

Gilly choked on a gasp. The little monkey leered up at Vornatti, its hands locked in a lewd self-caress.

"Impudence," Vornatti said, but there was laughter lurking beneath. "And paid for with my name, no doubt."

"I had to resort to it; you've kept me short of coin of late. If you'd given me jewelry, I could pawn it, as Mirabile undoubtedly has done with your bracelet," Maledicte said. "But here—" He brought up two silver-wrapped boxes, one small, one large, both ribbon-bedecked. "Chocolates from the Explorations."

He laid the big box on Vornatti's lap, untied the ribbon, and parted the tissue. Maledicte chose a chocolate for himself, popped it into his mouth with delight. "They're wonderful—try them, Vornatti. You too, Gilly." Maledicte tossed the small box to Gilly, who fielded it with quick hands. "Go on. Have it before dinner, be indulgent with us."

He held another to the old man's mouth. "A peace offering, my lord?" Vornatti's eyes met Maledicte's over the confection before accepting it; it collapsed under his tongue, and Maledicte let Vornatti lick the chocolate from his fingers without protest.

Maledicte sprawled across the velvet coverlet, his lacy sleeves foaming over the candy box. He crossed his booted feet, and fished for another chocolate. Vornatti smacked his hand. "Mine. But I'll share." Maledicte accepted a sweet from Vornatti's shaking hand, trapped it neatly with tongue and teeth, and sucked the sweet filling out from the darker coating. Vornatti watched him eat, and took another chocolate himself.

Gilly turned the package over in his hands; the label was DELIGHT'S, the confectionery shop where Aris bought the prince's candy. He held a piece in his hand and the smell rose temptingly and yet—

"Don't you want it?" Maledicte asked, lolling his head onto Vornatti's shoulder, letting Vornatti kiss the lingering traces of confection from his mouth.

Gilly took a bite. Sweetness spilled over his tongue, rich, smooth, cloying. He swallowed hard, as suddenly sickened as if he had found a worm in an apple. The gallows image lingered in his mind.

"Not to your taste, Gilly?" Maledicte said.

"Never mind about him," Vornatti said. "He's just ungrateful." At the warning note in the baron's voice, Maledicte curled closer to Vornatti.

"I'm grateful," he said, passing him another chocolate.

"Pretty little liar," Vornatti said, but the old man's thin-skinned cheeks flushed with pleasure. Gilly finished his chocolate in one bite, seeking distraction from Vornatti stroking the juncture of Maledicte's thigh and hip.

"Don't force yourself, Gilly," Maledicte said. "I sent oysters for our suppers. Will you join us, Vornatti?"

"I think not. I'll stay abed, eat chocolate and be an indulged old fool," Vornatti said, brought to a rare good humor by Maledicte's obedience. "But stay and let me feed you chocolates until the dinner bell sounds."

"Like a Kyrdic harem, only much less sandy," Maledicte said. "Should we invite Gilly to join us?"

"No," the two men said as one, and Maledicte laughed, even while Vornatti curled greedy hands around his shoulders.

Gilly's stomach churned at Maledicte sprawled so in Vornatti's bed, and yet he was afraid to go. Maledicte's giddy, uncharacteristic behavior struck him as dangerous.

The gong rang; Gilly jumped, the small foil box tumbling from his lap to the carpet. Maledicte disentangled himself from Vornatti's hands, lips rouged with chocolate liqueur, face flushed with something that might have been pleasure. Or well-masked rage.

"Come on, Gilly. Let's leave Vornatti to his desserts." Maledicte tugged Gilly from the room.

In the dining room, Gilly picked at his meal, eyeing the stuffed oysters with repugnance.

"Aren't you hungry?" Maledicte asked.

His face seemed luminescent in the candlelight, and dark wings spread out from his shoulders. Gilly rubbed his eyes, his aching head, and the vision was gone. But the room felt wavering and fluid, as if the walls were only curtains about to be drawn. He shook his head, the taste of chocolate strong in his mouth.

"What did you give me, Maledicte? What was in the chocolate?" Gilly asked, his voice rising.

"Shadowplay," Maledicte said, setting his fork down. "It's not harmful. It's only a sedative, though some claim it has visionary qualities."

"Why?"

"Because you'd recognize the taste of Laudable." Maledicte's voice was faintly surprised. The answer was not to the question Gilly meant—why drug him at all—but the room shivered; the overhead beams grew sputtering halos as if they were the masts of a ship beset by seafires. Gilly cupped his hands over his eyes.

"Are you seeing things? Tell me what you see."

Gilly peered through the swirling brightness that leaked from the candles, watching feathers sprout from Maledicte's skin like spring blossoms.

Maledicte crossed the space between them and sat on the table. Gilly looked up into his face. "Death in your eyes," he whispered.

"But not for you, never for you." The touch on his cheek was light and Maledicte was gone. Gilly rose; the floor fell away from him and he tumbled down, sliding across the room, rolling against the closed door. Scratching traveled through the wood, the scrabbling of a large bird. Gilly knelt, clawing at the knob. The door opened, and darkness rushed in on great black wings.

She crouched on the table, mouth agape, Her breathing like the gasps of a dying man. With each exhalation, the room darkened until the only light was one guttering candle, the flame streaming high and thin. The table became an altar, the disrupted meal Her offerings. Gilly crawled backward, trying to escape Her notice. She leaned over the edge of the table, Her pale feet dangling like gibbet corpses, Her wings upraised. "He is Mine. He will worship Me. He will love Me. Nothing you do will keep him from My kiss at the end." Her voice, a god's voice, seared his mind.

Gilly cried out and woke, head on the table, neck stiff, numb hands dangling off the sides of his chair. He touched the plate nearest him and found it cool. The candles had burned to half their length, spreading wax into the spillways below. The clock hands had jumped; hours had passed. He shoved back the chair with a shudder of protesting effort, ears still ringing. Staggering, he made his way from the dining room and down the hall.

Vornatti's door was closed. Gilly touched the blank, dark wood, and hesitated. He opened the door to darkness and cringed, but this darkness was only that of a room dimly lit. In the center of the room, Vornatti's bed was shrouded by the drawn bed curtains and the deafening silence within them. Gilly stumbled forward in the low light, reaching for the cloth. His fingers clenched velvet, but he could not bring himself to fling the panels back and accept their revelation. A clinking of glass on glass made him twitch galvanically.

Maledicte rose from the shadows of the wheeled chair, a goblet in his hand. The wine had darkened his lips to the color of old blood.

"Did you kill him?" Gilly said, his voice a rasp to match Maledicte's. "Tell me the truth, Mal. . . ." Gilly slumped against the wall, shivering. "Is he dead?"

Maledicte poured a small snifter of brandy and handed the glass to Gilly. "Your hands are shaking."

Gilly thought of murder done, and murderers caught red-handed, of cornered rats and poisons, but raised the glass to his lips and gulped the liquid without hesitation. The brandy warmed his tongue, his throat, his belly.

"Yes," Maledicte said, taking his seat again, setting his feet up on the bed, boots parting the hangings.

"How?" Gilly asked. "Poison? Or like *Kritos*?" His voice cracked, imagining the sheets sodden with blood.

"Peacefully." Maledicte drained his glass, poured another.

Gilly set his snifter down and yanked the drapes back, still expecting Vornatti to wake into furious complaint. He lifted the feather-heavy pillow from Vornatti's face, the fabric as malleable as liquid and as drowningly lethal. Vornatti's mouth was open, his eyes shut, his gnarled hands limp with a relaxation life and drugs had not granted. Gilly rubbed his wet face. "I should have warned you."

"When did he ever listen, Gilly?" Maledicte said.

"Why?"

"You know why." Maledicte leaned his head on the back of Gilly's shoulder, took his hands in his. Panic spiked him beyond brandy's ability to soothe. This murder might have freed Maledicte, but it cast Gilly into unemployment.

"You couldn't wait?" Gilly asked.

"To have Janus at hand and beyond my touch? Impossible. And time is fickle, Gilly, as was Vornatti. He would have grown bored with the victory handed him, might even have thrown me over for Mirabile, despite his promises. I thought him near death, but every month he seemed to improve. I could not chance it."

"You've gambled on other things," Gilly said.

"Not this," Maledicte said. "Gilly, I am in your hands. A murderer. What will you do?"

Gilly turned, freeing his hands from Maledicte's cool touch. He tilted Maledicte's face to meet his, to see what the dark eyes held: fear, hope, pain, the lashes spiked with dampness.

"Do you regret this?"

Maledicte met Gilly's eyes. "No."

"What would you have me do?" Gilly whispered.

"Nothing." Maledicte's voice was tight. "His death should pass without scrutiny; his habits were known to be precarious—drinking mixed with Elysia. But do find me his will. I need to be sure he didn't append some recent codicil. I wouldn't put it past Mirabile to finagle one out of him."

Gilly nodded, feeling oddly numb, as if the Shadowplay lingered yet and this was only another dream. He knelt and prised up the floorboard near the hearth, revealing the strongbox beneath.

Gilly lifted the parchment out, smoothing the creamy vellum from its rolled shape. He weighted one end with the strongbox, the other with his hand.

Maledicte knelt beside him, so close they were nearly bumping heads. Above them, the pillow Gilly had taken from Vornatti's face shifted and Gilly jumped to his feet, heart pounding.

Maledicte flattened the curling edge that Gilly's abrupt movement had allowed, and skimmed the elaborate language, sorting and reading. Gilly, turning back, thought again that Maledicte had the instinct of a solicitor.

Maledicte smiled for the first time since Gilly had entered the room. "Seems he was not so much a fool as that," Maledicte said. "Mirabile is nowhere mentioned. Nor are his Itarusine relatives. I suppose he held that grudge right and true enough."

Gilly slid the document away from Maledicte, sought out his own name, fearing, hoping. It was with the other servants'. Though his bequest was by far the largest, it still knotted his belly with resentment and fear. Tired of him, Gilly thought, his dismissal imminent. The sum allotted was a year's salary, no more. Enough to buy himself a berth to the Explorations, but not on the swift *Virga*. Enough to take him slowly away, and set him down in the Explorations, penniless, with no funds to return. Alone and friendless, he thought, as chilled as if a dash of blown snow had touched him; it would leave him without Maledicte.

"Don't worry, Gilly. You'll stay with me," Maledicte said, reading over Gilly's shoulder. "I told you. I'll take care of you."

"As a servant," Gilly said.

"As a friend." The quiet word resonated in this room, this city of purchase and patronage, manipulation and deception. The silence gave weight to the word, and Gilly realized with sudden disbelief that this was the measure of the city's moral decay—that his closest ally and dearest friend was a murderer, with more bodies yet to reap.

FLEDGLING

· 18 ·

ILLY AND MALEDICTE HAD BEEN returned from the funeral for only minutes; in silence both of them fled to the dining room and the warming comfort of the liquor on the sideboard. Maledicte poured two glasses, and raised a toast. "Done and be-damned," he said. Gilly swallowed his whiskey without a response, too shaken by Mirabile's conduct at the funeral. They had not expected her to attend at all, considered her safely rusticating in the country. But Brierly Westfall's sudden miscarriage had kept the Westfalls in the city, and Mirabile with them.

Still, funerals were not the ceremonies they once were. With the gods gone, there was no one to impress with their piety but themselves, and Vornatti's funeral was sparsely attended: Mirabile, Echo, two representatives from the palace, indistinguishable from each other, and Vornatti's solicitor, Bellington. There was no ritual, nothing but two cemetery workers covering the hole in the earth, shadowed by a chapel now used for harvest storage, and overlooked by the great stone god chairs, overgrown by weeds.

It was when the grave was nearly full that Mirabile had whispered, "You murdered him. To keep him from me. I would have shared everything with you—now we'll see what rumors I can spread, see how fast your welcome disappears."

"Do so, and I will comment on the timeliness of Brierly's miscarriage, your access to Harlot's Friend, and your hatred of the countryside. While everyone knows of your murderous past, they know nothing of mine," Maledicte said.

"Bastard," she hissed, trembling with frustrated rage, then as suddenly as a shadow chased by sunlight, her face cleared. "I'll strike a bargain with you. We'll keep each other's secrets, each other's counsel, and each other's company—"

"No. I've made one dangerous bargain already and it's consumed any desire to make another."

She growled under her breath, a distinct animal sound, and Maledicte cast a wary glance at her. She dimpled and said, her voice sweet again, "Mal, remember me, and this, the moment you've spurned me. I told you once before—I am as clever and as determined as you. I have been playing too gently, but that's done now. I have a mind to level the field. I know what you fear—"

Maledicte seized her shoulders, grip bruising, suddenly washed with rage at her nebulous threats, but instead of the fright he hoped to see, she laughed, honestly amused. "Such a savage," she said. "Is unthinking force always your solution when there are subtler resources to draw on?"

Heads were beginning to turn, and Maledicte felt trapped, unwilling to back away, conceding her this round, and equally unwilling to keep Echo's scrutiny on him. Gilly put his hands on Maledicte's arms, and Maledicte relaxed, given a reason to release her. Mirabile leaned forward, closing the distance between them once more, even as Maledicte attempted to back away and was blocked by Gilly.

Mirabile kissed his mouth, her lips cold on his, and he shivered. She left the gravesite, the only sign of her anger the fisted hands at her sides. Maledicte turned back, aware of Gilly muttering quietly to their coachman, and the man slipping away. Then it was done, and Maledicte and Gilly had come home, Gilly taking up the reins of the coach.

"You sent the coachman after her?" Maledicte said.

"She seemed too confident. I want to know where she goes," Gilly said.

"Yes," Maledicte agreed. Unsettled, he took refuge in peevishness granted by the front door opening, heralded by its usual creak and Livia's voice as she played butler. "Who's that now? All these cards and flowers, all this fuss for one old man—"

"It's Bellington," Gilly said, looking into the hall. "With Echo at his side."

He set down his glass; it clattered on the tray. "With Vornatti's death so sudden, with Last's dislike of you, with Mirabile spreading her venom, Echo will be looking for something actionable."

"I don't fear Echo," Maledicte said.

"You should. He has followers beyond that rabble of Particulars. Powerful men like Westfall and Last. Even Aris listens to him."

"So what do you counsel?" Maledicte said.

"Attend to Bellington's reading of the will without any asides or insults. Be silent as best you can and pretend to grieve. Please. Or Echo'll have you in jail." He ushered Maledicte into the hallway. From the library, Gilly heard the stilted tones of Echo conversing with Bellington.

"I could remove his threatening presence for good," Maledicte said. "A doctored drink—some of my stock is quite tasteless. It would be a small matter to—"

"No," Gilly yelped. "Are you mad?" He dropped his voice to the barest whisper. "And to discuss such a thing so close to Echo."

"He's nothing but a man. Not some avenging creature of a dark god," Maledicte said, a faint smile curling his mouth.

By the time Gilly had his panicked urge to laugh under control, Maledicte was greeting the two men, Echo first as was due his rank. "Lord Echo, what brings you here? I find it hard to imagine that you intend to pay your respects to Vornatti since you had none for him while he was alive."

Echo's dark eyes narrowed. "I find it odd that Vornatti took you in, and suspicious that he died so abruptly."

"The ways of the heart are not easily understood," Maledicte said. "Neither why he cared for me, nor why his heart stopped. But if it gives you pleasure, you may join me for the reading of the will."

Bellington started into speech, portly form rocking back onto his heels. "If it's your will that Lord Echo be privy to the contents, then I withdraw my objection."

Maledicte settled himself as Bellington took the will from his worn leather valise. Bellington coughed, face reddening. "You are familiar with the late baron's will?"

A tap on the door interrupted Maledicte's response, and drew a snarl from Echo. "Your servants don't know their place." He yanked the door open, startling Livia.

Behind her, Janus stood, elegant in the color the court called Last blue. Echo mimicked Livia's startlement and stepped back. "You visit a house of mourning?" Maledicte's smile bloomed, and Bellington coughed again.

"Aris sent me," Janus said, with a half bow in Echo's direction, "to carry his condolences." He held out a letter sealed in gold-edged blue. Echo moved to take it, and Maledicte forestalled him.

"First you pry into the will, now my correspondence? How deadly dull your life must be, Echo, to find mine so fascinating."

He claimed the missive from Janus, and Janus bent and brushed his lips over Maledicte's fingers. "He waits on a response, my dark cavalier."

Bellington stood, "Perhaps I should return—"

"Sit," Maledicte said, "read away. Let us hear my guardian's last thoughts."

"In broadest outlines, the entailed properties in Itarus and his title go to his next of kin, Dantalion Vornatti; his Antyrrian country estate, being a residence for life, reverts to the Crown; the Dove Street residence and his considerable fortune fall to you, Maledicte."

Echo grew more intent. As if sensing their master's mood, the Particulars in the garden straightened.

"Perhaps we should take another look at his cadaver," Echo said. "To leave a fortune to a stranger and slight his own blood—"

"If it pleases you. Only make sure you tamp down the grave dirt well after, or you'll find him up yet again, and burgled," Maledicte said, even while Janus stiffened minutely. Gilly's throat felt thick, and he concentrated on looking merely miserable, rather than guilty.

"By the gods, your tongue is foul—"

"Tell Aris," Maledicte said, his voice overriding Echo's. "Tell him I am only too glad to accept his condolences, and to accede to his request. With pleasure." The opened letter whispered stiffly in the close room, the vellum brushing Maledicte's sleeves.

"Perhaps Echo can deliver your reply," Janus said, "if he truly intends to petition Aris for an exhumation."

Echo stormed for the door, and Maledicte said, "Gilly, it seems Lord Echo has had a surfeit of our company. Show him out, and Bellington as well, please."

"Sir," Bellington said, hesitating. "We should go over the details. Besides the usual estate matters, there's the Antyrrian audit books to be dealt with. They need to be sent abroad to wait for the next auditor."

"Another day will suit, surely," Maledicte said.

Bellington nodded. "It may take some time for Itarus to name a replacement for Vornatti's post. I understand the court abroad is most competitive. Though I believe Dantalion Vornatti is in the running, if only for familiarity with the baron's script."

Gilly herded the men to the door. Bellington stepped out with the step of a man relieved of an onerous duty.

Janus nodded to Echo and said, "Shall I walk you to your coach, my lord?"

"No," Echo said, letting his gaze linger on the letter in Maledicte's hands.

Gilly shut the door and slumped against it, slid down to rest on the cool tiles of the foyer, exhausted.

A shadow came between him and the light and he looked up. Maledicte hesitated on the stair. "Are you well, Gilly?"

"Well enough for having Echo in the house three days after a murder."

"Watch yourself," Janus snapped. "Echo will be snooping for days. Only Aris's interest sent him off so soon."

"And sooner or later, someone will tell him of my chest of poisons and potions. It will be a sore disappointment to him that Vornatti died of nothing so exotic," Maledicte said.

He drifted up the stairs after Janus, paused again. "Gilly, I'll need your help."

Gilly nodded, wondering what Maledicte wanted now.

"Vornatti's Antyrrian ledgers need to be copied. The private ones that detail all the funds diverted back to Aris. You needn't worry about copying Vornatti's hand, just the information," Maledicte said, continuing up the stairs, untying his black cravat, slinging his black coat over the banister.

"It may take days," Gilly said. The private ledgers filled nearly an entire shelf.

"Then it takes days," Maledicte said. "Aris wishes to see those ledgers gone, and as he barters so nicely for them, I cannot help but think they may have other uses in the future. And don't fret, Gilly, I'll stay out from underfoot while you work."

"You're in mourning, Mal. Your activities must be curtailed—"

His only answer was the flutter of tossed paper as Maledicte continued on his path up the stairs.

Gilly smoothed the paper out, the thick foolscap, the weight of the seal against his palm letting him know that this was Aris's letter in truth, and not some convenient forgery.

> *Maledicte,*
> *Let me express my condolences for your loss, and relay an unusual request. As you have no doubt been aware, a financial agreement existed between myself and your guardian, wherein he arranged certain figures to the benefit of us both. As I cannot rely on the next auditor to be so amenable, please bring me those ledgers. In recompense, I am prepared to grant you dispensation from whatever scandal-broth your impetuous heart contrives to create.*
> *Aris*

The request, couched so openly, in a letter passed hand to hand, left Gilly breathless. The king was perhaps the fool the newspapers called him to think Maledicte's behavior might always be so easily condoned. Maledicte's own nature stirred trouble, but with Ani's wings urging him on, Maledicte was capable of anything. And Aris thought to dismiss all trouble with a smile and a gracious word. It went beyond foolishness and into madness.

ARIS ENTERED THE THRONE ROOM from the king's entrance at the rear of the dais. By the main door, two of the Kingsguard stood to attention, dressed in the armor the palace etiquette required, enamel over steel, Last blue over silver. The elaborate gate that closed off the anteroom was drawn back, showing Aris his petitioners—two Dainanders in their customary gray cloaks, and on the receiving end of their horrified gazes, Maledicte. Though he was dressed in gray as they were, it was entirely evident that he held none of their abstemious views: His grays were silk and satin, his hair curled and glistened; they wore wool and linen, and kept their hair cropped close.

Aris hid a smile as he nodded greetings. With Maledicte a visible reminder of Antyre's decadent court, the straitlaced Dainanders' eagerness to return home might outweigh their avarice. Aris waved Maledicte forward, and once he had entered, the guards shut the anteroom gate on the waiting emissaries.

Maledicte dropped into a bow as he approached Aris; it felt amused to Aris, as if Maledicte mocked the role of court and courtier, the positions of king and servant, when they were only two men.

Aris settled himself on his throne, conscious of his own smile. "You came. My request done?" His gaze flicked to the single book held in a gloved hand.

"Delivered to your quarters, I believe. Your Captain Jasper seemed most eager to relieve me of the burden." Maledicte offered up the ledger he held.

Aris opened it, and Maledicte said, "Careful, the ink may still be damp."

Wariness replaced the pleasure Aris had felt. He tapped the open book with an agitated finger, smudged the ink, and said, "So I see." He waited for an explanation.

"Vornatti's hand was crabbed and nigh unreadable, quite gave me the headache looking at them. I thought to spare you that pain."

"The originals?" Aris asked.

"Quite safe," Maledicte said. "I am careful of my possessions." The dark gaze that met his was confident, and under its power, Aris bit back his first instinct to shout for the guards.

Aris tore his eyes from those dark ones, and said, "My brother thinks you dangerous."

"What courtier is not?" Maledicte said. "I have a sword to let men's blood, and a wit to make them wish their wounds fatal. But I am hardly the only such in your court."

"I could wish otherwise," Aris said, impetuous himself. "It makes me feel less a shepherd of my people and more a serpent charmer."

Maledicte smiled, and uninvited, dropped to sit on the stair, looking up at Aris. "I am charmed," he said.

"And yet you deny me what I asked for."

Maledicte sighed, traced the horned image of Haith worked into the side of the throne. "Vornatti had the training of me, sire, and so I am constitutionally unable to part with anything of such potential value."

"Your intentions?" Aris's anger roiled, turning belly-up, and exposing that thread of betrayal and hurt that lay beneath it. This young courtier had drawn his liking from the first. Aris had imagined the sentiment returned.

"I have none."

"Then give them to me," Aris commanded.

"I will not," Maledicte said.

Aris let his breath out, stung and chilled at once. "Little fool. I am your king. Should I so command, you must obey. To do otherwise is treason."

"I will not," Maledicte repeated.

Aris put his hand beneath the mulish jaw and tilted the dark eyes to meet his own. "I could have the guards take your stubborn head from your shoulders." Aris slid his other hand around Maledicte's jawline, into the silken curls. "I do not think your stiff neck will prove obstacle enough for steel."

"Can you truly fault me for my caution? My craving for security in a world where I've known so little?" Maledicte met Aris's eyes without fear or apology. Aris contemplated the face turned up to his, his fingers moving idly through Maledicte's hair, feeling the fineness of his neck and skin, the sleek curve of the skull, the rough touch of the boy's scarred cheek against his fingers. Maledicte smelled of lilacs, and Aris found himself staring into the wide, dark eyes as if they were the only thing in the room.

Aris was suddenly, uncomfortably aware that he was breathing faster, that his touch had turned to a caress, that Maledicte had woken long-dormant desire he thought gone with his dead queen. He started to withdraw his hands, and Maledicte caught one in his own gloved hand, caged the palm over his mouth.

"Please, Aris." Maledicte's breath warmed Aris's palm, and Aris was wholly mindful of the soft brush of lips against his skin. The rasping voice was as intimate as any Aris had ever heard; that agile tongue swept out, licked ink from Aris's fingertips.

Aris took his hand away, hid the warmth of it against his side. Maledicte's lips curled.

"Leave us. We dismiss you from our presence." Aris took his refuge in unusual formality of speech, uncomfortably stirred.

Maledicte rose and bowed. He backed down the dais stairs, then bowed again and turned toward the door and the guards, the slim line of his back a gray smudge in the white room. Only after he had left was Aris able to recall the ledgers denied him. A brief spurt of bewildered irritation rushed his veins: Maledicte thought he required the ledgers to protect himself from Aris? When he had just proven to his satisfaction that words and touch alone would suffice?

*Women, by their nature, are more susceptible to sudden nerve-storms,
to crying out to the gods for succor. However, they are also fickle creatures, no more able to hold to one course than a ship without its sail, and
their petty outrages often die stillborn on their lips, forgotten as the next
emotion crests. Though there are histories of women summoning the aid
of gods, few are substantiated, and indeed, I have never met the woman
determined enough to deserve a god's attention.*

—Darian Chancel, "On Theology"

"GILLY, TELL ME ABOUT THE debutantes this year. The king
has it in mind for me to wed."

Janus was in smallclothes only, his hair sleek along the
thick column of his neck. Gilly held the shaving basin and mirror steady for him, studying Janus surreptitiously. Janus's skin was marked
with scars, wounds neglected and healed without care. The young noblemen
of the court had hides of gilt and marble; Janus recalled to mind the older
generation, the ones who had fought and bled, the ones who had their history etched into their skin. Gilly wondered if Maledicte's skin carried that
same violent history.

Watching, Maledicte lounged amid rumpled sheets, fully dressed, admiring Janus.

Janus nicked himself and flinched at the spot of bright blood. "You keep
this thing too damn sharp," he said.

"What purpose has a dull blade?" Maledicte said. "But I'll act your valet." He sat and smoothed the bedsheets, reaching for the razor.

"You're too fond of sharp edges to play barber," Janus said.

Maledicte subsided back into the massed pillows, propping himself on his elbows. "And so I find out how much you trust me."

Janus pounced, rolling Maledicte into his arms for a lazy kiss.

"You're bleeding on me," Maledicte said, rubbing the smear near his mouth. Janus bent, licked the smudge away.

"There are several acceptable candidates, depending on your intentions," Gilly said, unwilling to watch more of this play.

"I want my birthright," Janus said, voice muffled by the soft skin of Maledicte's throat. "The title and all it entails."

Maledicte wrestled free of Janus, sat behind him, tilted Janus's head back. "Consider while I shave him." Maledicte collected the basin and razor over Janus's objection.

"Amarantha Lovesy," Gilly said, after several moments of reflection.

"The duke of Love's daughter? She's no debutante, too old and serious-minded, mad about books and horses. Father told me of her," Janus said, nearly getting a mouthful of soap.

"And above a bastard's touch," Gilly said. "Except she's blotted her book, got caught with her skirts up with a stablehand. But she's got breeding, and she has a reasonable dowry. Besides being a counselor's daughter."

"Aris expects an heir. Is she barren?" Janus said.

Gilly shrugged. "Nothing's been said. But she's not so old as all that."

"Is she pretty, Gilly?" Janus asked. "I've not laid eyes on her yet."

Maledicte's fingers tensed about the razor.

Gilly recalled his first court attendance with Vornatti and his first sight of Amarantha. A girl near his own age and as far removed from his farming sisters as to be a separate race. Lady Perfection, the court called her. When her skirts had foamed over Gilly's boots in passing, he had nearly melted with desire.

"*Very* pretty," Maledicte said, before Gilly could.

"Beautiful," Gilly amended.

Maledicte snarled; his hands clenched about the razor's handle, and Janus put a hand up to keep the blade away.

"I suppose a beautiful wife is more palatable than an ugly one. Why hasn't she wed, Gilly?" Janus asked, still caging Maledicte's hand and the razor.

"Her father's holding out for a title. Even now. Rumor has it he's been thinking of an Itarusine duke, and so regain some of his money that's fled abroad with the Itarusine tithe. But your title might prove more tempting with its hint of the throne for future generations."

"Still, she's old," Janus said.

"If you don't want her, Gilly can bed her. He's already admitted to finding her desirable." Maledicte's voice was edged.

"I won't share with Gilly," Janus said.

His light eyes met Gilly's and Gilly deciphered the warning as clearly as if it had been spoken aloud. "I might find myself saddled with a farmboy's brat for heir."

Maledicte slapped him, a blow that reddened his newly shaved skin and filled the room with its impact. Janus winced and seized the razor again, tugging it from Maledicte's hand.

"Oh, then bed your beautiful wife yourself." Maledicte shoved Janus forward and surged off the bed. Soapy water splashed Janus's lap.

Janus ignored his tantrum and said to Gilly, "Amarantha it is, then." Wedding the Lovesy chit turns a necessary marriage into more than a way to please Aris. Love's support would be invaluable in my quest for the title."

"She has her pride. She might not accept," Gilly said, watching Maledicte's face. He touched Maledicte's wrist, intending to soothe, but Maledicte twitched away, all nerves and temper.

"Does she truly have a choice?" Janus asked. "With Aris urging me to wed, and her father eager to see her settled before she finds another stablehand to liven her days? Tell me, is she still considered respectable? I've no desire to be burdened with a socially unacceptable wife."

"She is Love's daughter," Gilly said. "Her sins can be forgotten with a ring."

"Enough," Maledicte said, voice cracking.

Janus's face softened; he held out his arms. "Come here, my dark cavalier." Maledicte dropped to his knees before Janus and put his head in his lap.

Janus stroked his dark hair, then said, "What else can I do, Mal? If not Amarantha, who then? Will there be anyone you accept?"

"I hate them all," Maledicte whispered, voice edged.

"So will I, I promise," Janus said, brushing aside Maledicte's hair to kiss the back of his nape.

Maledicte turned his mouth away when Janus sought it, but said, "Gilly, arrange for Janus to meet Amarantha. Find out where she goes, what she does, what she likes. Treat her as any other enemy we mean to vanquish."

GILLY RETURNED TO THE HOUSE in the afternoon after a series of meetings with his fellow servant-spies and informants. Though most of them had revolved around Amarantha, Gilly had taken the time to meet with a maid in the Westfalls' employ, to discover if Mirabile had yet returned. The answer had been no, but Gilly, watching the girl's eyes slip away from his, wondered if she were truthful. The last they had heard of Mirabile's doings had been the coachman's report. After Vornatti's funeral, he had followed her to the edge of the Relicts and balked while she delved farther in, her skirts vanishing into the winding rubble. The Relicts and their denizens should have been the end of her, but Gilly had uncomfortable doubts. Mirabile was a dangerous woman.

The castle of rooks on the roofline muttered growling agreement and Gilly shivered, slipping inside the house without looking upward, afraid of catching their black gaze. Inside, he found Livia waiting to intercept him. "Watch yourself, Gilly. Once Lord Last left—well, he's in a temper right enough. He threw the kettle at me. Broke the mirror on the landing, too."

Gilly looked up the dark stairs. "Why don't you go out?"

"Don't have to ask me twice," she said. Livia held out her hand, and Gilly, conscious that her pay wasn't due for another week, passed her a handful of coppers. "I'll give you a luna also, if you take the other two maids with you."

"Those dull mice?" she complained, but nodded.

Gilly took the stairs two at a time and paused. Livia hadn't said Maledicte had used the bronze serpent in the hall to break the mirror. The glass was still caged by the frame; only a few silvery fragments from the heart of the shattered mirror dotted the carpet. He stepped over them, tapped on Maledicte's door, and opened it on a curse.

Maledicte sat on the bed, sawing cravats apart with the shaving razor. The floor around him was littered with scraps of mangled linens and thrown objects: a boot on the hearth, the water basin beside the wall, a long splash before the upended kettle near the door. "Whose throat are you wishing cut?" Gilly asked.

"Mine," Maledicte said, his face blotched with tears and temper. Grief wrapped the sulky lines of his mouth. Gilly's heart turned over.

"His marriage," Gilly said.

Maledicte rubbed his swollen eyes. The razor moved perilously close to his skin and Gilly took it away, folding it closed.

Maledicte's eyes darkened. "I wasn't done."

"Why don't I pour you a drink instead?" Gilly looked over at the liquor tray, littered with broken crystal. "Or better yet, let's finish the job you've started, and frighten out Cook tonight. We'll raid her kitchen, find out what spirits she's been snaffling from your cellar."

"I'm not a child to be humored," Maledicte warned.

"Why shouldn't I humor you?" Gilly said. "You look like your heart is breaking."

Maledicte let Gilly tug him to his feet. "When he marries—"

"Shh," Gilly said. "It's remarkable how much improved things seem after a drink."

"An attitude like that, it's a marvel you're not a sot," Maledicte said, but allowed Gilly to lead him down the stairs, past the grand, empty, and shadowed rooms into the warm recesses of the kitchen. The cook looked up from her chopping, startled.

"We won't need you tonight," Gilly said.

The woman eyed Gilly, flickered her eyes over Maledicte's face, and pulled off her apron. "There's bread in the oven. Be a good boy, Gilly, and don't let it burn or you'll have no toast tomorrow."

When she had bustled away, Maledicte said, "She likes you."

"She's a motherly sort. If you weren't so off-putting, she'd never leave you be. She thinks you need feeding up."

"Is that motherly?" Maledicte said. "My mother wasn't like that." He settled down at the scarred wooden table, the unusual surroundings distracting him from his tantrum, and poked at the chopped almonds with the knife tip.

Gilly set a battered tin saucepan on the stove, checked the fire, and poured milk into the heating pan. "No?"

"She was just another Relicts whore. Like me." The tremble in the rasping voice sounded more like a rattlesnake warning than tears, but Gilly had memorized the nuances of his voice, and spun.

"Shh, shh, don't do that," Gilly said, daring to brush his lips over Maledicte's forehead as if he were no more than an unhappy sibling. "You're not that; you're an aristocrat."

"When he marries—all I become is his whore. Yet I chose this path. Vornatti didn't matter. I used him as he used me. But once I kill Last—what will I be if Janus is married? Exactly what my mother intended. A rich man's pet."

Gilly poured out the milk, added brandy with a liberal hand, and set it before him. "Never seen a pet with so many claws and teeth," Gilly said lightly. "Drink, and I'll tell you tales of the court."

Maledicte brought the cup to his lips, swallowed. "I don't know why I listen to your sentimental stories."

"Because you know I'll put up with your tempers and moods in return," Gilly said. "But if you're sick of love, I'll tell you about the sinking of the *Redoubtable* and the *Deviltry*."

"Is there blood?" Maledicte said.

"It was war," Gilly said, "There's always blood. This was during the first days of Xipos, when the gods were still with us. The *Redoubtable* was captained by Bellane, and the *Deviltry* by one of the Itarusine princes. Their cannons were loaded with iron, and their chests were packed with gold, the better to coax greedy Naga to their aid. They battled and bribed and bled, throwing sols overboard as often as they fired their cannons, and finally Scaled Naga, god of health and avarice, thrashing below in an agony of greed, raised Himself out of the sea and took it all. Ships, men, cannonballs, and two king's ransoms of gold. Bloody enough?"

"Mmm," Maledicte agreed on a hum of pleasure. "No one tried to reclaim the gold?"

"What the gods have touched is changed forever. Better left safely away from men's hands."

Gilly rose and fielded the hot bread from the oven, dropping it onto the cooling racks. He took one loaf to the table, found fresh-churned butter in the larder, and settled back at the table. He ripped a piece free, handed the warm bread to Maledicte. "I wager you've not eaten today, but wallowed in your temper."

"Don't lecture me," Maledicte said, but he reached out and slathered the butter on his bread.

"Eat, and I'll tell you another story. An older story of a knight and his squire and their petition to Espit to grant them a child of their own."

Maledicte rolled his eyes. "And back to love. Gilly, you're a romantic."

"It's an incurable disease," Gilly said, judging Maledicte's mood. His eyes were shadowed, drawn with weeping, but the sulkiness had left his mouth; even now his lips curled faintly.

Maledicte finished his cup of milk, walked over to the stove, and poured himself another. He sat down and ate chopped almonds and warmed bread, waiting. "Love stories are too often dull—"

"Should I take a leaf out of one of Vornatti's pornographic stories, give you ribaldry instead of romance?" Gilly teased.

"Whatever you want, Gilly, I am only your audience."

"There was a knight—" Gilly smiled as he told the story, not for the subject matter, but for Maledicte's reluctant attention, like a child coaxed into interest against his will. It was an old tale, and sad. The men's petition to Espit, the god of creation and despair, had been answered. A mare in the stables swelled with a human child. But during her birthing convulsions, the mare kicked the squire in the throat, and the sound of their daughter's first cry was mingled with the squire's death rattle.

Maledicte's eyes were shadowed again when he finished, his mouth down-drawn; Gilly took a rueful breath and retold it as farce, where the men petitioned Espit, the horse was a stallion; the two men ended pregnant, and the horse . . . well satisfied. Maledicte's moodiness gave way to laughter.

"I never guessed you knew tales like that," Maledicte said when his breath returned.

"I lived with the old bastard for eight years," Gilly said, "and before that I lived on a farm. It's only wonderful I don't talk like that all the time."

Maledicte stretched his arms across the table, his hands open. "Thank you, Gilly."

With Maledicte's bad temper assuaged for the moment, Gilly's thoughts turned to the wreckage upstairs. "Let's tidy up so that you'll have someplace to sleep without worrying about glass shards in your sheets." He tugged Maledicte to his feet, and herded him up the stairs, ignoring Maledicte's complaints and mocking claims of being aristocracy.

Maledicte held a handful of shredded lace, and Gilly had the linens stripped and piled neatly, still glittering with thrown porcelain, when Janus returned. Janus opened the door and paused.

Maledicte dropped his bundle, kicked it beneath the bedsteps.

Janus righted the hearthside chair and sank into it. "Temper again?"

"Better out than in, as Celia used to say."

"Celia used the axiom to excuse her drug fits," Janus said. He reached down, picked up the boot resting on the hearth, stroked the long scrape down its side.

"Are you angry?" Maledicte asked, crouching before Janus.

"They're your things," Janus said.

Gilly picked up the kettle; its spout was cracked and he added it to the wastebin.

After the effort Gilly had taken to soothe Maledicte, he was not inclined to let Janus rile him again so he busied himself around the room.

"What are you thinking about to make you so quiet?" Maledicte said, settling into Janus's lap.

"About boots. This one is ruined." He dropped it from his hands, wrapped his arms around Maledicte's waist. "At least, we consider it ruined. Now."

Maledicte touched the supple, scarred leather with slow fingertips, tracing the damage. "I haven't thought about that in years. We could have eaten off a pair of boots like this for a week."

"You ate boots?" Gilly asked.

"No, fool," Janus said. "We sold them for coppers, maybe lunas, if Mal did the haggling. Ragmen painted the flaws over, sold them at four times what they paid us."

"Can't eat boots, Gilly. They don't digest, and if you use them to flavor water, it only tastes like feet," Maledicte said. "If you could get the water at all. I was always thirsty in the Relicts."

Gilly sat down on the bedsteps.

"Had to put a pebble beneath your tongue to stave off thirst," Janus said.

"Rise in the dawn to wipe the dew from the walls. But so close to the sea, even dew tastes of salt," Maledicte said. "I haven't woken at dawn now in years."

"I did, at first, no matter that I was in a gilded cage. I woke with the sun, but there was always a pitcher of fresh water by my bed, and later, the maids came to bring me tea." Janus sighed into Maledicte's neck. "It seems so hard to recall being hungry."

"I remember hunger," Maledicte said. His mouth drew down as if he felt that bite in his belly now, bread and milk and nuts notwithstanding.

"You were always hungrier than I was," Janus said. "It's amazing you haven't gone to fat with the feasts you can have now." He raised his hand, circled Maledicte's wrist, spoke in a voice near dreaming. "It was so hard. And no one cared if we starved."

"Not our mothers," Maledicte said. "We're well rid of them."

"They ate what they would out of our hoard, and if there was nothing left, well then, wasn't it past time for us to go get more? Never mind that we had to steal or beg for it."

"You make me hungry now," Maledicte complained.

"I can't help you with past want, but if you don't mind a simple dinner, I can make that," Gilly said.

"Thank you, Gilly," Janus said.

Gilly startled at the lack of condescension in Janus's voice. Gilly nodded and went out the door, wondering what Janus was thinking. While Maledicte was all temper and secrets, Janus's apparent openness was still harder to read.

MALEDICTE UNDRESSED IN THE NEAR darkness of his bedchamber, the lamps both turned low, watching his shadow flicker and shrink. If he listened carefully, he could hear Gilly and Janus discussing Amarantha below in the unusual silence of a house emptied of servants. Maledicte chose not to make the effort, and let their words fade into a pleasant murmur like the crackling of a low-burning fire.

Carefully, he concealed his padded corset in the back of the wardrobe, trading it for a crisp white nightshirt. He caught sight of his reflection, ghostly in the mirror, and lingered, touching the snowy folds of cloth, the blunt cut of his unbound hair, and wondered, in a melancholy moment, if Amarantha hunted sleep attired in silks and lace.

But he wore silks aplenty during the day, and in the colors he chose. He went where he pleased; he carried a sword. The thought of the sword reassured him; the familiar lean length of it beckoned.

Unsheathing it, he sparred with shadows until the sulky set of his mouth shifted into a fierce grin, until the dark hair on his nape grew damp with the effort. Two final, quick slashes sliced the wicks from the oil lamps.

He woke to sumptuous darkness interrupted by wavering golden light, a flame in the room. His hand opened and closed, found the surety of the hilt in his palm. "Janus?"

"Who else?"

"I thought you were for home tonight," Maledicte said, opening the bed curtains to allow himself the sleepy pleasure of watching Janus undress by lamplight, all planes and angles, alternately shadowed and limned in flame. The fine hairs on his arms and legs gleamed.

"When I could be here?" He slid into bed, all warm limbs and skin, and Maledicte sighed into the feel of him.

"And you've brought your wardrobe with you," Maledicte said, catching sight of a valise by the door. He smiled and pushed Janus back into the nested pillows, arranging him for his own comfort before resting his head in the juncture of Janus's neck and shoulder.

Janus raised up enough to tug at the bed curtain, sealing them into a cocoon, then lay back again. "I've scandalized the court once by wearing the same clothes when I should not. I won't do so again. Damn."

"Hmm?" Maledicte said, half drowsing.

"I left the light burning."

"It will burn itself out," Maledicte said. "We're rich. We can waste lamp oil." He yawned, rubbed his cheek over Janus's chest and finally chose the spot over his heartbeat.

"It's not the oil, nor the light that bothers me," Janus said, tightening his arm around Maledicte's shoulders. "It's those cupids. Watching."

Maledicte's slackening mouth quirked into a smile; he let out a few puffs of silent laughter that stirred Janus's hair on the pillow. "I suppose we could hire someone to paint them over, but I loathe the smell of paint, and I hate the fuss and bother."

"You love fuss and bother," Janus said, tenting his elbow over his eyes. "As long as you're inflicting it." His voice slowed, relaxed; his body slowly untensed, stretching out to fill the space. "Rats take it!"

Maledicte jerked back to wakefulness. "What now?"

"Your damn sword bit me. Why in hell have you given it its own pillow?"

Janus sat up, dislodging Maledicte. A bleeding scratch etched the width of his biceps, a line of darkness against the paler skin, as if the night had left its own mark. "Look at that."

"I wanted company," Maledicte said.

"You have mine," Janus snapped, pushing the sword out of the bed with all the distaste of a man removing vermin.

Maledicte's mouth tightened as the sword hilt rasped along the edge of the bed before falling. "Don't dump it there. You'll wake in the morning and tread on it, and that will be my fault too. Get up and put it away."

"It's your sword," Janus said, dabbing at the scratch with the lace edge of the pillowcase.

"You left the lamp burning." Maledicte drew the blankets more firmly about his neck, burrowing after warmth. After a moment the sheets rustled and the mattress shifted as Janus ceded. Maledicte rolled over, stared at the ceiling, his mouth curling. "While you're up, will you—"

"Will I what?" Janus interrupted. "Make you tea? Bring you a biscuit?"

"Since you mention it, I am hungry."

"You should have stayed to dinner then," Janus said. "Gilly makes an acceptable cook."

Maledicte smiled. "Thank you, Janus, for being kinder to him."

"He has his place," Janus said. "As long as he realizes it's not in your bed, I have no quarrel with him." His face, exaggerated by faint light, stayed grim, belying his words. "Where do you keep this blade?"

"As with all my favorite possessions, I keep it near to hand," Maledicte said. "Set it beside the trunk. There are biscuits in the trunk also."

Janus paused, his hand on the lamp, then sighed. "Your sword by your bed, the sweets within reach—I am surprised you do not have Gilly sleeping outside your door. After all, he is also one of your favorite possessions." He fished the tin out and tossed two biscuits toward Maledicte's outstretched hands. "Will those suffice, or should I stay my hand on the lamp?"

"Put it out," Maledicte said, nibbling on the first biscuit, cupping his palm to catch the tender crumbs, keeping them from the sheets. Belated recognition of Janus's words filtered through his mind. "Gilly is no possession. You cannot own a friend."

"You own him as surely as you owned Roach," Janus said, moving through the darkness. He finagled his way beneath the sheets, drew the curtain shut. "I do not understand it," he said, tugging Maledicte into his arms. "I make friends easily. You offend people with every outborne breath, and yet you end with worshippers. Roach, Gilly, even Aris."

"And yourself?" Maledicte asked, wiping his fingers on the coverlet.

"No," Janus said, catching Maledicte's hands, and kissing the crumbs away. "I know you too well. I can only be your lover."

"Only," Maledicte said. "Isn't that everything? Let them follow me as they will. I will follow you."

· 20 ·

At ten o'clock in the morning, the elaborate lawns and paths of Jackal Park swarmed with aristocracy exercising their mounts and strolling along the rows of honored vendors permitted to hawk their wares in this playground. Maledicte clutched the reins and tightened his legs about his steed, trying not to collide with anyone, tensing as they passed the barricade that kept the antimachinist protestors from encroaching. If they shouted or threw stones, as they were wont to do—

"He'll have you off if you don't relax," Janus said, frowning. "Vornatti taught you dancing, dueling, and etiquette, but not horsemanship?"

"Vornatti tried," Maledicte said.

Janus sighed. He slowed his horse, reached out, and drew Maledicte's hands back on the reins. "Don't clench."

"They can't like being ridden," Maledicte said, but forced his hands to loosen. Beneath him, the horse stopped feeling like a pile of agitated muscle.

"Better," Janus said.

"Still, I don't see why we had to ride," Maledicte said. "And at such an hour."

"This is the hour to be seen, you know that," Janus said, shaking his hair free from his collar.

"I'd rather not be seen falling off a horse, thank you," Maledicte said acidly, but followed Janus along the hedge. The hedges, carved into hounds and hares, alternately pursued and fled as they passed. Ahead, the trail broadened to incorporate the promenading aristocracy, the small, decorative carriages, and more riders.

Beside him, Janus drove his horse into a sudden, flashy canter. At the end of the path, he slowed to a showy halt. Maledicte kept his horse to its nervous walk, glaring at the amused glances he garnered. A thin, dapper man in an Itarusine frock coat laughed aloud, teeth flashing within his neat ring of mustache and beard, and Maledicte spurred his horse forward, drawing up beside Janus. "Was there a purpose to that display?"

"Mating dance," Janus said, smiling. "The air is sweet, and courting is everywhere."

Maledicte's lips softened until he followed Janus's gaze and found it lingering on two well-attended women promenading along a side path. Their dresses were the height of fashion, and their eyes were raised, discreetly watching Janus.

The older woman was well into her fifties, Maledicte knew, but as unlined as powder and potions could make her. The younger woman's beauty needed no such aid. "And Amarantha Lovesy is easily impressed by horsemen," Maledicte finished.

"So they say," Janus said. "Will you excuse me? I do not think my chances so good that you should come with me."

"Then tell me why I accompanied you at all?" Maledicte said. "Why I must rise and ride with you, when I hate horses and despise mornings?" His horse crow-hopped beneath him, and Janus caught its bridle.

"I thought you'd prefer witnessing my wooing of Amarantha to imagining it."

"No," Maledicte said. He kicked his horse and sawed on the reins, trying to turn its head. Janus cantered away. Maledicte's horse, as restless as he at being deserted, made an attempt to follow. Maledicte yanked the reins; the horse danced beneath him, and Maledicte slacked his grip, clutching its mane.

"Too much beast for you? Perhaps you should join me for a stroll instead." Mirabile dimpled at him and tucked her gloved hand over the curve of boot and stirrup. Lacking his sword, Maledicte's hands knotted around the riding crop; he was startled to find her alive and well after her disappearance into the Relicts. Maledicte had not dwelled much on her threats, but to run across her of a sudden—he found himself remembering the animal fury in her eyes. To see her so poised now when he knew her enmity made him cat-nervous.

"No steed for you, Lady, or are the rumors true—have you sold your riding habits for pin money?" He was rewarded by the tightening of her rosebud lips.

"You'd best keep your grip on the reins, or you'll be at my feet before you know it."

"Take your hand away."

She stepped back, gloved hands spread wide, laughing. He was at a loss for her shifting moods, at her returning to his side time and time again, and the damn horse kept tugging at his hands. Maledicte could not keep himself from glancing over his shoulder, hoping for aid. But, now leading his steed, Janus was deep in conversation with the duchess of Love.

"He does the pretty very well," Mirabile said, leaning her weight against the horse's velvet side. "I hear he was quite well versed as a lover of women—do you suppose he's reverting to type?"

"Perhaps he already has, and the ladies were the anomaly," Maledicte said, lured into speech. "Some men lose all sense of self abroad, or so I'm told."

"So confident in his affections? I hope your loyalty is not misplaced. But let us not quarrel today. Instead, come and have tea with me."

"What have we to say to each other?" Maledicte said, his jaw tight.

"At the very least, tea would grant you an excuse to dismount. Come now, Mal. Is that horse really preferable to my company?" She leaned forward and blew into its flaring nostrils. The entire animal seized under him, going as rigid as a corpse, then it reared, hooves striking at the sky. Maledicte wrestled it down, panting, then dismounted with more haste than grace.

"I never did like having discourse on an unequal footing," she said, smiling.

Maledicte wound the reins in his hands, reconsidering. There was rage in her voice, barely contained. But he was unwilling to back down, or worse, attempt to remount beneath her gaze. He hoped to see Janus returning, escaping the vapid confines of polite first conversation between suitor and sought, but Janus lounged against a tree, one boot propped on a mounting block, smiling down at Amarantha. Even from a distance, Maledicte could see him working to hold Amarantha's interest. The duchess was his, but Amarantha looked away, plucking fitfully at her gloves.

Mirabile insinuated her hand into the crook of his arm. "Come and have tea," she said.

"It's early yet—" Maledicte said, looking at the angry shadows in her red-brown eyes. Something shifted and moved behind them, something sleek and dark, drowning his objections, as if her words were law.

"There, no protests," Mirabile said. "Such kindred spirits as we should be allies."

He walked with her, her hand around his elbow and caged by his free hand. Walking as if they were lovers. The horse? he wondered briefly, dragging his gaze away to look back. Had he loosed it in the park?

"Here we are," she said, settling herself onto a marble bench in the shade of a beech tree. A small table, its top a maze of inlaid tiles, had been laid out with a teapot, two cups of wafer-thin china, and a covered tray. Maledicte sat beside her, took the cup she handed him.

Shadows fell from the tree above, one crow and then another, followed by a slew of rooks, all come to scavenge for scraps. The two sets of birds squabbled and jabbered while Mirabile laughed and threw them tea cakes. Maledicte watched their glossy wings, the slick emptiness of their dark eyes. What could drive a noblewoman to the Relicts? He very much feared he had the answer.

"Your tea's growing cold," Mirabile said.

The same slick darkness rested in her eyes, Maledicte realized, the blank gaze of a predatory creature. The cup hovered at his lips, smelling of sweet jasmine and warmth, and reflecting the crow-blackness of his own gaze. He set it down with nervous fingers. "I am not thirsty," he said, standing.

She rose with him as if they were linked. She collected his cup and swallowed several mouthfuls. "There. In case your fearful heart cried poison, I have drunk from it as well." She folded his fingers around the cup again.

Her eyes on his, the hush of the leaves in the faint breeze, and the squabbling crows at his feet all conspired together, making him feel he had stumbled into a dream. But he looked at the shadows in her gaze and forced a smile. "No." He set down the cup; without looking back, he walked away, ignoring the quiver in his spine that urged him to run before her mask fell again and showed him more than he could bear to know.

GILLY WAS READING in the parlor when the front door shut with enough force to rattle a sour note out of the spinet. "How was the park?" Gilly asked, as the carved door opened.

"Vile," Maledicte said, settling down on a delicately curved love seat. "Janus went haring after Amarantha; Mirabile leeched onto me and tried to feed me dismal tea."

Gilly folded the pages of his new book closed with casual fingers, hoping to distract Maledicte from it. A moment's reflection showed him that Maledicte was unlikely to notice anything. "Mirabile? Are you well? You look . . . scared."

"I am no coward," Maledicte said, the words quick and hot, ragged in his throat. "At least, I never was before. But something was wrong. Mirabile's . . . changed. She had shadows in her eyes, Gilly."

"Shadows," Gilly parroted, heart sinking.

"I know, such melodrama," Maledicte said. "But I swear to you— No, I will think no more on it."

Gilly shivered, thinking of other eyes, all too often shadowed. "Mal, did you drink her tea?"

"No," Maledicte said, turning in his seat and gouging at the upholstery buttons. "I know there's no rule against declining tea, so you needn't frown at me like that."

"It might have been poisoned," Gilly said. "She hates you enough for that."

Maledicte paused in his destruction of the chair. "I sincerely hope it was. When I chose not to drink, she swallowed it. Perhaps she's ended herself?"

"Or found herself," Gilly said. "Shadows and poison. Mal—you said that she had changed. Could she have sought out Ani's aid as you did?"

"I never sought Her," Maledicte snapped. "As for Mirabile seeking Ani—" His hands clenched on the chair, his voice tightening as he rose. "It's those damned books you read. You see Her hand everywhere, when the simple fact is that I fled from Mirabile like a frightened child, afraid she'd pour poison down my throat."

Gilly seized Maledicte by the shoulders, stilled his restless pacing. Something moved over Maledicte's eyes, like the reflections of dark feathers, and Maledicte slumped.

"Let go of me."

"Ani supposedly protects Her own from poison," Gilly said. "Even had you drunk—"

"You say that—with stonethroat's effects branded in my voice? You have read far too many tales, Gilly."

"But that was before you sealed Her compact. Before you killed Kritos."

Maledicte said, "The only gift Ani brings is the only curse She brings, that of resolve and obsession. No more nonsense."

"And the sword?" Gilly said, watching Maledicte retrieve it from the divan where Janus had forced him to leave it before exiting the house. "She gave it to you. What might She have given Mirabile?"

"Gilly!" Maledicte said. "Are you trying to make me fear Mirabile more or less?"

Gilly sat, the book beneath him rustling as he did so, and Maledicte's attention shifted like a cat's. "What's that? Another tract on the dead gods?"

"It is," Gilly admitted, pulling it out and laying it on the floor between them. "Written by Mirabile's husband, as it occurs."

"I should have it burned," Maledicte said, looking at the gaudy cover with an expression composed equally of wariness and contempt.

"You gave me the money that bought the book. I suppose it's yours. Everything is, even me."

"No." Maledicte turned, the shadows fading from his face. "The money I gave you was only your share."

"An accomplice to murder," Gilly muttered.

Maledicte touched Gilly's cheek and said, "Don't fret, sweet Gilly. Or if you must, fret yourself to find something to entertain me until Janus returns."

Gilly's spirits lifted at the familiar petulance. Or so he told himself, dismissing the touch and casual endearment. Flushing, he cast about for diversion. "Want to learn to play the spinet?"

"No," Maledicte said. "Do you know how to play?"

"Vornatti had me take lessons when he thought it might be pleasant to have private entertainment on command. Before he decided his private entertainments didn't involve music."

"Then play for me. It can't be worse than the amateur talent they have at the courts."

Gilly sat at the spinet, but shifted on the seat, ill at ease. "Stop staring at my back. It's too much to ask of me, to play and to perform at the same time."

Maledicte rose and joined Gilly on the bench. "What if I sit here? Then you cannot mistake me for a critical audience."

Gilly set his hands on the keys and ran out a scale. The notes vibrated in the air, going flat as the untuned strings sounded. "Vornatti said my hands on the keys were too big. He was right."

"Excuses," Maledicte said. "I have found one thing you cannot do perfectly and you're ruining it by making reasonable excuses. Just play, Gilly."

Gilly turned his head to object and got lost in the sweep of dark hair sliding over Maledicte's cheek and throat. He took his hands from the keys, brushed Maledicte's hair away from his face.

"Are you going to play that instrument, Gilly?" Janus said from the doorway. "Or are you playing at fashionable music master instead?" At the palpable edge in Janus's voice, Gilly stood, leaving Maledicte possessor of the bench.

"I hear you made contact with Amarantha Lovesy," Gilly said. Behind him, Maledicte picked out notes at random.

Janus heaved a sigh, came into the room fully, and slung himself into a chair. "What a harridan. Despite her mother's enthusiasm, she made it clear the only reason she would even consider me was that she coveted Lastrest. All that beauty cannot mask her greed."

"Choose someone else," Maledicte said, head still bent over the keys, adding trembling dissonances to the air.

"What other wife could grant me a counselor's support so neatly? Lilia DeGuerre is wed and bred already, and Westfall has no child. No, I'll wed the bitch, and leave her in the country house she admires so much." Janus levered himself out of the chair, paced between Gilly and Maledicte.

"I thought we were to live at Lastrest," Maledicte said, eyes fixed on the spinet keys.

"It only needs to be for a little while. So many of the Last countesses have died of childbearing, we can create one more tragedy without much suspicion." Janus dropped a kiss on Maledicte's bent head, and pulled Maledicte from the bench. He lifted him onto the low stage. "But as for now—her parents will push her to accept my suit, we'll put my father in the ground, and you'll be consorting with an earl before you know it."

Maledicte smiled. "You hate her."

"Utterly. Set your heart at rest." Janus bent Maledicte over his arm to kiss his throat. "Gilly, give us a waltz."

"Please do," Maledicte added.

Gilly thumped out a waltz, ignoring his mistakes and the pitch of the untuned spinet.

Janus and Maledicte tussled for a moment, hands shifting and regripping, until Janus laughed and said, "Stop trying to lead, Mal." He raised his voice, carrying the tune himself, humming, a warm, intimate sound in the room. Maledicte leaned into Janus's arms.

When the waltz ended, Maledicte said, "Play something else, Gilly. Something that doesn't want an in-tune instrument."

"You don't ask for much," Gilly said. But he searched his memory for a folk jig of single notes at a time.

Janus shifted his grip, and Maledicte laughed, and then they were swinging each other like children, clasping each other's wrists, pulling and spinning until there was no dance, only the dizziness and laughter, Maledicte's voice disappearing under stonethroat's leash. Then Janus stumbled over the sword and swore. "Damn thing. Enough, Gilly."

Janus limped over and settled himself on the edge of the stage. "Why do you carry that in the house?"

"I like to," Maledicte said.

"Savage tastes, my dark cavalier," Janus said, rubbing his shin.

Maledicte rejoined Gilly and touched the keys with curious fingers. "We really should have it tuned." He tugged Gilly's hair. "Maybe even hire an instructor."

Gilly laughed. "Is that your subtle way of telling me I'm an abysmal player? I'm not used to such from you."

"Say better than some, worse than many," Maledicte said. "A thing of no moment since you are perfection itself in all other fields of endeavor." He tucked his legs up beneath him and sat on the floor.

"A compliment and a sting at once. I applaud you," Gilly said.

"Gilly, it's not too soon to invite the Lovesys to Lastrest, is it?" Janus said, interrupting their banter. "I intend to ask them to Lastrest tomorrow."

"Sudden, but acceptable," Gilly said. "They will be aware of Aris's command to wed."

"How long will you be gone?" Maledicte said, laughter wiped away as quickly as blown sand.

"The standard visit is a fortnight," Gilly said. "Add time for travel, laden with luggage and the stops noble ladies insist upon? Three weeks."

Maledicte said nothing, still curled up like a boy on the floor. Janus went to his knee. "Mal?"

"I will go with you," he said, his voice a bare whisper, as if he recognized the impossibility even as he said it. Gilly heard Maledicte's breath coming faster, realized that somehow this step had caught him unawares. Maledicte would have to release Janus from his side, and Gilly, looking at Maledicte's stricken face, wondered if Maledicte would allow it.

"It won't be straightaway. Not only must I inform Lastrest's staff, and Father, but the spoiled chit probably will require a week to pack," Janus said, kissing the dark hair, tilting the pale face and kissing the tight lips. "But I cannot bring you while I court her. For a title so close to king, the duke and duchess seem willing to overlook you, but that is far easier if you're not nearby."

Gilly caught Janus looking not at Maledicte, but at him, and with an expression very close to hatred. "Gilly will be here. He can tell you stories, play the spinet badly for you, make you laugh. I'll be back as soon as I can. Rats take it, love, how long can I stand to be apart from you? You may have me running back within a week."

Maledicte's shivering passed to Janus. Gilly saw their past in their trembling bodies, the pain that Maledicte felt when Janus was stolen from his side. Gilly was dwarfed by it, his own uncomfortable urges made irrelevant. He could not see himself anything but an unwelcomed interloper, and it was left to Janus to soothe Maledicte while Gilly sat, trapped at the bench.

· 2 1 ·

GILLY WALKED INTO THE COOLING EVENING, seeking to clear his head, and found his steps taking a familiar path into the city. At Sybarite Street, he turned toward the brothel with the ship drawn above the door. As it catered to sailors, Gilly found more than simple carnal amusement there; his fantasies of the Explorations were fed. But tonight he bypassed the salon, with its laughing, drinking sailors, and headed upstairs. He tapped on a closed door. It was the night he usually reserved, but he hadn't let her know he was coming. Just as he decided she was with someone, the door opened and Lizette stood there, rubbing her red hair out of her face and yawning. "Gilly, I thought you weren't coming." She kissed his mouth. He leaned into her warmth, her encircling arms.

"But you look so sad tonight," she said, drawing him into the room. "That love of yours giving you trouble?"

"Not mine at all," Gilly said. "Never was. There's someone else." He kissed her neck and stroked her shoulders beneath her silken robe.

She took herself out of his reach and lit the candles by the bed while he set lunas down on the dresser. "Well, she's a right fool then. You're sweet and gentle and generous."

Paid compliments though they were, Gilly relaxed under them. "My employer already gets those things from me, without needing my love."

Lizette drew back. "Your master's that courtier, ain't it? Why would you want someone like that?"

"I didn't know you followed the court," Gilly said, settling himself onto the smooth sheets. He paid extra for clean ones on his nights, and she'd been sure enough of his custom that they were freshly laundered, smelling of nothing more than the iron and a faint trace of her perfume.

"Not the courts, Gilly. Just you. I saw your man once. At a distance and all. Thinks he's a king, don't he, the way he walks. But pretty enough to be a girl."

"Watch yourself," Gilly said. "He's fast with a sword and doesn't like being called a girl. No matter his tastes."

"Mmm, well maybe he'd make a bad girl at that. Too scrawny. Not like me." She guided his hand to her voluptuous breasts. He bent his head to greet them with a kiss.

"Lizette," he murmured.

"That's it, Gilly-boy. Don't waste your thoughts on the likes of him."

He stopped her mouth with his and she tickled his ribs until he laughed. She rolled him over, teased him with her trailing hair until he growled and tangled his hands in her locks, pulling her to him, merging his body with hers, thinking yes, Lizette was right. This was simple. This was easy. This was welcoming and warm, and the only shadows in the room were those from flickering candle flames, not unseen gods. But he kept his eyes open, to make sure he didn't trade the vision of her warmth and curves for the cool, austere, and oft-imagined lines of Maledicte.

Still, once they'd finished, Gilly left her side after only a cursory attempt at sleep, haunted by the premonitory instinct that warned him he would only dream of Black-Winged Ani. Better awake than that. He slipped out into the night, wending his way home through the back streets, and came across Echo's Particulars rousting a drunken man from his stupor at the base of a fountain.

After a passing glance, Gilly paused and went back, exchanging coins for the drunken man's freedom. Briskly, he walked the man back and forth until he moaned, "At least in a cell, I could have obtained rest."

"I'm only trying to help," Gilly said.

"Help? Buy me a drink," the intercessor said, staggering away toward the nearest pub. Gilly hesitated before following; he had heard the old man speak, had seen his eyes when he recognized Ani in Maledicte; this might be his only chance for answers beyond his books and pamphlets.

Gilly sat down in the seat opposite him, wincing at the smells of old stew and drunken leftovers. The intercessor sighed. "The servant in Dove Street, correct?"

"Yes," Gilly said, "Your name, Intercessor?"

"Not that anymore," the man said. "I've given up shouting the truth to a city of the deaf and forgetful. I'll join them in their willful oblivion."

"I need your advice," Gilly said, gesturing to a barmaid when it looked as if the intercessor would walk away. The barmaid brought two ales to the table and the intercessor settled back.

"No one listens," the intercessor said, raising his drink, draining half of it.

"I listen. It's my job," Gilly said.

"It was mine once," the intercessor said. "I spoke for the gods. Filtering their words until my ears bled. And now—I'm forgotten along with them. You—do you understand how it was? To be like a child, forced to hear his parents come to blows? Months of strife and no surcease—only the visions of the gods battling each other. Intercessors died in their sleep. Others avoided sleep and went mad. Madder. Then came blessed silence—a silence that rendered our lives without meaning, except to bear the blame of Baxit's final message. On Xipos, we were stoned. In Itarus, Grigor rounded up the intercessors, sick, mad, despairing, and plunged them into a frozen sea. So now, when the gods stir again, there's none to hear. . . ."

"I hear," Gilly said, his voice ragged, remembering Ani claiming Maledicte in his dreams.

The intercessor paused, set the drink down, and looked at Gilly. "You do. But then, you should have been one of us. I can see it in your face. Do you dream of tombs, boy? Where the occupants lie sleeping, but restless?"

Gilly took a gulp of the sour ale, and said, "I do."

The intercessor pushed his empty tankard aside, and when Gilly would have gestured the barmaid back, the man shook his head, looking weary. "What would you know?"

"They're not dead, are they?" Gilly asked.

"They're gods and immortal," the intercessor said. "They've only withdrawn. Was that your question, because I believe you knew the answer already."

"I need to know how to break a compact between Black-Winged Ani and Her follower."

The intercessor gaped, then said, "She's a god, and Her compact is more binding than anything mortal man can understand. There is no escape save in fulfillment. Oh, perhaps you could distract Her with charms asking for Baxit's aid, Her opposing force, but even if He bestirred himself from His indolence, it would only buy you moments. It would not undo Her will."

"Nothing can be done?" Gilly asked, aware of the desperate edge to his voice. He hadn't understood how much he had hoped for another possibility until the intercessor scoffed at it.

"If you truly have a care for your friend, you will help him accomplish Her bloody goal and complete the Compact."

"He'll die," Gilly said. "I can't allow—"

"Die?" the intercessor said. "You've been reading *Vengeances* by the sensation-monger Grayle. Nothing but corrupt scholarship there."

"He'll survive then?" Gilly said, the relief enormous.

"Quicker he acts, the likelier it is. But Ani's compact takes a toll. She grants gifts. Grayle will have told you that in his own hysterical fashion. But She also takes. I once visited a woman who is kept walled in a country asylum. Years ago, she climbed a turret in her wedding gown, carrying a dagger in one hand. She should have fallen. She didn't. She killed her husband, waiting for his lover. But she was left with the mind of a child. Ani is a creature of instinct and emotion, violence and passion, not intellect.

"In Elisande's case, it was a kindness, I think. Her mindlessness. Others have taken their own lives after, unable to bear the remorse, the grief. Ani feeds on their triumph and leaves them nothing. Aid your boy or not, care for him after, but do not expect him to remain the same."

"There must be some way to fight," Gilly cried.

"There is none," the intercessor snapped. "Do not treat the gods as if they are human." He snagged Gilly's ale and gulped it down, then when Gilly continued to sit in mute misery, said, "Boy—let me warn you of one thing further. I have seen several compacts play out, and never have I seen Her shadow so strongly as I did in your master. Grayle, for all his melodrama, is right in one thing. A certain type of follower, strong-willed, fierce-natured, clever, might be enough to let Her manifest, creating Her Avatar, a mingling of god and man. A creature who could destroy the city.

"Most of Ani's children hunger and kill, the compact finished before danger ever arises. But the longer they delay, the more Ani invests of Herself, and the greater the gifts: Immunity to poison. Immunity to hurt. Witchcraft. Finally, transformation of the flesh. If your master is as strong as I fear, you'll not only lose him, but likely your own life, and the lives of all those around you."

Gilly fled the man's bleak eyes and sought the tranquil dark waters of the nighttime pier, contemplating flight. But his panic paled in the memory of dark eyes and a mouth coaxed to sulky laughter. When dawn crept over the sea in streaks of gray and yellow, he turned his steps back toward Dove Street and Maledicte.

The house was silent when he returned, creeping through the kitchen door. The sun just risen, even Cook was barely awake. Setting the tea to steep, she jumped at the sight of him, and the teapot clattered from the hearth.

"Sorry," Gilly said, recovering it before it spilled.

"So you should be, sneaking up on a body like that," she said. "Where've you been, Gilly lad?"

"Out," Gilly said. Without his asking, she poured him tea. Gilly took the kitchen mug in his hand. He drank it in one scalding gulp, then tipped the cup over.

It was not what he wanted to see, but in the wake of his conversation with the intercessor, he was not surprised to find that again the leaves gave him no shape but the gallows. He shivered in the warming kitchen. There would be nothing but the gallows tree until Maledicte's vengeance was done. He knew that now. Another death approached? *Let it be Last,* he thought, *and the end of it.*

"You're too levelheaded a lad to believe in such things," she said, wiping the leaves up with a dishrag.

"Thank you for the tea," he said, escaping her scolding.

A light limned the edge of the library door, spilled a faint dusting of gold over the dark, carpeted hall, and Gilly paused before pushing the door open.

"Maledicte?"

"Come look at this, will you?" Maledicte said, bent over the desk. "Vornatti's solicitor, Bellington, brought it over last night after you'd gone. He wanted coin for it. I'm not used to paying for information, Gilly. I gave him what he asked without haggling. If you're going to be gone all night, you need to teach me such things." The look Maledicte sent him was faintly accusatory.

"How much did you give him?" Gilly asked.

"Ten lunas," Maledicte said.

Gilly winced. "Oh, he'll be back then. I hope the information was worth it."

Maledicte took his hand from the scroll of paper and it coiled again. "It's from Vornatti's spies abroad. The same ones who told us of Janus's return. Read it, Gilly."

Gilly did so, fighting through the tight script. "Vornatti's cousin, Dantalion, has an agent in Antyre?"

"A solicitor, supposedly. Janus and I are torn on what it means that, though we know he's in the kingdom, he's made no attempt to challenge the will that disinherited his client. No one's heard of him at all."

Gilly sat down, nerves singing.

"Gilly, what do you call a solicitor who shirks the law in favor of secrecy and prying?" Maledicte said, eyes dark. "I have a word in mind."

"Assassin," Gilly breathed. "Mal, you must be careful. An Itarusine lord is a dangerous foe on his own, and Dantalion is a crony of Last, and so will know more about us than perhaps is safe. Last could tell him your haunts and your favorite pasttimes."

Maledicte said, "Should I mew myself up behind these walls? I do not want to be a prisoner, kept away from all my hard-won freedoms." He was weary; Gilly saw it in the droop of his mouth, the pallor of his skin.

"We will hire agents of our own to find this man. Once found, he'll be no threat. Assassins thrive on secrecy, and Dantalion will have to find another route to recoup his losses," Gilly said, taking the letter. "I'll send runners out, and you—go back to bed."

"I could crawl into his arms and stay there forever, were it not that our enemies would find us," Maledicte said. "I know the path I've taken, and yet it galls me that I have nothing but enemies at my back. Even I weary of the fight."

"You may have enemies to spare, but you have allies as well. Janus, myself, even the king." Gilly tugged Mal to his feet. "It will be well, how can it not be? Are you not the scourge of the court, the terror of Last?" He cupped Maledicte's face in his hands, and allowed himself to kiss Maledicte's forehead. "Go to bed."

Maledicte rubbed his cheek into Gilly's palm like a contented cat, then stiffened and freed himself. "I trust you are right, that finding the man is as good as killing him. Because I intend to do so. I have no time for Dantalion's nonsense. I have an earl to kill, and an earl to create. Fortunately, though I may tire, Ani does not, and Her blade is sharp," Maledicte said, with a sudden surge of strength, an angry glitter in the black eyes.

Gilly, chilled again, watched Maledicte leave the room, and thought of the gallows tree and blood spilled beneath.

22

Stillheart, mostly used to facilitate battlefield surgeries, is a chancy pow-
der at best. The correct dosage is notoriously difficult to quantify, and
many a surgeon has finished his task only to find that the corpselike still-
ness of his patient is nothing less than death in truth.

—*A Lady's Treatise*, attributed to Sofia Grigorian

A LITTLE PAST THE FASHIONABLE hour of the evening, Maledicte and Janus were still at home, sitting in moody silence in the library.

From the dining room, they heard the maids laying the table for their last meal together. Without a word, Maledicte rose from his seat and straddled Janus's lap. Janus tugged Maledicte closer, resting his chin in the dark, loose curls.

"Sir," the newest butler said, entering. "There is a solicitor to see you."

"Gilly said Bellington would be back. But so quickly? I must have over-paid him dramatically."

The butler coughed. "It is not Bellington, sir, but another gentleman and, from the cut of his coat, foreign. Shall I show him in?"

"Why not?" Maledicte stood, pushing away from Janus's chest. "Perhaps he's heard I sought him and chose to save me the effort." Maledicte collected the sword, strapping it to his hip, ready for use. "But show him into the din-ing room. I see no reason to hold back supper."

Janus said, "I mislike him coming to us. It seems counter to his mission."

"Never question fortune," Maledicte said. "But I agree, he must be a most confident gentleman indeed."

The man stood in the dining room, the lean, well-dressed man Maledicte had seen in the park. Laughing at him. Maledicte's mood darkened.

"Maledicte, and Lord Last, is it not? How gracious of you to receive me."

"How obliging of you to come to us," Maledicte said, faintly startled to see that the man's wary eyes fixed not on Maledicte and his sword, but on Janus.

"I've had a task to do first," he said, "but with that accomplished, I'm aware of how little Dantalion is paying me." Unasked, he took a seat at the table. Deliberately, he laid a pistol before him, like an unexpected part of their place setting. "It is primed," he said. "And quicker to hand than that blade of yours. Still, keep it sheathed and all will be well."

"You want money from me?" Maledicte said. "Like some distant relative come a-begging?"

"You have no relatives," the solicitor said. "Unless you count a Relict whore. Dantalion chose not to challenge the will outright, not with Ixion, and some say Aris himself, sotted on you. So I sought levers and found such a lovely one, I can barely believe it, even now."

Maledicte sat down, leaned forward. "Tell me."

The solicitor said, "Not until Ixion takes his seat. I know his reputation and I don't want him at my throat. I doubt you'd grant me my pension if I had to shoot him."

Maledicte's breath sailed out in a rush. When he took it back, there was nothing but rage filling him, pure, cold, and smelling of feathers. "So far you've told me nothing worth a copper." He poured himself a glass of wine, settled himself, hitching his hip to allow for the sword's presence.

"I sought information on this black-haired boy from the Relicts and found nothing at all. As if he never existed. But I did hear stories about Janus. I found a quick talker in a Relict rat called Roach—you know him? A useful boy, hungry for coin, and short on moral qualms. He agreed to act my courier for certain letters if I fail to return to him tonight." The solicitor reached out for a goblet. "Will you quench my thirst, *Sir* Maledicte?"

Maledicte poured the glass. The solicitor's eyes never left his hands. "Do I have your attention?"

Janus said, "Roach is a liar."

"Only an inadvertent one. He told me Miranda was dead. I thought nothing of it, until I saw you in the park, Maledicte."

Maledicte shuddered, shaken to the core by hearing that name unexpectedly voiced.

The solicitor laughed. "I couldn't believe it—there you were, in a crowd of blind men. No one takes the time to look past expectation anymore. No one but me. So tell me, girl, what do I do now? Tell Dantalion that the will is invalid, or tell him nothing, and let you take care of me?"

"I will kill you," Maledicte said, voice raw with outrage, nearly shaking. He sought control. Murder in an aristocratic house took concentrated effort and planning.

"You're nothing but a girl, and I won't let your man get close enough."

Gilly tapped and entered. "Mal, Cook's waiting to serve." He paused, eyeing the stranger at the table. "Mal?"

"This is Dantalion's solicitor, come to blackmail us. I see no reason he cannot stay, so long as he understands that talking business during dinner is a killing offense." Maledicte's thoughts raced, calculating risk against risk, exposure versus letting the man disappear back into the shadows.

"Your house, *sir*," the solicitor said. "But I'm afraid I've taken someone's place; the table is set for three."

"I'll eat in the kitchen," Gilly said.

"I think not," the solicitor said. "I will not trust any of you near my food's preparation. Come, sit beside me and share my plate."

Maledicte lowered his head to disguise his sudden chagrin. He wanted the man dead, wanted it so badly he was willing to take any risk, with Ani spurring him on. He met Janus's eyes, read the communication there, that they could kill the solicitor before he could do more than wound one of them, but the servants were one wall away, and secrets were hard to keep. Best for the man to die silent and quick. If Dantalion's man could not trust them with his food, neither could they trust him to leave this house and keep to his word.

Maledicte dropped his hand to his sword, and watched the solicitor's eyes follow the movement and narrow. Death wouldn't be by blade; the man was warier than his confidence painted him.

"What is for supper, Gilly?" Maledicte said, buying time and thinking there was always poison, an Itarusine's love, but all Maledicte's potions were upstairs.

"Oysters from market."

Maledicte leaned back as he was served, watching the solicitor, trying to judge whether his wariness was only the usual thing, weapon-focused, or something more troublesome. He picked up an oyster shell, feeling the sharp, rippled edge.

"Gilly, is it?" the solicitor said. "I'll let you have the first bite."

"Too late," Maledicte said, dropping the empty shell to his plate. "They're good, Gilly."

"So you say," Janus said, poking at his with open revulsion. "If you loved me, Mal, you'd never serve them, no matter Aris's strictures on imported foods. I've seen the harbors here. The water's vile."

"The price of tablestuffs is ridiculous; Itarus gets the lion's share and leaves us to squabble over the rest, driving the price beyond reason. The nobles should learn to eat rats, as we did. Cure their impecunious ways."

"Must you bring the past into every conversation, Mal?" Janus scowled. "And we *never* ate rats. Filthy animals."

The solicitor grinned. "Hard to convince everyone you're Quality when they picture you in rags and rubble."

Janus surged from his seat, hand tightening around his dull table knife. Gilly flinched. The solicitor's eyes swung in Janus's direction, even at that minimal threat; his hand found the pistol beside his plate.

"Sit down, Janus. Don't let him distress you. After all, your breeding, illicit though it was, is surely more genteel than his," Maledicte said.

Janus nodded at Maledicte. "Ever my voice of reason."

Maledicte smiled back. The temper tantrum had done what he needed, shown the solicitor's predilections toward conventional weaponry. After all, he had focused on Janus and the dull knife, rather than Maledicte with a better edge to hand.

"Gilly, I'm done. And you've had to share. Would you like my last oyster?" Maledicte rose; the solicitor watched him walk, watched Janus, and rested his hand on the pistol.

"Open your mouth, Gilly," Maledicte said, sitting on the arm of Gilly's chair. "I'll feed you." Distantly, he trusted Gilly would play along, but Ani spread Her wings and the feeling of imminent bloodshed was so pleasurable, he smiled.

Gilly raised his head, parted his lips, and Maledicte tipped the oyster down. "Good?"

"Yes," Gilly said, swallowing, lips pale.

Maledicte kissed his forehead, and as he did so, the solicitor said, "Not content with one man? You are a wanton creature—"

The quick, slicing kiss of the ragged oyster shell across his neck shocked him into silence, into groping for the trigger. The wound was not deep; the breadth of Gilly's body and the chair robbed Maledicte of a killing blow. The solicitor shoved his seat back, a hand covering the bloody line. Maledicte swung again before the solicitor could bring the pistol to bear, and the second blow was messier, deeper, and quite fatal.

Maledicte slammed the shell into the solicitor's gasping mouth, silencing any attempt at an outcry, and then shoved him over the back of his chair.

"Gilly, get the doors," Maledicte said.

Gilly started out of his shock and darted to the doors, locking them. Janus seized the pistol from the solicitor's thrashing hands. "Mind the trigger," Maledicte warned. They stepped back; the man convulsed in silence, boots kicking at the overturned chair until Janus righted it.

Gilly's hands were at his mouth, shaking. He picked up Maledicte's wineglass, and drained its contents. Still, his hands trembled.

Maledicte joined him, reached out for his hands; Gilly drew back, his eyes on Maledicte's bloody fingers. "Go then. Flee if you must. But it had to be done." Maledicte toed the corpse; the solicitor made a spasming gasp. Maledicte wrinkled his nose in distaste. Gilly paled and fled.

Janus settled back into his seat and began picking through his cooling dinner. "I must do something about Roach. I should have done it when he told me I'd killed you. But I'll do it before I go. The solicitor was right about that. Roach does love his coin."

"Roach was my friend." Maledicte picked up a cloth, wet it in the finger bowl, and started washing his hands.

"Roach's tongue is a danger. Those letters are a danger." Janus's voice soothed and coaxed.

"Roach's probably lost them already," Maledicte said. "Or drunk away the coin meant to frank them. But if you worry so, go find him and bring him back here."

"Then there'd be two who knew your identity and soon after, multitudes, when Roach slips your secret to Gilly, to the maids, to the gossips on the street."

"We could warn him not to talk."

But Maledicte knew that Roach's discretion was not to be relied upon. Even as a child, he let information slip at the worst moments. Might as well expect Ella to learn modesty. "We could send him away?"

"Where?" Janus said. "He can barely manage the skills of a Relict rat."

Maledicte closed his eyes, his heart pounding. Janus could have been killed. Or Gilly, if the pistol had misfired. "We haven't time to hunt him down. Not now. We have to dispose of the solicitor tonight."

"The timing is unfortunate," Janus agreed. "But inescapable. Intercepting the letters before they're sent, taking them from Roach, is feasible. Intercepting them after they're sent is not. The solicitor gave us no word on the recipients. Dantalion, Aris, Echo, Last? Who knows how many? But Roach is easy; you could lure Roach out."

"Go back to the Relicts and chance being recognized? How many men do you want to see dead tonight? I've killed one man already." And night in the Relicts meant Ella would be trolling. What if she saw him, recognized him—would she see Vornatti lingering on his skin, know what he had become? "If you must go after Roach, you'll do it on your own."

The doors opened and Gilly returned, pale-faced but steady. "I sent the butler on an errand." His mouth twisted. "I blamed your eccentric desire for some *absente* and never mind about the hour. We'll have to get the body out the door—" Gilly blanched again, and Maledicte went around the table to see what had disturbed him.

Janus peered over the table and swore.

"What a mess. Indoor bloodlettings are so unforgiving without the earth to soak up the fluids." Janus joined them, and looked down at the corpse. "Still, dead is dead. That's the crux of it. Gilly, get the floor cleaned before the blood sets. Mal, get his feet—no, wait." Janus cleared the table, then yanked the tablecloth free and laid it out on the floor. "Now."

Janus and Maledicte levered the body onto the cloth; Janus went through the solicitor's pocket with quick, agile fingers, sorting coin and rubbish, before allowing Maledicte to wind the cloth tight. He handed the mixed pile of currency to Gilly, who looked at it with horror before dumping it onto the table.

"Where to?" Maledicte said. "The docks and the sea beyond?"

"No," Gilly said, his voice ragged. "Too many eyes."

"Loath as I am to agree with Gilly, he's right," Janus said. "The docks rarely sleep, or the Relicts. Wrap him tight and I will take him courting with me."

Gilly asked, "Will you really do that?"

"What else is there to do? Bury him out back? His ghost will not haunt me, I assure you." Janus bent, checked for seepage.

"Gilly, go confine the maids to their quarters so we can fetch water from the laundry," Maledicte said.

With the servants out of the way, the cleaning went faster; Gilly brought water and soap and removed the blood from the carpet, while Maledicte and Janus practiced winding cloths. When they had finished, they headed to the attic to locate a suitable trunk.

Alone in the room, Gilly was aware of his hands shaking again, pale red to the wrists. He kept tasting the sweet firmness of the oyster in his throat, followed by the sound of the solicitor's blood-soaked gasp. Gilly swore off blackmail on the spot.

Janus's casual appropriation of the solicitor's purse and pistol lingered with him, the absentminded way he wiped the smeared gore on his fingers on the man's shirt. He contrasted it to Maledicte's hungry stillness and sudden violence and wondered, not for the first time, which of them was more dangerous.

The slam of the trunk hitting the exposed floorboards jarred him from his thoughts.

"There," Janus said, hefting the body up across his shoulders with deceptive ease. "Not a leak to be sprung." He forced the body into the trunk and snapped the lid closed. Bending, he picked up the trunk itself and carried it out toward the carriage house.

Gilly scrubbed at the carpet; the wet cloth, pink-tinged now, shredded.

"Gilly, it's enough," Maledicte said, kneeling beside him.

"I just don't want to be able to see the stain."

"A new rug is in order," Maledicte said. "I find I no longer like the looks of it myself. But it could have been Janus's blood spilled there, or yours, or mine. The fact that he underestimated me made him no less of a danger. I acted as I had to. Forgive me for involving you?"

Wadding up the cloth in his hands, Gilly nodded.

"Will you do one thing more for me tonight?"

"Yes," Gilly said, hearing Lizette in his mind—*why love him?*—and he could not answer it now either, sick to his stomach and frightened, yet he met Maledicte's dark eyes, and the tallies began: freedom, friendship, money, and the strange workings that created desire where there should be none.

"Three deaths to my hand now, and I am no closer to killing the earl of Last than I was three years ago," Maledicte said, quietly. "But I tell you, Gilly, no matter the outcome of this marriage, I will have Last dead within the cold season. But I must have my chance at him; Janus feels there is another danger. Will you go with him tonight? Aid him as you can?"

Maledicte's eyes were glossy; Gilly could not tell if they were wet with unshed tears, or with anticipation. But, bloody rags in hand, he swore again to aid Maledicte.

GILLY LOOKED OVER HIS SHOULDER, eliciting an exasperated sigh from Janus. "What are you expecting to see? The solicitor climbing free from the trunk? You'll have us off the road."

"Why did we bring it along?" Gilly said.

"Do you think Mal wanted it underfoot?" Janus said. "We'll start with the docks. I wager Roach has his roots there. When I saw him, he was cleaning salt from his clothes. He's a skinny thing and dark, taller than Mal, but not nearly so pretty."

"I met a boy with that name some months ago," Gilly said. "A would-be thief working in a tavern called the Horned Bull."

Janus's hands tensed so tightly around the edge of the seat that they seemed carved of alabaster. "You spoke to him?" His voice, as quietly knotted as his hands, made Gilly nervous.

"Not much," Gilly said, trying to make that unaccountable anger disappear, feeling out his words in increments of Janus's stiffening or loosening hands. "He offered to housebreak at DeGuerre's for a fee. I turned him down."

"Nothing else?"

"He mentioned you. Said you taught him to read. He doesn't like you.

Said you'd killed his girl. How are you going to get him to come to you?" Gilly said, clopping his tongue at the horses as they shied from a drunk staggering down the cobblestone streets.

Janus sighed. "He's greedy and lazy and undoubtedly in need of coin. I expect he's whoring somewhere, passing time and waiting for the solicitor to return."

"You think him a whore?" Gilly could not reconcile the feral, defiant boy in the street outside the tavern with a pliant whore. "He seemed too thin for that."

"They're not all like your pretty one," Janus said, "put in gilded rooms where they eat sweets and wait for their men. The Relict whores are so different you might not even recognize them as human. They're not." The bitter edge to Janus's voice kept Gilly silent.

"Mal fell ill once when we were children; I thought he would die. He couldn't stop coughing and shivered so violently that I could barely hold him. Ella dosed him with enough Laudable to damn near drown him because his moaning and shaking was scaring away her customers, who couldn't tell Relict fever from plague. I spent the night with him in my arms, curled beneath the bed, wondering if he was going to wake, and Ella spent the night fucking above us. One sailor after another. That was before she realized Mal was going to be beautiful. Then she cared. But I cared first, and Mal is mine."

The whole speech was a near rasp, so choked with rage that Gilly felt it was Maledicte telling him this slice of nightmare. He drove on wordlessly; he barely knew how to soothe Maledicte; Janus was a mystery still.

Beside him, Janus's ragged breathing steadied, but he didn't speak again until they were at the Horned Bull. "Go see if Roach still works there."

Gilly clambered off the bench and went inside. He nodded at the taverner and slipped into the kitchens.

"What do you want?" A heavyset woman looked up from the hearth where she was stirring a fish stew so old and salty Gilly could smell it across the room.

"Looking for Roach," Gilly said.

"He don't work here anymore. Not that he ever did more than rob our customers when they got too castaway to notice. Lift your purse, did he?"

"Something like that," Gilly said.

"Try down by the cheap brothels. He's like to be trying his hand at robbing drunken sailors. Sooner or later, he'll try the wrong man, get hisself killed. If Echo's Particulars don't catch him first. Stupid rat."

Gilly nodded his thanks, and continued out the back door, circling around the building, checking the shadows. A black-haired young man in cheap clothing stepped out of an expensive carriage, drawing Gilly's attention. The boy tossed a luna from palm to palm, and blew a kiss after the retreating coach. "Mal—" Gilly breathed, but even as he did so, he realized his error. The boy vamped at him, all painted lips and eyes, and headed into the tavern.

"Another Itarusine sailor's get, I'd imagine," Janus said, his voice velvet and sudden in Gilly's ear. "But a startling resemblance, nonetheless."

Gilly jumped. "Yes," he said.

Janus flashed a quick, malicious smile. "Though if I were you, I'd not tell Mal you mistook a rented boy for him."

"I'm not a fool," Gilly said.

Janus raised a brow. "What did they say, within?"

"That he had turned to robbing brothel customers." He climbed up onto the bench. Janus joined him and took up the reins.

"I bet he's not even stripping them of their boots," Janus said, urging the horses into a bone-jarring trot across the cobbles. "Let's finish this and go home. I shudder to think what Maledicte has done to the house this time."

"He has no regrets over the solicitor's death, and he's past the worst part of accepting your marriage. What is there to upset him?"

"With Maledicte, sometimes I think it's the shifting of the wind."

Gilly turned his head as they came onto Sybarite Street, smiled at the sight of the familiar door painted with the sailing ship.

"Thinking of your girl?" Janus said. "What's her name?"

"It doesn't matter," Gilly said, leery of Janus's interest.

Janus drove, avoiding the whores advertising in the street, avoiding the clusters of young men daring each other to bravery in the fields of love, the hired whisperers who haunted the street, murmuring of places where one could go to buy smuggled Itarusine whiskey or other illicit imports, and as the street grew darker and less well-kept, avoiding the rubble they could barely see. "Gilly, get down. Look for him. If you find him, don't waste time chatting, but bring him back. I'd do it, but I think you would not like being left with the trunk."

"No," Gilly agreed, dropping from the side of the carriage, and wandering into the dark alone, hunting for a half-remembered pickpocket. Abstraction lent an air of drunkenness he hadn't intended, and the first he knew of Roach's presence was the skinny wrist reaching for his purse, even as the stick missed Gilly's head entirely. "Stop that," Gilly said, grabbing the stick, the thin-boned wrist with practiced quickness.

"I remember you. What do you want?" Roach rubbed his wrist ruefully. "Caught me just as quick this time."

"Information. I'll pay," Gilly said. He closed his fist, opened it, and a silver luna caught the light, a strayed bit of starshine.

"All right then," Roach said, snatching the coin. "What do you want to know?"

"Not me, a friend. He's a poet, wants to write verses about the Relicts, wants it to be romantic." Gilly was surprised he even bothered to lie. The hunger in Roach's eyes, the lack of caution, spoke volumes. Roach didn't care for anything but the sight of silver.

"Verses about the Relicts? Is he touched?" Roach frowned. "Going to write about rats and boots and fever, is he?"

"No, he's another one who wants to write about Black-Winged Ani bringing down the Relicts for love," Gilly said, thinking he had been too long exposed to the court, finding it all too easy to envision his imaginary poet. He took Roach's arm in his hand.

"How much is he gonna pay?" Roach said.

"He's a poet without a patron. Not much. Maybe two lunas." More and even Roach might find suspicion, but Gilly had given him coin before, easy earnings, and this looked the same.

"Can't take too long. I'm meeting someone," Roach said, even as he followed in Gilly's wake.

"Ain't that a fancy rig?" Roach said as they approached the carriage. "And your man ain't got more coins than that?"

"Paper's expensive, as are quills," Gilly said.

"I bet they are," Roach said, turning over new thoughts. "Where's your fancy man?"

"He was here," Gilly said.

The reins were weighted with a cobble; the carriage door hung off the latch. Gilly wondered what had happened, a soundless struggle? Or had Janus simply grown bored with waiting?

Roach opened the carriage door and peered inside. "Ain't that fine."

Gilly picked up the reins and looked up to see Janus come out of a shadow, the knife aimed for Roach's nape. Gilly gasped, but Roach was already crumpling forward. Janus bent in the same quick economy of motion and shoved the body into the carriage, closing the door.

"Don't gape, get on the bench, and let's go." Janus swung himself up, setting the carriage to rocking, and held down his hand. "Gilly! Let's not attract more notice than the carriage will have already. Get up, or I leave you here."

Gilly saw the temper flaring in Janus's pinched nostrils, in the swelling blueness of his eyes, but he could not respond. He remembered Roach's desperate insouciance, the thinness of his arm beneath his hand, and his awe of the carriage, all snuffed out in one moment.

Janus snapped the reins and turned the carriage. "Last chance, Gilly. There is still some night left and I don't mean to spend it haranguing you when I could spend it in Mal's arms. No? Fine." The carriage wheels spattered loose bits of sand and gravel over Gilly's boots. He watched it go, and only then started the long walk home.

It was nearer dawn than midnight when he opened the doors and crept through dark halls. As he approached the stairs, a light flared and smoked, setting shadows to dancing in the narrow stairwell. "Do you realize you always use the servants' stairs when you're upset?"

Maledicte was still dressed as he had been for dinner; dark splotches remained where the blood stained his cuffs.

"Did you know he was going to kill him when you sent me?" Gilly asked. His voice shook. He took a seat on the riser below Maledicte when the tremble in his voice reached his legs.

"Yes," Maledicte said, looking away.

"Why?" Gilly cried. "He was just a boy. The solicitor I understand, Kritos, even Vornatti, but this boy . . ."

"He knew things Janus thought best left unsaid, a gossip as deadly as Mirabile," Maledicte said, setting the lamp on the stairs above his head, haloing them both.

Maledicte's voice was all Gilly heard. He refused to look at him, not wanting to be distracted by the dark eyes, by the lush mouth, by his own desire. "You killed the solicitor. Who else would think to talk to a rat? Why not pay him to go away? Or send him to the sea as aristocrats have done as long as there have been sailing vessels and inconvenient people—" Gilly's voice broke.

The lamp flared and popped as impurities in the oil burned, and in the silence after those small explosions, Maledicte said, "There was more to it, Gilly. I was scared, and Janus was so sure. But he never liked Roach. Not ever." Maledicte let his breath out in a shivering gust, as if he had caught Gilly's quaking.

"Don't ever send me out again to lure someone to their death," Gilly said. "I cannot do that. I will aid you in any other capacity I can. But please, Mal—don't make me kill for you."

"Hush." Maledicte drew Gilly's head into his lap, stroked back the fair hair, streaked damp with night fogs. "I promise. Never again. Not ever. I'm so sorry, Gilly. So sorry."

He smoothed the pale hair, spreading it over his lap like a gilt mesh, until Gilly's trembling ceased, and the lamp was beginning to gutter, unaware of Janus standing at the top of the staircase.

23

ARIS PAUSED IN THE FOYER of the Westfall city estate and watched Westfall's face, never as restrained as
the other nobility, reveal his surprise as Aris nodded
and moved on, dog and guards in tow. Aris smiled; he was surprised himself. Westfall's periodic afternoon parties were really no such
thing. If the attendees found amusements, it was through avoiding Westfall,
who used the occasions to argue his interest in the equality of the classes, his
remarkable engines, and the future world to come.

"Sire," Lord Echo said, stepping alongside him. "I didn't think to see you
here."

"I'm sure that will be a sentiment I hear frequently this afternoon. And
I'm equally sure that Westfall's cause will draw new interest. I do like to keep
my counselors content," Aris said, and while true, it was far from the entirety
of the truth: He had attended for one reason only.

"Thus you attend an affair you have little interest in," Echo said, with the
ease of long acquaintance.

"It's the industrial aspect that flummoxes me, Dominick," Aris said. "How
Adam thinks that machines that increase the rate of production will aid us
when the problem remains the same—that our profits are not our own. I see
little reason to benefit Itarus."

"Eventually the terms of surrender will end, our concessions fulfilled,"
Echo said.

"And in the meantime, Westfall's engines will replace the working poor."
Aris shook his head. "What both you and Westfall forget is that a country is
not built on machines, but its people. All of them."

"The poor are—"

Aris put a hand up, halting Echo. "If you'll excuse me, I came here to ap-
pease Adam, not listen to his ideas. And I think you spend too much time
among the sordid types of our city. It makes you bitter, unable to see that
good exists on all levels. My offer still stands. Join my Kingsguard and I'll see
you at its head."

"Your Kingsguard, sire, is not a thinking thing, but an army. I prefer to
solve problems."

"As you will, then," Aris said. When Echo would have followed, Aris
shook his head, and Echo dropped back. Aris moved on, unimpeded, as the
small crowd bowed before him. So many familiar faces turned toward him,
and yet the one he wished to see eluded him. He frowned at the sight of
Mirabile whispering into Brierly's ear, wondering what poison the woman
cared to spread now, and if her presence meant Maledicte's absence. Aris
tapped his fingers impatiently against his thigh, and Bane trotted forward to
pant heavily by his side.

Aris slipped into the cool hallways, still seeking. He had expected to see
more of Maledicte, now that the young man held the ledgers over his head.
Until Janus had left Murne with Amarantha Lovesy, Aris had expected
Maledicte to use the ledgers to derail Aris's requirement that Janus wed. Perhaps Maledicte had been in earnest after all, when he claimed he had no intentions of using the ledgers against Aris. Aris wanted badly to believe that,
and not simply for the safety of Antyre.

He finally found Maledicte studying a portrait of a fair-haired woman in
Westfall's family gallery. Maledicte frowned and spoke quietly to his servant.

"Lady Rosamunde, Celia Rosamunde's mother, and Janus's grandmother.
I believe she was a distant cousin of the Westfalls." The servant's words came
clear as Aris approached.

Maledicte seemed uncharacteristically at a loss for words, lips parting.
He touched the painting. "Celia looks much like her."

"The whole point of aristocratic breeding," the servant said. "Put a stamp of
heredity on the children's faces, even if it requires inbreeding and creates idiots."

The guard coughed, and the servant turned, paling. He dropped to his knee. Maledicte's smile faded, his eyes growing wary. He put a hand on his servant's shoulder.

"You may rise," Aris said. "Your sentiments are not new, I assure you. If I spent all my time punishing them, I'd have no time left to rule."

The servant nodded and stood, uncertain.

"You may leave us," Aris said. The servant glanced at Maledicte for permission, caught himself, and bowed again before leaving.

Maledicte shook his head. "He'll be fretted for weeks about that. It's my fault entirely. I've allowed him to be as free with his thoughts as he likes."

"It's not his thoughts that will see him in trouble," Aris said, "but his tongue."

"Still—it's pleasant to have an honest opinion," Maledicte said. "Rare and pleasant." He turned back to the wall of portraits.

"Yes," Aris said, nearly a whisper, startled again at the warmth he felt near this lad. He cleared his throat. "I have to admit to some surprise at finding you here. Adam's afternoon entertainments are known to be deadly bores."

"Then why do you attend?" Maledicte asked, frowning at another painting of a corpulent gentleman in furs.

"I asked for the attendee list," Aris said. "Once I saw that you meant to attend—" Pleased, he watched a fragile blush touch Maledicte's cheek.

"Oh, and what have I to say that lures you to brave such dullness as egalitarianism and economics?" Maledicte asked, his tone a little stiff.

Aris caught Maledicte's quick glance at the guard and changed the subject. "I thought you might tell me how goes Janus's courting? Michel knows nothing. And Amarantha—"

"You ask me that?" Maledicte said, his voice dropping to an offended hush. "Do you think Janus pauses in his wooing to send me accounts of it?"

"I don't know what to think," Aris said, his own temper sparking. "Janus has sent no word. To be honest, I had not expected such a political choice of wife from him. I thought him unconcerned with court ways and yet . . . Amarantha is a difficult woman at best."

"But very beautiful," Maledicte said, his tone still distant. "And perhaps he thought the choice would be pleasing to you. A counselor's daughter."

"You hold his wooing her against me," Aris said. The weight of his distress startled him. But what had he expected?

"We all do what we must," Maledicte said, and to Aris, the quiet weariness in his voice sounded like forgiveness.

"Still, I hate to think I played a part in making you unhappy. Were it in my power—I'd grant your wishes." Daring, he stroked the soft curls clustered at Maledicte's nape.

"I don't believe you would," Maledicte said, lips curling into a slow smile.

"No?" Aris said. "Won't you tell me what drives you? What brought you to my court?"

Maledicte looked up through dark lashes, his eyes merciless. "Janus."

"Just that," Aris sighed. He took a step back. "Is it true what the gossips say? That you knew him before? That you were—"

"A Relict rat?" Maledicte finished. "I fear my secrets are no secrets at all. But I'd rather not discuss that, if you'll indulge this wish. The past is past, Aris."

"No," Aris said. "It's never past. Not when everything reminds you of what you've done or lost." He cupped Maledicte's chin, brushed his thumb over the soft lips, and watched the dark eyes shade yet darker. "Was I wrong?" he whispered. "To surrender Xipos to Itarus, to barter our future away for our present?"

Maledicte laughed. "You ask me? The war was before my time, sire."

That young? Aris thought, finding it a strange relief that here was one person who could not force him to relive the pains of his past. He drew closer.

Maledicte's eyes flickered over Aris's shoulder.

"He's only my guard," Aris said. "He doesn't matter."

Maledicte slipped from his grasp. "Aris—how can you say that here? In Westfall's home, where all men are equal?" The mockery seemed evenly apportioned between Westfall's follies and Aris's own.

A sudden shout tore the quiet, and the mutter of voices in the next rooms rose.

The guard swore; the mastiff lunged to attention, pushing between Aris and Maledicte, growling. His hackles bristled.

"Find out," Aris said, resting a hand on Bane's withers. "I'm safe enough."

Another mocking smile bloomed in response. "Do you think your counselors, your *brother* would agree to that? Alone with me—and safe?"

"Why must it matter so much what they think?" Aris said, answering the tone and not the words. He felt suffocated.

"Because, sire," Maledicte said, "you belong to them, not they to you."

Aris knew the truth of that by the weight it left on his heart.

"Do you still think my company safe?" Maledicte asked, reaching out. He laid his hand over the king's. Bane's growling ceased.

Aris couldn't tell if it were his hand trembling or the hound beneath it. "Safe enough," Aris whispered. He leaned forward to taste Maledicte's lips, to see if they were as sweet as they looked, or as bitter as the words he spoke.

"Nothing of importance, sire," the guard said, returning. Maledicte stepped away. "Lady Mirabile's hem was torn by a servant. Done deliberately, she swore. Your brother is taking the whip to him now."

"That temper of his," Aris said, shaking his head. "Find out whose servant I will need to replace."

"It's yours, Maledicte." The guard acknowledged Maledicte's presence for the first time.

Rage washed Maledicte's face, transforming it so utterly that Aris froze and Bane keened uncertainly. Courtier or not, Maledicte ran from the room like an arrow in flight. "Go!" Aris said to the guard, but to protect Maledicte from Michel or the reverse, he didn't know. Hand wrapped around Bane's collar, he followed more discreetly.

The green lines of the garden maze were marred with the violence. West-fall dithered, plucking at Last's sleeve, while Last worked the whip back into his palm. Beside him, Mirabile watched, a tiny smile on her lips.

The servant knelt, half-fallen, pressed back against the hedge, his shirt torn and the skin beneath bloody. He put his hand to the wound, heedless of the whip being drawn back again, and the look of such utter shock on his face told Aris that whatever flaws Maledicte had, beating his servants was not one of them.

Maledicte interposed his slender shape between Aris's sight and the servant. A faint growl of pleasure rose from Last's throat as he set the whip flying again. The whistle of it sang in the air. "No, Michel, I forbid it," Aris shouted, but the stroke had been sent.

Turning as if possessed of a snake's quickness, Maledicte moved to meet the lash head-on. Aris flinched, but when the snap-crack of contact sounded, the scene had changed. Maledicte held the lash's tip in his hand, firm against Last's tugging. The air darkened and drew close.

Last put his weight into the effort to free the whip, his face purpling with rage and embarrassment. Maledicte stood unbudging, his face remote. His other hand dropped to the hilt of his sword and drew a fist length of steel.

Bane growled, low and uncertain, crowding against Aris's hip, nudging Aris's numb fingers.

Maledicte's gaze, as black as city smoke, fell on him and Aris looked away, unable to meet the empty rage in it. Then Maledicte's dark lashes fell and rose and he was simply another courtier in a temper. He released his grip on the hilt; the sheath swallowed the blade.

"If this is a taste of your vaunted equality, Westfall," Maledicte said, "and the people you choose to build futures with, I don't fancy your chances."

Westfall flushed.

"You insult the king," Last said.

"Do I?" Maledicte asked, tugging his servant to his feet and supporting him. "I thought I insulted you."

Last snarled, his hand clenched on the whip handle again. "I will insure that Janus never sees you again."

"Janus cannot leave me alone. He's mad for the touch of my hands, my mouth; he begs for me at night. When you are dead, I will lie in your bed while you lie in the ground, one more unmourned ancestor, and I will be free to do as I see fit," he said, his voice so laced with venom that Aris half expected to see Last finally subject to apoplexy.

"May I take my leave, sire?" Maledicte asked but turned away without waiting for an answer.

"Mal," Aris said, his voice rough. "Are you—hurt? Your hand is bloody."

"It's not mine," Maledicte said, closing his fingers over the clotting gore. He turned his head and said something softly to the servant, and then they made their way out of the garden. Mirabile dropped a curtsy as Maledicte neared her, and he widened his path to give her a wide berth. Aris watched and worried. Maledicte had faced Last without hesitation or the merest sign of fear, yet skirted Mirabile. Her expression was no longer that pleased half smile, content that a man was whipped for her whim, but something darker, and far more calculating. She swept back into the house, her skirts trailing behind her, undamaged despite her claims otherwise. Aris frowned.

"It's witchcraft," Last spat, drawing his attention. "Did you not hear anything he said?"

"I heard a young man in a temper, showing remarkable loyalty to a servant," Aris said. He turned his unease on his brother, and his tone was cold and unwelcoming.

"You are witched. Do you think I failed to notice you seeking him out? Ask yourself what draws you so?" Last said again, and as if he meant it more than angry words. "Ask yourself what kind of man can take the lash's touch unscathed?"

"A proud one who refuses to acknowledge hurt," Aris said. "What man brings a whip to beat a clumsy servant and turns it on a peer of the realm? I think you've been too much in the city, Michel. Some rest might suit you. Go home to Lastrest."

Last grated out, "As you command, sire." He turned toward the stables, and said, more temperately, "He is dangerous, Aris. I hope you never have cause to regret the license you grant him."

"Michel," Aris said, his temper fading, but Last walked away. Aris sighed, and sat on a garden bench, taking care to choose one that did not overlook the hedge where blood still spattered the leaves and lawn.

MICHEL IXION, EARL OF LAST, lay in wait. He had arrived at Lastrest to find that Janus and Lady Amarantha were riding the grounds, but his temper demanded instant expression. So instead of busying himself with his correspondence, his bills, his petitioners, he sat in his reading room, the double doors wide to the hall and the front door, the leaded windows opened over rosebushes and the smoothly clipped lawn, waiting for the first sound of their return.

A day and a half's hard travel and distance from Maledicte's insolent mouth had not eased his temper; firecracker spurts of rage still flared beneath his outward composure.

He heard the hoofbeats first, drumming toward the stable, hooves spattering the fine gravel of the drive, and he frowned. They should have more care for the tender hooves of his livestock. Even as he thought that, he heard a woman's voice raised and the horses slowed.

Some minutes later, the front doors opened and two sets of footsteps rang against the marble floor of the foyer. He rose and went into the hall. Janus and Amarantha dallied there, shedding gloves. Amarantha's cheeks were flushed, and Last thought the heat under her skin due to temper and not exertion, judging so from the rigidity of Janus's smiling countenance, from the slap of her leather gloves striking the hall table.

"Janus, I must speak with you at once," he said, in lieu of greeting.

"If you must," Janus said.

"At once," Last repeated, irritated anew at Janus's laconic acknowledgment.

Amarantha said, in a remote tone, "Courtesy is owed to one's elders."

Janus's face went brittle; then he recovered his smile. "Father, have you met Lady Amarantha?" Janus said, drawing her forward. "I believe you well acquainted with her parents."

"It's been some time since I've last had the pleasure," the earl said, frustrated in his desire to speak his mind at once. He bowed with careful formality.

Lady Amarantha shrugged out of her riding coat, ignored Janus's waiting hand, and dropped it over her gloves. She curtsied and held her hand toward Last. "I remember you, of course. Father speaks highly of you. I am most grateful for your hospitality, my lord. This is a lovely and well-ordered estate."

Last took her hand in his and raised her curled fingers to his mouth, thinking that Lovesy's daughter had grown into an uncommonly pretty woman. "I hope Janus has been making you welcome."

"He has done his best," Amarantha said. "If you will excuse me, I will change." She nodded again in the earl's direction before ascending the broad stairs.

"She seems a bit short with you," Last said, bemusement doing what time had not, cooling his temper. "What have you done?"

"Nothing pleasing, according to her," Janus said, looking after the retreating tail of her riding habit. "However, I have vowed reform."

"Yes," Last said, his brows folding downward again. "Come with me." He led the way into the study, closing the doors behind them.

"I am at your disposal," Janus said, sketching a bow, darkening the earl's frown.

"Perhaps she finds your manner flippant. It is remarkable that Lovesy will even consider a match. Were I you, I would not jeopardize my chances with mannerisms borrowed from a scandalous source." Last closed the windows, and turned the key of the gas lamp up to push away the resultant dimness.

"Maledicte, you mean," Janus said, sitting opposite Last's study desk.

"I do," Last said, his temper flaring like a wick touched by flame. He took his chair, aware of protesting stiffness in his hips and other joints. Once, the journey from the city to Lastrest took him a day, galloping on horseback. Now, a carriage trip left him stiff and sore.

"This marriage of yours is well thought," he said, testing Janus's mood, since the calm face revealed nothing. "Despite the story we have put about, you are nothing but a bastard."

"And Amarantha is no longer virgin. Which is more scorned by the court? Bastard or slut?" Boredom flashed over his face; he stifled a yawn.

"You will not speak of a lady in that fashion." The earl continued, "I am not as unquestioning as Aris. To truly convince me of your sincerity to the line of Last, you must end your unsuitable alliance with that creature and eradicate the unfortunate influence he has had on your tongue and manners. Or I will take steps of my own."

Janus smiled. "Every boy sows his wild oats to the distress of his parents. Actresses, whores, dancers, peasants . . . scandalous courtiers. I daresay Mal's attraction will pall; for now, I find too much enjoyment in his company to be rid of him so precipitously. But I will endeavor to convince Lady Amarantha and yourself of my sincerity toward the line of Last."

"Your creature thinks to set up house here," the earl said, his tone darkening at the memory.

Janus sighed. "Such a wild mouth on him. He says things merely for effect and to watch people rage. You must have pleased him mightily."

"Until I took the whip to him," Last said.

The distant amusement in Janus's face vanished, then reappeared so quickly that if Last had not been studying Janus closely, he would have missed it. The realization chilled him. His son was not only a stranger, but an able liar. Last was forced to recognize that he could not believe anything Janus said. That phantom blaze in the pale eyes, that hot rage, convinced the earl of one thing: Maledicte, wretched creature that he was, spoke truth. More truth than he had from this stranger sitting across from him. Dread seeped into his bones, quenching his anger with caution.

"Go away," Last said, rising from his seat. To make too much of the conversation would be to reveal his shock, so he resorted to a simpler anger. "Repair your tongue before you speak with Amarantha again. We will discuss your influences when you are in more of a humor to take this seriously."

"Sir." Janus bowed and left the room.

Last sat alone in his study, thinking. Perhaps Maledicte, with his open enmity, was the lesser danger. Resolve tightened his mouth, shook the last trepidation from his mind. Janus would not find his way to the title so easy. Last would insure that.

A folded letter caught his attention; discarded a week ago, now it beckoned him. Dantalion bemoaned that his agent had disappeared and asked counsel. Last had further advice for him now.

Looking up from his work with quill and parchment, he saw Lady Amarantha descend the stairs in a wash of buttery yellow that set off her pale beauty like a diamond set in gold. Rising, Last went to the window, broke off the first scarlet blossom to hand, and met her in the hall.

· 24 ·

W HAT SAYS JANUS?" GILLY ASKED, twisting in his seat, testing the sting and pull of healing scabs. He glanced over the emptied plates and soiled silverware to Maledicte, lounging in his chair, boots on the table, letter in hand.

"Stop squirming, you'll have them open again. And as you were such a baby about their bandaging, I'd prefer not to do it again," Maledicte said without looking up. His booted feet knocked over his wineglass as he shifted; his brows furrowed as he squinted at the letter, a little beyond the range of candlelight.

"Janus says that all is well, save that Last and Amarantha are trying to drown him in examples of proper etiquette. He asks if I am well, after Last's assault with the whip—hmm, some misunderstanding there, I see, though perhaps Last has rewritten his memories."

"I don't wonder at it," Gilly said. "There seems to be a good deal of that in the court." Maledicte shrugged, leaving Gilly to his own dark memories, that he had not gone within ten feet of Mirabile, fearing her nails, her temper, and yet, they all believed her when she spoke against him. He fisted his hands, wishing it were only that her words had the weight of aristocracy behind them, and fearing it was more.

Maledicte continued reading. "He writes that Amarantha is a difficult woman but that Last seems inclined to make the match work, spending time with Amarantha when Janus cannot." Maledicte reached for his glass, chuffed in disgust when he found it tipped and his fingers wet. He rose and went to the sideboard to pour himself another glassful.

"I don't like that," Gilly said.

"No," Maledicte agreed, concern pinching his features. "Are you going out tonight?"

"I meant to. I'll stay if you want me." Gilly reconsidered his visit to Lizette's. He felt as if he were back in the country, watching his family race to protect their crops from a looming storm.

"And deprive you of your fun? No, if I do that, you'll make do with Livia, and I'm running low on Harlot's Friend. I swear you are a worse rake than Vornatti."

"Quantity makes up for quality," Gilly said, startled as the words came out of his mouth, unsure of his own meaning. Belated awareness dawned red and hot on his face and neck. He pulled his glass back to him and drank, avoiding Maledicte's eyes, trying not to let Maledicte see his hunger. Quality, he thought, letting his eyes rest on Maledicte's pale hands.

Maledicte laughed. "And they think my tongue vicious. If that is the case, by all means, go to your girl."

"I can stay," Gilly said.

"Don't be foolish," Maledicte said. "Go on, then. She'll be disappointed, otherwise."

"Only at the lack of coin," Gilly said, conscious that he wronged Lizette, but torn between her softness and the odd coziness of being alone with Maledicte.

"You sell yourself short," Maledicte said. "Those shoulders, that sweet face."

His gaze raked Gilly from head to toe in a speculative, appreciative fashion and a second flush of embarrassment rushed Gilly's skin.

Gilly remembered Maledicte bandaging the whip's stripe, bent so close that his hair had brushed Gilly's bared chest. It had been that touch that set him squirming. He stood, half-naked, with Maledicte's light fingers on him, and yet Gilly had never so much as seen the white lines of Maledicte's shoulders or the sinews of his back or thigh.

Gilly had shifted from foot to foot until Maledicte laughed. "If you're that agile, you can't be much hurt," he had said, "But really, Gilly, did no one ever teach you to step away from the whip?" He stroked the last plaster into place; it tugged the skin taut over his ribs. Gilly winced, desire and embarrassment forgotten.

"This hurts out of all reason," he said.

"It's the hatred behind it that festers," Maledicte said. "Be glad you were not born a sailor on one of your beloved ships, or you would have felt the whip long ago."

"Not I," Gilly said, "I would have been a perfect sailor. They would have made me first mate by now."

Maledicte laughed. "With your hair bleached white, and your skin burned brown, running around in torn breeches—" He smiled at Gilly with a considering light in his eyes and Gilly felt warmth bloom deep within his body. Maledicte stepped closer, stroked Gilly's cheek, and Gilly's ardor cooled. He moved away from the touch, from Maledicte's hand.

Shadows chased themselves across Maledicte's eyes.

"Your hand," Gilly said. "Where you caught the whip—your injury's gone without a mark. I still bleed."

Gilly remembered that now, as he dithered between leaving and staying, the storm-cloud feel of fate in the air, and the lingering presence of Ani in Maledicte's eyes.

"What, a compliment renders you dumb?" Maledicte said.

Gilly flickered a smile, and nodded. "I will go out."

He shrugged on his coat against the evening's coolness and opened the front door, startling a young messenger, hand upraised to knock. Gilly closed his eyes in acknowledgment. The storm, he thought, had come.

"Message?" the boy squeaked, still nervous.

"Yes," Gilly said, "I'll take it." He handed the boy a coin, and went back in, holding the sheet sealed with blue wax as if the weight of the world hung from it.

"Not gone?" Maledicte said.

"Janus sent this," Gilly said. He dropped it before Maledicte, on the white tablecloth marred with spilled wine.

Maledicte broke the seal. He let the note fall to the table, his face white, his fingers clenching on open air as if he would do battle if he only had the blade at his side.

Gilly recognized Janus's black scrawl at once. There was only one line on the note.

Father wed Amarantha Lovesy last night.

"I should have killed him the moment he first stepped within my reach and damned the consequences," Maledicte said, surging to his feet.

"Only a setback," Gilly said, trying to keep the bloody light in Maledicte's eyes from flooding outward.

Maledicte hurled first his plate against the door, then Gilly's; at the shattering china, a maid poked her head in and as quickly withdrew it. "Setback? Last has wed. Had he ever intended Janus to follow him, he would never have married. It is more than a counter, Gilly, it's Last's declaration that he will stymie us any fashion he can. I've waited too long, too lulled by your talk of consequences and Janus's mercenary considerations and caution."

"And how will you kill Last? His murder will be treason, Mal. Janus might well inherit by murder, it's happened before, but you . . . you would be forced to flee. Alone. Or do you think Janus would give up a title for—"

"Get out, Gilly," Maledicte said, voice thinned to a thread. The sword bloomed in his hand and the black light rose in his eyes.

Gilly edged away from the blade that tracked him, from the insane anger in dark eyes, until he reached the door.

In the center of the room, Maledicte sparred with shadows that crawled out from the walls to meet him. Maledicte shivered as if in a fit, the shadows ripping at the touch of the blade, spilling slow darkness. Kritos's dark shape, last seen lunging toward them in an alley, rose up behind Maledicte, and Gilly gasped. But Maledicte turned like a somnambulist and struck him down once more. Remembered triumph lit his face and he slowed his swordplay, tension in his eyes slackening, his lips parting. He shuddered all over, and he pressed the sword into the floor, skewering Kritos's corpse. He slumped. The shadows hovered.

Gilly returned in a rush, bearing Maledicte away from the blade, grabbing the slender shoulders hard enough that he knew Maledicte would bear bruises tomorrow, if Ani allowed it. Maledicte emitted a wordless shriek of rage, a vibration in the ravaged throat, and then Gilly was holding a madman.

Gilly yowled as Maledicte's teeth bloodied his knuckles, as Maledicte's elbows found his sore ribs. But he held on, like trying to cage a raptor, pinning it without damaging the fragile bones, all the time aware of the beak and the talons and the snapping edges of wings pulled taut.

"You cannot give in to this," Gilly said, his mouth near choked with Maledicte's hair. "Now, more than ever, you need reason and patience, not blind rage. You must be cunning, must be clever, must be careful." His breath was rapid, his words mere pants of air and sound, and he wondered if they still contained meaning. He pinned Maledicte's arms behind his back, unnerved at the bowstring tension in them. If he let go, what would happen?

"Ani loves blood for blood alone. Vengeance begets death and nothing more. You tell me She does not rule you—make me believe it. Or you'll end as others have, mad or dead." In a desperate hope, he whispered one of the little paeans to Baxit, god of indolence and reason. Either aspect would aid Gilly now.

Maledicte went limp in his hands, slumping forward like a puppet freed from its strings. Gilly, taking the sudden weight in his arms, found his pulse hammering with more anxiety. Was this a feint? If he let go, would he find Maledicte coming back at him and with the sword in his hand? Beneath him, Maledicte grumbled.

"Mal?"

"Get off me," Maledicte said. "What are you doing? Trying to wrench my arms out of true over a few broken plates?"

Gilly slackened his vise-grip on Maledicte's wrists, feeling like a bullyboy, aware of how Maledicte's slender bones ground beneath his hands.

Gilly released him and Maledicte turned, his face filled with simple irritation. "Rats take it, Gilly. If you're not even going to let me throw a tantrum in my own house, there'll be no fun left at all in being wealthy."

"A tantrum," Gilly said. "Is that what you call it?"

"Two broken plates. And you knock me down," Maledicte said. "And my sword? Were you trying to break it, wedging it in the floor like that? You've bloodied your knuckles on it and serve you right. I need it to kill Last."

Maledicte stepped over and put his hand on the hilt, tugging it free. Gilly flinched, but Maledicte only complained, "I've lost the sheath again."

"It's probably still abovestairs in your room," Gilly said, his lips numb with shock. Did Maledicte remember nothing of the moments between broken crockery and Gilly's hold?

"I don't carry the blade unsheathed. I am not the callow boy I once was." Maledicte sat at the table, laid the blade out before him, ran his fingers down the steel, sheeting blood from the blade as if the shadows had been flesh enough to bleed.

"Gilly?" Maledicte said. "Did you hurt yourself badly on it?" A faint tremor touched his fingers.

Gilly touched his own hands, scraped and bloodied, hands that had never touched the blade at all. "You came down without the blade," Gilly said. "It came down later."

"Ridiculous," Maledicte said, his tone so uninflected that Gilly had no way of telling if Maledicte believed him or not. "It's only a sword. But think how useful it would be to have one that heeled like a dog." Maledicte's lips lifted in a movement too faint to be smile or snarl, though it held something of both, and more, the death's-head rictus of a gallows corpse. Gilly, picking up the largest pieces of shattered china, flinched at his expression, and watched his blood roll over the porcelain. For the first time in a long, long while, Gilly found himself frightened of Maledicte and the violence that eddied around him like storm winds, merciless to friend or foe alike.

JANUS ARRIVED JUST AFTER TWILIGHT. Gilly opened the door to him silently, still listening to the quiet voice within himself warning that Ani was gaining Her ascendancy with each passing day.

"Where is Maledicte?"

"In his rooms."

Janus hesitated on the stair. "Angry?"

"Possessed," Gilly said. The ugly word hung between them.

"Rats eat your nonsense." Janus turned. "Maledicte is no one's creature; there is no god of love and vengeance anymore."

"Maledicte made his vow to Her. He's bound to Her as surely as he's bound to you."

Janus's face flushed, quick temper rising in his cheeks, then fading. "You know so little of him. Maledicte has an odd and morbid sense of humor, prone to elaborate charades."

"I know him well enough to declare that humor, like perspective, is something Maledicte lacks," Gilly said.

"Perspective?" Janus said, eyes paling further yet, until Gilly was minded of distant lightning.

"He is determined to see you earl, even at the cost of his own life, while you sit back and allow him the risk—"

Gilly didn't see Janus move as much as felt the rush. Then his back slammed against the flocked wallpaper with enough force to set little motes of color floating free. His head and ears rang with the impact. Like an insect pinned, he struggled until Janus's gloved fingers closed on his throat. Janus pinched the pulse on either side of Gilly's neck with delicate inquiry, his face placid, his eyes mad.

"I could choke your life away and Maledicte would forgive me. He would forgive me anything. Remember that before you speak so. You know nothing of me if you think I would endanger Maledicte. Do you not listen? I've told you time and time again. He's mine." Janus released Gilly, ghosted past him and up the stairs.

Gilly shuddered, left to himself in the empty hall. Again the *Virga* crept into his mind, the siren song of sea and sail.

MALEDICTE HEARD THE DOOR open and close, unheralded, and knew, without looking away from the window, that Janus had entered. Only he made himself so free in Maledicte's home. But numbed with rage, Maledicte waited for Janus to come to him. Janus's hands rested on his shoulders, turning him, drawing him close. "Janus," Maledicte whispered.

Janus buried his face in Maledicte's neck. "I am sorry," he said, his voice roughed with exhaustion. "Sorry I did not win her hand. Sorry I made mincemeat of my duty. Though by the gods, I am not sorry to see her tongue hitched to another."

"Will you loose me on him now?" Maledicte said, raising his eyes to Janus's. "He plots against us, Janus. He'll have you prisoner, soon enough, confined to Lastrest or the town house, watched and spied upon."

"He already does that," Janus said. "Haven't I crept away from their wedding reception? But kill him? Not without a plan."

Maledicte stepped out of the warm circle of his arms. "My blade, his heart. What more plan do I need? Set me free to act. Didn't I rid us of Kritos?"

"Kritos was a rogue and a gambler. That he died as he did was not worthy of comment or even much concern. To beard Last, who rarely leaves the courts, or his estates, is a far thornier problem."

"I want him dead. Need him dead. Blood flows the same regardless of one's surroundings. If it goes wrong, if suspicion brands us guilty, we can quit the earldom entirely. We'll gut his estate and live like kings in the Explorations."

"Flee like rats? Die like rats, when the money runs out?" Janus said, shaking Maledicte. "I'll not revisit that life again." His hands stilled on Maledicte's shoulders, caressed where they had bruised. "You remember hardship. Even were you minded to risk it again, it would be worse than you think, knowing what we do now. The taste of fresh bread in the morning. The warmth of fireplaces in the winter." Janus kissed Maledicte's mouth when he started to speak again, sealing the words away with his tongue.

Janus walked him back toward the bed, and when their lips parted, continued, "The softness of silk on our skin, the luxury of sheets and velvet coverlets. It's more than luxury, Mal. It's safety."

Maledicte fell back into the feather mattress, his shirt falling open, the corset sliding down to his waist. Janus pinned Maledicte's hands above his head, buried them in the soft drape of down pillows. "I will endeavor to put Last in the path of your blade, winkle him out of his secure areas, but you must wait for it. I don't intend to lose you to a verdict of treason."

Maledicte looked up at the pale eyes, kissed the fine scattering of gold down at the back of Janus's neck. "Make it soon?"

"Very soon," Janus whispered. "My dark and bloodthirsty cavalier."

"Time is our enemy," Maledicte said. "Amarantha must not—"

"Shh," Janus said, "It's been near a fortnight without you."

Maledicte gave himself over to the familiar, marvelous touch; sighing, moaning, biting where such response was called for, and all the time he thought of Last's machinations working against them. Again he found himself balancing the simple act of vengeance and flight weighed opposite this elaborate charade of parry and counterthrust, of politics and power. The rushing pleasure that lit Janus's face only dimly touched Maledicte, lost in his thoughts of blood and patience.

Janus disentangled himself from the loose knot of their legs, stretched, and said, a little crossly, "Even whores feign their pleasures."

Maledicte stroked the furrow on Janus's brow. "Whores do not have such schedules and schemes as I do. Amarantha is a threat to us. But to kill *her* would be to only delay the problem. Until you deliver Last to my blade, she might quicken and deprive you of your birthright. We must keep her barren until I have Last's heart spitted." He slipped from Janus's grasp, the comforting softness of the bedsheets, and opened his chest of poisons. Dragging his finger along the vials until they sang, he found the first glimmer of pleasure. It wasn't death, but it was a small vengeance even if it moved through Amarantha instead of Last.

He pulled out a handful of waxed paper twists, each pale green at their heart, and returned to the bed, spilling the papers out between them. "Harlot's Friend," he said. "You recognize it?"

"Yes," Janus said. "Our mothers used such to prevent pregnancy. But Mal, how am I to get her to drink it daily?"

"Daily prevents. Monthly—she'll miscarry if she's gravid. Rougher on her, but far easier for you. All you need do is slip it into her wine. Though I warn you now, Janus, I will not tolerate a wait of months."

Janus tucked the twists of paper into his pockets, sat up and began straightening his clothes, fastening buttons and retying laces.

"Janus?"

"I'd best be back before my absence is noted. Now that Father feels he has the upper hand, he has laid new strictures on me."

"Were he dead, he could set no such rules."

"Mal—" Janus warned.

Maledicte looked away. "If you're bent on leaving, there are fresh linens in my armoire. You'd best have one. I've clawed your cravat past discretion."

Janus searched out the snowy lengths of cloths, sorted through them while Maledicte watched with an amused eye. "The one on the end is starched silk, if that's what your pampered skin demands."

"Tie it for me," Janus said.

Maledicte let the sheets unwind and reached out. "Ever the aristocrat—lift your chin more, hmm? I wear my linens to disguise. You will not leave yours off even for a covert jaunt across town."

"Dress is the easiest aspect of rank to mimic and a visible sign of breeding," Janus said, rising to check his appearance. He ran his fingers through his hair, smoothing the sleek locks. "Westfall may gad about town like a rustic in shirtsleeves and open collar . . . he has ten impeccable generations behind him. But if I appear with a veneer of dust marring the shine on my boots, it is because I am only a bastard, aping my betters." Janus curled his mouth in a smile unlike his usual pleasant one. "But a title will change that. Or at least take the whispers from my hearing."

Maledicte moved Janus's sweep of hair aside, kissed the nape of the neck, silk stiff under his lips. "When will you be back?"

"Two nights from now. Father and Amarantha attend another wedding reception," Janus said. "I will creep out of my window like some lovesick suitor, and come courting."

"Promise?" Maledicte asked.

Janus turned, cupped Maledicte's face in his hands, pressed their foreheads together. "I swear."

LOOKING OUT over the crowded room, the Duke of Love turned to Last and said, "Has your son forgiven you? I saw him only briefly and thought him a little grim."

"It matters not," Last said, sipping from his glass. "His spirit has been too independent for my tastes. This may chasten him. He is too much Celia's son, willful and selfish."

"Some of that may be due to venal influences," Love said.

"Maledicte," Last growled. "That damned . . . I'd see him gone, only Aris is unaccountably fond of him."

"Yes," Love said. "Have you seen this week's paper? And Poole's scurrilous caricature? I've set Echo on the artist, but unless Aris objects, nothing will come of it."

"I missed it," Last said. "But it can hardly be worse than Poole's previous images, my brother the king of slavering hounds."

"It's vile," Love said, drew Last aside, and into the quiet recesses of his study. He unfolded the broadsheet.

Last's mouth parted and his cheeks flushed. The image was drawn with careful simplicity, not the usual cluttered style of the artist, but something designed to be quickly memorable. Maledicte, all dark hair and lush mouth, lounged on the throne, his sword naked in one hand, and in the other—a long leash fastened about Aris's neck. Aris himself had been drawn so that his face was nearly witless, blindly turning away from the corpse labeled Vornatti at his feet, looking up at Maledicte with adoration. Last's hand crumpled the page. "Tell Echo to jail Poole. We'll see if he has influence enough to free himself. And then we'll know who aids him in spreading such slander."

"Mirabile, no doubt, started the rumor; her whispers have increased ten-fold in scope. And people believe where before they only listened," Love said. "But that still leaves us with the ultimate source of your troubles and mine. Maledicte."

Last sighed. "I thought that problem solved once. Dantalion, Vornatti's displaced heir, sent an assassin, but either the man failed or was bought. I believe Dantalion plans to handle it himself once his position as Antyre's new auditor is official."

"A foreign assassin on our shores? Dantalion hunting our courtiers?" Love said, scowling. "Itarus is too free with their manners and too blatant in their hatreds. You should have mentioned such to me or Captain Jasper at once. Had he succeeded with Maledicte, he might have turned his attentions to the throne. Itarus would reward an assassin well for Aris. Still—" He raised his head and met Last's eyes. "The idea is sound. Perhaps we can accomplish the task on our own. I have a manservant who might be of assistance. A man I've used before to rid myself of a troublesome stableboy. Why not a troublesome courtier?"

Last smiled. "Do this thing, and I'll renegotiate Amarantha's bride portion."

Love said, "Let me grant you this as a wedding gift. All you need do is insure Janus's absence from Maledicte's side. Despite his posturing, I think the boy only a stripling. On his own, he should prove no threat."

*L*ATE AT NIGHT, the town house fell into silence as the maids retired, the cook settled to sleep, and the empty butler's chambers cooled. In his bedroom, Maledicte alone sat awake. In the hall below, the great clock tolled out the quarter hour, and Maledicte set his book aside. With every chimed note, Janus's promised arrival grew less likely. With every chime a new fear took hold.

Perhaps Last had drugged Janus and sent him abroad, a prisoner until Amarantha's worthiness could be proved. Or maybe Last had chosen to gamble the future entirely on Amarantha and had drowned Janus like an unwanted cat. The old wounds on Maledicte's side and face burned, a scorching reminder that Last had defeated Miranda before, had robbed her of Janus before.

Before Me—Ani's whisper throbbed in his blood, turning fears to fury, but without any comfort. Janus had no such protection. Ani's wings sheltered Maledicte only. Maledicte picked up the sword, dancing his way across the room with it, stabbing and slicing as if his fears could be defeated by bladework. Were Gilly home and dreaming, Maledicte would creep in to find solace in the placid face. He would wake him to hear him grumble and find his fears pushed back by the familiar voice. But Gilly was out, visiting the damned brothel girl.

With a flourish of the blade, Maledicte whirled and took his sudden temper out on the heavy mahogany door. Red wood peeled back like parting flesh and Maledicte sighed.

He discarded the sword, a little ashamed of his tantrums, ashamed of his doubts and fears. Janus would come.

Behind him, the air shifted, the dark scent of the night fogs creeping in. Maledicte turned to see the windows parting and a man surging through. He leaped for the sword, his fingers falling short as the assassin lunged forward, and tumbled them both across the room. Maledicte fell to his knees beneath the brute's weight, and, snarling, turned to claw at his face.

The garrote caught him by surprise, still warm where the assassin had held it close. It fell over his head, and, sword forgotten, Maledicte strove instead to deter the closing noose. His hands changed direction, forcing panic away for planning. Instead of clawing at the assassin, he clawed at the wire, managing to slip a hand up between the tightening loop and his neck.

Maledicte wheezed for breath, forcing his hand farther through the loop, skinning the flesh on his forearm, and nearing the elbow. If he could only get the wire past his elbow, he could slip out of it, its chokehold vanished with the inclusion of shoulder and rib. But the wire tightened, making it hard to muster the energy needed. Doggedly, breathlessly, Maledicte wormed his arm up another inch; the assassin rolled them both forward and put his knees in Maledicte's back.

Maledicte could see the sword now, only a yard away, and thought if Gilly were right, if the sword could come to him at will, now would be the time above all. Maledicte's last breath faded and fled, scorching his lungs with its haste. Where was Ani's aid now? Or was this assailant unworthy of Her notice, being no part of their bargain. . . . Maledicte's blood drummed in his ears; he clawed backward, one-handed, trying to find leverage.

The door flew open and the assassin's grip slackened in surprise.

Maledicte sucked in air, put his shoulder up, and squirmed through the garrote loop, heading for the sword. His hand was on it when he heard the crash. Turning on unsteady feet, he saw Gilly holding the downstairs poker and standing above the assassin. One look at the huddled form and Maledicte dropped the blade. "You saved me the effort. Do I thank you?" he croaked.

White to the lips, Gilly held his death grip on the dripping iron of the poker as if frozen in horror and Maledicte repented his flippant words.

He took Gilly by the shirtsleeve and steered him away from the corpse, opening his fingers and letting the poker fall.

"I saw him, a shadow going through the window. I didn't think I'd make it." Gilly's voice trembled and faded like an amateur singer at her debut.

"You did," Maledicte said, pressing Gilly back into the softness of the chair, tucking a blanket around his shoulders. "You're shaking." His own composure was returning, the familiar rush of breath and anger, both so essential to him.

"I just— Did I kill him?"

"He's not like to rise after you knocked that piece of skull loose. Tell me, did you ever play at stick as a child?" Maledicte poured a glass of brandy for Gilly, curled his fingers around the heavy crystal.

Gilly raised the glass to his lips, managed a sip, and then let it settle in his lap again. "Are you hurt?"

"Only knocked about." Maledicte sat down on the bed and rubbed his throat with tentative fingers. His other hand drummed and twitched with residual nervousness and he started to his feet again.

Gilly passed him the brandy glass. Maledicte tossed it back, coughing as the liquor hit strained flesh.

"He's the duke of Love's man," Gilly said, shifting in his seat so that his head rested against the sheltering side. "I recognized him as I struck. I forget his name, but not his face."

"The duke? What wrong have I done him?" Maledicte felt as bewildered as a child, the clarity of battle gone.

"The king's favor, perhaps," Gilly said. "The scandal of it. Or Last may have borrowed him."

"Last," Maledicte said, rather more pleased than not to gain another reason to hate the man. He knelt beside the body and began rifling the assassin's clothing. An inner pocket yielded a note on expensive parchment. He unfolded it, trying to keep the blood sliding down his arm from obscuring the words.

"What is that?" Gilly said, roused from his shock by the sound of paper. He took it from Maledicte's hands. "It's instructions, but no names, not even yours."

"Well then, if he can't be useful, let's get him out of here. I swear he's beginning to stink." Maledicte picked up the poker. "Do you have a lucifer on you?"

"You're not going to burn him?"

Maledicte found a reluctant smile at Gilly's evident horror. "Only the blood and hair on the poker. He's far too fresh for that kind of thing. But I am open to suggestions, Gilly. The night will not last forever, and I am tired. You know everything; tell me what to do with him." Maledicte's tone was soft, conciliatory.

"I never had to know how to dispose of corpses until I took service with you," Gilly said. He stared down at the body, at the ruined head, and flexed his fingers. "We bluff."

THEY STAGGERED QUIETLY down the dim, carpeted hall, past the sweeping main staircase, to the narrow attic stairs, the corpse hanging heavy between them. Gilly's hands, wet with sweat, slipped on the man's booted ankles, and he made a hasty catch to prevent them from banging on the stair riser. Maledicte, breathing harshly, signaled a rest, propping the corpse's torso up along the wall. Gilly looked away from the staring eyes, hating that this was his idea, and so disallowed him complaint—his idea to turn the assassin into an unlucky thief who had fallen to his death.

Maledicte, kicking speculatively at the cooling body, had suggested his bedroom window as the "thief's" point of attempted entry, but Gilly pointed out the plush lawn and rose beds below. A man might break his neck, but not open his brain box in such a fall to such a surface.

So they carried his weight toward the high attic window, where the decaying trellis made plausible both an attempt at entry and the successive fall to the stone path below.

Maledicte's other suggestion—that they claim self-defense, and allow Echo the pleasure of removing the body—Gilly had rejected out of hand, citing the inadvisability of allowing Echo within Maledicte's rooms at all, given the man's desire to prove Maledicte culpable of something, anything. Gilly had held his breath until Maledicte agreed, but knew from the look in the sharp, dark eyes that his real motive had not gone unnoticed: If it were a thief and an accident, then Gilly would not have to dwell on the thing he had done. . . .

Gilly looked up to find the dull shine of the corpse's eyes fixed on him. Something slick and wet slid down the dead face, reminding him of a melting waxwork. Gilly fought bile. No wonder the aristocrats dueled; they could kill someone and be away, even as the body fell. They never had to tidy up after. Maledicte's cold fingers touched his wrist, startling him.

"Stop gawping. You've been blooded now and no distress on your part will undo it. Take his ankles and be done with your vapors," Maledicte said. "But let me go up the stairs first. If we take him head down, we'll have to clean the stairs after. The night is long enough without that."

Death—aristocrats turned it into sport, Gilly thought savagely. He took a step too fast and Maledicte stumbled.

Too near the top and the maid's rooms to apologize, Gilly merely shrugged. Maledicte tugged again and started up, his hair and eyes slipping into shadows, then the shadows flowing forward and enveloping them entire.

At the top of the stairs, they hesitated, looking for thin lines of light that might betoken a maid still awake. But the darkness was near absolute; only the faint gleam of night sky sketched out the floor beams as they crept by the maids' rooms and up the last half stairs to the attic proper.

Maledicte set the body down with a sigh, stretched his hands up to the roof, easing his back and shoulders. "Why are the dead so damn heavy?"

"Awkward, not heavy," Gilly said. "You or I could have carried him alone, were it not for the stairs and our own squeamishness. Cradled like a lover, there'd be little difficulty." Though looking again at Maledicte's slight form, he doubted his words.

"He's stiffening," Maledicte said, prodding the corpse, then locking his grip around the assassin's chest so that his hands met and knotted into each other, white-knuckled. "Let's finish this."

Gilly shifted his grip from dead ankles to thighs, trying to take more of the weight, seeing the tension in Maledicte's hands echoed in his neck and shoulders.

"I am going to make Love regret this," Maledicte panted as they maneuvered the body up to the narrow windowsill.

The corpse stuck for a moment, then it dropped with a rustle of ivy and the sudden burst of black wings. Maledicte and Gilly jumped back as a handful of rooks came in the window, their sleep disturbed, their wings beating like Gilly's startled heartbeat.

"Did you know they were nesting there?" Gilly asked, when the last rook had found its way back into the sky.

"It's convenient. Gives him a lovely reason to have been startled and fall to his death. You've done well by me tonight, Gilly. My lucky piece, faithful friend." Maledicte brushed Gilly's cheek with his lips.

Gilly found himself wondering what all his distress had been for. An assassin who would have killed Maledicte?

Down below, the blurred black shape of the assassin, broken on the pale stones, shifted and seethed. Gilly flinched, and looked at Maledicte, startled at the apparent movement and sick at the thought that perhaps they had dropped a living man. But Maledicte merely smiled and Gilly realized the moving blackness was not the man, but the man covered in feeding rooks.

ONCE AGAIN, MALEDICTE FOUND HIMSELF at the heart of scandal; the young courtier nearly burgled by the duke of Love's own valet. As if that were not enough to keep tongues wagging, the confrontation between Maledicte and the duke, which started with mutual recriminations and threats, ended in Love's apoplexy and death. And all, rumor had it, without Maledicte even needing to draw his sword, or raise his voice. There were bets laid, trying to guess what it was Maledicte had said. Some rumors said it wasn't words, but the rudeness that had kept Maledicte from allowing Love and Echo entrance, kept them standing in the cold, morning drizzle. Brierly Westfall, Mirabile's sweet-voiced mouthpiece, said she had heard that Maledicte cursed Love's family. Others claimed he mocked Love's pride and so sent him into apoplectic rage.

When the bets grew high enough midweek, Maledicte entered the game himself, swearing he would tell them what he had said, if the victor would split the spoils. He visited the Horned Bull, over Gilly's objections of discretion and propriety, and went through the betting book himself, finally awarding a young poet the purse. "It wasn't so much," Maledicte said, smiling at the wildest fancies of witchcraft and exotic poisons. "All I did was bar my door and tell Love it was in fear that, as his man was a sneak thief, why should the master be any better? Love had a weak heart. His own temper undid him."

Poole, the caricaturist, still ensconced in Stones, made the scene his next work when he heard of it: Maledicte, cloaked in shadow, ringed by sly faces, with coins spilled before them all. He captioned it "Betting on Death," and behind Maledicte's image, the horned brow of Haith, god of death and victory, loomed. Gilly fussed when he saw it, but Maledicte only grinned.

"You must be more discreet, stay home and be—"

"Besieged by visitors curious to see where first Love's man and then himself died? No, Gilly, that's begun to pall."

But in the midst of all the notes Maledicte received, the invitations to scandalous gatherings, the reawakening interest in the dark cavalier who had been silent for a season, one omission stood out. From Janus, there had been nothing, and Gilly knew it was that which had driven Maledicte out and about, courting his attention.

When Janus came, it was days later and late at night. He came cloaked in secrets and wearing all the signs of a late appointment to a lover's rendezvous, dark linens, newly applied scent, and barbered cheeks.

Gilly let him in and Janus swept into the parlor as if he knew that since the attack Maledicte had not slept well within his bedchamber. Gilly, following Janus, resented his glib assurance of welcome, even a week late; he was appeased at Janus's sudden pause at the sight of Maledicte stretched out on the chaise longue beside the spinet. All in dove gray, Maledicte embodied both demureness and danger.

"Was it an assassin? The duke's man?" Janus said, dropping his cloak over a chair, ignoring the slow slide of velvet-trimmed wool as it puddled over the edge and fell to the floor. Gilly picked it up, draped it again.

"The duke's man. Your father's hand. Sit, if you're not going to drink; Gilly's teaching me to cheat at pennywhist."

Janus bent to kiss Maledicte and Maledicte turned his head like an affronted maid, refusing to be turned up sweet.

"That's a servant's game," Janus said, seemingly willing to humor Maledicte's mood. He settled himself on the chaise, bumping his hip against Maledicte's.

"Victory is victory, no matter the stakes." Maledicte stood, stretched in another series of deliberate movements.

Watching, always watching, Gilly was reminded of smoldering fires in Maledicte's stillness, of hot lampblack, of the mountainous volcanoes abroad, rumbling.

"The body," Janus said. "Why the charade?" He gripped Maledicte's hand, tugged him back to the seat, settled him between his thighs.

"I thought a dead burglar would be less commented on than a dead assassin," Gilly answered when Maledicte did not.

"I wish you had waited," Janus said.

"Wait, always wait. How you love that song. Should I have just propped him in a closet?" The edge rose in Maledicte's voice suddenly. "Or send a card, begging Last's pardon, but could Janus come aid me—I seem to have a corpse in my bedchamber? I was sick of the sight of him, and Gilly was just sick. And you were not here."

"Father changed his plans and kept me at his side, late into the night, going over land management for land I may never own while I acted the obedient son. But I'm done with that," Janus said, nestling his face into Maledicte's hair. His eyes grew blue and bright. "Is your sword sharp?"

"No," Gilly said, "No."

"Don't tease," Maledicte said, after a frozen moment.

"I am in deadly earnest," Janus said. "He tried to kill you. He cannot be allowed to try it again. I have flushed our quarry, Mal, goaded them into movement. It is time to hunt."

"You're hiding something," Gilly accused, meeting the gas-flame blue eyes with his own. He wouldn't flinch. Not anymore.

Janus slapped his gloves back and forth in his palms. "Only that I gambled on our plan, our odds of success, when I am not entirely sanguine of the result. I am not a gambler by nature. But after Father's attempt on Maledicte's life, waiting seemed even more of a fool's game."

"What did you do?" Gilly asked.

"I poured Amarantha a drink, taking care that she saw—"

"What does it matter?" Maledicte interrupted. "Just tell me where—"

"The docks," Janus said. "To the *Winter's Kiss* and thence to Itarus, where they can ally with another who wishes you dead."

"Dantalion," Gilly said in Maledicte's place.

Maledicte seemed uncaring, eyes half closed, a smile curling his mouth. A man lost in a delightful dream of murder. He opened his eyes, pure triumph simmering in their depths. "You doubt those odds, Janus? I'll slaughter Last ere he ever sets foot on the *Kiss*."

"You cannot run into the night waving your sword like a barbarian," Gilly

said, standing before the door into the hall and the city outside as if to bar
their way.

"Don't fret, Gilly. It does you no good and cannot change what we do,"
Maledicte said.

"We could hire footpads to kill Last for us. Take a page from his book,"
Janus said.

"No," Maledicte said, rising again, as slim as his sword. "What joy is there
in blood spilled by proxy?"

"But sword wounds look like nothing else. If you made it appear accidental, an attempted robbery or some such—"

"Burn it," Maledicte said, settling his sword around his narrow hips. "I
have been patient. I will be so no longer."

"I set a boy to watch the house," Janus said. "He'll send word when Last
leaves. You'll wait that long." Half command, half entreaty, it worked well
enough that Maledicte stopped in his forward path toward the door.

Maledicte paced the confines of the hallway, much like the caged animals
of the city gardens, waiting, refusing to be drawn into further speech, though
Gilly tried. It was nearly dawn before the message came, a one-word note.
Now. Maledicte was out the door before the paper had fluttered to the tiles.

The rooks fled the roof, creeling and calling; in the stables, the horses
shrieked as if their stalls were afire. Maledicte turned and walked into the retreating night, following the sting of salt in the air, and dragging shadows
after him like the sweep of dark wings.

THE EARL OF LAST SWUNG down out of the carriage and gestured his
coachman onward to the silent quay and the waiting Itarusine ship, distinctive with its ice-breaking prow. The tiger dropped from his post behind the
carriage, not the usual skinny lad to run messages but a man Gilly's size.
While Last looked after the coachman and crew now unloading his valises,
the tiger kept watch, peering into shadows, a hand on his knife. In a dark
niche of broken wall and alley, Maledicte's eyes narrowed. Did Last think a
single, extra guard would be enough? Even one so large—Maledicte had
long ago stopped fearing men who outweighed him. They all bled the same.
Insult lanced through him; that Last, who supposedly feared for his life,
would rely on only one guard and his coachman for protection.

The dank, morning fogs hugging the streets and pier reached pale tendrils into Maledicte's lair and wrapped a cloak of obscurity around Last's form. Maledicte welcomed the warming trickle of hatred creeping through his heart and brain, Ani's shared rage eclipsing all else. The foggy fingers touching him slowly tinted to the ink of starless night. He stepped out of his lair, onto the pier, eyes focused on the tall blur that was Last, and the shadows in the alley followed him out, spreading soundlessly, blanketing the wharf in untimely dark.

The tiger, for all his jumping at shadows, was woefully unprepared when Maledicte emerged, blade already drawn and moving. The size, the strength, all for show, Maledicte thought dimly, as he moved past the man falling to the street, blood pouring from his ruined throat. Last would have done better to bring a hound, which at least could have been counted on to bark.

"Last," he said, when he was a swordstrike away.

The earl spun, one hand clenched the haft of his cane, the other the handle, while he quickly sought sign of the guard. Finding no one, he twisted the cane. It clicked and showed a faint gleam of metal. No surprise showed on his features, only resignation and rage. "He set you on? So be it. You will not dispose of me so easily as you think."

Maledicte lunged without response, thrusting the blade forward. It made an eager hiss all its own, and the earl parried, using his cane to deflect the blow. The wood split, revealing the sword beneath.

The earl shoved, using the steel core as a lever, and forced Maledicte's retreat, giving him a moment to strip the sword of its ruined sheath. Maledicte danced forward, and Last evaded the next blow by pivoting on one heel. Last called for help, but the words were swallowed by the black fogs. "Witchcraft," he spat. "You're nothing without it. You couldn't take me without the god's aid."

"All She does is hold the world at bay," Maledicte said, lunging. His sword bit into the bulky coat. Last winced, then clamped the fabric close, trying to use it to disarm Maledicte.

Maledicte hung on to his blade, slipped back, and Last ripped the hampering greatcoat off with a quick agility that made Maledicte snarl.

Last snapped the weighted edge into Maledicte's face. Maledicte ducked away with no space to spare and ripped the coat from Last's hand, enraged that the man thought to use it as a shield.

At this long-delayed moment, it became apparent that the earl of Last was a swordsman of some skill, and, of course, was possessed of the urge to stay alive. But Maledicte, shadowed and dark, moving as if he had no more limitations than the fog itself, was merely possessed. Gradually, strike after strike, he began to win.

The darkness was as complete as if the deepest sea had reached up and drowned the city. In its black embrace, Maledicte's world narrowed to the ring of steel on steel and their panting breaths. There wasn't even room for rage or triumph; with Last dancing so well with him, all Maledicte could feel was the enjoyment of physical exertion, and the breath-stealing anticipation of blood. The dark sword, ghostly in the fogs, swooped forward and took a bite; Maledicte moaned for Last, the pleasure deep in his belly surfacing. Last cursed and stumbled back, bleeding along his upper arm.

The fog carried the muffled prayers of frightened sailors. Nearby, the coachman called out but Last had Maledicte's sword pressing him, and no breath to answer.

Last gained ground, took them from the treacherous slick wood of the quay to the cobbled edge of pier and street, but the effort left him bleeding from arm and thigh.

His face, set in lines of desperate concentration, broke and filled with a wild triumph as the coachman blundered into their duelists' circle. Maledicte danced back and turned, the blade flying from his hand to strike home in the coachman's chest. The primed pistol dropped from the coachman's hand, falling onto the cobbles with a crimson roar, its shot spent. Maledicte's pleasure turned to anger. The coachman thought to interfere; who might next?

Last lunged forward, his blade aimed for the sweat-wet cravat at Maledicte's neck and Maledicte slipped away in time to save his neck, if not his waistcoat and shirt. The fabric ripped, the dark brocade, the pale linen, the dense cotton, all rent with one swift stroke, baring Maledicte's moon-white flesh and ending with one drop of blood blooming and fading at his collarbone.

Maledicte growled at the touch of the fog on his skin. He was a body's length from the coachman's corpse and his sword, and his temper was turning foul.

This went on too long; every minute brought Last closer to reprieve. The pistol shot would have been heard, and though the fog played havoc with sound, eventually they would be found. Even now, Maledicte heard a woman shrieking, a high, shrill sound that set his teeth on edge. Last hesitated, his face confounded; Maledicte lunged in a long, low dive for his distant sword, even as Last shook the astonishment from his face, and returned to the fight.

Last's blade missed his tumbling form by a hair's breadth. More silk ripped; the riband holding his hair slithered down his neck and pointed out how close the blade had come, but the coachman's body and Maledicte's sword were within reach. Maledicte's hand closed on the sharp-feathered hilt of his sword and it slipped from flesh and bone as if a human body were just another hilt.

Maledicte shook the hair from his face and backed Last toward the pier. The duel was done. The set blankness on Last's face told Maledicte such, the fear unmasked in blue eyes. Maledicte darted out with his blade, a bird's quick stoop for prey, narrowed his vision to Last's throat. The man parried at the last, but Maledicte's blade shrieked over steel and sliced through Last's ear.

"Who are you?" Last gasped.

"Is that what ails you?" Maledicte laughed, trying to imagine what Last saw. His hair falling loose, shadowing his eyes, the feral snarl of teeth and tongue, the pale skin and delicate breasts bared to the night air. . . . Were Last less of an aristocrat, he would fear less, but in his experience, women were nothing but playthings and pawns. That one could wield a sword and more, fight him to the death, would be beyond his experience.

"Who are you?" he cried again.

"Black-Winged Ani." The name forced itself free of Maledicte's throat without his willing it.

Last staggered and Maledicte punched the sword into his chest, twisted the blade for the pleasure of hearing the man cry out as he fell. Blood welled, bubbling through Last's sweat-soaked linens, spurting against the fabric as blood and air fought to escape. Left alone, Last would bleed to death. Maledicte knelt beside him, touching the wound. "Is it your heart I've hit, or your lungs? You took my heart once."

"I will not beg," Last said, a rough whisper, blood frothing his mouth.

"Nor did I, and it made little difference." Maledicte brought his hand to his mouth and nose, smelling the hot tang of blood. He licked his fingers; blood warmed his raw throat, meeting his thirst, but not slaking it.

Dizzy with rage, he stood. It was not enough. Maledicte swayed, wondering whose hunger he felt, whose bloodlust. Last was near dead and in a moment Maledicte would finish the deed, his revenge accomplished in blood and shadows. But he felt nowhere near sated, and inside his belly, wings fluttered.

A bare gasp behind him reminded him of Last's physical presence and he turned, wanting to see the light fade in his eyes, the life leave. But Last was not alone. Another man had found his way to the heart of the fogs.

"Filth," Last gasped, "come to see your leman kill me? I should have killed you at birth."

Janus bent and slit his throat ear to ear.

"He was mine!" Maledicte said, rage erasing his voice so that all he could do was whisper.

"You were too slow. I was worried about you. And rightly, I see, mooning about, half-naked," Janus said. He tugged the gaping sides of Maledicte's shirt together. Maledicte's fingers curled into a fist and, feather-blind, he struck. Janus reeled, licking his split lip, eyes darkening. "What matters who killed him? You made him bleed, you made him fear you."

"He was mine," Maledicte said, "Mine." He tightened his hand on the sword hilt; it seemed to surge in his hand. He lunged and buried the sword in Last's body once more. Janus spun, stepping out of range. Maledicte wrenched the sword through Last's guts, hoping for some final groan, some final hurt he could wring out.

"Enough, Mal," Janus said.

Maledicte, not listening, pulled the sword from Last's chest, then sheathed it when he realized that all he wanted was to spill blood and that the only person within reach was Janus. He stared out at the sea, dark waters surging and receding, at the ships slowly becoming visible as the fog thinned and faded. The shining figurehead of the *Winter's Kiss*, a young man seemingly carved of ice, glimmered as the fogs parted. Gilly would like that one, he thought, and with that the rage faded. The earl was dead. His vengeance done, Maledicte stared down into the blank eyes, the gaping, slack mouth. Ani's touch subsided into sulky confusion.

Maledicte watched the body, waiting for some sign, his eyes never leaving the corpse, though Janus spoke his name twice, then finally in exasperation—"Miranda!"

She turned, searching for words to explain her dismay. The earl of Last was dead and her victory was as meaningless as when she first heard his name. Last—it had meant nothing to her then. Dead, he meant nothing to her now.

"Over your tantrum?" Janus asked. "Grab his ankles and let's sink him into the water; we'll weight his coat with cobbles and delay the discovery that much longer."

Maledicte mutely did as Janus said. He watched the body drop by slow degrees deeper into the water, fading. "What are you doing here?"

"Aiding you," Janus said. "Amarantha?"

"She's here?" Maledicte said.

"Aboard the *Kiss*, I suspect," Janus said, lips thinning. "Well, there's no help for that. Unless we want to fight the entire crew."

We could, Ani whispered. *Turn the waters red.*

Maledicte shook his head, and at Janus's imperious wave, went over to help him with disposing of Last's men.

They were still stooped, the sagging weight of the burly tiger held between them, when two sailors came out of the night, drunk and staggering. They blinked and one of them frowned. "Milord Last, is that you?" Janus pulled his cloak over his pale hair, and traded a glance with Maledicte, one that needed no special communion to be understood. The sailors had to disappear. Maledicte reclaimed his sword and flew at them, and they, panicking, headed not for the safety of the ship, but back into the dark streets. Janus yanked his cravat up over his nose and cheeks and followed as silent and supple as a cat. Maledicte still gained on the two sailors, moving as light and quick as a shattering of glass.

He darted through a shadowed alley and tore the shadows after him. Looking behind him, one sailor tried to sign an avert charm and stumbled. Maledicte pounced, jamming his head against the rocks. He freed his sword from the hilt, and Janus, flashing by, said, "Not the sword."

Maledicte snarled but balked, understanding. The sailor struggled to rise, and Maledicte picked up a rock. He brought it crashing down on the man's skull, heard the wet crack, and remembered Miranda's lectures. He bent over the corpse and plucked the few lunas left from the bag.

Janus returned, out of breath, but dragging the second sailor behind him. He dropped the body near the other. "Did you get his purse?" he asked.

Maledicte nodded.

"Then let's leave this. There's no great mystery to drunken sailors being set upon for coin," Janus said. "And I need to be home, setting arnica to my mouth. A bruise might be hard to explain, should Last surface with the next tide." His tone invited apology, but Maledicte denied him that.

In truth, Maledicte wouldn't be able to apologize even were he so inclined. This final death stole his voice; he fought a surprising urge for tears. The sailor was no part of his revenge. Just a man visiting the city whores and finding his pleasure where he could.

Janus glanced at him and said coldly, "If Ella had had her way, you'd be bedding men like this." He tugged Maledicte closer, and wound a narrow strip of cording around his waist, cinching the fabric closed. "Try not to run into Gilly, hmm?"

Maledicte touched the dead man's belt and nodded. He strode off into the darkness, heading for home, clinging to the shadows of the Relicts like a ghost, daring someone to confront him, to recognize him. Invoked by Janus's words, he almost expected to see Ella staggering out of an alley, shaking down her skirts. Maledicte wondered what would happen then. Would Ella even see Miranda in Maledicte's guise? Most like, she'd not even look, but scuttle away, recognizing danger, if not her child. Maledicte wondered briefly if Ella had grieved when Miranda left, if she had meant anything to her at all, beyond merchandise.

Sudden thoughts stilled his feet, left him numb. Miranda was nothing, a rat, but Janus—Celia knew Last had taken him—why had she not followed? Surely the gossip reached this far—surely she knew that Janus had come into coin. . . . Her absence meant she was either dead or so far lost in her Laudable dreams she might as well be dead. And what befell Celia undoubtedly befell Ella. Maledicte shed a shaky breath and went on, dreading his past rising up to meet him. But alleys passed in these uncanny fogs, peopled only in his imagination; Maledicte saw no one.

He arrived home and crept in through the kitchen. Cook drowsed in her chair, and fresh dough rose on the counter. The dark, sour scent of the yeast made his stomach clench. He fled the kitchen, halting when he found Gilly dozing on the main stair, a guttering candle spilling wax over the riser. Maledicte backed away, and crept up the servants' stairs.

It was done, he thought as he stripped the bloody shirt from his flesh.

Even now, Last plagued him, the cloth sticking to his skin, making its removal close to pain.

Done, and Janus to be earl. Maledicte winced. If they escaped conviction. He ripped off the ruined corset and dropped it in the pile of stiffening cloth.

Naked, he fumbled to the hearth, searching for lucifers. He thrust the fabric into the fireplace. Kneeling, he blew at the struggling flame and succeeded only in scattering the fine ash left behind from last season's fire. It stung his eyes and brought him to tears again.

Why this weakness? Why this grief? Maledicte could not understand it. No such thing had plagued him before.

Daylight showed through the curtained glass of his rooms, and, despairing, he sloshed the brandy over the slow-singeing clothes. Then and only then did the room fill with the stink of burning blood and embroidery. Some of the rigidity left Maledicte's shoulders. He scrubbed his face with cold washwater, trying to wipe the ashes away. The cloth came away speckled with red as well as black, and he squeezed it out until the basin turned pink. The face, the figure that looked back at him from the glass was that of a madwoman and he refused to let his eyes rest on it. He was Maledicte, the dark cavalier, Last's scourge. Ani's servant. *Still* Her servant. And with Last dead, whose blood could release him?

Daylight reminded him that the maid would come to bring fresh water and morning tea. The clothes had best be burnt by then, burnt to ashes. He stirred them with the poker, set glowing sparks free to sting his bare arms and hands. These faint pains woke him from his stupor, and he dressed with his usual elaborate care. Fine leather breeches laced along the thighs and belly for the fashionable fit. Another corset, secreted in the space that once held Vornatti's will, bound his chest and thickened his narrow waist. He layered on the shirt, finest lawn, and the brocade vest, tied his cravat in a reasonable facsimile of the popular Leaffall, and called it done just as Gilly's familiar tap sounded on the door. "Mal?" Anxiety laced his voice.

At his invitation Gilly came in and coughed. "What are you burning?" he asked, flinging the windows open without waiting for permission. He poked at the black remains of the fire, and said, "Oh. Did you do it then? Kill him?" His voice grew tentative and pained. "Were you seen? What happens next?"

Maledicte hefted the brandy bottle, but the liquor was gone, fed to the fire. "It's all ashes," he said. "Nothing but ashes. Can you tell me why this should be so unsatisfying?" He took the poker from Gilly and stirred the fire, breaking the charred fabric into black dust. "I plotted this death for years. Gloated over it, imagined it, fed my rage on it. And it's ashes in my mouth."

"Ani goads you, spurs you on to mad rages, and when you've done as She wished, She recedes, taking it all for Herself. And you're left with nothing but the aftermath of blood. Now that your vengeance is done, She'll have left you completely." Gilly let out his breath and studied the carpet beneath his boots, scuffing at soot that had spilled out with the withdrawn fire-iron. "Most of Her previous children have gone mad with Her loss." His voice shook.

Maledicte said, "Gilly. Look at me and tell me She's left me. That Ani's mark is gone. You who see it so clearly. My compact completed—that I am no longer Her stalking horse."

Gilly sucked in his breath. He touched the shadows under Maledicte's dark eyes, and then looked into the shadows in the eyes themselves. "No. She rides you still."

"The earl is dead, but She lingers. Is this all my future holds? Blood and fighting? I wanted Janus back and I have that. I wanted riches enough to never starve. I have that. If this night's bloody work remains a mystery, Janus will be earl, and there will be nothing left to need." He wrenched his chin from Gilly's grip, and collapsed into the chair beside the fire.

"Janus will always want more. He's near as hungry as Ani Herself," Gilly said, bitterness in his tone. "Why is Ani still with you? What happened, Mal?"

"It's all ashes," Maledicte repeated. He slumped, his face in his hands, tears in his throat.

"I know something that is all ashes, without question," Gilly said, changing his mood with an audible effort. "What did you do, clean the hearth with your hair?"

Distracted, Maledicte touched his hair, and frowned at the dusting it left on his fingers. Gilly collected the ivory-backed brush from the dresser and said, "Lean forward."

Maledicte bent his head, letting his hair dangle over the hearth, and Gilly brushed the ashes out, brushed until Maledicte's hair gleamed like a rook's wing.

"What color ribbon do you want?" Gilly said. "Your usual black, or something more dramatic?"

"Black will do," Maledicte said. "I am expecting Echo at any moment. Even if Last obliges by staying disposed of, his disappearance will cause comment. And that means Echo again. I never thought how apt his name was before—he keeps returning, my words distorted on his lips."

Gilly gathered the dark strands into a queue, tied it off at Maledicte's nape, making a neat knot and letting the ribbons dangle. "What will you say?"

"It hardly matters," Maledicte said. "I am not the only one with animus against Last, and until his body surfaces, Echo will be hard pressed to charge me with a crime. He'll assume I killed Last. But he'll have to prove it—and he'll find no witness to the deed."

Gilly frowned, thinking beyond his immediate worries for Maledicte's sanity, for the compact still unfinished. "I'll send out runners and spies, those who can differentiate whispered fact from wishful rumor. We'll know what Echo plans before he does. And Amarantha?"

"On the *Kiss*, we think," Maledicte said.

"I'll send a letter in her wake, then, asking Vornatti's spies in Itarus to keep their ears open. If she's abroad, she'll seek Dantalion as Last would have done." Gilly sucked in a breath, beginning to hope that, Ani's lingering presence notwithstanding, Last's murder had been accomplished without jeopardizing Maledicte's neck.

· 27 ·

GILLY PACED OUTSIDE MALEDICTE'S ROOM, waiting. It was the dark night of the year, and superstition held that the unshriven dead returned on the Dark Solstice. Once there had been solemn ceremonies to placate the dead, but in the bored hands of the aristocracy, the Dark Solstice had become another excuse to play.

Did the dead come back and to the court, Gilly thought, they would return to their graves, ashamed for the antics of the attics-to-let and the debauched, for the gamblers who took advantage of their costumes to cheat with abandon. Though none was truly masked in the select crowd, caught in the nets of well-recognized foible and mannerism, they could pretend and act accordingly. Despite his creeping unease at the idea of Vornatti's ghostly step sounding in the hall, Gilly wished Maledicte had chosen not to attend, not when Mirabile had paved their path with rumors centering on Last's disappearance and Maledicte's possible role in it.

The Dark Masque, though, had put a spark into Maledicte's eyes, replacing the sullen temper and brooding fits Maledicte had been prone to since Last's death. Gilly had expected to see only release in Maledicte's eyes after the earl's death; everything the boy had craved was granted. Janus, his lover; the earl of Last, dead. Gilly knew where his own unease lay; Ani's continuing presence as obvious now as it had ever been, darkening Maledicte's nights, sending him into muttering rages and long bouts of sword practice against enemies only he could see.

Perhaps, it was simply that the changes had proved fickle and fleeting. Janus was Maledicte's, true, but Janus was also at Aris's beck and call, and Aris still hunted him a wife. The earl was dead, but earl was a title and it could be bestowed else—

The floorboards creaked along the stairwell; Gilly twitched but didn't take his eyes from the closed door. For one moment he even wished Janus here, waiting in this dim hall. On the darkest night, Gilly would prefer to spend it in Lizette's arms, letting the flame of her hair warm him like sunlight, letting the ampleness of her charms drive dead men from his mind. But Janus attended the masque as part of the king's entourage, and not Maledicte's escort. Gilly believed that it wasn't the masque itself that had brought the smile to Maledicte's face, but the simple fact that he would see Janus this evening, after a long month where Maledicte had seen Janus only rarely.

The stairs creaked again and Gilly turned his head in time to see a gray figure slip away. For a bone-shuddering moment, he believed in the dead as wholeheartedly as a child, but it was only Livia, stealing down the main stairs to avoid Cook's watchful eye.

"What do you think?" Maledicte asked, ghosting from his room.

Gilly shivered, caught by the dark eyes behind the raven mask. It was as if he saw Maledicte for the first time, and he was surprised all over again at how lovely Maledicte was. The lush mouth beneath the jutting black beak curled in amusement, changing the shape of the face. For one dizzying moment, Gilly saw a woman in a mask, behind the mask.

"Speechless?" Maledicte asked, the harsh rasp of his voice breaking the illusion. He stepped closer and the rook feathers sewn into his coat glimmered and shifted green, gold, and returned to black. The scent of dusty feathers washed over Gilly, the sweet pungency of lilac. He imagined touching the lush mouth, and the sudden violence of his desire made him quake.

Lizette teased him often about his love for Maledicte, and he allowed it, acknowledging his fascination, and acknowledging that Maledicte was not his. A bittersweet pang. But tonight, for the first time, he wondered if he could change that, wondered why his heart and body had run so counter to his tastes. He took Maledicte's slim shoulders in his hands, the feathers rustling against his palms, and drew him closer.

Maledicte looked up, inquiring and impatient. "Say something. I thought you would like the feathers. And what a time I had collecting them." Gilly imagined kissing the sulkiness from Maledicte's mouth, but the beaked mask was more than proof against such incursions.

"Do you think it wise to parade your allegiance with Black-Winged Ani?" he asked instead.

"It's not the fashion to believe in gods, remember?" Maledicte said, pushing away from Gilly. He paused in his path down the hall, and said, "Come along, Gilly. We're running late, and we must get you a mask. Should Vornatti come hunting for someone to tend his needs, I will not have him find you."

ONCE AGAIN THE TWO HALF-MOON courts were opened to each other, Aris's sunrise half and the nobles' secretive twilight. But the whirl of time and sky was fractured, made into mazes with hanging mirrors, swaying gently in the press of bodies, reflecting dizzying views of gilded traceries on the walls and the movement of the revelers, clad in fantastic concoctions limited only by their pockets or sense—lace and leather, masks and fur, and gems.

Small groups clustered near these illusory walls, where once they could have expected the gods' eyes to peer out at them, overseeing the Dark Solstice and its intersection of the living and the dead. Now the mirrors only served to double the attendees' numbers and the only ghosts were their own cloudy reflections. Masked royal servants, clad in gray velvet, moved like wraiths through the crowd, a reminder of the deaths the aristocrats evaded.

In the heart of the room, a raised dais stood, draped from above with a pale gray cloth that shimmered like rain in moonlight. The gilded chairs on it were empty, the backs of the chairs draped in black—the only symbol of mourning Aris allowed himself for a brother not proved dead.

Maledicte's face was stern behind the mask; his mouth, starred by a small velvet feather, grew tighter as he scanned the room, dismissing the crowd one costumed aristocrat at a time. In turn, Gilly noticed how few faces, even shielded, braved Maledicte's gaze.

"Janus will be on the dais with Aris," Gilly said. "Do you know his mask?"

"Do you think a mask can hide him from me?"

The royal dais became a hive of motion, of servants moving back and forth. Through their smoky shapes, behind the silvery drapes, the diminished family of Last could be seen. Aris, in festival white, nonetheless wore black armbands, and his mask was shaped like Sorrow.

Adiran sat at his father's right, in the queen's chair, which dwarfed his fragile body. On either side, the mastiffs, tongues lolling, watched the crowds, gulping foodstuffs that Adiran tossed them. A servant, clumsy with nervousness, stumbled over his own feet, and Hela chastised him with a deep, sudden bark. Adi giggled, tugged at her ears, holding his mask on with his other hand. He wore only a half-mask, white satin, trimmed with blue, and kept pushing it up his forehead, ruffling his hair.

Behind him, hands on the high back of the throne, was a dog-masked man with blue eyes. Adi looked up at him and barked, echoing Hela with a curious, imitative precision. Janus smiled and straightened his cousin's mask once again. He raised his head and met Maledicte's gaze, smiling.

"Will you dance?" a woman asked in Maledicte's ear, her hands on his shoulders, her breath on his nape.

Despite the dulcet words, there was a edge to the voice that Maledicte recognized. He knew her, mask or no mask.

"What reason will you give me, lady?" he asked, taking in her costume, the twin to his own in spirit if not in shade. Where Maledicte's feathers were unseasonably black, Mirabile's were unnaturally white, though more in tune with fashion. Her beaked mask had rubies crusted around the eyeholes, the only spark of color about her. Even her hair had been powdered to whiteness.

"Think how well we will look," she coaxed.

"Is that more important than enmity and spite?" Despite his glibness, her presence made him wary. He had not forgotten his atypical docility alongside her in Jackal Park, the way he had bent to the certainty in her eyes. Time had not diminished that strength.

"Infinitely," she said, holding out her hands. He had been wrong about the rubies being her only color. Her ungloved hands showed red nails, painted like any harlot's.

Maledicte drew back, turned, and found his path thwarted by a swaying mirror. Reflected in it, Janus bowed over a young woman's hand, drew her into a dance with a smile while Aris looked on approvingly. Mirabile ghosted up, a shimmer of red-eyed white in the mirror, and Maledicte found his hands entwined with hers as the dance began.

They danced in silence, Maledicte fighting the drowning sensation of being nothing more than her shadow, of having as little mind as a shadow— He forced through the numbness finally, his voice rough, "What do you want?"

"Found your tongue, I see," Mirabile said. Her lips curled in approval. "I was sure you would."

"Found my tongue, my will, and my senses," Maledicte said. He forced his steps to a halt, and freed his hands. "I am done with you—"

"Don't be ridiculous," Mirabile said, and fit herself back into his arms as if his rejection had only been a flirt within the dance pattern. "You ask me what I want? Nothing so dire as to make you frown so. I only wish to aid you. And in doing so, aid myself. Our common goal—" Her eyes darkened as his grip tightened, grinding the small bones of her hands together, but showed no other sign of pain.

Maledicte said, "What have we in common? *Nothing.*"

"Nearly everything," she said.

Mask to mask, Maledicte faltered a step, seeing Ani mirrored in her, and made no reply. She smiled sweetly, savagely at him, and said, swaying close, her voice a whisper, "You think your task is done, your compact fulfilled? When Last's death is not on your hands, but on those of your impetuous lover, who stole your kill?"

For one moment, Maledicte knew sympathy for Gilly, who preached caution with an ever-increasing avidity. For Mirabile to speak so in the king's presence, among witnesses, for her even to *know*— Maledicte shivered, suddenly unsure of who he held in his arms, Mirabile, the vicious-tongued harridan, or Ani Herself. The pale feathers on her costume brushed his, whispering.

Mirabile leaned in, warmed his cheek with her breath, and said, "Intercessors dream of the gods through an imperfect window, but I am one of Ani's chosen, and I . . . I dream of you. I saw you in the blurred shadows of sleep, you and Ixion, killing him."

"How dull your wits have become," Maledicte said. "To think to entertain me with past events that I experienced for myself." His mouth dried with unease. Once he had chastised Gilly for dreaming of him; to have Mirabile doing the same was far less bearable. Were they not the cynosure of the room, he would claw her eyes out that she not see him, tear her tongue out that she not speak of him.

"Now, now," she said. "Ixion favored you when he struck, whether you know it or not. To keep Ani close, clutched in your heart, can only be a boon. She grants such gifts—" Mirabile's eyes fluttered, opened again, russet eyes red-tinted as if they had taken on some of the rubies' bloody splendor. "Everything you ask, She grants, and all you need do is allow Her in as deep as She will go. You've asked so very little of Her, caught up in your petty obsession with Ixion. My advice is simple. Forgo this business of love and settle into power."

"Such things you say," Maledicte said. "I believe you are mad." Over the wheeling of the dance, the flashing mirrors, the rustling of feathers meeting feathers, he saw Gilly watching, concern etched in his furrowed brow.

"Why play the fool?" she said. "We are kin, the children of the carrion crow. Be my complement, my comrade, and we will do as we will. Isn't it seductive, my dark cavalier, to see the knowledge in their eyes—that their lives are in your hands or mine?"

"Your hands are too dainty for such work," Maledicte said. "You're only a spoiled aristocrat and delusional with despair. A gift of dreaming? Dreams are useless compared to a blade."

She tensed her fingers on his hands, digging her nails into the skin until blood welled.

"Weakling," she said. "Gifted and you do nothing with it. Take power for yourself—it will not satisfy you otherwise. Will you watch your lover rise, and stay weak as a woman, at his mercy?"

Maledicte stared at the distortion in her fine features as she shivered with rage. It touched ice to his bones, the realization that she was his mirror, or worse, his future. She had given herself wholly to Ani, and she was as terrible as a specter.

"Ani drives you mad," Maledicte said. "I will not join you on that road. Your vaunted alliance would be only to lull me into complacency so you could stab me in the back."

"Knife work is your métier. I prefer subtler arts. But you doubt me, doubt my skills?" She smiled, her eyes going distant. "The ice," she said, "breaks under the ship's prow. Shall I see what can be stirred to the surface? Bring your sins to light? I shall prove my skills to you, tonight," she said, curtseying and disappearing behind the nearest partition.

Sweat broke out along Maledicte's back and brow. Cold settled in his stomach. His hands shook, and he jammed them against his sides, striding purposefully for the doors and outside air. Gilly shadowed him, and Maledicte turned. "Back off, Gilly. I'm in a killing mood."

"You're bleeding," Gilly said, flinching as Maledicte snarled.

Maledicte forced his temper down, the pain radiating up his torn hands, and said plainly, "I believe the bitch poisoned me. *Tested* me." He moved onward to the balcony, shivering, hunching his shoulders against that spreading internal chill.

"Mal—" Gilly said, voice tight.

"I'm thirsty," Maledicte said. "Bring me a drink." His hand swung again and again to his sword hilt; droplets of blood flecked the marble floor. Maledicte leaned over the edge of the rail, panting a little, then recovered his poise. "Go on, Gilly. I'll be here. I've got my mask, after all, to protect me from death."

On the balcony, Maledicte watched the small wounds puff and swell with a near-indifferent eye, though he shook with chill and his feathers grew spiky with his sweat. Numbness swept over him, stiffening his legs, arms, and face, as if the chill in his veins had turned to ice. His breath labored. Then a convulsive shudder shook him and the small wounds spat back blood and something darker, something that trickled like a spill of greenish syrup. It pooled on the stone at his feet, and when it was done, he licked the scratches closed.

"Mal?" Janus came out of the light, into the shadows on the balcony, and Maledicte rose from his crouch.

"Here."

"And hale? Gilly spun me a tale of poison," Janus said, setting the glass on the balcony railing. It chattered and clinked against the stone. The velvet quality to his voice was ruffled. "I should have known he lied."

"Gilly so rarely lies," Maledicte said, picking up the glass and draining it. His raw throat eased.

Janus sucked his breath in, grabbed Maledicte to him, touching his damp skin and peering into his eyes. "You seem well enough."

"Yes," Maledicte said, curling into Janus's arms. Their hearts beat steadily against each other's: Janus's slowing as his fright eased, and Maledicte's speeding up from the dirge it had been dragged into by Mirabile's poison.

Janus sighed into Maledicte's hair, bent to kiss him, and finding the mask's black beak in his way, pushed it off.

Maledicte moved into Janus, pressing against him as if they could become one creature. Give up love for power? Mirabile was madder than he thought.

Too soon, Janus broke the embrace. "I must return."

"I have not touched you in weeks. A single kiss is all you spare me? Was this only an interlude in your quest for social acceptance?" Maledicte's fear made him bitter. The poison came too close, woke fears long dormant, reminding him that the world could separate them at any time, and still, Janus chose to play games. "Should I thank you for the time you've condescended to grant me?"

"Mal," Janus said. "I'm only trying to keep tabs on what is being said regarding Last, assuring Aris that you are blameless in Last's disappearance. And with Echo replacing Love as Counselor, I have much to defend against. But I'll come home tonight. I've missed you." He tugged Maledicte's hands to his chest, pressed them to his heart. Maledicte brought Janus's mouth to his again. The kiss lingered, but once more Janus broke it, this time walking away into the court.

Maledicte stared after him for a hungry moment, wishing he could make Janus see that they needed none of this. Let them retire to Lastrest, out of Mirabile's threats and entreaties, out of sight of Aris and his attempts to continue the line. But he had sworn to aid Janus, and Janus wanted the court, the title— Aris would likely reward a marriage with the title, once Last's death was accepted, and though that was what they wished, the idea of it woke some slow-burning worry in Maledicte's chest that he couldn't understand.

Spying Janus's earlier dance partner, the tiny girl dressed as a wood nymph in green and gold, with a veil instead of a mask, Maledicte deserted the balcony abruptly.

He made his bow before the wood nymph's chaperone and took the nymph's hands. A mask was no aid to the little doll girl; her lack of inches made her obvious.

They danced in stifling silence for a full four measures before Maledicte said, "If you hate me so much that you can't be bothered to be civil, I wonder why you agreed to dance at all. Surely no one would fault you for turning me away."

She looked up at him and flushed, the redness visible through the fine pale linen of her veil. Maledicte waited until the color had faded, then provoked it again. "Can't you answer me? Or were you never trained to talk?"

"Mother's desperate," she said in a breathless rush. "I have six younger sisters waiting for me to wed."

"Does she think to attach me?" he asked, incredulous. "I might as well be the plague for a chit like you." Compared to these noblewomen, Ella was an amateur schemer when it came to profiting from her daughter.

She lowered her head and mumbled some words that, though unintelligible, made her flush again.

Impatient, he tilted her head up, his bare fingers beneath the delicate veil. Her heart raced beneath his fingertips. "Be brave, girl. You're masked. Perhaps I don't even know who you are—as improbable as it seems."

The girl either took heart or umbrage, it was hard to tell, but the result was the same. She raised her head, a grim determination settling on her blurred face, and said. "She wants me to wed Lord Last."

Maledicte's temper turned in his belly. "Brazen or desperate indeed. To use Janus's lover to meet him. Does she want me to tell you what pleases him? What makes him sweat and cry out? What his skin feels like under my lips? What he says to me while we're abed?"

The girl's breathing quickened in shock. Such plain speaking was hard enough to hear for a maiden; for Maledicte to speak with such venom undid her composure completely. Her shoulders shook, and the veil over her eyes grew damp and dark with tears.

"Stop that," Maledicte said. "I will not have you start another scandal with me at the heart of it."

She stopped struggling, and he loosened his painful tourniquet on her arm. They took another round of the dance without any speech; the spots of moisture on the veil shrank and dried, leaving only quivering lips and shaking hands to convey the shock she still felt.

"I think your mother must be mad," he said, though mad brought to mind not a matchmaking aristocrat, but Mirabile with her red eyes and bloody nails.

"Why—" The girl paused, then continued, her voice gaining strength, "Why are you so cruel? I've never said a thing to hurt you. But you'll say anything to hurt me. You have every reason to be kind. You're handsome, and rich, and no one tells you what to do."

"You've never met my Gilly, if you think no one dictates to me," Maledicte said.

The dance ended and he bowed, but stayed at her side. She blanched as he drew her toward one curtained partition, a seat at the nexus of three mirrors. "Your virtue is safe," Maledicte said. "I merely want a word with you."

She nodded, biting her lips so hard that he thought the veil might darken with blood. He tugged it away from her face entirely, watched her eyes widen like morning-glories at sunrise.

He sat down in one of the quilted chairs, still holding her arm so that she had to bend with him. He drew her closer, put his lips by her ear. "Your mother may want Janus for you. Aris may want the same. But if you take Janus from me—" His breath hissed out at the very thought. "If you take him, I'll kill you. Best say no, should he come courting."

She whimpered and he said, "We are understood?"

Backing away, she stumbled and nearly fell, stepping on her skirts in her haste to be out of his reach. Heads turned as she floundered across the floor, toward the shelter of her abigail and the cluster of debutantes drinking toasts to the dawn, safely arrived.

Mirabile passed through the debutantes with a word here, a touch there, and a smile for Maledicte cast over her shoulder as she bypassed the nymph sobbing in her chaperone's arms.

"That was not well done of you," Gilly said. "Besides being a cousin to Westfall, Psyke Bellane is a gentle, inoffensive girl."

"Gentle, yes. Inoffensive?" Maledicte said, "No. But killing her would be like crushing a sparrow, so easy as to arouse more pity than satisfaction. By warning her off, I've done both of us a kindness."

"Only you could argue that way," Gilly said.

Maledicte pulled his mask off, dropped it to the marble floor. "I've had enough. I'm going home."

Gilly's response was drowned in the sudden tolling of deep bells. This close to the palace, the sound was as powerful as the tide and as inexorable.

Maledicte turned to catch Janus's eyes and met Aris's instead, and saw the quick shattering in them. Maledicte flinched.

"Last," Gilly whispered. "The unshriven dead."

"Hush, Gilly," Maledicte said, taking his hand. "Hush."

On the dais, Adiran, startled by the clamor, clapped his hands over his ears and wailed, his voice rising over the low pitch of the bells like a descant. Aris pulled him into his lap, soothing him. Jasper and Echo moved toward Aris at a trot.

The bells faded into silence though the mirrors still shivered with their echoes. In the sudden hush, a startled shriek rang out as a debutante fainted in her escort's grip. Gilly stepped closer to Maledicte, and Maledicte tightened his grip on Gilly's trembling fingers. "Shh, Gilly."

The girl's abigail fanned her face, and her escort chafed her wrists, ever more frantically. He looked up with wide eyes. "She's not breathing."

Before his words stopped sounding, a second girl fell, an heiress of some repute. By the time her people converged around her, the first debutante was dead.

On the dais, Aris stood and started as if he could see Death walking the floor. Jasper gestured madly and the Kingsguard enclosed the king, surrounding him. Hela barked, long, deep, and hoarse, the sound reminiscent of the death bells, and Janus closed her muzzle with his hand. Aris nodded his shaky thanks and they fled the court. As the king's doors sealed tight behind him, the chaos spread unchecked, as a third, then fourth girl collapsed.

In the doorway, shadowed by the rising sun, Mirabile smiled at Maledicte, and dropped the tiniest of curtsies, a performer acknowledging praise.

FLIGHT

ARIS LOOKED DOWN AT THE wreck of a body resting on the marble slab, lying between Haith's sculpted hands, sheltering in the grasp of the god. Though pains had been taken with the corpse, the worst of the torn and waterlogged flesh hidden beneath the blue cloak, still the face was barely human. Only the chill of the winter sea had kept flesh and bone together, and Aris, remembering his first horrified look at the sea dreck his brother had become, knew that beneath the softening cloak were sections of bare bone.

"Sire," a kingsguard said, "the courtier Maledicte has arrived. Where will you receive him?"

"Bring him here," Aris said.

The guard's sandy brows rose nearly to his hairline, but he merely nodded. Aris turned his attention back to his brother's body, barely hearing the man leave.

"So it came to this," he said. "Nearly alone, our family winnowed by time . . . You should have been the older, Michel," Aris said, feeling as if a weight had settled over his neck and shoulders, sinking toward his heart. "You would have made a better king than I, I think, shortsighted and reactionary though you were. Antyre loves me not, and more, respects me not. You would have forced respect on them. Or fear. And I would not be left with this—" Footsteps echoed in the hall, the shuffle of feet on stone.

Aris raised his head. Few enough people came down the winding, dark hallways toward the chapel that he knew who it must be.

Maledicte dropped a bow. "You sent for me?" Behind him, a guard lurked.

"Yes," Aris said, his throat rough. Maledicte's eyes were heavy-lidded, his hair loosely and hastily tied back. Small jet feathers sieved from them, and Aris remembered the two dancers, one black, one white, whirling around the ballroom, heads bent close together. His hands fisted.

"Come and see what has befallen my brother," Aris said, stepping away from the bier.

Maledicte came forward, wavering like one of the shadows in the dimly lit room. He leaned over the ruined head, and stepped back, his pale face expressionless.

"Does it satisfy you to see him dead?" Aris said. "I know you hated him, though never the why of it."

"Yes," Maledicte said.

"Give me your hand," Aris said.

Maledicte proffered his right hand. Aris seized it and tugged him back to the edge of the bier. The sickly sweet odor of putrefaction washed over them, driving Maledicte's perfume back. His hand in Aris's struggled. Maledicte turned his face away, leaving Aris to speak to the wing of dark hair sheltering him.

"Touch him," Aris said, voice ragged. The guard leaned forward to watch, witness. Maledicte resisted, and Aris yanked his arm forward, stretching it toward the body. Tears started in his eyes.

Maledicte turned, caged Aris's prisoning hands with his free hand, stopping him. "A learned man so wild with grief," Maledicte whispered, his voice meant only for Aris's ears. Maledicte's dark lashes lifted; the black eyes met Aris's and Aris shivered. "Which superstition are we chasing, sire? Is Last supposed to bleed at my touch?" He freed his hand from Aris's grip, as gently and precisely as a pickpocket liberating coins.

"I doubt you can claim squeamishness."

"Why don't you ask me?" Maledicte said.

"You must do it," Aris said, looking away from the sweet mouth turned down in distaste, hardening his ears to the intimacy of that raspy voice, so close, sounding so caring. False or not, it made Aris tremble.

Maledicte stepped forward and touched his fingers to Last's forehead, then touched the sodden fabric over Last's heart. Then he spread his hand to show Aris the unmarked flesh. "I did not kill your brother."

Aris no longer knew what to believe, his mind as cold and as numb as Last's corpse. As cold as the fallen debutantes, awaiting their spring burials. He only knew that death had come to his country on Maledicte's heels, that any member of his court must be an able liar, well versed in apparent sincerity, and that Maledicte had an unsavory reputation as a swordsman and blackmailer. The one Aris could testify to, thinking of the damning Antyrrian audit ledgers kept hidden by this boy's pale hands, weapons more worrying to Aris than the blade.

As for the sword—those delicate hands were smooth, barely callused, and Aris knew that reputations were often based on gossip. Neither Aris, nor any of his guards, had ever seen Maledicte dueling. Even Echo, ready to condemn, had qualms imagining Last taken by Maledicte's sword. Last himself granted no aid; though he had spoken out against Maledicte in life, his body, caught up in the *Fleur's* anchor and dragged along the keel before breaking free, was too mangled to make any mute accusations.

Aris covered his eyes as if he could blot out the images, blot out the panic surging in his blood.

Aris shivered as Maledicte put his hand on his arm, unasked. He heard the guards shifting uneasily, but said nothing, instead allowing Maledicte to tow him away from the bier. He opened his eyes to see what expression he could catch on Maledicte's face, as if he could sneak up on verity when it eluded words, but learned nothing new, save that compassion sat uneasily on Maledicte's clever face.

"I thought you meant to question him, sire," Echo said, arriving in the doorway on an upswing of anger. Aris put another body width between himself and Maledicte.

Maledicte said, "Ask at will. I will give you no more difficulty."

"The debutantes," Aris said, his words overriding Echo's attempt to take control of the room. "Had you anything to do with their deaths?"

"No," Maledicte said, startled and frowning. In the background, Echo scoffed, and it was to him that Maledicte addressed the rest. "I am no killer of feckless girls."

"Whispers speak of a evil pact between yourself and Mirabile," Echo said, coming closer.

"Are you serving as counselor of gossip?" Maledicte asked, his customary acid eating into his tone.

"You danced with her," Echo said, "your heads bent close as if you shared secrets and schemes—"

"Never with her," Maledicte said. "She's quite crazed. Send for her, Echo. I doubt she'll deny her wrongdoing."

"I sent Jasper to collect her," Aris said, noting the lack of concern in Maledicte's gaze. "Echo, it's early. Let us continue this later, after we've spoken to Mirabile . . ." He drew Maledicte away from Echo, closer to himself, and lowered his voice. "I will see you out of this, but you will repay me with your discretion and silence this winter. I want no gossip to reach my ears of your doings."

"Such a thing you ask of me," Maledicte said. "Surely, it is not within my power to still idle tongues—"

"Enough," Aris said, in no mood for banter, not with his brother's corpse so near, not with the young man suspected of killing him. "The court is closed. Until spring comes and wipes away death with life, there will be no balls, no celebrations, no masques. The nobles will rusticate in their country homes, or in town estates should they feel inclined. You will do likewise. Do so and I will give you Janus."

"He's not yours to bestow," Maledicte said.

"But his absence is mine to command. I could see him mewed at Lastrest, trapped in mourning clothes and customs. Or I could keep him at my side exclusively—" Aris trailed off. In the dimly lit room, cold with death and pain, Maledicte's burgeoning anger felt huge, a looming, dark presence. Echo moved closer, hand dropping to his sword hilt.

"Little fool," Aris said, seizing Maledicte's shoulders and shaking him with all his pent-up frustrations. "Do not force me to heed the whispers."

Maledicte suffered the shaking meekly, his hair falling from its loose queue and hiding his face. His harsh voice came like a whisper of scale on stone. "I will be discreet, sire, to the best of my ability, which is not inconsiderable, you'll agree?"

"Aris," Echo objected. "Better to hold him until we see what Mirabile has to say—"

"Are you so eager to keep me from my luncheon and my books?" Maledicte asked. Aris felt like one of his dogs gone to point. The specter of the ledgers had been in the room since Maledicte's entrance. He had expected Maledicte to invoke their power sooner, and more bluntly. This reminder, so gently spoken, could be a threat, or merely a reminder that Maledicte could, indeed, be discreet.

"Go then," Aris said. His hand, still resting on Maledicte's shoulder, lifted and twined the dark hair around his fingers, turning his face up for study. It wasn't innocence that greeted him; Aris would have distrusted such an expression on Maledicte's face, but there was no triumph either. Its lack softened Aris's offense. "Go on then. Off with you. Let me hear nothing of you but praise, and come back in the spring."

Maledicte bowed, his hair slipping through Aris's grasp.

"Sire—" Echo objected, but never had time to finish. Jasper returned, white-faced, two guards walking behind him, their hands on their pistols, their gazes nervous, as if they had seen devils.

"Jasper?" Aris asked, his voice unsteady. "What's happened?"

"Westfall's dead . . . his house afire—"

"The antimachinists? They dared to—"

Jasper wiped a hand over his mouth and his sweating face as he interrupted his king. "Not them. Mirabile's run mad, sire. She's killed them both, poisoned Brierly and murdered Westfall. She took his eyes and heart." He shuddered. "We saw her, gown bloodstained from hem to hip, as if she'd been wading through blood. But before we could lay hands on her, she was gone, like a shadow disappearing under the noon sun.

"Gone," Aris repeated, dumbly.

"It's witchcraft, sire, I swear. No matter that the gods are gone . . . she's found some way to touch power, and no one will be safe until she's stopped."

Aris sank onto the bench, looking up at the painted gods, and for the first time in thirty years offered a whisper of a prayer to Baxit, praying that reason would return to his kingdom.

· 29 ·

THE FIRST SIGNS OF SPRING inside the city limits were the groans and creaking of the ice breaking up near the docks, moaning like live things in torment. Maledicte had slept badly this winter, and would have slept a good deal worse, saving Janus's presence and the gossip mill turning from him to Mirabile. As the Dark Solstice deaths faded in urgent memory, his rumored part in it fell beneath the waves of Mirabile's continued depredations.

The slaughter of the Westfalls paled beside the subsequent deaths of the four kingsguards who had run her to ground. All four men were found rent and eyeless, and on that violent topic, tongues wagged. Mirabile, some cried, was a phantom, returned to plague the living. A witch, cried others, and one who meant to curse the aristocracy. Others, more cautious, whispered of returned gods and Ani's touch, whispered so quietly that only Gilly, sifting information, heard that rumor.

One further tidbit kept bored tongues busy. The whisper that Aris had chosen Janus to replace Westfall as counselor. The rumors claimed first that this was merely Aris's way of leashing his scandalous nephew and keeping the last of a line close. More acidly voiced rumors said that Aris always liked one of his counselors to be in touch with the common folk, and what was more common than a bastard?

Still the season passed, with Janus often at the palace, acting as Aris's aide. It was Janus who greeted foreign merchants at the dock, haggling for

Aris, and spurning the bulk of the Itarusine cargo. And it was Janus, or so it was murmured, who met with Captain Tarrant, that pardoned war pirate, to strike a surreptitious bargain, smuggling those same spurned Itarusine goods into the country, thus relieving the exorbitant prices on staples, and silencing some of the protesting poor. But if Janus spent his days at Aris's beck and call, his nights were Maledicte's exclusively.

Even with Janus's near-constant presence, Gilly knew that Maledicte was more often haunted than not, nights given over to nightmares, and saw, with increasing regularity, the shadows drifting in Maledicte's eyes as Ani, stymied, made Herself felt in a hundred small black tantrums and nightmares. From the brittle tension that rose between Maledicte and Janus, from the near-resentful looks Maledicte cast Janus on occasion, Gilly thought he understood what had happened. As of yet, he had not found a tactful way to ask for confirmation.

Tonight, Gilly came in with the groaning of the ice, feeling as grave as if it were he doing the moaning. He had, in his hand, the instrument that would shatter their fragile peace.

"Do you know you have frost in your hair?" Maledicte said, lounging in the hall with a glass of wine in his hand. "And you look chilled through." Maledicte set his glass down on the empty receiving salver. As Aris had requested, Maledicte had refused to attend any of the makeshift festivities, though in truth, few had requested his presence. Maledicte dusted the frost from Gilly's coat and sleeves. Parchment crackled like breaking ice, and Maledicte tugged the paper from Gilly's hand.

"What's this? A note from Lizette? Does your ladybird know how to write?" Maledicte teased. Gilly reached for the letter, but Maledicte evaded him.

Taking up his glass again, Maledicte propped himself against the wall, and began to read the gathered gossip and speculation Gilly paid Bellington for.

The glass splintered in his hand. "When did you know about this?" Maledicte demanded.

"Just this afternoon," Gilly said. "I got word from the solicitor and went down to the docks to talk to the captain of the *Kiss*. He confirmed it, said she was showing signs even on the journey out."

Maledicte let out a strangled sound—whimper, snarl, or both together, combined of rage and despair. "We should have thrown her into the sea with her damned husband. But who would have calculated the odds to be so against us? Five years it took for Last to seed his previous wife, and several slips after that. But Amarantha—wife for a bare sennight—" His breath sobbed in his chest, unequal to his rage.

"What's the matter now, the soup served cold?" Janus asked, coming into the hall. As he looked from Gilly to Maledicte, the bored humor drained from his face.

"The countess of Last, Amarantha Ixion, is near to term with your father's child, and she returns to lay claim to the estate and title." Maledicte belatedly noticed the broken glass in his hand. He opened his clenched fist, let the shards patter down like rain from his unmarred skin.

Janus blanched. "A blow to be sure." He raised his hand to his forehead, rubbed the narrow spot between his eyes. "Is it Father's child for sure? Not some bastard thing she's using to gain control of the estate?"

"If it is not your father's babe, it is so close that we will never prove otherwise," Gilly said.

"What do we do?" Maledicte said. "If the child is born, if it is a boy, our plans are thrown over, Janus."

Janus stroked Maledicte's dark hair. "You'll just have to kill her before she gives birth. But be careful, Mal. Aris seems most . . . interested in your activities. Echo counsels mistrust, while I scoff, and yet we only attain stalemate. Best we heed Aris's obsession, and be discreet in her death."

WHEN ARIS SENT A RUNNER to Janus, informing him that he would be sent to meet Amarantha's ship with the royal carriage and a slew of guards, Maledicte said, "I don't suppose you could drown her by accident." He said it with no particular energy, lounging on the chaise, slowly moving to fill the area that Janus had vacated.

"No," Janus said, though his lips quirked.

Maledicte marked the smile with one of his own. "At least we know that Aris holds you innocent of your father's fate, to send you to fetch Amarantha."

"He sends me with an armed escort. That argues no particular trust," Janus said, pulling his coat on, settling the shoulders, and checking the lines in the mirror.

"Well, you did murder Last," Maledicte said.

Watching from the chair beside the parlor door, Gilly raised his head sharply. Janus cast him a baleful look, and spoke to Maledicte. "We are not discussing this again. You killed him, I merely sped him on his way."

"All your own way," Maledicte said, still lazily. "The fun of patricide and treason and none of the blame."

Janus stooped, pulled Maledicte up, and shook him, once. "Enough. What do you want me to do to apologize?"

Maledicte smiled at him. "I can't think of anything."

"I can," Gilly said, drawing two sets of eyes to him. "Wouldn't it be appropriate to have a welcoming celebration? Urge Aris to hold one."

"She wouldn't attend," Maledicte said. "The letters our spies sent said she had become quite mad with suspicion. To expect her to attend a ball, where others have died—"

"Take it up with the king. If Aris commands it, she will attend," Gilly said, his mouth dry as he argued for murder. But if Janus meant to see Amarantha dead, Gilly would do what he could to ensure Maledicte's survival. Without a plan, Maledicte would be far too prone to give in to Ani's careless bloodlust. And unlike Last, a pregnant Countess would rarely be alone.

Gilly let out a shaky breath. Perhaps this was a second chance to free Maledicte from Ani's touch. There was no earl of Last, but Amarantha was the titular head of the line—perhaps her death would be enough; perhaps whatever had been done the first time to invalidate Last's death, Maledicte could undo. It came to him, suddenly, that he was hoping for the death of a woman with child, and his whole body rang with the shock of it.

Janus paced the room. "If Aris agreed, it would be a well-guarded thing, Mal. I doubt you could you kill her there."

"Mirabile did well enough," Maledicte said. "You gave me aid when none was wanted, Janus. Give me aid now when I ask for it. Our enemies grow like the hydra. One dead, two created. Let's destroy this head before we have to kill an infant as well." Maledicte's voice shifted.

"Be as honest with yourself as you were with me when you accused me of patricide. Were Amarantha not gravid, you would not need to raise your sword. Infanticide is your goal, Mal. Can you stomach it?"

"I have no choice," Maledicte said, "if you would be earl."

After Janus left, Maledicte sank onto the chaise and covered his eyes. Gilly went to his side, hesitant, then reaching out, took one hand. Maledicte's fingers curled around Gilly's.

"He killed Last?" Gilly asked, shying away from future murders in favor of past ones. But the confirmation of his fear laced his heart with dismay. If Janus had done so, was it any wonder that Ani lingered, foul-tempered and growing? "That could not have satisfied Ani."

"In all your books," Maledicte said pensively, "all your pamphlets and gossip, have you ever heard that Ani can be satisfied? Mirabile seemed to think otherwise."

"Tell me what happened," Gilly asked. "How you meant to kill Last, and instead had Janus kill Last and some sailors."

Maledicte raised his eyes, ringed with sudden weariness. "If you know that, you know it all. We should have taken Amarantha then. If I had, I would not be facing this now."

"You could wait," Gilly said. "Perhaps the child will be female, or, like Adiran, will be born flawed, unable to inherit. Or it may die of its own accord, as Last's most recent son did. Murdering Last is one thing, this is another."

"Enough, Gilly, I am done with talking about it. If Amarantha attends the party, she dies." Maledicte burst from the chair, yanking his hand from Gilly's, and stormed toward the door. He paused at the last moment and turned back, his voice ragged and wild. "I cannot have this, Gilly. I cannot take on your conscience. I need to be free to draw blood at will, be it man, woman, or babe. As there are deaths behind me, that is all that is before me as well. Do not weaken me."

. . . he withdrew his knife and stabbed her thrice, seeking her heart, but she merely mocked his prowess with the blade, for Ani's unnatural children scoff at injury and fear no man. She clawed out his eyes with sharpened nails and when dawn came, she was found still feasting on his heart . . .

—Grayle's *Book of Vengeances,* "The Savage of Issey"

S NOW SPOTTED THE FIRST BRAVE leaves of the spring crocus. Maledicte looked up at the leaden sky, and at the faint sparks of spiraling white drifting down to edge the palace grounds. "Spring?"

Gilly, attending him, said, "Snow's not unheard of this early in the season. But it is damaging to silk. Best go in now."

Maledicte smiled at him. "Oh yes, because spotted silk is a terrible sin." The fey cheerfulness to his manner made Gilly's stomach ache. He had seen this before. It was as if Ani, knowing Maledicte's plans, was curled up in sulky approval, sated before the act as She never was after.

"I think you just don't want to be alone in the dark with a murderer," Maledicte said, tugging Gilly's tied-back tail of hair.

"Mal, hush," Gilly said, looking around. No one was within earshot, but his heart pounded all the same. Halfway to the king's court, in the winter-riven lines of the garden, with the stables at their back—Gilly couldn't imagine what Maledicte was playing at.

"Admit it, Gilly. You fear me."

"Fear *for* you," Gilly said, taking Maledicte's arm and pulling him deeper into the skeleton of the garden. He pressed Maledicte back into the prickly embrace of a hedge, its leaves only faint smudges of starting greenery, and said, "What ails you?"

Maledicte closed his eyes, letting the snow lay ephemeral patterns on his skin. Gilly touched Maledicte's cheek. Had it not been for the quick, cold nip of snow melt, the dampness on his palm could have been tears. "Mal?"

"I am," Maledicte said, opening dark eyes. "I am afraid to be alone in the dark by myself."

Tongue caught, Gilly could say nothing.

"I do things I never expected I could. And that's cause enough to fear, but more, I do not feel alone in my own mind, in my own skin. She's there, wanting out. It's getting crowded, Gilly. The person I was, the person I am, and the crow. We're all jostling for ascendancy, and I don't know who's going to win."

Gilly opened his mouth; Maledicte put his gloved hand over it. "Listen, Gilly. If Ani wins, leave me. Don't stay. I would never hurt you, but She would devour you entire. Promise me."

Gilly shook his head, and Maledicte frowned. Footsteps crunched on the seashell paths as a coachman walked steadily into the dark, undoubtedly heading for the wall the stable staff used as a privy. "Come on," Maledicte said, ducking under Gilly's caging arms.

Turning in the direction of the court, Gilly found himself walking alone. Maledicte had gone back the way they had come, heading into the stables.

Gilly caught up, trying to move soundlessly, grimacing with the effort. Maledicte smiled at him when he arrived. "Watch for anyone coming?" He went down the silent rows of detached coaches. Twenty feet away, stableboys fed horses, rubbed them down, and cleaned the stalls.

Maledicte ghosted along the rows of coaches until he reached the glossy blue of Last's coach, gone drowned and greenish in the flickering lamplight. Maledicte climbed onto the coachman's bench and insinuated his hand into the juncture of carriage and seat, recovering a worn flask. He joined Gilly again in the sheltering darkness of an unused stall. "Hold this," he said. He stripped off his jacket and felt inside the seams. Gilly watched, mouth falling open. As Maledicte pulled out two tiny crystal vials, Gilly said in a furious whisper, "You brought poison to court? After what happened to those girls? You are mad."

"We're not in court," Maledicte said, "and these vials never will be." He levered out the wax stopper and trickled a thin syrup into the coachman's flask. Closing the flask's lid, he sloshed it gently.

"You're going to poison the coachman?" Gilly said.

"Would you prefer me to stalk into the court and strike Amarantha dead by blade, or pour her a drink and have her fall at my feet? This way is more chancy, but far more likely to pass as accidental."

Maledicte sloshed the flask a moment more, then opened it and sniffed. "Perfect."

"And if he drinks it all now? While waiting for his masters?"

"I'm counting on it," Maledicte said. "Janus is supposed to goad Amarantha into flight. Failing that, my presence alone should do it." He looked over Gilly's shoulder and scowled. Two stableboys had skived off their chores and crept into the coach aisle, and were playing dice in the carriages' shadows.

"Rats take it," Maledicte muttered.

"We've time," Gilly said.

"That we do not," Maledicte said. "Dantalion is too careful. He will not allow his coachman to linger in the yard with the others, playing cards. He'll want him here. Guarding the carriage against saboteurs."

"Give it to me, then," Gilly said. "I look enough like a coachman. I'll return it; those boys won't remember me at all."

Maledicte relinquished his hold on the flask and Gilly sauntered out into the lamplit alley between coaches. The two boys paused in their game, bodies wary, ready to bolt should Gilly show any signs of noticing them.

Gilly realized halfway to Last's coach that his was more than a little errand that Maledicte could not do, that what he was doing would result in at least one man's death, maybe more. But the fear that if he balked Maledicte would choose a more dangerous path kept him from freezing in his tracks. "Don't ask me to kill for you," he had said once. Now it seemed he volunteered.

Feeling as if he ascended the gallows, Gilly climbed to the bench. He had just reached to return the flask when he heard the cry. "Hoy! What're you doing?"

He turned, aware of the two stableboys scattering—directed at them or not, the words were too close to the ones they dreaded—and found Dantalion's coachman staring up at him.

"Get off of there—hey, that's mine," he said, his indignation darkening to suspicion and anger. He held out his hand for the flask and Gilly, seeing no alternative, put it in his hand.

"What were you doing with that?"

Gilly, reaching for a plausible explanation, was forestalled by Maledicte. "I asked him to find me a drink," Maledicte said.

"There's fancy guff inside. What d'you need mine for?" The coachman scowled at the slim aristocratic shape.

"The last time drink was taken within those walls, people fell dead. Call me overcautious," Maledicte said, leaning against the stall.

"Mirabile killed fillies," the coachman said, but after another sneering look, he continued, "though you've got more than a touch of the mare about you, don't you?"

Maledicte's cheeks flushed, and he dropped his hand to where his sword hilt would have been, had he not left it in the hay when he removed his jacket.

Assessing that motion, the coachman paused. "You're that one, aren't you? That cursed cavalier my master natters on about. Maybe you'd better have my flask after all. Take a drink of it, just in case." He tossed it to Maledicte.

"Too gracious," Maledicte said, tilting the tarnished metal to his lips.

Gilly's heart was in his mouth, choking back protest, as he watched for the trick, the movement that betrayed that Maledicte was not really swallowing mouthfuls of his own poison. A trickle of adulterated whiskey ran from the edge of his mouth, and it was too much for the coachman.

"Here! Leave me some. Gi' me that." He snatched it from Maledicte's hand. He shook the flask, and swore. "Drank near half of it, damn you."

Maledicte wiped his mouth with a lazy hand. "That stuff's rot; you really should get your employer to give you better."

The coachman spat on the floor, and Maledicte moved the tip of his polished boot away from the glistening, wet spot with a moue of distaste. "And people find my manners lamentable? Gilly, bring my coat with you." He stalked off without waiting for reply.

"I don't envy you your master, boy," the coachman said.

Gilly jammed his shaking hands into his coat pockets. "He pays well." His words were near as hoarse as Maledicte's, tight with dread. Dread that Maledicte drank his own brew. Dread that the coachman would drink and die and make Gilly a murderer.

Gilly cast a frantic glance into the gardens, but Maledicte had disappeared from sight. His stomach clenched to the point of pain, imagining Maledicte fallen, convulsing. Would Ani protect him? With Last's death denied Her?

He snatched up Maledicte's coat, hearing a faint rip as the embroidery snagged on the baled hay, and hurried toward the stable doors. Gilly looked back once to see the coachman take a great pull from his flask, making Gilly a murderer.

After a few panicky moments, he found Maledicte back in the quiet shadows of the thorny hedge again. His eyes glittered like black water. "Did he drink?" Maledicte asked. Coatless, he seemed smaller, more fragile than he was.

"Did you?" Gilly asked, his voice trembling, a bare whisper.

"You saw me," Maledicte said.

Gilly tugged at him. "Let's go home. We'll find you the antidote. Or maybe you won't really need one. Ani protects Her own, right? But we can't risk it."

Maledicte slipped from his grip. "Gilly, I've already taken it. Two vials, remember? You were afraid I was dying? I don't trust Ani that far. And I'm not stupid enough to die in an attempt on Amarantha's life. Not when it's a chancy death at best. I think I'm offend—"

Gilly seized him close, held him, heart beating against his own. This close, Maledicte surprised him by not being awkwardly tall or broad; he fit as snugly in his arms as Livia did. Maledicte sagged against him, giving Gilly license to let his hands rove down across the narrow back and slender hips, pulling him closer still. Maledicte looked up at him, and Gilly bent; at the last, Maledicte avoided his mouth. Gilly's kiss ended on the slightly slick length of the scar on his jaw. He tasted the flesh there, a tongue tip at a time, and Maledicte made a faint sound in his arms, of appreciation or protest, Gilly wasn't sure.

Gilly's clever fingers transmitted a piece of information to him. "You wear a corset?"

"I eat too much," Maledicte muttered, and while he didn't take himself from Gilly's arms, nonetheless Gilly was aware of some wary withdrawal.

Gilly touched the line of his jaw, guided Maledicte's mouth toward his own, but even as he did, desire faltered to curiosity. The lean bones of Maledicte's arms and legs argued against such a need.

Maledicte's sigh against his skin stifled curiosity, and Gilly pressed his suit, aware of his own hunger made evident in the fit of his breeches, his thighs against Maledicte's.

"Let me go," Maledicte said. "Enough, Gilly." The whisper was faint enough that Gilly could ignore it if he chose. But while the tremble in Maledicte's back, the kneading of his hands on Gilly's chest urged him on, Gilly was all too aware that Maledicte's desire did not equal his own, that if they were to step apart, there would be no telltale swelling to mar the smooth fit of Maledicte's breeches.

"Gilly," Maledicte's voice was more urgent. "Let me go, or I'll make a eunuch of you."

Startled, Gilly released him. Maledicte staggered away, fell to his knees, and vomited in the hedges. Snow hares rustled and darted away from his sudden descent into their domain. Gilly crouched beside him and Maledicte gasped that he was well. Gilly drew Maledicte's hair from his face while he was sick.

Maledicte rose and took steps back to the main path, sat down on a stone bench, covered with a thin drifting of blown snow. He wet his hands with it, the snow melting at his touch, and wiped his face. "Sometimes the antidote is worse than the poison."

Gilly sat down heavily by his side, his heart feeling overtaxed. "I thought you were dying."

"We've had this conversation," Maledicte said. "And it led us—" He put snow in his mouth like a child. It reddened his lips.

"Led us where?" Gilly asked. It hurt to do so, to probe at the disconnection between them, but he was no more capable of not asking than he was of walking away.

"Astray," Maledicte said. "Decidedly astray." He leaned his elbows on his knees, traced images in the frost at their feet. Raven wings, eyes, a sword. "I am his entirely, remember. What I do, I do for him." His mouth twisted, as if he found the fact not as much of a boon as it once was.

"And he'll be looking for you," Gilly said, standing and holding out an arm.

Maledicte hesitated, then took Gilly's arm. As they walked toward the yellow glow of candlelight and warmth, the drifting voices that held an edge of fear, Maledicte said, "Besides, Gilly, I'm no partner for you. You need a nice girl, one who'll give you babies, not ask you to kill them."

Gilly let out his breath. "Lizette's a whore, and no fonder of me than she is of my money, and our little Livia's a spy. Yet I care for them both. So what's the addition of one murderer to my affections?"

"Livia—a spy?" Maledicte said, his eyes hooded by speculation.

Gilly bit his lip, but words once said were impossible to cage again. "She has far more coin than she should and she creeps out nights. And none of our trinkets or teaspoons are missing. Unless she's thieving other houses, it's information she's selling."

"A spy," Maledicte said, dismay in his voice. "And we have such secrets to sell." He drifted up the lawn, boots leaving dark tracks in the rime, and paused. "Perhaps we can turn it to our advantage. Do nothing directly until we know who's buying."

"Dantalion," Gilly suggested.

"Or Mad Mirabile, or even Aris, as unpalatable as that thought is. We'd best find out."

Gilly nodded, a little shamed that he had needed telling.

Maledicte looked toward the lit rooms, spills of light raying out like slow lightning, flickering in the wakes of skirts and coats, and his mouth tipped into a deeper frown. This near, they could hear the forced gaiety, the musicians sawing out newly written tunes, lest anyone be reminded of the Dark Night deaths. "Gilly, go prepare the coach. I will enter only long enough to spook Amarantha, if Janus has not already done so. Tonight, I prefer my nest."

MALEDICTE WIPED HIS MOUTH one last time; the bitter taste of bile, tannic fluids, and belladonna lingered. He climbed the wide steps from the garden and gained access to the balconies, unwilling to enter under the watchful, fearful eyes of the other attendees. Seen through the open doors of the ballroom, Janus danced attendance on Psyke Bellane, his eyes alight with an amusement she didn't share.

White around her rosebud lips, the china doll curtsied and attempted to take her leave. Janus stopped her with another question, a hand on her silk-draped arm, smiling down at her. Her chaperone watched with a smile. When Janus lifted his hand from her sleeve, she flew like a dove.

"What kept you?" Janus said, turning as if he had sensed Maledicte's approach. "I've had to entertain myself with sweet, scared Psyke. What did you say to her?"

"Nothing she took seriously enough," Maledicte said, watching the slight girl slip through the crowds. He fought an absurd sense of betrayal, as if he had expected Psyke to forswear Janus simply because the time spent listening to Maledicte's threats had spared her from Mirabile's touch.

He swayed on his feet a moment, off balance by the imagined weight of his hatred. Janus smiled at him and led him back out to the seclusion of topiary and stone.

"You look so fierce," Janus said, kissing Maledicte's throat and cheek. Maledicte turned his head to avoid his lips, thinking of toxins on his, feeling as if he'd stumbled into an odd, repetitive dream world. Turn from Gilly's warmth, turn from Janus's arms; face the cold wind and the dark alone. He dreaded Ani rising up through his throat, stabbing out from his mouth, the long beak terrible and gore-smeared, Her wings scratching through his chest, pushing out past his lungs and ribs, dragging him up into the night sky, a soaring, bloody puppet. Distantly, Maledicte realized some of the belladonna must have lingered beyond the antidote, sparking hallucinations.

"What kept you?" Janus asked.

"Gilly kissed me in the snow gardens," Maledicte said. "He killed the coachman and kissed me. . . ." He shook his head, shaking the moment from his mind. "I fear his ethics have been severely compromised by our association."

Janus shook him. "Mal, are you mad?"

"Yes," Maledicte said. "I think I must be." Lips moving against the roughness of the brocade, Maledicte imagined the threads snaking out to drag him into Janus's skin.

"To let Gilly kiss you, I must agree," Janus snapped, pushing Maledicte away. He paced a quick circle and then came back, blue eyes smoldering. "Do you want him, desire him? Is that it? Why you would risk all for a tumble? In the king's garden? Tell me, Mal—do you love him?"

Janus's hushed words sounded wounded, stripped of strength, but Maledicte, dark-dreaming with the belladonna's aid, saw what the low tones disguised—the red cloud settling around his bright form, splintering out from the steady flame of rage behind his pale eyes.

"You are all my desires," Maledicte said, twining his arms about Janus's neck. "And so I told him. That I am yours and yours alone. Though you are not exclusive to me . . . you will marry."

"And why shouldn't you?" Janus twitched within Maledicte's arms at the familiar deep voice. Maledicte felt near panic himself—how long had Aris been listening? Behind the king, Psyke stood in the doorway. Maledicte fought a growl—had she led the king to Janus?

"Sire," Maledicte said, sinking into a bow.

Beside him, Janus nodded. "Uncle."

"I would speak with Maledicte," Aris said. "Janus, I owe Psyke this dance. Please take my place."

Janus bowed and left, Psyke on his arm once more; Maledicte stood as still as a wild creature unexpectedly cornered. His heart pounded. Inside him, Ani stretched Her wings, whispering. His fingers itched for the sword hilt, for its cold security, with a desire not his own.

"Be easy," Aris said, settling himself onto a bench with visible weariness. "You are in the fortunate position of the king requesting a favor." Aris patted the bench.

Maledicte slipped over to him, sat on the very edge of the stone, among the carved vinework. "You want me to marry?"

"All men should marry, if only to see themselves through others' eyes. Wedding Aurora changed the way I saw my kingdom and myself. Under her tutelage, I saw my court as it was—decadent, violent, concerned more with matters of style than of state. We have chosen to mirror Itarus, but we have chosen to reflect only their surface. Their courtiers vie and kill, but they further the kingdom as a whole, whereas my court—cares only for entertainment." He sighed, breath loud in the night; frosty clouds carried his words away, scented with the sting of wine.

"Aurora was a queen to be revered. She knew we had to change, and I did so. I have attempted to make the court do so as well, and failed on that count."

"Such foolish heads can be led," Maledicte said. "Make them bend to your will."

Aris laughed. "I am merely a king and not a god." His laughter faded into bitterness. "And while some kings can ape gods, make their will and their people's one and the same, I am all too aware that I am only a man. But I understand Baxit, who looked on His own court and despaired, who forced the gods into oblivion. Were it not for Adiran, for other innocents who would suffer, I could do the same. Stop the struggle and let us fall—"

Maledicte shivered. Aris's face, so like Janus's in structure, might have been uncarved marble for all that Maledicte could learn of his mood in it.

"Were it not for love—" Aris said, his gloved hand touching Maledicte's chin, his voice thinned by exhaustion. Then his mouth claimed Maledicte's, his lips not tentative like his words, but so fierce that Maledicte felt Ani dwarfed beneath the sensation. It wasn't simple desire that Maledicte felt in Aris's hunger, but bleakness, a desperate attempt to quicken the blood.

Aris's tongue touched his, wine-rich, and Maledicte shoved him away, panic racing in his veins. It was done without grace or subtlety, but all he could think was what if the belladonna lacing his mouth was enough to kill a king? He fell off the bench, awkward in fright and dismay.

Maledicte knelt on the cold, damp stone, silent and waiting, his agile tongue gone dry along with his bravado, tracing the tangling lines of the stony vines.

"It is bewitchment," Aris said, "that feeds this fascination. But I think one of my own making."

His voice, empty of any emotion but despair, wicked some of the dread from Maledicte's spine. "Aris," Maledicte breathed.

"Shh," Aris said, laying his hand over Maledicte's mouth, then taking it away as if desire would spill over again. "I will be done with this nonsense, and ask my favor of you. The Lady Amarantha fears you. Fears your eyes on her belly, beyond all reason. I would have you avoid my court until her child is born."

"Exile?" Maledicte said, striving to put some flippancy in his voice, striving to restore himself. He was Maledicte, the unflappable, dark cavalier. Why should a weary king and a despairing kiss have had the power to overset him so? "On a woman's whims—you are a gentle man indeed."

"It is my brother's child," Aris said. "Antyre's future."

"I will do as you ask," Maledicte said, rising to his feet and stepping toward the balustrade. "But you know, Aris, you needn't have asked my compliance. You could have demanded it." Without waiting for leave, Maledicte dropped down the few feet to the garden and fled back to the stables, to Gilly, who was fiddling with harness straps and buckles.

"Done so soon?" Gilly asked, without looking up from his hands.

"Yes," Maledicte said. He leaned against a mossy wall and closed his eyes, stopped fighting the belladonna; it took him into the dark clouds above, a raven's-eye view of the city wheeling and spinning beneath him. He wouldn't want to be in any coach driven by a man hallucinating the way he was. "Poor Aris," Maledicte murmured, thinking of the king with distant regret. "If only I could trust it to be a girl—"

"Are we waiting for Janus?" Gilly called back, busy with the harness.

"No. He'll have to chase Amarantha away. I've been banned," Maledicte said, sliding down the wall, pressing his back against it until the stone's dampness sank through the layers of silk and linen, touching his skin with the intimacy he had denied Gilly and Aris. Gilly spoke but Maledicte heard only the comforting sound of his voice, watching as coaches came and went in the spaces of his blinking.

"Come on now," Gilly murmured in his ear, pulling him to his feet. "You've dozed enough to miss Amarantha on the move. Best we leave before her coachman spies us lurking. . . . Mal, you're shaking," he said, his calm slipping away.

Maledicte's thoughts tangled in his mind, strangling the words of reassurance in his throat.

"The antidote *is* working?" Gilly said.

Again, Maledicte's response died stillborn. That the belladonna was more potent than he had thought, that the antidote was less effective than he had been led to believe, that Ani sulked and shirked Her aid.

Clutching the hilt of his sword, Maledicte staggered to the coach. Gilly caught him, his words lost in the rushing murmur of Maledicte's blood. Gilly bundled him into the coach, tucked him round with heavy warmth, and shut the door.

"Ani," Maledicte whispered. Inside his heart, his belly, his bones, the whisper of wings stirred and rustled, sounding their susurrant reassurance. Maledicte sprawled across the seat, wrapped in the rough leather of Gilly's greatcoat. Rocked by the movement of the coach, he slipped into waking dreams.

Ani pressed out through his ribs, sending out long feathers to row through the air. Rising, She soared above Maledicte's coach, the cold winds parting beneath Her strokes. She rose above the wide streets of the palace surrounds, the smooth cobbles glistening like scales beneath Her. Circling above the palace, She watched the coaches moving like bright beetles, finally spotting Her goal—the glossy blue coach, its color robbed by darkness, trundling slowly along the cobbled road out of the city.

How afraid Amarantha must be, She gloated, to brave the overnight journey to Lastrest with a weary coachman. Flanking the coach, four kings-guards on gray horses and Dantalion on a blood-colored bay insured her safe passage.

As She neared, the coachman yanked on the reins, frightening the team into arrhythmic canters. His face blanched. The kingsguard wheeled their mounts and wheeled them again, confusion and concern written on their faces.

"She's there!" the coachman screamed, his voice spiraling into the sky like a prayer. She reveled in it, dropping closer. The kingsguards gaped at the road, at the sky, at the trees alongside; Dantalion kept his eyes where it mattered—the coach. He drew his steed nearer the door, preparing to dis-mount and climb aboard. But the coachman snapped the reins, lashed out with the whip, and set the horses to a panicked gallop, leaving Dantalion still reaching for the frame.

Caught flat-footed, the kingsguards milled for a moment, a tangle of reins and stirrups and pistoning hooves, then they streamed after the sway-ing coach. Dantalion was a length ahead and gaining when She opened Her wings to their fullest extent, spreading the stench of carrion fields, the sweet rot of the grave. The horses reared and frothed. Two kingsguards were thrown, rolling hastily to avoid being trampled by their maddened horses.

Dantalion savagely held his horse to his will, but he lost ground, and the coach hurtled away, Amarantha's screams trailing in its wake. The coachman still peered over his shoulder, panicked, trusting the horses to stay on the road. Their hooves pounded out the cadence of a frantic heart.

Her feathers sliced the air, driving Her over and beyond the coach. The coachman's head swiveled, his mouth slackened. She wheeled, soared, and came back at the coach. The coachman's face, seen head-on, was that of a ghost, gibbering and hollow-eyed.

He sawed on the reins and the stressed leather snapped. Kicking their heels, heads flat out and flecked with foam, the horses bolted. The coach tipped to the left, putting one edge in the dirt, skidding, rolling, broken wheels crashing through the enamel and gilt, and coming to a shuddering halt. Lying in the road, the coachman whimpered, "Ani." She devoured his prayer, his worship.

Dantalion gained the scene, his mouth taut with rage. He dismounted his chastened horse, tied it to a piece of the wreckage, and started sorting through the remains of the coach. Lifting the door, he found Amarantha, her eyes staring at the sky, her belly huge. Dantalion knelt. . . .

"Mal?"

The voice distracted Her, and the scene faltered. Strong hands confined Her, dragging Her away, Her feathers dwindling, Her sight gone. She protested.

"Easy, Mal," Gilly murmured in his ear. "Or you'll have us tumbling down the stairs."

Blinking, Maledicte pieced the details together. That steady rush and thump was not the downbeat of wings, but Gilly's chest beneath his cheek, the swaying sense of flight nothing but Gilly's slow ascent up the staircase, cradling Maledicte in his arms. The shattering of wood and wheel was the damage done by Maledicte's trailing scabbard against the delicate ornaments in the railing. "Put me down."

"Two more steps," Gilly said, tightening his grip.

Maledicte tensed, uncomfortable with such proximity to Gilly, too aware of secrets, Janus's potential arrival, and his own weakness that urged him to slide his arms around Gilly's neck.

At the top of the stairs, Gilly set him down, patiently making sure he had his balance before stepping back. Throughout it all, his eyes never met Maledicte's. "Are you well now? Your shaking has stopped."

"Yes," Maledicte said.

"I thought you were immune to poisons."

"I'm not dead, am I?" Maledicte croaked; his throat felt stiff, as if it wanted to voice words not his own, to finish Ani's triumphant cry.

Gilly nodded, eyes sluing toward the stairs and the front hall.

"Thank you, Gilly," Maledicte said, touching his cheek.

Beneath his fingers, Gilly flinched. "I'm going out," he said.

"Are you well?" Maledicte asked.

"No," Gilly said. "I killed a man tonight. You nearly poisoned yourself, and all the way back, I listened to Ani ranting in your voice. All I want is to be someplace far from death. I know Lizette won't ask me to kill anyone."

"Gilly," Maledicte said, "don't—"

"Don't what? Don't feel guilt? Don't dream of them? The coachman, Amarantha, the babe? My head is already full of Vornatti, Kritos, that assassin, Love's man, and poor Roach."

"I need you," Maledicte said. "You agreed it had to be done. I didn't ask you to kill him."

Gilly sighed. "I know. But tonight, I didn't kill for you, in your defense. Tonight, I killed to make Janus's path easier. And I can't think of a single reason I should let myself be used by him, the way he's using you."

Maledicte shoved him, despair replaced with something stronger, hotter, more palatable. Gilly stumbled backward, missed the top step, and fell. He caught the railing with one quick hand before he fell more than a few risers. He righted himself, looked up at Maledicte.

Breathing quickly, Maledicte waited, aching for the fight. For something he could win. Once, he would have been able to use words to sway Gilly, but he found nothing to say now, all churned under Ani's wings.

"And you worried that Ani would hurt me," Gilly said. "That was all you."

"Gilly," Maledicte said, voice a thread of sound, forcing words through the rage that choked him.

"Think about what you want and need of me. I will not kill for Janus. If that's what you want, you'll have to find a new ally."

"No," Maledicte said. He stretched a hand out, but Gilly had already turned and finished going down the stairs. The door shut with a bang.

His hands fisted. Gilly just didn't understand. He would apologize, explain that so close to their goal, he was unsettled, make him the promise he'd made before: that Gilly wouldn't have to kill for him. This time, he'd make sure it was kept. If Gilly returned. If the blood on his hands hadn't been too much for his honest nature.

Blond hair gleamed in the light and Maledicte's breath caught. "Gilly?"

"No," Janus said. "What are you doing on the stairs? Come down, let's wait out the night and see death in with the morning."

Maledicte stretched his hand out, and Janus tugged him to his feet, kissed his temple, driving away his moodiness, his anger and fear at Gilly. "What did Aris want of you?"

"Nothing," Maledicte said, then laughed. "He asked me to stay out of the court while Amarantha was attending."

Janus smiled. "You promised, of course."

"Knowing what I know, how could I not?" Maledicte leaned against Janus, and they went down the stairs, through the quiet house, hand in hand.

· 31 ·

PINK HAD JUST CREPT INTO the sky when the great bells of the palace began to toll. Maledicte, dozing against Janus's shoulder, sat upright, anticipation chasing the last sleep from his face. Janus turned his head, smiling. "A sweet sound of funeral bells in the air. You've done it. Amarantha's dead."

Maledicte didn't respond, too caught up in the deep, slow voice of the bells. When they came to a stop, like a faltering heartbeat finding rest at last, Maledicte let out his pent breath in a languorous sigh. "It's done. Finally done." A bubble of lightness started in his belly, a seed of relief.

Janus kissed his forehead, his mouth. "Thank you, my cavalier, my dark swordsman. Now you may rest your sword."

The relief in Maledicte's belly refused to grow. Even as he murmured agreement, he wondered if Janus could sense his forebodings. Would Ani leave him now?

When he closed his eyes and listened to the dark recesses of Miranda's body, he believed Ani had taken root like a child not easily ridded by potions and poison. "What will I do?" he said aloud.

"Anything you like," Janus said. "We've won, Mal." At the hushed velvet quality in his voice, a tone saved for long moments between the sheets, whispers in the dark, Maledicte let the last of his tightwire energy drain away.

Were Gilly in the room, he might see past the disguise now, see beyond his expectations. In Maledicte's softening limbs and giddy smile, in the way he folded himself into Janus's arms . . . all these had more in common with Miranda than any courtier. But Gilly was still gone from the town house, though no longer closeted in Lizette's sheltering embrace. Instead, he roamed the early-morning streets, seeking information the bells could not give him—was the coachman alive?

What he heard, in whispers from servant to servant, from merchant to customer, and finally from the broadsheet criers, sent him home, running through the narrow streets.

MALEDICTE RESTED HIS HEAD in Janus's lap, let his eyes drift closed. Janus trailed his fingers through Maledicte's hair, planning aloud. "I'll need to attend Aris. There may be questions. Amarantha made no secret of her fears—"

The sound made them both stiffen, made Maledicte raise his head, eyes flaring dark and wild. "What is that?" The bright carillon continued, ringing off stone and rebounding, filling the air. Tumbling off the chaise, Maledicte put his hands over his ears. Within him, Ani twisted, churned, waking to malevolence.

Gilly burst into the room, and Maledicte looked up, near blind with nameless anxiety. "What is that sound, Gilly? What is it?"

Gilly panted for breath, his chest shuddering, too distraught to mince words. "A child has been born to the royal family," he said, staring at Maledicte's face, as white as milk or marble. "Dantalion cut him from her belly. The bells mean they expect him to live."

Maledicte screamed, the sound soaring up over the bells, ripping free of the confines of his maimed throat, beyond human range. Outside, the rooks burst into panicked flight, wheeling and setting dark flickers behind the window glass. Janus released him, face blank in alarm and chagrin.

"Gilly, are you sure?" Janus said, but Gilly had no time for Janus, no time for anything but the swelling blackness in the slim form before him. Gilly stroked countercharms in the air with all the fervor of a country intercessor, but the empty wildness in Maledicte's eyes remained unchanged.

"The earl is dead . . . Long live the earl . . . I will not allow it." The voice was barely recognizable as human; it raised hackles along Gilly's nape, the rattle and rasp of it like old bones, like his dream of Ani brought to life.

"Maledicte," he breathed. "Please."

Sword drawn, Maledicte moved toward the door, inexorably dragging the shadows after him. "Stop him," Gilly said.

Janus reached out with alarming casualness and seized Maledicte's arm, his face annoyed. "Mal, enough with the melodrama. We need to—" He sucked in his breath and lunged back as the sword sliced toward his belly. Gilly leaped forward, taking advantage of Maledicte's half-turned body, taking that slim form in his rush and bearing it to the floor. Maledicte shrieked again, thwarted blood in his voice; the rooks crashed through the windows, shredding themselves on the glass, pelting them with bone and feather and blood.

"The sword," Gilly gasped, trying to keep Maledicte down, when it felt as if Maledicte was as muscular and as agile as a serpent. If the countercharms were worthless, removing the sword from Maledicte's grip might be the only chance left. Sliding over Maledicte's back, he pushed Maledicte's arm out, spreading the sword hand farther away from himself.

Janus, assessing, shook himself and then stamped on Maledicte's outspread hand. Despite his desperation, Gilly winced when the bones cracked. In an elegant motion, as well suited to a dance as to a duel, Janus swept the sword across the floor with a booted foot.

"Elysia, in the butler's pantry," Gilly panted.

Maledicte, heedless or insensible of the pain, heaved himself to his hands and knees, reaching for the sword. Gilly exhaled, made himself heavy, thought of immovable boulders, of nets. Janus's footsteps moved swiftly away, and Gilly thought *hurry, hurry.* He could not hold him much longer; with every pulse of his heart, Maledicte gained on the sword.

Gilly yanked Maledicte's leading arm up and back, spilling him from his inexorable crawl. Then Maledicte slipped sideways, rolled, got his knees between his body and Gilly's, and kicked. The blow was all out of proportion painful; Maledicte shook free of Gilly's spasming fingers, and only Janus's quick grasp saved the sword from making its way back to Maledicte. Janus backed away, the sword held awkwardly in his grip, bloodying his fingers, the Elysia bottle in the other hand, the syringe slipping through the cage of his hand. Gilly made a gasping effort and caught it, rolling clear of the space between them.

"That's mine," Maledicte growled; as if Ani tired of the pretense, of the games, the sword twisted in Janus's hand and clattered across the floor, skidding up against Maledicte's boot. He scooped it up with his foot, kicking it into the air, and caught it with his sword hand.

The bones reknitted, the tendons flexed, and the sword shifted to a better grip. Janus dropped the Elysia bottle, staring at Maledicte's burgeoning shadow, at the drift of bloody feathers saturating the air. Maledicte stepped forward and broke the bottle underfoot.

Janus met Gilly's eyes and for once, his poise was stripped from him. "Keep him here," Gilly said.

Janus stepped between Maledicte and the door. Faintly, a frown crossed the blank mask of Maledicte's face. Gilly wished it concern, but was far more afraid that the emotion was outrage.

"Hold him!" he called, then ran for the stairs and Maledicte's rooms. Slamming the door back, heedless of damage, he started searching for the poison chest. Below him, steel crashed against steel, and Gilly wondered, his heart in his throat, how much time Janus could grant him. More, how little time would pass before Janus realized that he was preventing Maledicte from his goal, a goal that Janus wholeheartedly craved.

The chest in his hands, Gilly pawed through the contents carelessly. All the little crystal vials seemed maddeningly identical to his frantic eyes. But beneath them, a bottle, bigger than the others, caught his attention—what had Maledicte planned for that? Shaking the question off, he snatched it and bolted for the parlor.

Janus, backed against the door, panted, holding Maledicte at bay with the parlor poker; Janus's sword, notched and scarred, lay trembling across the room. Feathers littered the air as the maddened rooks spilled unceasingly into the room.

Gilly gritted his teeth and pulled off his shirt. He soaked the fabric with the bottle's contents. Janus lunged and ducked and parried, the poker thrust punching Maledicte's sternum. When Maledicte staggered, Gilly flung the cloth over Maledicte's head, pressing the fabric close to his face, his bared teeth.

The sword stroked back and Gilly leaned into Maledicte's body, trying to hide in the shelter of his back. In his arms, Maledicte contorted and fought.

Gilly, holding his breath, had time for the single despairing thought that this was not going to succeed, that Maledicte would step free and slash his way to the palace.

Janus took advantage of Maledicte's cloth blindness to strike another blow, breaking the delicate elbow joint and sending the sword spinning away. In Gilly's arms, Maledicte collapsed all at once.

Gilly fell with him, sprawled on the floor, nerves singing, shaking as with an ague. The living rooks fled. Janus kicked a few of their bodies out of their way with a fastidious foot and knelt beside Gilly and Maledicte. He lifted the cloth and wrinkled his nose.

"Ether," Gilly said, but Janus wasn't listening. He touched Maledicte's slack face, the hand that had been broken, the elbow that even now mended itself.

Finally he looked up and met Gilly's eyes. "What the devil was that?" His voice was a near whisper, as if he feared Maledicte would wake. "I hurt him. I broke his hand, I broke his ribs, his elbow, and nothing mattered."

"She's insane, and infinitely more powerful than we are." Gilly dragged the cloth back over Maledicte's face. "Fortunately, Maledicte is not, being mere bone and blood like the rest of us . . . no matter how powerful She is."

"She?" Janus said, his sword in his hand, though when it had been recovered, Gilly couldn't say. Janus's expression was blank.

"The danger's past, I believe. You can put that away," Gilly said. "She, my lord Last, is Black-Winged Ani." He shifted his weight, dragged a dead rook out from beneath his knee, and settled back again. "And She grants Her followers certain abilities. Freedom from poison, from injury, and all She asks is their bodies. The longer the vengeance takes, the stronger She grows. She has no cares beside the shedding of blood."

"But he fell to the ether," Janus said. "None of your nonsense, Gilly. . . ."

"I think immunity from poison is a mistranslation," Gilly said. "It affects him, but not for long."

"She can heal wounds? All wounds?" Janus said, touching Maledicte's shrouded form again.

"Some say so," Gilly said. In his arms, Maledicte stirred, despite the ether-soaked cloth over his nose and mouth. Gilly put his hand back to the bottle and soaked the cloth again. Maledicte subsided.

"Be careful, Gilly," Janus snapped. "He's not very big. You'll kill—" The wolf paleness of his eyes flickered, the shock of belief hitting home. "Will he wake maddened?"

"I don't know. I don't think so. I think it takes effort for Her to manifest Herself. I think it had to do with the belladonna Mal drank last night."

"Belladonna," Janus said, his voice low. "How much of it?"

"Enough to kill," Gilly said. "All for you."

Janus made a small, choked sound, his face whitening. He gathered Maledicte into his arms and put his face into Maledicte's neck, rocking them both.

Stiffly, Gilly stood, and surveyed the wreckage. Another mess too difficult to explain to the few servants they had remaining. He picked up one dead bird by its wing, dropped it out the shattered windows.

Behind him, Janus whispered, "I'm so sorry I hurt you."

"Didn't hurt." The ghost of a whisper turned Gilly about. Maledicte's eyelids flickered. "Like pain in a dream. Not real."

Janus grunted with effort but brought both himself and Maledicte off the floor in a single movement, Maledicte cradled in his arms. "Real or not, you need to rest."

Maledicte slipped from Janus's arms, and picked up the sword, flexing his hand around it, parrying with a few still floating feathers. "See, not hurt."

Janus and Gilly tensed, and Maledicte smiled at them both as acidly as he had ever smiled at his enemies. "I would have had it done, had you two not balked me."

"You would have died," Gilly said. Despite the guilt this relationship had sparked, it was nothing compared to the pain of imagining the loss of it.

"Would I? With Her touch on me?" Maledicte shrugged as if it were a matter of no import, and sheathed the sword. "Perhaps, but not until the babe was dead. My release from Ani is contingent upon my vengeance."

"We want more than simple vengeance, remember," Janus said. "We want the court, the title, the safety."

"I remember," Maledicte said. He sat down at the spinet, flicked a wing from the stained keys, and pressed a few notes, oddly muted. He reached inward, tugged another bird free from the strings, and dropped it to the floor. "Ani doesn't care."

· 3 2 ·

ARIS STOOD BESIDE THE EMPTY CRADLE, rocking it with a trembling hand. In the chair next to it, the wet nurse, holding the infant against her, shot nervous glances at the king and the attendant guards.

"Adi was never so small," he said aloud. The woman opened her mouth and closed it again. Against her breast, the baby suckled. In the corner of the nursery, Adi played with Hela, uninterested in the new baby, or in the newly partitioned section of his domain.

"Speak, if you would," Aris said.

"Your son was a full-term child, and this one, this little one—it is a miracle he survived at all." She rocked the child; his lips rolled back, showing pink gums and a milky tongue.

"He must be whole." His voice broke on the last word, as he wondered if his brother's child would be another Adiran. Sound of body, lacking mind. Right now, he could not decide which would be better. He needed an heir, a child of sound mind and blameless parentage, and yet—if the babe were deficient, there was no danger to him. And Aris, who had seen the wreckage of the coach, the twisted wood and wheel, the coachman's broken body, Amarantha's gutted flesh, knew there was an undeniable danger.

Fleeing, he had sought the sanctuary of the nursery, away from the fearsome images evoked by the wreckage, away from the horror of Jasper's reports. Dantalion had come in with the child just after dawn, the infant still bloody in his arms, but alive. Jasper had brought Amarantha's body in and laid her respectfully down, his fair face flushed and distraught. "He didn't wait, sire. Not for her to live or die. He just cut her open and took the babe. Left her body like refuse on the road."

At first, Aris had been nearly afraid to look on the child, afraid that Jasper's words would have left a taint of atrocity on the boy, but the child was an infant pure and sweet. Briefly, Aris let himself remember that too-short moment when Aurora had held Adiran up to him, smiling. Before they knew she was dying. Before Adi's flaws became apparent.

Gingerly, he touched the infant's soft skull, cupped it, warm and pulsing, in the cradle of his palm. He owed Dantalion's decisiveness for this moment, but still he could not trust the man. Last night, only last night, he had heard Dantalion extolling the virtues of culling the Itarusine children, insuring that only the fittest lived. The ones found wanting were plunged into the icy seas. Aris had thought of his sweet Adiran and had fled the court room.

"Sire," Jasper said, entering and dropping his voice to lower tones immediately on seeing the sleeping child. Echo followed him in and averted his gaze from the blushing wet nurse.

"Have you found the cause of the accident?" Aris asked, but lost parts of their answers, studying the delicate veins in the child's eyelids.

"Coachman spooked . . . lost control of the reins, though why—" Jasper said.

"We've questioned the stablehands . . ." Echo said. "And found silver embroidery thread in an unused stall."

"Which means little," Jasper said. "Could be off livery, could be signs of a noble girl's dalliance. Silver's popular this year—"

"Maledicte made it so," Echo said.

Aris took the child from the nurse with a careful hand. The infant curled his fingers around Aris's forefinger, and he smiled. "A good grip. And I believe I saw a glimmer of awareness in his face."

"He's a right one," the nurse said. "Small but perfect."

"He is," Aris said, veering between joy and worry. An heir. A release from his burden. But such a court to leave a beautiful child—

Behind him, Echo and Jasper's voices rose, growing harsh and brittle as they argued with each other.

"I tell you, you cannot blame your favorite in this matter," Jasper said. "You cannot blame a death on a man who did not attend."

"And you—I suppose you see the hand of witchcraft in this?" Echo spat. "Your Mad Mirabile creeping onto the palace grounds, still in her ballgown, poisoning the coachman with her spells? The same spells you blame for allowing her to escape your net?"

"Perhaps if you could be convinced to share your resources with my men—" Jasper said. "We are at home in the palace, and in the main thoroughfares of the city. The alleys and Relicts are your Particulars' job, and yet they've not found her either. But that has nothing to do with this. I think you must admit—"

"To you, nothing," Echo said.

"We need look elsewhere. Amarantha feared—" Jasper flinched under Aris's sudden gaze.

"Feared who?" Aris asked.

"More than one man," Jasper said, refusing to meet the king's eyes.

"Your bastard nephew," Echo said, unafraid of Aris. "Your newest counselor. She feared Janus but I still believe the blame lies where it is most obvious. Maledicte."

"Echo, you seem slow to learn. Maledicte did not attend the ball," Jasper said.

Aris laid the infant down, his throat suddenly numb and cold. He forced the words from his throat, but frozen, they did not carry above their argument. "He was there." Aris rocked the cradle, all the while remembering the rough silk feel of Maledicte's lips against his. "I saw him coming from the gardens and stable."

Jasper and Echo fell silent, staring at him.

"He was there, his eyes wild, his manner—" Aris trailed off, knowing himself for a fool at last. He sank down onto the padded bench that Adi often napped on, and covered his eyes. He had looked the other way when Kritos died, when Vornatti died, neither man long for the world, a debt-ridden gambler and an old roué.

Even when Last fell, Aris had sought other foes, had looked into the dark eyes and thought, shamefully, that perhaps Last was not entirely innocent of his own death. After all, the enmity had been mutual and undeniable. Maledicte might have only defended himself. Aris had even presumed that with Last's death, Maledicte had no one to hate, and so was defanged.

But hate, Aris knew, was addictive; why had he never considered that? Instead, he had accepted gentle blackmail from the lad with mute passivity, trusting Maledicte to need no more than diversion from scandal. He had even, Baxit forgive him, found it almost a game of wits between them.

"Echo," he said, his voice rough. "You blame him. Tell me what motive he held." He had been a fool perhaps, but one capable of learning.

"Janus," Echo said. "What he does, he does for him." He held up a hand at Aris's protest. "I don't know that Janus understands what kind of man he's allied himself with."

"Janus," Aris said, "is one of my counselors and my nephew. Your peer. He has never given me reason to distrust him. Perhaps, like me, he is only too trusting."

"I'll send the guard for Maledicte—"

"No," Aris said. The refusal came instinctively. There were the ledgers to worry about. They would have to be recovered before any steps could be taken. But Echo waited impatiently on an explanation. "He thinks too quickly for that. I would deprive him of time to prepare glib assurances. Jasper and I will go to him and see if I can surprise truth from his lips."

Echo said, "If it were as easy as that, I'd have had truth from him long ago. We should simply arrest him, and let him prove his innocence."

"I'd rather you prove his guilt before I see a member of the court imprisoned," Aris said. Echo glowered, and Aris forced himself to the intricate steps of manipulation so necessary to his court. "Find me incontrovertible proof of a crime committed, Echo, and you may have him. Talk to Dantalion, who knows more of poisons than I would like, being an Itarusine. Ask him if he knows of a potion to send a coachman mad. I will ask Maledicte the same."

He leaned over the cradle once more, breathing deeply, as if the child's innocence would not only grant him clarity and strength, but wisdom.

ARIS RETURNED from the Dove Street town house, having gone to confront Maledicte over Echo's objections. The visit had been fruitless and unsettling, Maledicte not at home and the house and hall so spattered with rook feathers and blood that it seemed a nigh-impossible task for the manservant left to clean them away. Shaken, Aris retreated without attempting a hunt for the ledgers. At the palace, he found one member of that eccentric household in the nursery, leaning over the sleeping infant, alone. Nearby, Adiran sang quietly and stacked blocks. "What do you call him?" Janus said, without looking up. "My brother. . . ."

Half-formed fear melted at the interest in Janus's blue eyes. Aris came forward, and joined his small family.

"Auron," he said. "After my wife."

Janus touched the sleeping baby's soft mouth with a finger that dwarfed it. Aris watched as Janus rocked the cradle, setting it to sea-tide swaying until Auron opened cloudy blue eyes.

"Auron Ixion," Janus said, "Welcome, your grace."

Aris let his breath out in a steady hiss.

"It's true, isn't it?" Janus said. "Little brother is the earl. I am only a bastard."

"Janus, you will always have a place at court, always be cared for," Aris said. "My counselor."

"I know that, Uncle," Janus said. "I wonder if Auron will feel the same. . . ." He smiled and said, "If he's as sweet-natured as Adi, as kind as you, I will never want for anything."

Aris said, "I thought to name you guardian to Auron and one of his regents, should I not live to see his ascension."

He saw sudden startlement in the pale eyes. "I, guardian?"

"Who better than family?" Aris said.

"I think most of your court would say who is not better . . . but if it is your will, I am honored," Janus said, sinking to his knee before Aris.

"Two caveats," Aris said. "Two conditions fulfilled before I name you guardian."

"Sire?" Janus said, face growing still.

"Do you know where Maledicte is?" Aris asked.

"At this moment?" Janus asked. "No."

Aris studied Janus, seeking honesty, seeking rebelliousness. Instead, he saw only resignation and a glimmer of anticipated pain. "He will be questioned in Amarantha's death."

"He had no reason to injure her," Janus said.

"None at all?" Aris said. "Not even for you?"

Janus's eyes widened and he laughed. "Once Amarantha wed Last instead of me, Maledicte ceased to notice her at all. As for more . . . elaborate motives . . ." He paused, as if feeling his way. "I am not unaware that had Auron died, it might have been seen as beneficial to myself. But this sequence of events? No, if you want inducements to violence, consider Dantalion himself. He saved the babe. He put Antyre in Itarus's debt. He will collect."

"You know what he will ask?" Aris said, gesturing for Janus to rise. He grew dizzy looking into the pale depths of Janus's eyes, so like water shifting beneath thin ice.

"The Itarusine court is much occupied with honor. Dantalion's disinheritance must rankle like salt in an open wound. But if you owe him a boon, and if Maledicte is suspect and out of favor—"

"You think Dantalion would kill Amarantha merely to regain his inheritance?" Aris leaned against the wall, jostling the cradle and setting Auron to fussing. Absently, he smoothed the blanket, stroked the soft skin until the drowsy complaint stopped.

"Men have done worse for less. Still, I think it more likely the accident was only that, and Dantalion capitalizes on it, cleverly shaping events to his benefit," Janus said.

"Maledicte hated Michel and he died. Amarantha believed he sought her death as well and she is dead. Elaborations aside, how do you know he did not kill them both?"

"I was with Maledicte when Father died. I swear he did not strike the blow. As for Amarantha—did Maledicte ride after the carriage like a highwayman, shatter their wheels all unseen and send them to their deaths? Or are you imagining poison in a court so fearful that no one partakes of refreshments since the Dark Solstice?"

"If I had those answers," Aris said. "There would be no need for this conversation. But Maledicte—"

Auron made a sleepy sound of contentment, and Janus smiled down at him. "He's perfect, isn't he?"

Aris hewed doggedly to the topic. "Janus. My first condition—Maledicte holds some books for me that I would require returned."

Janus nodded understanding. "The Antyrrian audits. I believe I can put my hands on them. Your second stipulation, sire?"

"Should you become guardian, you will not be allowed the freedom you have now. You will not live in Maledicte's house, but the palace only. You will never bring him here, and indeed I prefer you not see him at all. His situation becomes too—irregular."

"A perfect model of a courtier," Janus murmured.

"With an empty house full of blood and feathers," Aris said.

Janus flinched, his composure faltering. For once, Aris could read a thought in his nephew's face—astonishment and dismay that Aris had visited Maledicte's house. "An accident," he said. "Startled birds, nothing of moment—"

"Janus," Aris said. "It has been borne in on me that I've been a fool. I would like to see you escape that same realization. Of late, I have done nothing for Antyre but watch it, dreamlike, crumble. I've woken now; I have Auron and his future to protect. Do not think me blind."

Janus worried his lower lip like a schoolboy, and Aris felt some of his anger mellow. "Whatever hold Maledicte has on you, whatever has happened, with your knowledge or not, it stops now.

"If you must keep him, you may. But you will do so as men keep mistresses, discreetly, and never at the expense of your own responsibilities. I will find you a wife, and you will wed her. And should you misstep—"

"What, then," Janus said. "Banishment?"

"Yes," Aris said. "But not for you. Your slightest misdeed will see Maledicte sent beyond your reach."

*A*LONE AT A TABLE IN THE BACK, Maledicte surveyed the tavern with an incredulous eye. The Seadog had been the height of imagined luxury to him and to Janus not so long ago. They used to peer in at the smoky rooms, at the jewel tones of firelight on Naga's scales fetched up from the deeps, on sea buoys hanging from the crossbeams like necklaces of great sea creatures. The men themselves all seemed made of coin, scattering moon spills of silver over the teak bar with careless fingers. Miranda, who rarely held more than one luna in her palm, and that clutched tight, had leaned against Janus's shoulder and marveled at such wealth.

Now the Seadog was evident for what it was, a run-down shanty near the edge of the pier, patronized only for its proximity to the salt-weary sailors and by nobles recovering from their visits at the cheapest brothels, the drug dens, and gaming tables so rigged that two nights running saw them in different surroundings. Even now, Maledicte watched two young nobles ruefully and dazedly taking stock of themselves, cataloguing damage done to their purses or persons.

Fools, he thought. They might think themselves beggared, but their clothes, their boots, even their perfumed hair meant money down here, and yet, they stood in the heart of the lamplight.

He sank farther back into his corner, into the dark shadows of his dimly turned lamp. It cast a dying glow over his table, made the bottle burn with hidden lights. Maledicte poured the contents into his glass, straining it through sugared mesh.

"You never got that here," Janus said, settling into the seat opposite him.

Maledicte paused in his pouring and smiled, taking up a broken chunk of brown sugar, and grating it over the whole. "No, *absente* is definitely beyond the Dog's cellar." He took a sip, but the warmth that moved through him had less to do with the liquor than Janus's arrival. "You found me."

"Always," Janus said. "Though I admit to a few false starts before I remembered the Seadog. Vile place, really." Janus studied the smoky room with a contemptuous glance.

"We thought it so fine," Maledicte said. He closed his eyes, trying to overlay one image on another.

"We were fools," Janus said, taking the bottle from Maledicte's grasp. "And *absente* is nearly as vile. It drives men mad."

"I'm already mad," Maledicte said, a whisper in the lamplight. "Haven't you realized? Gilly does. And as for the *absente*—I haven't offered you any, so you needn't sneer at it."

Janus edged his seat around the table, drawing closer to Maledicte. "Mal, I need you to listen to me."

"I always do," Maledicte said, taking another languid sip. Janus removed the glass from his hands, set it on the floor beside him.

"Aris went to Dove Street and found the house as we left it, bloodied," he said. "Aris suspects that you caused Amarantha's death, more so than he ever did for Last. I don't understand why, but you must be prepared. What will you say if he charges you in her death?" Before Maledicte could answer, Janus leaned in. "I did my best, shifting his eye to Dantalion, but can you keep it there?"

Maledicte stroked the line of Janus's jaw, admiring the gold-stubbled sheen in the lamplight. "I suppose. Best just to stay clear as long as I can." He frowned, reaching for his glass on the floor. Right now, its bitterness leavened with sweet suited his mood.

Janus said, more to himself than to Maledicte, "Who knew he would grow so suspicious so swiftly?"

"We should have planned for it," Maledicte said. "Even the most docile of men might choke on the death we served him. Still, had I known—I would have let him kiss me longer, instead of fleeing like a virtuous maid."

"You let Aris—" Janus said, rage flickering in his eyes. "You risked the intimacy, the scrutiny? He's no stripling to be blinded to the difference between man and woman. In his arms—"

"He discovered nothing, near drunk on his own unhappiness," Maledicte said, allowing Janus to tug Maledicte into sharing his seat. "And I? I was thinking of you dancing attendance on Psyke. He took me by surprise and meant little of it. Unreasoning jealousy will be your downfall," Maledicte said, shifting his weight until he sat on Janus's lap. "So possessive of what's yours . . ."

Janus cut his words off with a kiss, careless of spectators. Maledicte laughed against his lips and the triumph in it bled through. "But you're mine too, aren't you? It's still just us against the world."

"Of course," Janus said, drawing his mouth back to his. "Of course."

Maledicte turned his mouth up for Janus's kiss, closed his eyes at the familiar warmth of Janus's tongue touching his own.

"Such a tender moment." The voice cut into their intimacy, and Maledicte felt Janus stiffen with recognition. A dark man, heavyset and tall, his words accented in the Itarusine manner. Maledicte stood and smiled. "You must be Dantalion, Vornatti's despised kin."

"And you, Maledicte," Dantalion said, eyes widening slightly. "You, the dark cavalier of Aris's court? A puling youth with a sword too good for him?"

Maledicte's hand dropped to the sword hilt, even though he saw Echo appear behind Dantalion. "Janus, next time, try to avoid leading the bores to us?" Despite his easy words, he felt the surging wingbeat in his blood, the rage that they dared interrupt an all-too-rare moment of pleasure. He knew he should feel caution; Dantalion and Echo were an alliance that meant him nothing but ill.

"My uncle's catamite," Dantalion said. "I'd heard such things about you. I nearly believed them, but you're barely worth my sword at all."

The other patrons, sailors and scattered nobles, watched with avid eyes in dulled faces.

"Mal," Janus said, laying a restraining hand on his forearm. "You mustn't."

"But I *want* to," Maledicte said. His eyes never left Dantalion's. He felt the dreamy tone lace his voice, the languor of the *absente* reaching his head. All he wanted at this moment was the sound of steel and sweep of flashing metal. He savored the unwinding of Ani's coiled hatred, its warmth seeping through his bones.

"Waiting for an excuse?" Dantalion asked, then struck. Janus tried to deflect the blow, but Dantalion was too close and too fast. Maledicte caught Dantalion's fist in his own. Dantalion's eyes grew thoughtful at the speed of it.

"That will do," Maledicte said, releasing the man's fist. "Shall we duel?"

"No," Janus said, rising, interposing himself between the two men.

"I never thought you a coward, Ixion," Dantalion said. "And I had planned on spitting you next."

Maledicte drew his sword in quick economy of motion, evading Janus's grasp. "You have to take me first," he said.

"Mal," Janus said, voice low. "I don't like this. It reeks of calculation. Echo is trying to—"

Maledicte grinned at him. "I don't care." He wondered what was in his face that made Janus blanch so, but lost that in the delight welling in him. To be free of another cur that nipped at his heels—the lure was too great to deny.

"Outside, think you?" he asked Dantalion.

"The cobbles are slick with dew," Dantalion said, shaking his head. "And the alleys too full of those who would interrupt our sport for the coin we carry. No, we'll stick to tradition and the dueling grounds at the park."

Janus grasped Maledicte's hand once more, held him back when he would have followed. "It's a trap, Mal." As if to underscore his words, Maledicte noticed Echo slipping away, his task obviously accomplished.

"It doesn't matter," Maledicte said, touching Janus's cheek. "Don't you see that? If not now, then later. Dantalion means to see us all dead."

"But now, when you're near drunk on *absente*—"

"Drunk on blood," Maledicte whispered into Janus's ear, laughed at the expression on his face, the whisper of feathers in his mind. He pulled free of his grip and followed Dantalion into the gray-dawning sky.

DAWN BATHED THE MEN in the park in pearly light and cast their shadows like spider-legged creatures over the lawn. Maledicte stood before Dantalion, sword unsheathed, dangling lazily from his hand.

Dantalion leaned close and spoke at length, his words lost in distance, but Maledicte's face darkened. All that, Aris saw as the carriage drew close, and more, Janus pacing madly behind the fighters. Janus drew forward and Maledicte pushed him back, his eyes never leaving Dantalion's blade.

Echo was right, Aris thought. Maledicte did intend to duel Dantalion, flaunting his disobedience. But as they approached, Aris found himself dwelling not on the illegality of it, but the monstrously uneven odds. Dantalion was head and shoulders above Maledicte, and muscled with it.

Beside him, Echo sank back into the seat, smiling. Dantalion's blade was of the Itarusine style, heavy and curved, the length of a man's arm. A savage weapon. And Maledicte's dark, slim blade seemed more a child's toy in comparison, though wickedly sharp.

Dantalion stepped forward, and the duel began.

"Should we intervene, sire?" Jasper said. "Before it goes further?"

"We can always cry halt," Echo coaxed. "I am interested in seeing Maledicte's ability."

Aris nodded, his eyes on the two figures. Maledicte made a sound like a laugh; it carried over the still air, and raised the hackles on Aris's neck. It wasn't a sound he associated with men, but the sound of feeding birds on a battlefield. Dantalion took a hasty step back as Maledicte darted in, as agile as a crow in flight.

Dantalion struck back, his great curved sword carving the air, but missed Maledicte entirely. His blade bit only Maledicte's black-fluttering sleeves.

Maledicte danced forward, his sword skidding along the width of Dantalion's blade, raising sparks of outraged metal, and ending with a little flourish at the end that nearly touched Dantalion's shoulder. Dantalion jerked back, pivoted his weight, and came on again, thrusting, parrying, slicing at Maledicte's delicate form.

Dantalion dripped sweat, growing ponderous under his own weight. Maledicte, facing him, seemed as intangible as a shadow. His blade wavered, judged, and then they were moving again; Maledicte thrust forward, extending his arm, his blade, and kept himself out of range of the returned slash. His blade took the force of Dantalion's parry, unyielding. Aris let out his breath, watched the narrow focus of concentration on Maledicte's face, the dark glee in his eyes, and knew Dantalion was going to lose. That Maledicte had enough skill to have killed Last and anyone else he chose.

"End it," Aris said.

Maledicte swept forward, danced under Dantalion's swing, not bothering to parry, and put his blade across Dantalion's throat. Dantalion jerked back at the last second, and the blade left only a wet red line behind.

"In the king's name," the guard called, spurring his steed forward. "Halt!"

Maledicte fell back, out of the reach of Dantalion's sword, his teeth bared. "Your salvation," he spat, spreading his arms like wings, inviting Dantalion's stroke. "Too much a coward to finish this?"

Dantalion lunged, and Maledicte flowed backward until Dantalion was overextended. The sword slipping past him, Maledicte reached out with his free hand and caught Dantalion's arm against his body, prisoning it, the sword useless. With agile fingers, Maledicte pinched the nerve inside Dantalion's elbow; Dantalion cried out and dropped his blade.

Aris breathed a sigh of relief to see the battle so neatly won, and then Maledicte reached forward with his sword hand and inscribed the same line over Dantalion's heaving throat.

This time, the blood was not content to spill over a thin trench, but spouted instead. Maledicte released Dantalion's arm and grabbed his hair, yanking his head farther back, widening that bloody smile. Blood sprayed Maledicte's face, his shirt, his sword, and ran in steaming droplets onto the fresh spring grass.

Aris froze; the duel had been won. Had Aris any remaining doubts about Maledicte as a killer, they were gone now. Watching the blood fountain under Maledicte's manipulation, he found it impossible to see any trace of the impetuous young cavalier he had so often declared him to be.

When the blood slowed, Maledicte shoved Dantalion's body away. He wiped his blade on the grass, tore handfuls of the grass up to wash the mask of blood from his skin. When the guard put his sword at his back and commanded him to be still, Maledicte settled the sword on the ground. He stood, bloody hands dangling; the sword quivered on the grass.

"Your Majesty," he said.

"I cried halt," Aris said.

"He would have killed me had it been his chance," Maledicte said, his voice uninflected, a quiet rasp. "He has tried to do so by proxy, and would have done so again. Should I have turned my back on a dangerous enemy?"

"If you had proof, you could have petitioned me," Aris said.

"Proof is all too often hard to find," Maledicte said, his words a bitter echo of Aris's own.

Janus said, "Dantalion forced the fight." He put his arms around Maledicte, heedless of blood, heedless of the guardsman's expression.

Aris sat silent, and Janus said, "Uncle," a quiet plea, his eyes eloquent.

"I asked for your discretion," Aris said. "This is very far from discreet. A member of the foreign courts, murdered—and it was murder I saw, Maledicte, you had him disarmed, and yet you struck. . . ." Aris rubbed his hands over his face.

Echo said, "I'll have him taken to Stones immediately."

"No," Janus said, his voice as abrupt, as commanding as Aris's was not. "You set Dantalion on; you are as guilty of his death as Maledicte. Please, Aris, let me take Maledicte home. Let him be prisoned there until you decide his fate."

Aris could not think around the blood in his mind, this surfeit of death. But Echo had presumed—that was as clear to him as Maledicte's act of murder. And the ledgers were not yet in his hands. To act now would risk them.

"No, I see no need for the cells. Not yet. Take him home, Janus. Remember our bargain. I am more desirous than ever of you fulfilling your end." Nerving himself, Aris stepped down from the coach, and joined the two men. He reached out and touched Maledicte's blood-spattered face. Blank black eyes looked back at him, as enigmatic as a starless night. "Maledicte, tell me why."

"Death to us all," Maledicte whispered. "My blood, then Janus's, then my poor Gilly's. That's what Dantalion promised." The gaze sharpened, lifted, held Aris's eyes with their intensity. "He boasted of killing her, of granting you an heir. How long do you think you would have survived? Or the babe? After all, Adiran is the son of Aurora Vornatti, and if Janus died, if you died, then Dantalion was Adiran's nearest kin, an Itarusine nobleman, hungry for power and blood."

"You speak treason," Echo spat.

"Do I?" Maledicte said, voice fading to a bare thread of sound. "I thought I only repeated it."

Aris frowned, and nodded to his guards. "My guards will see you home."

ILLY MET THEM at the door to the town house, blanching at the blood spray on Maledicte's clothing. "What happened?" Janus slapped him hard, twice, and would have done so a third time but for the sudden hiss of the black blade unsheathing. He lowered his hand. Maledicte lowered the sword.

"Don't take your temper out on him," Maledicte said, slipping past them and disappearing into the library. Their footsteps followed him in like distant drums, their words like the ocean, quiet, senseless, repetitive. He slung himself into a chair, and watched them argue, wondering if he would need to intervene again. He supposed he should be angry, but all he felt was the wet seep of blood through the linen shirt, and the numbed weariness in his soul.

He interrupted their quarreling to say, "Gilly, run me a bath, please. I'm all over blood. And when you're done with that—I have another errand for you. I want you to take our funds from the banks and hide them where Aris and his guards can't reach. I've heard enough of Itarusine ways to know they'll attempt to take recompense for Dantalion's death in a monetary way."

Janus opened his mouth to object and Maledicte rounded on him savagely. "You allowed Aris to send guards to follow me home. You cannot object to the steps I choose to take now."

MALEDICTE LEANED FORWARD in the warmth of the bathwater, setting off small, tidal sloshes. Tinged red and perceptibly cooling, still the water was soothing, as soothing as Janus's slow detangling of Maledicte's blood-matted hair. Mindlessly, he trailed his fingers through the water, and grimaced at the bloody foam sheeting out of his hair.

"You were a fool to kill Dantalion," Janus said quietly, as if he kept close rein on his temper. He paused in his ministrations, trading fingers for a wide-toothed comb, ivory overlaid with silver. "Twice a fool to kill him in such a manner—to show Aris the blood on your blade. Aris could see you hanged."

"No fear of that," Maledicte said. "Ani is more potent than kings. I'll slip the gallows knot yet."

Maledicte reached for the sponge and rinsed his arm, removing a streak of blood that had so far evaded the water. Tension curled in his belly at the sight.

"You are mad," Janus said. "I accept Black-Winged Ani as your patron—I have seen the evidence myself—but that's no reason to overthrow sense. I need you to be clever, and all you think of is blood."

"Your doing," Maledicte said. "I would have been content with Last's death, had you not robbed me of it. Instead, I must kill again and again to keep the ground we've gained. Is it any wonder it's become habit?" Ani's offense mingled with his own and his words grew edged; beneath the water, his hands fisted. "But I'd give it all up in a heartbeat. For you. But you—you made a bargain with Aris," Maledicte said, letting the sponge drift. "You promised him— What exactly did you promise him?"

"Discretion, as he said," Janus said, but the shift of his eyes told Maledicte more than he wanted to know.

"How much discretion?" he asked. "To not live here at my side? To not walk beside me in the public streets? To not acknowledge me at all? Did you promise to set me aside?"

Janus stood and claimed a towel. "The water's grown cold. You're all over gooseflesh."

"It's not the water's chill," Maledicte said, but rose and allowed Janus to wrap him in warmth. "Tell me how things have changed with Amarantha's death. With Dantalion's. The longer you balk, the more I fear what you've done."

Janus sat down on the edge of the tub, looked up with clear blue eyes. "In exchange for staying third counselor and guardian to Auron, I am to live in the palace. I am not to see you more often than a man sees a mistress. I am not to take you about in public. I am to wed and—"

Maledicte dropped the towel, wrapped himself in a dressing gown, tying the sash with angry jerks. "You are to play Aris's lapdog. You ruled the Relics, and yet you'll take such orders from the king, just to play second fiddle to a true-born infant?"

Janus said, lowering his face, his eyes blazing, "To be kept at arm's distance when I am this close to power, to fortune, to everything we've ever wanted, galls me. But I must act the part. And act it well and for some time. Were little Auron to die so soon in my guardianship, it would ruin us far more than his survival. Aris—" He frowned. "Aris doesn't trust me. So I will live in the palace, act the dutiful guardian, fond older brother. But I will visit you—"

"Like a whore set up in a bijou," Maledicte said. "How Ella would laugh—you, who she blamed for my recalcitrance to sell my body; you making me a whore when she could not. Except you don't have to pay for me or my rent. She wouldn't like that at all. . . . Please, tell me you'll set me up in a fashionable part of town, my dear. I would so hate to cross paths with my mother."

"Ella's long cold," Janus said quietly, hands dabbling in the bloodied water.

Maledicte's breath caught, startled out of his rage for the moment. He had always known that Ella would not have survived to the fullness of old age, but had never thought of her as dead. Just gone. But Janus's voice held more than that simple understanding.

"You went back," Maledicte said, remembering. "You told me you found R-Roach—" He couldn't help the tiny stagger in his voice, but he went on. "Did—did you find them too?"

"Yes," Janus said. "It wasn't hard. Once I realized they could tell me nothing of you—"

"You killed them," Maledicte said, eyes on his blood-tinged bath. His heart gave a sudden, unexpected lurch; his ears rang.

"The moment Last reclaimed me, Celia's life was forfeit. I could not have her dogging my heels, begging for coin, for her precious rank, her Laudable-addled mind making hash of my plans. And Ella, who had the poor taste to scream when I killed Celia—do not tell me you will cry for her; not that selfish woman who gave you nothing beyond your bare existence." Janus's blue eyes simmered with heat, the expression recalling kicks and curses, and days spent scrounging for scraps while the two of them plotted and seethed.

Untrue, Maledicte thought numbly. Ella had given Miranda one precious gift, even unknowingly, when she had opened her door to an aristocratic castoff and her infant son. A gift so valued that some of its virtue rubbed off on the giver: Maledicte's heart, tangled in loathing and contempt, still held room for that spark of gratitude. He could not have killed Ella. But Janus—

Maledicte shuddered all over, temper surging back. "How is it that you raise your blade to whomever you choose, and I—I only garner censure and suspicion? You walk the courts and I might be banished, impoverished, or hanged."

"I will never let that happen," Janus said.

Maledicte threw the robe off, began dressing with shaking hands. "And how will you prevent it? Time may be on your side, allowing you to worm your way into acceptance, but it's my enemy. Banished, impoverished, or hanged; none of them appeals to me overmuch. Janus, let's give this up. We did in the Relicts, remember, when our plans went wrong or grew too dangerous." At the sight of Janus shaking his head, Maledicte tried entreaty though it stuck in his throat like dusty feathers. "Janus, you're all I have. All I value."

"Be rid of Gilly, and I'll believe you. You trust him with everything. Sometimes I think you trust him more than me. Giving him control over your accounts, really Mal . . ."

"This isn't about him," Maledicte said. "It's about Auron, about claiming your birthright, about making our future. We've failed at claiming your title. I see no way to succeed."

"When you gained Ani's favor, you lost your mind," Janus said. "There's always a way."

"So you say, and yet the babe lives, his future safeguarded by one who should be the wolf. You've been playing dog too long. Aris holds your leash, and you fawn at his feet, saving your teeth for those weaker than yourself, helpless women . . ." Maledicte heard his voice, hoarse and ranting, taunting Janus as if he were one of his enemies, willing his words to bruise and sting, and wondered what was becoming of him. In the rippling water, he thought he saw the reflection of dark wings.

Janus slapped him, knocking him back against the edge of the tub. Maledicte growled low in his throat and launched himself at Janus, knocking over the vanity, sending them sprawling. The shaving mirror broke, scattering their reflections across the floor, their tangled bodies distorted in its shards. Fighting for control, Janus twisted Maledicte's arm behind his back.

Pain erupted in his shoulder and Maledicte grabbed a handful of mirror glass, heedless of the stinging slice against his palm, and swung. For the second time that day, blood stained his hand. His own and Janus's. The pressure on his arm eased and Maledicte turned, remorse sickening him.

Janus mopped his shoulder with his sleeve, blood dripping onto his forearm. "That's two battles in one day," Janus said. "A record even for your temper."

Maledicte curled his fingers into his palms, aware of the blood sliding between them. He fumbled for words, tried to control his angry breathing. "Let me see," Maledicte said, his temper vanishing under concern and shame. "I'll get bandages."

"Don't bother," Janus said, blue eyes smoldering. He twisted Maledicte's hand over and studied the gash in the palm, watched the welling blood slow and stop with a calculating eye. "You don't need it, and I'll get mine cleaned elsewhere. With the mood you're in, I'd get *arsenixa* on the bandage."

"No," Maledicte said. "Janus, I'd never hurt—"

Janus smiled, a thin, tight thing. "Maybe not, but I can do it myself."

Maledicte slumped back against the floor, watching as Janus raided his room for bandages, alum powder, and aloe.

"You're going back to the palace," Maledicte said.

"I have to go play lapdog to Aris," Janus said, his tone savage as he bandaged the wound. "You need to trust me, Miranda. Once you trusted me implicitly. Do so again, and all will be well. You forget that there is no separation between us. No plans for me, and plans for you. There's only us, though you seem to fear otherwise. Your job done, you must let me work, now. You must be patient. You used to know how."

Maledicte trailed into the bedroom, sat down by the fire. "I used to be someone else."

Janus poured him a tumbler of whiskey and folded his fingers around it. "You're becoming maudlin." He sat beside Maledicte, the temper still in his eyes, though less bright, less hot. "We must lull Aris. You need to give me time to undo the damage you did by killing Dantalion."

Maledicte nodded, drinking deeply. "But you won't stay." He forced his voice level, when he wanted to beg. It felt like years ago, lying in the street rubble, watching Ella's gift, her Janus, taken from her; now Janus took himself away, and she was more powerless than before.

Janus shook his head. "I must prove myself to Aris."

After Janus left, Maledicte tilted the rest of the whiskey past his lips, and then poured himself another. He stared into the empty fireplace until the darkness settled into the room, filling it with the sound of wings. The house creaked, Livia going on tiptoe out the door. In the kitchen, Cook sluiced down the tables. Eventually silence fell, and still, Gilly had not returned. Maledicte swallowed the last of a third whiskey and fled the house.

·35·

GILLY AND LIZETTE TUMBLED AND teased each other over
the sheets, but Gilly's pleasure was leavened by guilt. He was
all too aware that he should have returned to the town house,
that Janus was not to be relied upon, and that Maledicte's temper was uncertain at best. But he dreaded the fraught rooms and the lingering presence of Black-Winged Ani. So when Lizette hailed him on the
street, he gave in to temptation, and followed her home as shamelessly as an
alley cat. Tonight, Lizette's simple charms were panacea for what ailed him.
He was bent between her breasts, making her laugh, making her gasp, when
she stiffened in his arms.

"Get out, you. Wrong room." She held Gilly's head to her chest, but the
shiver up his spine had already warned him. There was no surprise in him
when he heard the raspy voice responding.

"No," Maledicte said. "This is the right room. But there are too many
people in it." His words still held their bite, but their customary precision
had been traded for a drinker's slur. Gilly turned, drawing the sheets to his
chest like a maiden under a lecher's stare, though Maledicte's gaze lingered
on Lizette and not him.

"Well, she's clean enough, I suppose, if a little overripe. I expected the
worst, it took me so long to get directions to this brothel. And she's red-
headed. Predictable, Gilly."

"Mal—what are you doing here?"

Maledicte ignored him. "Go away," he told Lizette.

"He's paid for me. You leave." Her eyes were slightly protuberant; from the study of her throat, Maledicte considered squeezing her neck, making them pop.

Gilly intervened. "It's all right, Lizette. The money's yours. Just leave us." His heart pounded in his chest, but for what cause? Fear for Lizette's safety, or anticipation at being alone with Maledicte?

"You still want the room? Cause Ma's going to want to know." Lizette drew her dressing gown on, and Gilly, seeing it through Maledicte's critical eyes, was aware of the clash of violet silk against her ruddy skin and hair.

"Go away," Maledicte repeated. He stumbled forward, ripped the sword from his belt, dropped it on the floor, sat down, and pulled off his boots. With a last moue, Lizette left, banging the door behind her. Maledicte shot the bolt, locking them in, and leaned against the door.

The silence grew, and Gilly, tiring of waiting, said, "I thought you housebound."

"The guards only watched me go," Maledicte said. "Perhaps they followed and are downstairs, sampling the house delights on Aris's coin."

"Janus?" Gilly asked.

"The palace. But I came here to be away from all that." He crawled onto the bed, swaying, his balance shot, and lay down beside Gilly. He studied the draped shape of Gilly's body. "I came to let you distract me."

Drunk, Gilly thought, and wondered how much whiskey it took to override Ani's effect on poison. But even as he wondered, Maledicte's eyes lost the glassy quality they had held a moment ago, growing sharper, darker.

Gilly forced a laugh. Distract him. Maledicte had driven him to distraction and now all he could think about was the nearness of Maledicte's body to his. He could not think of a story now to save his life. "How am I to do that?"

Maledicte rolled over in a swift move that belied his drunkenness, pinned Gilly, and kissed him, like the fierce first kiss of a child. Gasping, Gilly clutched Maledicte's neck, brought his mouth back down, and deepened the kiss. He tasted whiskey on Maledicte's tongue, like the sting within a liqueur-laced chocolate.

Maledicte slid the sheet down, followed the retreating fabric with his mouth and tongue and teeth, no child's kiss this. Gilly groaned at the blaze of hot breath on bare skin, his hands clutching the thick layers of brocaded jacket and vest, embroidered shirt. He tangled his hands in Maledicte's hair, drew him up for another kiss, tasting the sweet, hungry mouth, as pliant as any woman's, but coupled with the sinew and strength of the body pressed to his.

Maledicte shuddered against him, and Gilly bit at his neck, tasting starched silk. He lipped Maledicte's delicate fingers, ran his hands over the sleek shoulders knotted with muscle, and groaned again, nearly undone by the combination of female and male, of softness and steel. Maledicte laughed, a soft cat-rasp of pleasure, and rolled over, caging Gilly's hands beneath his flesh. Gilly knelt up, crawled over him, pressing his face into the black curls at his nape, licking, biting. Some blood scent still lingered in the dark hair, and Gilly moaned. Maledicte rocked back beneath him, rough embroidery scratching teasingly against Gilly's flushed skin. He gripped Maledicte's hips, pressed closer, and was rewarded with a breathy gasp that might have been his name.

Drowning in the scent of his black hair, fumbling blindly, Gilly unwound Maledicte's cravat, kissed his bared nape, craned around, and tried for the divot at the heart of his collarbone. Maledicte turned, sought Gilly's mouth again, agile hands slipping down Gilly's flanks, pulling him closer. Gilly reached for the vest buttons between them, that maddening barrier of silk and wool, and Maledicte pulled away in a convulsive movement. "Ugh. I can taste her on you." He rolled away from Gilly's questing hands, put his back to Gilly.

Gilly had no way of knowing that this was untrue, that the only thing Maledicte tasted was the warm salt of Gilly's flesh, the flavor of a beating heart. But belated caution skulked into Maledicte's mind—if Gilly uncovered Miranda's secret, what would Janus do?

All Gilly knew, felt, was his pounding heart, his aching body. Breathing faster, he tried to tug Maledicte back into his arms, but Maledicte snarled, "Get off me."

"Mal—" Gilly said, his word a plea, a breath, a groan.

Maledicte huddled himself up, a slim line condensing itself. "Leave me alone. Let me sleep." Maledicte's voice was rougher than usual, thicker. Gilly wondered if he would see tears or desire as the cause if he forced Maledicte to face him. Belated recognition of the words filtered into his mind.

"Are you staying?"

"Why not? It's late, I'm drunk, and the bed seems free of vermin. My apologies if I ruined your sport. But more fool you if you paid her before you took your pleasures."

Gilly stared at the ceiling, counting the crystal stars pasted on it. Lizette's client list. Each star a patron. In the center of the ceiling was his own favored patronage, marked out in spirals and dots, a constellation made of desire. Lizette swore the constellation was one seen in the Explorations, taught to her by a sailor, but Gilly had no proof of that. Not yet. Perhaps not ever.

Beside him, Maledicte's breath steadied and quieted.

"Mal?" Gilly said.

When he was met with silence, he pulled the quilt off the floor where he and Lizette had dropped it, and draped it over Maledicte. He bent to tuck it around Maledicte's shoulders and hesitated, finding Maledicte watching him with steady black eyes. "Here," Gilly said, awkwardly finishing the motion, aware of the rough silk of Maledicte's hair pinned between his fingers and the coverlet.

"I'm not cold."

"Colder than marble," Gilly said. He stroked the smooth cheek, feeling the dip and sway of the flesh between cheekbone and scarred jaw. "You should go back to Dove Street."

"I don't want to."

"Petulant as a child," Gilly said. "But if you won't, you won't. It would serve you right if I brought Lizette back in."

"Don't," Maledicte said. "Please."

"I won't. Best move over some, you're going to fall off the edge."

Gilly slid beneath the sheets, unwound them as best he could, allowing for Maledicte's weight atop them. Gingerly, he stroked the softness of Maledicte's hair fanning out over the pillows. When Maledicte didn't object, he tucked himself around that slim form, and felt the tension rise and fall in Maledicte's bones.

Snuggled together in such surroundings, Gilly found himself wondering if this was how it had been for Maledicte and Janus. Away from the town house, this moment felt fragile, endangered by any opening door, by the rumble of voices down the hall, by the shouts of laughter and anger that rose from the streets. No wonder they clung to each other, he thought, they grew up with no haven but each other. Still, he thought, the situation was no longer the same.

"I've been thinking about the Explorations again," Gilly said, testing the waters.

In his arms, Maledicte made a sound of protest more felt than heard. It gave Gilly courage.

"I want you to come with me. The *Virga* sails in five months, just before the fall. We could ride out beneath its tall sails, out through the harbor, into the deep waters where it's so blue you can't tell sea from sky. We could watch sea beasts at play; the great whales spouting and diving, and stranger creatures still, so strange that no sailor ever mentions them unless you've seen them already for fear of being mocked. We'd land in a new world. No Relicts, no court, just the land and the sky and the stars. The sailors say it's a different sky entirely down there, that it never goes black, just to darker and darker shades of blue—"

"And do what?" Maledicte whispered. "Live like paupers? Or fish for a living, at the mercy of storm and sea?"

"I'd be a chocolate farmer," Gilly said, inventing on the spot. "Feed you sweets for breakfast, until you grew fat or sick from them."

Maledicte laughed, his warm breath brushing Gilly's forearm, raising the hairs on it and on his neck. "Dreamer."

"But not a fool," Gilly said. "Before I go, I'd buy up small luxuries here, to take with me. Sell them to the Antyrrian émigrés over there, desperate for a taste of home, and use the money for things exotic to Antyre and send them back for sale. Feathers for gowns and hats, pelts for pelisses, illustrations. Maybe I'd even write a book for the libraries." His words came stiff and slow, awkward as his stories never were, fearful of being mocked. It was the first time he'd spoken aloud of his dreams. And even then he balked at spilling it all, that he would include Maledicte as more than a whim. That he couldn't imagine life without him.

"A trader overseas," Maledicte said.

"I know, a dreamer," Gilly said.

Maledicte rose up, turned, and kissed Gilly's forehead, stroked his cheek. He slid back into Gilly's loose embrace, and only once his face was hidden again did Gilly hear him speak. "What about Janus?"

If Gilly's words of salt and sea and sky carried sunlight and tropical flavors, the mention of Janus brought the first taste of winter into the room.

Heart pounding, realizing that Maledicte was tempted, Gilly said, "Can't you forget him?" His words were a whisper. Vornatti died for voicing a similar thought, but Gilly gambled that Maledicte was far fonder of him.

"I could easier forget my own name," Maledicte said. "He needs me."

"I need you," Gilly said, sudden hunger darkening his voice to a growl, rolling Maledicte to face him.

Maledicte scowled. "You want me. Which is not the same thing at all."

Gilly started to protest and Maledicte put a hand over his mouth. "Listen to me, Gilly. When you'd had me, what then? You'd be as weary of me as you were of the old bastard . . . you'd be longing for your sweet-fleshed, sweet-tempered maids and not a dark-natured creature like myself."

Gilly kissed the fingers overlying his mouth in soundless retort. Maledicte withdrew his hand. "No, Gilly. Leave me be. I'm tired beyond belief. . . ." He tried to unravel himself from the blanket but Gilly stopped him.

"Shh, just sleep. I'll guard your sleep. Even from myself." Gilly forced a lightness into his voice he didn't feel, was rewarded with Maledicte relaxing into his embrace. He lay with Maledicte a swaddled bundle in his arms, and tried to sort out the truth of it. Was Maledicte right, would he repent of this unseasonal desire? Gilly couldn't imagine doing so, but when he slept his dreams were full of Black-Winged Ani cradled in his arms, covered in blood.

MALEDICTE WOKE, rubbed grit from his dry eyes, and took a startled breath at finding himself in the brothel. The corset pinched his ribs and he gasped. Untangling himself from the blankets, he staggered to the washstand, stared at his reflection in the still water. Gilly. Maledicte turned, breathing shallowly, breathing with small hitches of pain. In the emptiness of the room, he shucked out of the crumpled coat, the vest, and reached into his shirt to loosen the first laces on his corset. The relief was as sweet as the memory of his restraint. Janus would have killed him. Like Roach. Like Ella. Salt stung his eyes.

He splashed water on his face. The water was tepid but clear. Gilly must have asked them to bring another basin when he was done washing and shaving. Without Gilly's presence, the room seemed too full of the whore's trade, draggled lace, fine fabrics worn thin with use, the narrow bed and sagging mattress, the cloying odor of rose-scented powder and sweat in the air. If Maledicte had been less fortunate, less determined, without Janus to aid him, Ella might have sold Miranda to a place like this.

Nausea churned in his belly. Never to this, he thought. He would spill blood on the roads first, turn highwayman and waylay rich men's coaches. The thought calmed him; the sword on the bed soothed him with its bird's-eye glitter.

The door opened behind him. In the mirror, water blurring his vision, he saw Lizette enter. "What do you want?"

Lizette grinned. "Gilly said to make you comfortable. I came to offer you a razor."

Aware of the dampness at his throat and the loosened laces around his chest, Maledicte took up his vest, buttoning it with his back to her. "I hardly think to be here long enough to require one."

"I would be amazed if you did," she said. She closed the door, leaned against it much as he had last night. He remembered that. The stability of the rough wood when his heart was pounding with possibilities.

"Have you something to say?" Maledicte settled his coat as best he could, adjusting the shoulders. His head throbbed, imagining her laughing over how he had routed her from her bed to lie with his servant.

"Poor Gilly," she said. "His head's in a swivet about you, desiring you, loving you." The scorn in her eyes took away any sweetness left in her face. "And he don't know the first thing about you, does he, *my lady?*"

Maledicte's breath stopped. All his worries about Gilly knowing, about the court finding out, about Aris looking at him without preconceptions, just *once*, and it was this whore who guessed. "I've killed one man for suggesting I was effeminate. What makes you—"

"Whores know things, we've got eyes for artifice, don't we? Appearances is our trade, more'n anything else. How to look better, smaller, fuller—each of us has played the man at least once, going out with a fellow where we wouldn't be wanted or escorting ourselves places where women don't walk alone. You're just better than most. Without that sword though, you're nothing but a tall, skinny—"

"Shut your mouth," Maledicte said. He grabbed the sword, yanked it free, then fought to resheathe it. He didn't need to murder her. Whores were easily bought.

"Or you'll shut it for me?" She vamped at him, flashing her skirts, wrinkling her nose, fluttering her eyelashes.

Maledicte grabbed her neck and slammed her into the door.

She coughed, then laughed. "Rough play do it for you? You'll be disappointed with Gilly then. He's a sweetheart, through and through, my Gilly is—"

"Shut up," Maledicte said, pinching his fingers inward like the claws of a crab, collecting her attention along with the air in her windpipe.

Wary now, she opened her mouth to cry out. As quickly as she did, he barred her mouth with his fingers. "Listen to me, Lizette. Should you unmask me, I will make you suffer. I know Itarusine potions to make your blood surge and foam within your skin, seeking egress. You'll bleed and keep bleeding from your eyes, your mouth, your overused sex . . . and you'll suffer pain you can't imagine. You'll die slowly while your blood swells like the surf and your skin splits to make way for it. And when you're dead, even the crows won't touch your flesh." He released her. "And no one will even care. Or investigate. You'll be just another dead whore."

She slid down the door, soiled violet silk and blotchy face. "I wasn't going to say nothing. Whores don't say nothing."

"Not if they're wise." Maledicte stepped back. She wiped her teary eyes and nose with the edge of her gown, looking up at him. He put a hand to her shoulder and she flinched. "I see you understand me."

He left the door sagging open, left Lizette huddled on the floor, and went home.

GILLY, LOUNGING IN THE LIBRARY, looked up at the bang of the door. He folded the broadsheet, set it down at his feet. "Did you sleep well?" He doubted it, the way Maledicte clung to the shadows of the room, pulling curtains.

"Did you send Lizette in to me?" Maledicte asked.

Gilly winced at the ugly edge in Maledicte's voice. "No. But the greedy little cat probably liked the rich looks of you. Did she wake you?"

"The screeching of the matron did, rousting some sailors who outstayed their coin. Don't I give you enough to establish a bijou in a peaceful neighborhood?"

"Woke up temperamental, that's obvious," Gilly said. Aware that Maledicte hadn't yet met his eyes, Gilly wondered what ailed him, embarrassment or anger. "Come here." When Maledicte hesitated, he repeated himself. "Come here."

Maledicte stood before him, stiff and spiky like a child uncertain of chastisement.

"Woke with a head, I've no doubts," Gilly said. "Poor Mal. You were very drunk last night. I am amazed Ani allowed it."

Maledicte knelt before Gilly. "You're not angry?"

"No," Gilly said. Why should he be angry? He knew something he hadn't known before, that Maledicte desired him. That knowledge made him lazy and content. He stroked Maledicte's neck, his shoulders, his dark hair. Maledicte laid his head in Gilly's lap, sighing.

"I'm sorry you woke unpleasantly," Gilly said, separating strands of dark hair and twining them again. "You looked so peaceful when I left."

"That was your mistake," Janus said. Gilly flinched in his seat, felt Maledicte carry the movement through. "When Mal is peaceful, it's always deceptive. Usually means he's going to kill someone."

"I have to wash," Maledicte said. "Those sheets probably had fleas." He pushed away from Gilly's loose embrace.

Janus snagged his arm, studied him with a sapphirine gaze. "Aris restricted you to these four walls. You went out?"

"You disobey him at will. Why shouldn't I?" Maledicte said, twitching his arm free.

"I am not on sufferance," Janus said.

"Aren't you?" Maledicte said.

Janus's face darkened, and Maledicte sighed. "My temper is foul today, Janus, so go cautiously."

"I remind you," Janus said. "Aris has guards watching the house, watching you. Remember that, should you feel the need to draw your blade."

Maledicte shivered; his hands clenched, but he made no further response to the tightening noose of suspicion he found himself in. Instead, he drew Janus's head down and kissed him fiercely, after a quick, burdened glance at Gilly.

"I'm tired. You need to time your visits better. Until then, Gilly will take care of me." Maledicte slipped out of Janus's arms and went upstairs.

Janus smiled thinly at Gilly, and prowled the room, unspeaking. Gilly rose to go and Janus forestalled him. "Something you want to confess to me, Gilly? You're jumpy today. As if you had a guilty conscience."

"Is yours any more pristine?" Gilly countered.

"Do I need to tell you again to stay away from Maledicte? He's more than you can handle."

"I handled things well enough last night," Gilly said.

The sudden blankness in Janus's face gave him enough warning to duck the blow. But then Janus seized his shoulders in a grip that trembled with rage; Gilly felt bruises starting.

"You dared," Janus said.

"Why shouldn't I?" Gilly said. "If you can change your appetite from women for Mal's sake, why can I not do the same? He was willing enough."

The tension in Janus's arms eased enough for Gilly to free himself. What he had said that defused the worst of Janus's temper, Gilly didn't know, and he found himself regretting it. This fight had been a long time coming, and he welcomed it as much as he feared it.

"Get out," Janus said.

"This is my house," Gilly said. "You go." He grinned. His heart raced with exhilaration and fear. He found Maledicte's evil genius poking him, as if the night spent together had left him with more than frustrated desire. "Of course, you could stay. Could hit me again, threaten to kill me. Again. But I know why you balk . . . you are not so sure that Mal would forgive you—"

Janus struck and Gilly blocked, catching the fist in his own grip, twisting it. "No more idle threats, Janus. I've gotten your measure. Maledicte's love protects me from you. And he does love me, whether he wants to or not."

"Then be honest with me," Janus said. "You mean to steal him from me."

Gilly said, "Your love will send him to blood and death."

"You don't care about the blood, about the court. All you care about is having him for yourself. Don't dress your motives in fine words. You want him."

"I do," Gilly said.

"I'll kill you first," Janus said.

"And that brings us around to where we started this quarrel," Gilly said. "Like two dogs fighting over a bitch in season."

"That's a flattering thought. Be sure to share it with Mal. He'll gut you for me," Janus said.

"He promised he'd never hurt me. I believe him. He may be many things, but he's not a liar."

"He'd forgive me anything," Janus said.

"Are you willing to test it?" Gilly said. He stepped back, raised his arms wide, inviting Janus. "Not that you'd have it all your own way. I may not be a swordsman, but I outreach you."

Janus snarled. "You forget your place. Maledicte may call you friend, but you are a servant born, and a servant until death."

"And you haven't forgotten yours?" Gilly asked. "You're so far out of your place that you're dangling from a rope marked treason."

Janus hissed, his hand clenching around his sword, but as soon as his knuckles whitened, they relaxed, the rage cresting and disappearing as if it had never been. He turned a placid face to Gilly, leaving him off-balance. Where did the rage go? Where would Janus vent it? Not on Maledicte, surely; it was no longer safe to do so.

Gilly put his back to Janus and walked out, though his skin crawled. If Janus could be rid of him by accident or manipulation, Maledicte's protection would be useless. And Janus's anger, though better controlled than Maledicte's, always erupted in the end.

He listened for Janus's footsteps in the hall, in case Janus chose to continue their quarrel. But instead, he heard them going up the stairs, chasing after Maledicte.

· 36 ·

For a most enlightening murder, in times when subtlety is not as prized
as spectacle, one can do no better than to seek out tincture Precatorius,
imported from the Explorations. A single death by its means is always·
enough to open the eyes of the most recalcitrant subject.

—A Lady's Treatise, *attributed to Sofia Grigorian*

*T*HE MESSENGER ARRIVED EARLY in the morning, rousting
Gilly from his bed after a night full of stealthy leavings, first Livia
creeping out yet again, then Janus seeking the palace. Sleepily,
Gilly paid the boy and flipped open the note, curious to see which of their
spies had something to report, or if perhaps the coachman hadn't lost Livia
this time—the girl was clever and careful. But the terse lines didn't involve
Maledicte and his schemes at all. The note, straggling words written in a
hand unused to a pen, read simply: *Lizette very sick. Need help.* Gilly crumpled
the quarter sheet of cheap paper in his fist, releasing the scent of the brothel
and desperation.

Gilly was torn between agitation and irritation. Lizette had been furious with Maledicte's intrusion and threats, had failed to meet with him
last night, sent Ma Desire herself down to make her sentiments known.
He half suspected this emergency mere stratagem, showing whether he
valued her.

When he entered, he smelled the hot tang of blood over all the other odors, and knew the need was real. The madam met him at the door, her skirts splotched with blood.

"It's too late," she said. "She's gone."

"Gone," Gilly repeated, and went where the madam beckoned.

Lizette's boudoir was drenched. The blood, mostly stiff and browning, still had a few spots of freshness to it. One rivulet dripped slowly from the bed.

Her back arched; her eyes were open but obscured by blood, her hands locked on the sheets in her last spasm. Gilly gagged. *Lizette.*

"What happened?"

"Poison," Ma Desire said.

"Poison," Gilly repeated, his ears numbing.

"She got a box of chocolates, last night, after she sent you away. She ate them up, didn't she, most of them at once. And a note—didn't I read it for her." She spoke to the room at large, though Gilly was the only one listening. Over by the hearth, another whore, her hands gloved, shoved bloody sheets into the fireplace. A second girl scrubbed at the spots on Lizette's finest dress, attempting to salvage it.

"Said as how you were sorry. That she should forgive you. Real gentlemanly, it was."

"I didn't send it," Gilly said. But he might as well have, he thought. Somehow this blame fell at his door.

"Figured that out when she started to bleed. She knew then who done it."

"Who?" Gilly said.

The madam turned her head, studied the room with a speaking silence. Gilly's breath shuddered out of him. Throat tight, he reached into his pocket for coins.

" 'Tain't for me," Ma Desire said, as she tucked them into her bodice. "For her. Someone's got to pay for the burying."

"Who did this?" Beneath the grief, a flicker of anger grew. He was not Janus, was not Maledicte, to find forgiveness of anything.

"She raved about your other lover, your highborn lady, said the crows were at her, tearing her insides. She felt their beaks. Said your lover had warned her. Said she'd bleed. Said Black-Winged Ani was killing her sure. Said she stole the crow's man and doomed herself. That true?"

"What?" Gilly said, his mind quaking away from the ruined woman on the bed, the fevered words attributed to her. Maledicte? Maledicte found killing offenses entirely too easily, Gilly thought, sick at heart. And penned at home with watchful guards, unable to bring the sword to bear, a box of poisoned sweets would be all too easy to arrange.

"That you're one of Black Ani's creatures."

"No," Gilly said. "My master—my friend—" His voice broke. He sat on the bed, touched Lizette's distorted face, cold, waxy, and faintly sticky.

"You want to protect yourself. There's charms and such," she said. "You're a good boy. Don't get caught up in the crow's feathers." She reached out, touched his hair, the hardness fading from her face. "You was good to my girl."

THE KINGSGUARDS POSTED near the house eyed him curiously as he pounded up the entry stairs, slamming the door open, but did no more than watch.

Inside, Maledicte, muted in gray wool with a scarlet shirt peeking out, sat to luncheon, his head bent over a book. Gilly paused, the anger in him churning, and he bypassed the dining room for the main stairs. He pushed open Maledicte's doors, ransacked drawers and wardrobe until he found the wooden case that held the poisons and dumped them across the bed, greenish-gray powder spilling out of white twists, dusting his hands. He rummaged through the small vials, looking for the one that could make flesh melt to blood.

"You've only been out for a few hours," Maledicte said from the doorway. "Surely no one's offended you so badly in that time that you would turn to poison. But if they have, let me know, and I'll take care of it for you."

Gilly's hand closed around the vial. A scant few purple drops clung to the curved bottom. "You didn't have to kill her. All you had to do was ask me to give her up. I would have done anything for you. I have done everything for you."

"Gilly?"

Gilly threw the vial at him. Maledicte caught it easily, looked at it with wary eyes. "Precatorius syrup. She bled to death, as you threatened."

"Lizette." Just her name drew Maledicte's supple mouth into a scowl.

To Gilly, it felt like confession. "She bled out and your bottle is near empty. Why kill her like that? Why make her suffer? Why kill her at all?" Gilly's eyes blurred with tears.

"Is she worth all this fuss? She was just a whore." Maledicte's face twisted. "A creature without value."

Gilly's fingers clenched; he raised his fist, and dropped it. Maledicte hadn't flinched.

"I liked her. She was uncomplicated and mouthy. What did she do to you? What did she say? Did she laugh at you? Give me a reason—" He raised his hand to Maledicte's cheek. "Please." He needed something, anything to stop the rage and pain churning inside him. He waited in frozen silence for Maledicte's response, waited to be freed to anger or bittersweet relief.

"I didn't kill the bitch," Maledicte said, slapping Gilly's hand away. "Are you my hanging judge? Go away, Gilly."

"Chocolate and poison. A sweet with a sting. A note she couldn't read but had my name on it. It apologized for our interrupted sport. You expect me to believe you didn't do this?"

"Burn your soul, I—" His voice refused to rise, the rasp giving way to forced silence. Thwarted, Maledicte bared his teeth and shoved past Gilly like a departing evil spirit. The parlor door downstairs slammed with a sound of cracking glass, leaving Gilly cut off from his answers. Small crashes shattered silence like distant cannonfire as Maledicte took his temper out on frangibles.

Gilly's own rage simmered and roiled. He fled the house, past the lurking guards, and into the city. He was nearly into the merchants' streets before the fog of temper and pain cleared way for a single thought. Maledicte had never denied his wrongdoings before. Still, it was Maledicte's bottle that had been emptied. . . .

Gilly moaned, resting his sweating face against his hands. He forgot that he had enemies himself, one of whom resided under the same roof, privy to Lizette's existence, to her location, to Gilly's thrice-weekly visits. Grim, Gilly traced his way back in the twilight. He would ask once again, and this time, he would listen.

The door was not locked against him as he half expected it to be. The parlor was awash in wreckage, as if it was the spill point for the tides' refuse. The mirrored door was broken; winking glass met Gilly's gaze from every angle; the spinet stool lay beneath the lintel, one leg snapped.

Gilly's boot crunched in the soft pile of the rugs. A curled bit of porcelain stuck out from beneath his boot. He picked it up—a small porcelain arm. The silk thread and dangling stick were all that told him he held the remains of one of a series of puppeteer figures. He raised his eyes to their shelf. Not one remained, and though he found more identifiable pieces, a dog's head with a high, ruffled collar, a serpent's rattle, a minuscule puppet's puppet with its arms snapped off, he found no whole survivor. Some of them had been broken so fiercely it seemed as if Maledicte had attempted to grind them underfoot.

Gilly set down his handful of parts on the curtained altar with a speculative expression. Janus had gifted Maledicte with these puppets. Maledicte held them dear. Or had. Likened himself to the puppeteer of the gods, but perhaps he felt more a puppet today.

Gilly ascended the stairs to the first level, turning the gas lamps to glowing life as he went.

"Maledicte?" Gilly called. The house was as hushed as if Gilly was the only breathing thing within its walls, and his heart beat faster. "Maledicte?" In the hallway, Gilly hesitated, then chose to climb the dark attic steps. Faint glimmers of porcelain dust traced a footstep six steps before him and he took the rest of the stairs with more surety.

Cool evening air swirled down, whistled under the attic door. Gilly pushed it open. The attic window gaped with jagged glass. Maledicte sat before it, perched on a pile of trunks. The heavy sweep of his scarlet shirt, the sleeves uncorded, unrestrained by a jacket, draped like bloody wings. His knees were drawn up, wrists crossed over their peaks.

"I'm sorry, Gilly." Maledicte turned his head to look back over his shoulder; the heavy hair whispered and shifted. His face gleamed in the faint starshine and reflected gaslight straining through the city fogs.

A scrabble and the brushed, whiskery sound of feathers kept Gilly from instant speech as the rooks hopped his foot and lifted off, one wheeling out the window, the other perching on the pile of discarded clothing. It dipped its beak, exposed a rent in an embroidered jacket, and flew out the window, trailing golden strands.

"I didn't know you cared so much about her," Maledicte said. His voice was muffled; he laid his head into the space between his arms. "I hated her."

Gilly sat on a low trunk, peering up at the huddled shape. "You didn't even know her. I barely knew her beyond her profession. How could you know her enough to hate her?"

"She came in while I was washing, teasing me. I told her to go away. She wouldn't, just leaned against the wall, her dress falling off her breasts, flaunting herself. I tried to scare her away and she laughed at me. I only did it to make her stop."

"So instead of stabbing her there, you came home and sent her poisoned chocolates, leaving her time to spread the story. No, you came home. You spoke to Janus. And Janus killed her."

"No," Maledicte said. "Gilly, you have all the evidence. What more do you want? I am a murderer after all, several times over."

Gilly let out his breath; it left blueness in the chill air. "Tell me you killed her. Tell me you sent death to her, wrapped in pink paper."

Maledicte stared down at Gilly. "I killed Lizette."

The shadows made patchwork of his face, created dark holes where his eyes should shine, and his voice was as calm as ever. Yet Gilly felt his pulse jump, his breath catch as he recognized the lie. Maledicte, the competent killer, was a bad liar, more used to half truth and misdirection.

"I'm sorry, Gilly," Maledicte said. He levered himself to his feet, standing before the open window. He stretched forward, slipped a clenched fist out into the night sky, rainwater washing over his fist, and then he opened it. Small, and glittering malevolently, the carved puppet of Ani plunged to the street below. Maledicte swayed in its wake and Gilly put a steadying hand on his ankle.

"Sorry for something you didn't do." Gilly plucked Maledicte from the chests, and let him go, listening to him stumble down the stairs. Gilly looked out the window, down to where the statue had disappeared.

"You'd forgive him anything," Gilly said. "Even making me believe you killed her. Trying to set us at odds." Bile twisted in his belly at the sheer callousness of it, at turning Lizette's life into a pawn move. In the attic's soothing darkness, Gilly, like Maledicte before him, crouched and wept. If he had any doubts before—he had none now. Janus was a killer, and like his father, like Dantalion, preferred to smile and kill at a distance.

Gilly bowed his head. The fault, after all, was his. He had goaded Janus, knowing that the man would retaliate. But to imply that Maledicte was to blame— Outrage settled the anger in his belly to a steady flame.

His fisted hands touched the stiff, dark patches of Lizette's blood, transferred when he sat beside her corpse, and he turned to seek his bath. But through the broken window, he heard the coach draw up outside, the horses' hooves loud on the cobbles. *Janus*, he thought, and decided to put off his cleaning in favor of confrontation.

When Gilly reached the entry hall, he found Maledicte, blank-faced and white, facing Lord Echo and a brace of Particulars.

"I have a warrant sworn out for your arrest," Echo said, smiling grimly, his hand on his pistol.

"In what matter?" Maledicte asked. "You've sought to blame me for so—"

"One incontrovertible death. The murder of Dantalion Vornatti."

ARDLY MURDER," MALEDICTE SAID. "A duel."

"His blood, your sword. You cannot deny that."

"Why would I deny it? When I enjoyed myself so much?" Maledicte said, though in truth he had almost forgotten it. Dantalion's death swallowed under Ani's blood tide; to find himself accountable for it now— His hands shook but his voice remained light. He tightened the small muscles in his hands, and they too obeyed his will, stilling. The sword hilt shifted against his palm, though he wasn't aware of seeking it out. The feathers coaxed and whispered against his skin. Gilly's clothes, scented with Lizette's passing, kept blood in Maledicte's mind.

There were only three men after all. He could have his sword through the protruding belly of the nearest Particular without much effort, spill the blood out and dance toward the young Particular to Echo's left. Already his dewy skin paled at the audacity of arresting a nobleman. If Maledicte gutted the first man, the youngster would bolt. He'd lay sols on the matter. Only Echo promised a fight.

Maledicte sucked air through his teeth, felt it cool the furnace of his blood. Yes or no. Fight or fly—he'd have to chase the stripling if he fled. He'd had enough of witnesses. But three were manageable.

"Maledicte," Echo said. "Lay down your sword."

"If I choose otherwise?" Maledicte said, still listening to the clock of his blood, ticking away.

Echo pulled his pistol, cocked it, and leveled it at Gilly's chest. "Do I need to use your friend as a surety for your behavior? Should I see one gesture that speaks of weapon, poison, or even enchantment, I will kill him."

Rage reddened Maledicte's vision; his heartbeat, reacting, deafened him. *Kill them all*, Ani whispered. *Bathe in their blood. Feast on their eyes. Even Gilly. He mistrusted you after all, accused you of something you never did.* The sword rose in the sheath; his fingers coiled down, touched the cool metal of the blade itself.

The violent simplicity of the idea held Maledicte hostage. *Kill them all.*

Maledicte felt the movement in the air and he spun on instinct, the sword free of the sheath, registering the shock in Echo's face even as he did so. It was Gilly moving, only Gilly, and instead of slicing skin and bone, Maledicte twisted the blade, letting the flat of the sword strike Gilly's broad wrist. It welted the skin and left a fine line of blood where the edge had nipped. But the hand was whole, the wrist entire, the fingers closing on his shoulder. Maledicte panted, watching that slow beading of blood on Gilly's fair skin.

"Maledicte," Gilly said. "Be still." He stepped past him, blocked Maledicte's view of Echo. "Does the king know you're here?"

"The king can call me off—he has that privilege. But he need not set me on. There were many witnesses." Echo smiled. "Maledicte is mine."

Behind Gilly's sheltering back, Maledicte started shaking again, this time beyond his ability to control. Stonegate Prison. How could he accomplish Ani's goal then? How could he even survive, locked in the dark, with constant company—how could he be Maledicte?

The thin thought crossed his mind, a ghost of reason. Echo had not shot Gilly, though Maledicte had drawn his sword; Echo bluffed.

Maledicte bolted for the stairs, for the scent of the sky, and Echo shouted. Behind him, Maledicte heard the report of a gun, but no outcry from Gilly. If he hadn't been so desperate, he could have wept with relief. But trying to think around the flapping blackness of Ani's rioting emotions left him little but the frantic intellect of a cornered rat.

Echo's hard hands grabbed his shoulders and Maledicte kicked back in a Relict rat's dirty blow. But Echo, though he faltered, was wise enough to have anticipated such a trick. Maledicte twisted to bring the blade to bear, freeing himself from Echo's clawing grasp, and found himself borne back into the wall by Gilly.

Maledicte fought Gilly's grip, breath sobbing in his throat. Ani whispered, *Kill him and be gone*. Maledicte gasped his refusal, even as Gilly pulled him closer, clutched him to his body, pressing him between his solid warmth and the unyielding wall.

"Mal," Gilly said. "Maledicte, please. If you flee now, there will be no Janus, no future, only blood and death." Gilly's breath warmed his cheek; his fingers traced soothing patterns on his wrists and back.

Over Gilly's shoulder Maledicte saw the two Particulars nervously watching, saw Echo's eyes narrow, and Maledicte hissed at him. Echo took an involuntary step back and Maledicte laughed.

"Hush," Gilly said. "Hush, this is what we'll do. Where one man can be paid to do his duty, another can be paid to ease your way. Go with Echo. It'll be only temporary."

Maledicte burrowed into Gilly's warmth, listened to the heartbeat pounding beneath his ear, not as calm as the words Gilly spoke. Beneath the patterns Gilly traced, Maledicte felt Ani retreat, muttering, leaving Maledicte drained but capable of thought.

"You won't leave me there?" Maledicte said.

"No," Gilly whispered, stroking Maledicte's hair, heedless of Echo's furious gaze. "I promise," Gilly said, "I will always come for you."

"Tell him."

"Yes," Gilly said.

"He'll get me free," Maledicte said.

Gilly nodded. Maledicte reversed his grip on the sword; Echo raised his pistol again, but lowered it as Maledicte handed the sword to Gilly hilt-first. "Take care of this. I'll need it again." Then he stepped past Gilly's sheltering arms, and into the rough grasp of the Particulars.

AN HOUR LATER, shoved into a filthy communal cell, Maledicte reminded himself of the satisfaction that had filled him when he had taken Dantalion's throat, reminding himself that the bloodlust had been worth the price he paid now. The remembered smell of blood kept away the stink of unwashed bodies, of rank straw, of fouled water and illness, soothed the panicky flutter of his heart.

The cell fell silent at his entrance. In his fine clothing, his perfumed hair, he was a world away from their existence. Usually the nobles met with Damastes, the jailer, handed over their valuables for a private cell, for fresh water, for a mouthful of bread not gone blue. But Echo had brushed by the jailer, ignoring the man's covetous looks at Maledicte's finery, and forced Maledicte into the common cell. The rattle and thump of the heavy door woke those who had learned to be wary, and made others flinch in their sleep. Maledicte's heart leaped again at the long rattle of chains being drawn through iron rings, the wooden bar sealing the cell door shut behind him. Caging him. His mouth dried.

Two women, huddled in the corner, averted their eyes, pulling ragged shawls up to cover their faces. Beside them, a man rose to his feet, bare arms showing the dark ink of a conscripted soldier, a survivor of Xipos Island, and undoubtedly an enemy of the aristocracy that had used him and discarded him. Wary, Maledicte watched him stand. "You're even taller than my Gilly," he said aloud. The torchlight wavered through the grill on the door, casting ruddy shadows into the room.

"And you're dressed for pleasure, not prison," the man said, his voice equal to Maledicte's rasp. "Those shiny buttons, that stickpin—hope you won't mind sharing."

"I do," Maledicte said. His hand itched for his sword, but when he was Miranda he'd taken on grown men, unarmed, save for a stick. Though even Miranda, half-mad with starvation, might have balked at this fellow.

The man lumbered at him, meaty hands outstretched, and Maledicte laughed. Snatching up a handful of stiff straw, he lunged to meet him, stuck his makeshift weapon into the man's eyesockets, and twisted. The man screamed, his voice gone high and hoarse. "You're too slow and fat," Maledicte said.

He pivoted, aware of others slowly joining the fray, eager for revenge on a noble, for the temptation of riches enough to pay off their petty crimes or debts.

In the back of his mind, Miranda began to panic—she knew what happened to girls who got overwhelmed, torn down—but Ani raised Her wings and Maledicte let his will slip away, gave himself entirely over to Her hungers.

He reached up to the thrashing giant, climbed his shirt, and bit through the skin at his neck. The man fell, whimpering, covering his bloody neck. Ani spat the tiny scraps of flesh out and they were lost on the floor.

The other men hesitated a moment, and Ani grinned a bloody smile at them. In the corner, the women gibbered, whether in support or terror he couldn't tell. Ani sucked in a breath, took in the foul vapors of the room, of the death lingering in corners, and spat it all back out. Black foam flecked the floor where his spit landed, splashed on their faces.

"Rot you," Maledicte said. "Rot you all."

They backed off, hands touching their faces, wiping the spittle away as if it burned them.

Maledicte's throat itched as if his saliva had been caustic. He reached for a water pail, skimmed the top of it, and drank the clearer water below. Where his lips touched the dipper, the metal blackened, Ani moving through him in waves of heat.

"What's all this?" the jailer said from the doorway, keys jangling self-importantly. He checked on seeing the big man whimpering in the middle of the floor. Maledicte looked at Damastes blankly for a moment, trying to re-cover the courtly ways that Ani had eclipsed.

"He wanted to share the things I'm saving for you," Maledicte said, touching his jeweled cuffs, his gemstone-buttoned vest, the fine weave of his coat.

"You shouldn't be in here. Not with the likes of them. You're Quality," Damastes said. "Quality"—he drew the word out again, raising his head to stare Maledicte down. His eyes were the color of dirty slate, and oddly opaque, his hair a faded brown, as if he took his coloring from the stone and earth around them.

"I've always thought so." Maledicte said. "Shall we adjourn to your office? Maybe have some wine sent in. That water is foul." His flippancy felt strained.

The jailer nodded, his eyes assessing. "Yes, let's talk about your situation." He bowed with as much mockery as Maledicte had ever managed, and ges-tured him out of the common cell.

As Maledicte passed through the doorway, guards fell in step beside him from the places on either side of the door, letting Maledicte see that as greedy as Damastes was, he was also wary.

Echo and his damned interference again, Maledicte thought. The jailer was unlikely to treat his other noble patrons with such caution. Too often now, Echo had created obstacles for him. Maledicte, walking down the nar-row hallway, ignored the stone walls, the damp, spending his thoughts on sweeter dreams of killing Echo. His fingers curled, seeking the hilt of his sword, and for a moment, the familiar memories of it were so strong, so real that he felt the weight of the blade waiting, smelled the steel tang of it in the dank air.

His hand snatched at empty air; he faltered in his steps as the sense of steel faded to nothing, like smoke in his grasp. "Keep moving," a guard said, reaching out to prod Maledicte into motion. Maledicte evaded the careless hand and started up the uneven stairs he had been pushed down barely an hour before.

The jailer's office and quarters were only cells with their walls knocked out, leaving cut masonry edges visible. Narrow windows allowed an unbarred view over the approaching street, but were too thin to permit egress. Around the room, heaped on elegant furniture, jumbled piles of aristocratic castoffs gave the impression of a disorganized pawnshop. Small jewels spilled over the edge of a mahogany dresser, gleaming like water, pouring into the half-open drawers. A riot of chairs made the room a maze of gilded legs and scrollwork, of tapestry and velvet and leather. At the heart of the room, a clerk's desk, all pigeonholes and paperwork, rested. A fireplace peeked out from behind a stack of dust-felted books.

Idly, Maledicte bent and picked up a pocket watch from a pile of others. Lapis sails, a nacre ship, enameled on washed gold. He swung it from his hands, the chain slipping through his fingers with the heft of a living serpent.

"Sit," Damastes said.

Tucking the watch and chain up his cuff with the same economy of motion that he had used while card-sharping, Maledicte felt more at ease. If the jailer and his guards missed his small theft, they were not so observant as he feared. He turned his attention to choosing a chair, looking at gilded legs, carved frogs, or lions rampant on leather.

"This is not a shop for your perusal," the jailer said, brows drawing down over hooded eyes.

"No," Maledicte said. "A shop would be better organized, and considerably cleaner." He hauled a lady's chair up, all delicate legs and filigree, took care to sprawl over it, overflowing it.

Damastes sat in a velvet chair opposite, put his filthy boots up on a carved ivory footstool that creaked under their weight. Maledicte flickered his eyes downward, studied the worn soles of the jailer's boots.

"All this plunder and you need new boots," Maledicte said. "Is it false economy that hinders you, or do you just not know a decent shop?" Over the man's shoulder, he watched the night sky split by darting bats and the sleek flow of rooks.

He was minded to draw this bickering out as long as he could, lulled by the sight of the sky. Only underground for minutes and already he felt buried alive. It was Ani within him who loathed the dirt, he knew; the underground dark had always been Miranda's friend, her kingdom found beneath the beds, beneath the rubble, beneath the storm-cloud overhangs of stone eaves.

Damastes grinned at him, brown teeth in a turned-down smile. "Say what you want. I've been abused by aristocrats before—but remember, you're here to beg for my favors."

"Is that what drives you?" Maledicte said. "All this stolen wealth and it means only humbled aristocrats to you? You're a fool. You could buy yourself a title abroad and live like a lord. If it's begging you want, I have nothing to offer you."

"Make him kneel," Damastes said, his strange, slaty eyes hardening.

They reached for him; Maledicte evaded their hands, stepping behind a wing chair, making them stumble over the heaped greatcoats he pushed from its seat.

"No need," Maledicte said. "I'm tired of my clothes being manhandled. First my Gilly, who should know better, and Echo, then that oaf in the cells. I see no reason to add two more pairs of damp handprints to my coat. You want me to kneel?"

Maledicte searched out a clean spot on the floor, finding one just as the guards reached for him again. He dropped, letting them grope the air. He grinned at Damastes. "Here I am. Kneeling before you . . . but very far from begging, I assure you."

The jailer surged out of his chair, a thin hand knotting into a fist, and paused, his shoulders rising and falling with a laden breath. "I could break you," he said, his voice striving to match Maledicte's insouciance.

"My bones perhaps," Maledicte said. "But what then? Will you gamble that I am to be incarcerated forever? Or will you strike me, and see me freed tomorrow, full of rancor? My lover does not care to see me abused."

"Your lover—the king's nephew," the jailer said.

"No secret there, an old scandal in the court."

"You're as much a bauble as any of these jewels," Damastes said. "A favored possession. Close to royalty. You've been bedded on crested sheets."

"Sometimes in crested carriages," Maledicte agreed, all silken tones, like steel withdrawing.

"A collectible and rare. They say even Aris has touched you—" The jailer's voice dropped to a whisper; he darted a quick glance at his guards.

"That would be indiscriminate of me, surely, to bed both nephew and uncle," Maledicte said, relaxing into the familiar thrust and parry of spite and gossip. Damastes was simply another fool to be manipulated.

"To add you to my collection, to have something that was theirs . . . I could—" The jailer paused, an ugly, triumphant light in his eyes. He touched Maledicte's throat, drew closer, a hand on his own breeches.

Maledicte smiled. "My teeth are as sharp as my wit."

Damastes took his hand away. Maledicte shrugged, a loose liquid thing, as if he had been only chatting with friends. "Are we not to barter at all? Or have you brought me here only to enact the worst examples of boring pornographies?"

He made no attempt to lower his voice and Damastes snapped, "Shut up, or I'll gag you."

"Back to the cell, then?" Maledicte said. "You'll never get your trophies that way."

"What have you got?" the jailer said grudgingly, sinking back into his seat.

"No furniture, I'm afraid, I haven't been here long enough to have furnishings brought, nor do I intend to be. But then, this room is rather bewildered with furniture. All I have is the usual bric-a-brac of a gentleman's life."

He turned out his purse. "Two sols, how lucky for you—enough to get your boots resoled. After all, gold is no trophy, gold spends. A stickpin, ruby, jet, and silver." He dropped it onto the desk. "Had I known I was to be arrested, I would have worn one I liked less. Jet buttons on my waistcoat. Cuff links, ruby again." They landed beside the stickpin, rolled, and fell to the floor with faint thumps.

"In my pockets, well, Gilly says it's the mark of a gentleman to have nothing marring the line of my coat, but luckily for you, I am not so much a gentleman as all that. A luna and a snuffbox"—he frowned—"that I stole from Dantalion's corpse. I'd be careful with it. Knowing the man's reputation, I'd expect it to be full of something that would do you no good at all to inhale."

He tugged at his coat sleeves, and withdrew another handful of small objects. "Broken porcelain, nothing to interest you there, I'm afraid. That looks to be it. What do you think? Enough for a solitary cell aboveground? That bottle of wine we discussed?"

Damastes jerked his head at the guards. One left and returned with an opened bottle, passed it to Maledicte. Maledicte sniffed, and made a face, acting the spoiled lord. "Adequate, I suppose." He drank deeply, taking the dryness from his throat, the scratching sensation that the dirt was trying to crawl into his mouth. He craved the night air, fouled with fog as it was, yearned to go over and put his face to the windows.

"All right then," the jailer said. "Bargaining's concluded. Guards, take him back to the common cell."

Maledicte snarled, caught flat-footed long enough for the first guard to take hold of his arm. The second guard caught the bottle square in the jaw, and fell backward, teeth broken and bleeding.

Damastes swung himself over the desk, and helped pin Maledicte, knees digging into Maledicte's back. He said, "You're right. Sols do spend. And Echo gave me plenty of them to keep you caged with the other rats." He wrenched Maledicte's head up by his hair. "If you want out of that cell, you'll have to beg."

Maledicte struggled, clawing and kicking, until Damastes called for more guards to secure him. Even with the shock still ringing through his body that he had misread Damastes so, Maledicte growled, "You'll be dead before I ever come begging to you." The jailer's hand swung around, crashing across Maledicte's face and ear. When the ringing stopped, Maledicte ran his tongue over his bloody lip, and spat the blood back at him.

They dragged him down the stairs and threw him into the cells. He crawled away from the door into a dark corner, his head swimming, his body aching, and in his chest, Ani and Miranda vying for panic. Miranda felt the corset loosening as a result of the rough handling, her bladder already protesting the water and wine, and wondered how long she could hold out, how she could repair the corset strings without attracting notice.

A shadow crossed her. She raised her head and hissed; the men, allies of the earlier oaf, backed away. But she knew they'd watch and wait for their chance.

Ani flapped wings through him, setting his heart to racing, his blood pumping; he wanted to fly, but there was no escape from the surrounding earth and stone. He whimpered but swallowed the sound, and refused to make another.

Gilly would tell Janus. Janus would get him out. They wouldn't leave him here. Gilly hadn't believed him when he confessed to killing Lizette. He would come, tell him tales to soothe him, make him laugh. Maledicte sank back against the stone, felt a small impact in his forearm, and reached trembling fingers up his sleeve. The pocket watch spun on the end of the chain, catching the faint torchlight from the hall, making a small sun and sea in the dimness of the prison cell. He refused to acknowledge the pressing walls and earth, choosing to dwell on images of the sea and sky and Gilly's low voice telling him improbable stories.

Ani, displaced by Miranda's panic, by Maledicte's careful control, spread outward, seeking egress.

Across the room, one of the predatory men began to beat his head against the stone to the rhythm of Maledicte's imaginary oarsmen. The sleeping prisoners whimpered without waking. By the time the needs of his body sent him into knotted coils, no one was left to notice. The oaf staved his head in with a sudden last blow. Around his fallen body, his two allies stood and began to beat out the same fatal rhythm. One woman screamed, her face welting up with black bruises that burst when she touched them. People scattered away from her, shrieking, some of them already blistering.

Maledicte dragged over a chamber pot and used it without worry, still imagining the blueness of the sea, and gulls reeling overhead, but sounding like rooks.

· 38 ·

AT FIRST LIGHT, Gilly sought the palace, slipping through the maze to the dark side of the king's ballroom, skirting it until he saw the house servants at their morning chores. He followed a maidservant burdened by wet linens to the rear entrance of the residential side of the palace. Following her in, he was halted not by an upper servant, which he had expected, but by an armed guard.

"You're not employed here. What's your business?" the guard asked.

"Message for Janus Ixion, Lord Last," Gilly said.

"You can leave a message at the front gate," the guard said, then scowled. "Wait, I know you. Your master's Maledicte. I saw you going in and out of his home."

Gilly nodded when his startled hesitation made any other answer a lie. But he was dismayed at his own incompetence; he hadn't recognized the guard, though he had passed him more than once. Such notice used to be his task. He hoped the guard was less aware of Maledicte's current status, of his arrest—or that, even if aware, had no reason to deny a message.

The guard said, "Ixion's in quarters next to the nursery. You know where that is?"

"Yes," Gilly lied, gambling that it was better to be familiar with the palace. He strode away, unwilling to give the guard a chance to decide that Gilly should wait, and wait, and wait for Janus. Not while Maledicte was prisoned.

"You," the guard said. Gilly turned. "You take the servants' stairs." He pointed to the small doors Gilly had passed.

Gilly bent his head, and went into the labyrinthine world of the palace servants. Dark, ill-lit, and narrow, the stairs rose at a leg-burning angle, then suddenly veered. Heat flushed Gilly's skin, and he thought he must be behind a fireplace. He found himself dallying on the stairs, trying to map the castle in his mind. He acknowledged that he didn't want to see Janus at all. He shouldn't have had to, except that when Gilly had gone to retrieve the Antyrrian audit ledgers, intending to use them to buy Maledicte's freedom, he found them gone.

Hidden as they had been in the recesses of Maledicte's bedchamber, Gilly had no doubts that Janus had used them for his own purpose. Without the ledgers for leverage, Gilly had tried bribing the jailer directly, but the man refused his coin. So Gilly was left to beg aid from Lizette's murderer, from the man who had taken Maledicte's security for his own.

Coupled with that loathing, fear crawled along his spine. If Janus had faulted Gilly for Maledicte's behavior before, what would he think now, when he learned of Maledicte's arrest?

"Be wary," Gilly whispered to himself. "Be careful."

He found the nursery door by the simple expedient of the two guards flanking it. These guards wore mail as well as leathers, pistols as well as swords. Gilly shuddered. Aris knew the babe was still threatened. For a brief moment Gilly found himself heart-glad of Maledicte's imprisonment, the murderous plan stymied. But he had come to release Maledicte. . . .

"Janus Ixion." Despite himself, he couldn't help the growl that came out. He had expected them to allow him to pass farther down the hallway, toward Janus's quarters, but the guards opened the nursery door with little more than a glance.

Gilly's unruly emotions, fear, loathing, and worry, gave way to a far simpler one. Wonder. So this was how royal children lived. The long room was appointed as richly as any room he had ever seen, adorned with tapestries and carpets, ornate furniture and shelves full of books tooled in gold.

The carpets piled thickly enough across the floor in a careless riot of scarlet, lapis, and gold that even the most clumsy child could find no injury in falling. At one end of the room, opened windows overlooked the gardens below, their panes barred with iron. But even the iron had been wrapped with batting to protect the children from hurt. A firescreen locked to the stone fireplace attested to more precautionary measures. At the opposite end of the room, wide doors, paned with mirrors, stood closed.

Near them, reflected in bits and pieces, the heart of all these small worries, Adiran played with painted blocks, stacking them with an air of weary boredom. The mastiff beside him whuffed at Gilly, halting his approach.

Gilly had heard about Adiran, of course, had shared that knowledge with Maledicte long ago. Gossip about the king's son could fill every ear in the kingdom were all the rumors spoken at once, but he had never seen him so close. Disbelief shaded his thoughts. Adiran seemed hale and entire; then the boy looked up at him with such exquisite vacuity that Gilly's breath lodged in his throat.

Adiran stood, and approached like an uncertain pup, cautiously pleased. Behind him, the mirrored doors flashed, scattering reflections as they opened.

"He thinks you're the servant who brings him his morning sweet," Janus said, standing framed within the mirrored doors.

"Oh," Gilly said, as Adiran reached out and tugged at his pockets, then held up an empty hand. Gilly obediently searched his pockets, finding coin, but no candy. His fingers closed on something smooth and cool, and he brought it out to look at it. The porcelain puppeteer, least damaged by Maledicte's temper, barely chipped by Her fall from the attic. He handed Black-Winged Ani to Adiran, who cupped Her wings in his hands and laughed. He returned to his building, placing the puppet atop the blocks.

Gilly watched the boy, horribly aware of Janus's eyes on him, of his own simmering anger in this peaceful place.

"So you came to give little Adi a toy Aris will surely dislike—or is there another reason?"

"Maledicte's been arrested. He was taken to Stones last night. Echo has seen to it that money alone will not free him; the guards turned my offering away without a moment's thought. It wants an influence that seems to have gone missing." Gilly turned to see the result of his blunt words.

"I'll see Echo gutted and spread on the docks for the gulls," Janus said, a whisper of rage. "And you—where were you that you allowed this to happen?"

Gilly, unused to lying, found a lie on his lips now, a lie to serve two purposes, to shield him from Janus's wrath and a small, barbed retaliation for Janus's actions. "With Lizette. Seeing what could be done to ease her passing."

"You should never have left him," Janus said.

"It's you he wants. Not me. And you're here." His voice cracked, bitter with the taste of it, and Janus curled his mouth into a smile. Gilly drove it away with his next words. "Tell me, Janus, did you buy this position with the ledgers? Trade Maledicte's security for your own power?"

"I had little choice. Maledicte's impatience has seen him ruined. What good would it do us to have me fall alongside?"

"Ani rides him too fiercely for patience or reason. Your doing also, I believe." Goading Janus wasn't wise, Gilly thought, but he seemed unable to stop, and worse, unable to provoke the reaction he wanted: guilt.

"Maledicte and Ani are not the same creature. What he lacks in patience he should make up in trust. But he doesn't understand. . . ." Janus turned, looked back in at Auron's small, huddled form. "Guardian to the earl is not so different from being the earl. By the time Auron is grown enough to take the title, well, boys of that age are notoriously careless. Carriage racing, dueling, drinking in the bad parts of town . . . It'll be as much a wonder if he survives his first year as a young man as it was that he survived the carriage wreck."

Gilly's breath knotted at the pale serenity in Janus's eyes, at the pleasant tone to his words. Surely there should be some outward taint, some hint of the viciousness beneath, but even knowing Janus as he did, knowing what lay beneath the mask, Gilly's first impression of Janus still lingered, a bored, amiable young aristocrat.

Though aghast at Auron's coolly planned fate, Gilly refused to let it distract him from his current purpose. "What about Maledicte? Will you free him or is he simply a casualty of your schemes?"

"Don't be insulting." Janus said, frowning.

"Then you'd best go soon," Gilly said. "Best sweep down on them like an avenging godling and remove Mal before they stop to think that king's nephew or no—your influence is fragile, your breeding suspect, and your pockets to let."

Janus's hands clenched, but his voice remained pleasant. "You're aping your betters, Gilly. Trying to sound like him. You haven't the tongue for it."

Any rejoinder Gilly would have made was stifled by the guards opening the door, not the crack they opened it for Gilly, but flinging it wide, stepping back.

Aris came into the room, dressed casually, breeches and linens under a dressing gown. Adiran cried, "Papa," and flung himself on the king.

Gilly dropped to his knees, shivering, and when he looked up, Aris was watching him, startlement in his eyes, as if Gilly's master had been much on his mind.

The weariness and drawn lines of the king's face made Gilly's guilty heart turn over. How many of those lines had Gilly helped put there?

"You've brought the news, then," Aris said.

"Sire," Gilly said in agreement.

"Then you've done your duty and we need not keep you," Aris said.

Gilly bowed out and headed for the servants' stairs, shaken, and desperately worried.

In the darkness of the servants' stairwell, Gilly hesitated, seeing again the other doors. They would open into other rooms. Once, Gilly earned his pocket money by gathering secrets, by being unobtrusive and silent, by sneaking and prying himself, instead of paying others to do so. He should never have stopped his snooping, he thought bitterly now. He should have had word of the warrant signed for Maledicte's arrest—but either his spies had failed or the message had been intercepted, his fault either way.

Gilly tried to judge which door would allow him to eavesdrop without being caught. He eased open the next door, the one that should be Janus's and therefore empty. The room was cool and dim; he listened for movement and heard nothing. He leaned up against the interior wall, near the hearth, and the white-clad maid he had taken for a curtain in the dull light made a quick squeak of surprise. Gilly put his hand over her mouth. "Shh, I'm just here to listen. Like you."

"It's the only way," she said, keeping her voice low. "That one has a temper on him, if you don't watch out—best to know his moods well ahead."

"The king?" Gilly said, though he knew the answer.

"He never notices us at all—it's the bastard you've got to watch."

Gilly leaned closer to the wall, drowning her words in the rumble of voices filtered through plaster and brick.

"—in charge, and his holdings seized," Aris said.

"With your approval? Echo is sure of himself, but not so confident as all that," Janus said.

"With my approval," Aris said, and Janus hissed out his breath. "Maledicte cannot escape punishment, Janus."

"I'll secure his release."

"It will be impossible to do so without my permission."

Behind the wall, Gilly gritted his teeth, trying to think of who he could bribe or blackmail and failing that, how to free Maledicte without permission at all.

". . . prison," Janus said, in quiet tones. "Is there no alternative?"

"Want to watch?" the maidservant said.

Gilly nodded again. She tugged at a brick, gingerly sliding it out.

"They'll see the hole," Gilly said, his hand on hers, halting her progress.

She put her hand to his lips, rough with brick dust, and shook her head. She pulled the brick out completely, cradled it in her apron pocket.

Gilly, picturing the infant's room from the narrow slice he'd seen over Janus's shoulder, recalled the extensive firescreen that spread beyond the confines of the hearth, encompassing much of the wall.

He peered through, saw the two men standing beside the cradle, their words clearer now.

"Janus, don't take on so," Aris said. "I never meant his imprisonment to last. A few days locked alone in a cell, and Maledicte will be more amenable to his fate."

Seen through the woven mesh of the firescreen, Janus's face was as still as marble, his eyes as blank as Adiran's blue-sky ones. The expression stirred familiar notes in Gilly's head.

"Enlighten me as to your plans?" Janus asked.

"He will live," Aris said. "Though for all practical purposes, he is dead to you.

"There's a village called Ennisere on the north coast. It's a cold place, and desolate, but I have comfortable holdings there. I will send Maledicte there with a competence to live on, servants to care for his whims and to watch over him. It will be a prison, Janus, but one far more pleasant than Stones. And you will never see him again." He raised a hand as if Janus had started to interrupt, but Gilly could see that Janus's face was as frozen as lakewater in winter. "He should have been hanged, Janus."

Janus let his breath out. "May I at least take him from the cells, tell him what you've done for him?"

"I would prefer . . ."

"We fought, Uncle, the last time we were together. Will you deny me the chance to apologize to him? To leave us both with a sweeter memory?" Janus's tendons were white in his neck, white in his hands as he dared to interrupt the king.

Aris turned Janus's face up to his, searched the open eyes for signs of rebellion, and then nodded. "A brief meeting only. And my guards will go with you, should his temper hold sway."

"Thank you, Uncle," Janus said, and Gilly was horrified by the clear blueness in Janus's eyes. He had placed the memory, placed that empty exaltation in Maledicte's eyes in the moments when he turned to murder.

"Do not thank me," Aris said. "I should have taken Michel's advice in this instance. Maledicte is not fit for civilized society. Take a wife, Janus, and if you crave your male flesh, take a lover, but one less disposed to mayhem and more disposed to discretion." His mouth firmed, then relaxed. "Janus, it is for the best. Such a companion is not fit for a counselor."

"As you say," Janus said. His eyes reminded Gilly of heat lightning, and he wondered that the king couldn't see or feel the danger. All that rage, ruthlessly tamped down, until Janus found something, someone to release it on.

Gilly slotted the brick back into place, keeping his hands from trembling by the greater fear that if his hands shook, made the brick chatter, Janus would see him.

"Stay out of his way," Gilly urged the maid.

"No fear," she said. "I've seen that look before. Do you know your way back to the street?"

"I came by carriage," Gilly said.

"Aren't you the one?" she said. "Your master treats you well then. It's a pity he's not likely to need another maid."

Gilly kissed her cheek and she giggled at him before ushering him down the stairs. Each step down, Gilly thought giddily, was one step closer to Maledicte's side. Aris meant to send servants of his own, but surely Gilly would be allowed to attend Maledicte's needs in Ennisere. Still, his happiness was bittersweet; Gilly knew Maledicte would rail at the prison, no mat-

ter how fine the cage, and Ani would drive him mad, and as for himself—his
distant dream of the Explorations died in his chest.

He rested against the dark walls, trying to sort the mixture of relief and
glee, of pain and dismay, of fear and doubt into some more palatable sensation, and failed. Long minutes later, he let himself out of the servants' stairwell and headed for the stables.

At the carriage, the door was open. Gilly hesitated at the unexpected
sight, and while he did so, Janus stepped out. "You took your sweet time," he
said. "Get in."

"I'll walk," Gilly said, mistrustful of Janus's smile.

"Don't you want to help Maledicte?" Janus said. Again the storm flickers
washed his eyes.

"I don't see the guards Aris spoke of, your escort to the prison," Gilly said.

"Eavesdropper," Janus said, without heat. "But you dally. I thought you'd
be chafing at the bit, ready to seek banishment with him all to yourself."

Gilly stifled all reply, mistrusting that hot light still luminous in Janus's gaze.

"Do come on. I have errands aplenty. Before we release Mal, lock him
into the Kingsguard's care, I want to go to the town house to take what we
can salvage. The king's competency is likely to be adequate, but Maledicte is
most particular."

"He'll want the sword," Gilly said, thinking of it left waiting for Maledicte's return.

"Didn't Echo take it from him?" Janus said.

"Maledicte gave it to me for safekeeping," Gilly said.

Janus fingered his own sword thoughtfully. "Well, I'm not one to take his
toys from him. We'll collect it, and load the carriage with his possessions
while we're at it. Or do you want to explain to him how he comes to be a
hundred miles from the nearest tailor and without his favorite vest?" Janus
climbed back into the carriage, leaned against the seat, and said. "Go up and
drive, Gilly."

Gilly, relieved not to be closed in the carriage with Janus, did as he was
told. The town house stable, when they arrived, was emptied of horses. The
door to the house was marked with Echo's seal, but Gilly ignored it. In the
entry hall, Maledicte's sword rested on the marble table where calling cards
usually littered the surface, as if it too waited a response.

Janus picked up the sheathed sword, swearing as the feathered hilt bit through his thin gloves. His voice echoed in the house, striking no response from the shadows. When Gilly looked into the kitchen below, Cook's belongings had gone. He wondered who the little maids would work for now, wondered if Livia had smelled this coming, as cunning as a rat, and had found herself a new place.

Janus came into the kitchen after him, his boots ringing on the stone floor. "Tell me something, Gilly. How could Maledicte give you the blade if you weren't here?" The sudden storm feel of the room caught Gilly by surprise. Janus thrust Ani's sheathed sword at him hard enough to break ribs; Gilly flung himself backward, tripping over the raised brick hearth.

"You allowed his capture and blame me for it," Janus said. "He'd be free now, fought through them all, but for you—how did you manage it? Did you drug him again?"

Gilly said, "They would have killed him, Janus. This way he lives."

"Killed him, when he heals, when poison flees his blood? I have my own plans set in motion, and you had to interfere. You and he go north, banished together? Mal said you were intelligent—did you plan this? Itarusines make long plans, and Vornatti had the training of you—" Janus dropped the sword, unsheathed his own. Gilly grabbed the abandoned rolling pin, and took the strike on its marble surface. The sword skidded, shrieking, and Gilly pushed back, throwing the pin at Janus.

Watching the blade, he missed the bare-handed blow that hit his neck and shoulder, stiffening them into instant pain, and hurling him off balance. In desperation, Gilly threw himself forward, landing a blow of his own that split his knuckles and Janus's lip. Rage swept him and he forgot he was facing a man with a sword, bent on extracting at least a small measure of Lizette's pain from Janus.

Janus's head rocked with the blow; he spat blood at him, and said, "Fool. You'll break your hand before you hurt me that way."

Gilly punched out again, and Janus used his momentum against him, letting the rush take them both to the ground among a smashing of the cook's old chair. Rolling to land atop, Janus put his knees in Gilly's belly, bearing down, his hands sliding around Gilly's neck, the sword dropped and forgotten.

Already breathless from the exigencies of the fight, Gilly began to gasp in earnest. He pried Janus's hands away, doing his best to break the thumbs, and Janus let go. Gilly sucked in air, tried to push Janus's weight off of him, and barely avoided the elbow aimed at his face.

Janus's hands wound through Gilly's hair, and pounded his head into the floor, then the edge of the hearth. The room reeled, spinning into a moment's dull blackness; his vision cleared to Janus risen above him. Janus kicked him in the jaw, setting off another bout of spinning dizziness. Gilly knew he had to rise—another blow caught his shoulder as he tried to roll to hands and knees, tried to reach either sword.

The next kick cracked ribs and dropped him to his belly. There was blood in his mouth and dripping into his eyes; Gilly crawled up again, the kitchen spinning and dipping as if it were a galley in a shipwreck and not one safely at shore.

The explosion of pain in his side staggered him. He kept his balance, but barely, trying to pull himself up the table legs, wondering when Janus was going to remember the swords. The next blow, to the side of his knee, sent him writhing to the floor. Vision tunneling and clearing, pain a tide washing over him, he could barely make out Janus standing above him, incandescent as flame, grinning.

Gilly knew he was dead; it gave him breath enough to say, "Maledicte—"

"I'm going to give you to the sea. He'll think you abandoned him, took his coin and fled to the Explorations. He'll hate you for it," Janus said.

Gilly struggled to his feet, rested his hands on his thighs, his right leg buckling, and said, "Rot you, he'll know otherwise."

Janus drew back a moment, and Gilly stumbled toward the kitchen door and outside, hoping for a witness, even for the Kingsguard or Echo. A faint rasp of metal set him to fumbling for the handle, the iron slick in his palms, when Janus stepped behind him, as patient and as mad as an outcast wolf. He raised his sword. Gilly closed his eyes, whispered, "Mal."

· 39 ·

As the door to the communal cell opened, Maledicte looked up from his seat on the corpses of those who'd died overnight. Damastes slammed the door shut again and Ani, who'd seen the dark welts on his face, laughed through Maledicte's throat, flecking his lips with blood. Above him, in other cells, people screamed and wept as Ani's glee rose through the darkness and touched their dreams.

There were rough sounds of argument in the hall and then the door opened again.

"What a mess you've made," Janus said, holding the keys in a casual hand. "Damastes is cowering in his quarters, muttering about rat fever and devils; the kingsguard refused to come inside at all, and here you sit, laughing." Though insouciant, his voice held a hint of tremor.

"Janus." The name worked some of its old magic, driving some of the madness back; he fled his throne of corpses, belatedly repulsed.

"I brought your sword," Janus said. "Thought you might like to come out and use it."

Maledicte joined Janus at the door, each slow step returning him to himself. He took the sword in his hand, grimaced at the blood on his skin, and said, "I hope Gilly has a bath run. And despite his wishes, I am never wearing gray again, it's far too funereal." He forced the words out, trying to collect the courtier's mask about him, but finding that it didn't fit as well as it had.

"Are you unhurt?" Janus asked.

"I am," Maledicte said. "Some of these others cannot say the same. And I want my belongings back."

Janus drew him into the hall, folded him into his arms. "That jailer—Damastes, he didn't find out?"

"No," Maledicte said. He shivered in Janus's arms. "Let's go. I want to see the sky." Tears streaked his face, ran through the dirt and blood; he only noticed them when they trickled into his mouth, bitter with dust.

"Of course," Janus said, kissing Maledicte's mouth, delaying their exit.

Maledicte leaned against Janus, smelling the clean heat of the sun on his skin, tasting the sweetness of his tongue against his own. It pushed more of Ani's madness away, increased his shaking. "Janus, call for a physician."

"I thought you unhurt?" Janus held Maledicte at arm's length.

Maledicte shrugged under that piercing gaze. "For them. I don't know what I let loose in there."

"It's an outbreak of rat fever. Common enough in prisons. You're no witch, Mal, god-driven or not. And as for them? They're nothing," Janus said. "They would have rotted here regardless. Come now, Mal, shelve such unreasonable concerns and dry your tears—or do you want Damastes to see them?"

Maledicte let his breath out in relief as Janus reminded him of an enemy to face, shunted the poisonous guilt back, let Ani dissolve it with the clean heat of Her hatred. "He put us underground." His fingers tightened around the sword hilt; his mouth drew into a hungry grin.

"Mmm," Janus said. "Why don't *I* go talk to Damastes, get your things back? Let you wait in the carriage."

"The Kingsguard," Maledicte said, the words filtering through slowly, as if he was still half lost in nightmares. "Why are they here?"

"Did you truly think there would be no penalty?" Janus said. "The town house is sealed against you. They are here to escort you to a hotel, and to make sure you don't leave it. We're just trading one cell for another." Bitterness seeped through his voice.

"I cannot live in a hotel forever," Maledicte said. "What has Aris planned?"

Janus urged him up the stairs without answering, and Maledicte, sheathed in dirt and stone, was willing to allow evasion, eager to make the sky his own again.

"Look there," Janus said, laughing. "Damastes is not such a fool as all that." The piled belongings near the door sparkled in the low light. Maledicte swept them up into his hands, then passed them to Janus, preferring to keep his blade ready.

Maledicte stepped out into afternoon sunlight and winced. The Kingsguard standing beside Last's carriage stood to attention, then drew back as they saw the naked blade in Maledicte's hand.

"Where's Gilly?" Maledicte asked. "I thought sure he'd be here."

Janus helped him into the carriage, and Maledicte picked up the sheath lurking on the seat cushions. He buckled it on and sighed.

Janus gave the coachman the signal to go, and settled beside Maledicte. A kingsguard passed alongside the window, and Maledicte put his hand on the hilt of the sword.

"Take these back," Janus said, distracting him from contemplations of flight and murder.

The scatter of small stones and coins made him release the sword so he could catch them before they tumbled from his lap. Moodily, Maledicte sorted buttons from cuff links, stickpin from coins. The pocket watch fell into his fingers again and he pulled it out, setting it to spinning in the sunlight. "You never answered me. Where is Gilly?"

Janus's silence went on a moment too long, long enough for Maledicte's interest to turn to concern. "Janus, tell me."

"I haven't seen him," Janus said, tapping the watch in Maledicte's hands, making it swing. "When Aris told me of your arrest, I went to the town house to collect your belongings. The house was empty. No one had stayed behind—all the rooms were stripped. Your accounts too, undoubtedly. I told you your trust was misplaced."

"Gilly," Maledicte whispered, clutching that sudden hurt to his heart. Ani, Her attention diverted from the sky by his pain, turned the hurt around, studied it, and let it drop. There was nothing to be mined; Maledicte had already replaced the pain with wariness and hope. Gilly would return.

"He's fled," Janus said. "Count on it. Gone to the sea as he threatened to do so often."

Janus studied the guards maneuvering outside, his expression hidden. Maledicte turned Janus to face him, stared into the guileless blue eyes, and felt his heart constrict. Roach, Celia, and Ella—all had been helpless before Janus. "Did you . . . did you kill him?"

"Burn it, Mal," Janus said, irritation drawing his brows down, his lips thinning. "I begged Aris to free you, swore promises I hate to keep, and all you can ask is if I've killed your servant? I did not. Likely he's decided that our ways are too rough for his tender heart."

"Lizette died," Maledicte said. "Seemingly at my hand. Why did you do it?"

Janus cast another glance outside the carriage, at the kingsguard nearest, and leaned forward. "You know why. To punish Gilly, since you won't let me lay a hand on him. You should be glad of my restraint. And why you sought the brothel in the first place—"

"You murdered Ella, and kept it from me . . . I despise secrets from you," Maledicte said, waiting. When Janus only shrugged irritably, Maledicte asked, "What is it that Aris has planned? You seem remarkably loath to mention it."

"Ennisere," Janus said. "You're to live out your time there, on an estate staffed by guards."

Maledicte thought of maps and distance, but his knowledge was sketchy. Vornatti had taught him about the city and its fashionable retreats. Janus had told him about Itarus, and Gilly had sweetened his dreams with descriptions of the Explorations. Ennisere meant nothing, a foggy blur on an unfinished map of the world. "What of you?"

"I stay at Aris's side, and work to further our plans."

"*Your* plans," Maledicte said. "My plan was always simple, god-guided. Kill the earl of Last, and reclaim you. And I have yet to do the first. That child survives—"

Janus said, "Listen Mal, listen to me. I have my schemes. You're correct. Maledicte is ruined. So let Aris send you to Ennisere, bide your patience only a little. I know of a black-haired boy with pale skin, a poor mirror of you. We'll kill him, leave his body at Ennisere, and you can become Miranda again, and return to my side."

"You're a fool," Maledicte said. "Miranda with a ruined voice, a distinctive scar, and no antecedents? You may play puppets with the king but he is not so mindless as all that." He could not keep the threads of his argument together, losing them in the pale calculation in Janus's eyes, the clatter of hooves outside the carriage, the line of blood marring Janus's mouth. "You're bruised."

Janus touched his mouth. "You struck me, don't you recall?"

The blood was fresher than that, Maledicte thought, but that too was sucked away in the skirl of feathers within him. Above the coach, the rooks swarmed, darkening the sky prematurely with their wings. "Where's Gilly?" he asked again.

The coach drew up to the hotel; the horses milled uncertainly as the kingsmen conferred. Finally, two guards dismounted, flanked Maledicte as he and Janus went up the front stair. At the desk, the owner made a surreptitious charm against evil, and Maledicte smiled at him, showing all his teeth.

"The second floor," the guard said. "Go ahead of us."

Maledicte walked into the rooms without protest. The quarters were roomy enough, a bedchamber, a valet's chamber, sitting room, and bath. He peered out the window, drawing back the curtain. "No balcony. No trellis."

"It's a prison, Mal," Janus said, taking a seat on the bed, and waving the guards out irritably. They shut the door, but Maledicte could hear the faint jingle of their mail as they leaned against the wall.

"So it is," Maledicte said, dropping the curtain. "When am I transported north?"

"Tomorrow," Janus began and Maledicte growled.

"So soon?" He paced the room, boot heels muffled against the carpet, the blade swinging freely. "For how long?"

"Until Aris—"

"What? Until Aris dies—" Maledicte's voice rasped in the quiet room, and Janus pressed his hand close over his mouth.

"Hush," he said. "The guards are just outside."

"You're taking it all from me," Maledicte said. "I wanted the earl dead and you denied me, and I wanted you. Now you're walking away, because the king asks it of you. Why can't we just flee? Kill the guards and run for it?"

"A Last doesn't run, he conquers," Janus said.

Maledicte let his breath out in a hiss. "You choose playing for power over me."

"Not over—" Janus said. "With. I want both. You must be patient. Let me plan since your sense seems to have been buried with Amarantha. Trust me. I'll win through. See us both rich and powerful."

"It's all gone wrong in my head. It's all beaks and wings and blood. . . .

Where's Gilly? He can make it better," Maledicte said, slumping back onto the feather mattress.

Janus kissed his forehead. "You're overtired, overwrought. You should never have had to go to Stones."

"Not underground," Maledicte said. "Wings want sky."

"Not anywhere within those walls. But your discomfort will be repaid. I promise that."

Maledicte nodded, the words washing over him like the empty chatter of songbirds, soothing but meaningless. He let Janus undress him like a child, stood docilely in the hip bath while Janus sponged the filth of Stones from his body. He tangled his hands in Janus's pale hair, kissed his mouth, and let his mind drift away entirely. Janus laid him over the bed, kissing, stroking, soothing, and Maledicte clutched him close. When they were done and dressed, Janus gone, Maledicte sat by the window, staring at the sky.

Gilly kept creeping into his mind, the earnest eyes, the worried half frown that had become his common expression; his image was displaced only by Janus, and the slow ache that grew inside Maledicte. He couldn't keep them in his mind at the same moment; when he tried, all he saw was blood.

Across the room, the sword muttered and whispered until he cradled it in his lap. "I will, I promised you. In exchange for the sword. I'll spill his blood yet." Outside, the rooks settled atop the hotel, their chatter quieting.

ROCKING WATER, AND THE STINK of salt brine and tarred ropes, woke Gilly. He opened his eyes to a room made of shadows and lapping water, fractured and shivering with the pulsing of his aching head.

Alive. Why? Gilly wondered. There'd been murder enough in his face and strength enough in his hands.

Gilly tried to raise himself on limbs that were too numb to support him, and fell forward, splashing face-first into dark water. Panic woke him from his stupor. He scrambled back on unwieldy legs, sucked in air, and reassessed. His hands were knotted in a nest of twine and hemp, his ankles likewise. He was in the bilge of a ship. Gilly let out his breath in horrified understanding. A conscripted sailor.

Was death not enough for Janus; was it suffering he wanted? In the dark hold, dizzy and sick, surrounded by dank water and the strange oil scent of piled metal, Gilly found himself thinking with a clarity that surprised him. He'd been sold for a luna or two to line Janus's pockets, and more, the ability to tell Maledicte that he hadn't killed Gilly should Maledicte ask. Gone to sea finally, Gilly thought, and shuddered. Janus had piled the irony even higher; the strange metal shapes could only be bound for the Explorations, to build one of Westfall's engines there.

He started picking the ropes apart with his teeth, the tar and sodden hemp making him gag. They were still near shore; the slapping of the waves against pilings and other nearby hulls told him that. He had friends on nearly every pier, sailors, harbor clerks, dockworkers, who might aid him. If only he could get free. . . .

The shadows in the bilge massed and roiled as if they were water, stirred by an unseen tide. In the distance, Gilly heard a crow's call carried on the shrieks of gulls. The shadows seemed to vibrate to its resonance; the pain in Gilly's head crested and blurred his vision.

He chewed diligently at the knots linking his hands until they gave, but didn't fuss himself with the tight, salt-sodden loops left about his wrists. Though they chafed and burned, they could wait. He bent to work on the cords around his ankles and a rook flew out of the shadows on silent wings.

It landed on a jut of scrap metal, its talons making no sound as they contracted. Its eyes were matte black, as empty as a doll's, lacking the shine of a living creature's, and Gilly swallowed. It opened its beak, fluffed its wings, and bloomed bigger, a crow now, birthed of shadows.

"Mal—" Gilly whispered. The bird fluttered to the edge of the bilge, to the narrow ladder that rose to the deck and freedom. It fluffed its wings, again, and waited, rasping its beak against the splintered wood.

Gilly bent back to the ropes at his ankles, though keeping his head down increased the spinning languor of his body. He wanted nothing so much as to lie down. Instead, he dragged himself to the other side of the bilge and the aid implicit in the metal scraps. The right tool would be quicker than teeth surely, and far more efficient than fingers numbed by swollen wrists.

The ropes parted, surrendered strand by tarred strand, shredding with maddening slowness. When Gilly looked to share his triumph with the crow, he was alone. A flicker of movement pulled his attention upward.

"Mal—" he breathed again. The bird-shade, caught in midtransformation, flopped, wings unwieldy, folding inward, stretching itself tall and thin. A familiar human shape darted up the last rungs of the ladder, pausing for a bare moment to look back before flowing out onto the deck.

Gilly dragged himself to the ladder, up the first rung, sweat collecting on his abused body, chilling him like a layer of hoarfrost. His senses reeled and swam, nearly deserting him entirely. He felt as if he wandered in a dream.

"Mal," he whispered. Was it Last's window he was climbing to, hunting the nameless boy, ivy brittle under his gloved fingers, and snowmelt refreezing in his eyelashes, making him blink cold tears? Or was it underground, going further back, before everything he knew, following a staggering boy, newly hatched from Ani's wings, the sword naked and gleaming in his hands as he climbed into the Relicts.

"Mal," Gilly repeated, pulling himself up another rung, chasing that delicate phantom. Time stopped, sped up, shadows and light shifting across Gilly's vision left him standing at the king's palace, looking up at the high tower, at the slim shape, as black as the blade, standing at bay. Gilly reached up to climb to his aid, and his hand struck empty air. The salt smell of the sea woke him from his dreaming. "Mal. . . ."

No vision this, but a fate he wanted to escape. The foredeck bristled with sailors, drinking away their last hours ashore, telling each other stories, and repairing the fishing nets that would keep them fed on the long journey. The gangplank lay stretched to the pier before them, for easy access to the Relicts' bars and whores.

Once Gilly would have considered the crew good company. Now, he could only think of them as enemies, and all he could hope was that they had drunk enough to be careless. But so castaway as to watch him escape before their very eyes? He doubted it.

Gilly clung to the top of the ladder, leaned his head against the salt-scoured planks, watched the sun burning down into the sea, setting shadows roaming over the deck. He had lost all sense of time. Were it not for the spider constellation sparking to life in the sky, he could believe he'd slept for years, lost in the bilge.

The shadow, *his* shadow, divorced itself from its brethren on the deck, and flowed toward him. Not so human-shaped now, it bled outward like watered ink, growing fuzzed around the edges. It wafted toward him, swallowed him in an embrace chilly and dank, and a voice breathed into his skin, like no voice he'd ever heard before. *Hurry.*

Staggering like a drunkard, Gilly gave his fate to the shadow and wandered toward the sailors, toward the gangplank with its lure of safety beyond. Though it made his flesh crawl, and his heart pound as hard as his battered head, he made his way past the sailors and to the gangplank. They made no sign that they had noticed anything out of the ordinary way, not even when the worn plank sagged and moaned beneath his weight.

The water below him churned in odd eddies, dark and flecked with luminous foam, splashing upward toward him. He fixed his faltering vision on the pier, and at the end of it, waiting by a coach, a pale face in shadow.

Maledicte, Gilly thought on a crest of relief, come to take him home, and showing a rare subtlety for once, coaxing him from beneath the eyes of the sailors, rather than forcing Gilly's freedom at swordspoint.

The water beneath him surged, a sudden high tide rising as he descended, and it slapped salt water over his feet, his ankles, and burned the shadow away. Naga's touch inimical to Ani's uncommonly delicate working.

Gilly urged himself onward, finally reaching the salt-weathered planks of the pier. He stumbled, pushed himself to his feet, concentrated on walking normally. With the cloaking shadow gone, he thought the illusion might have gone with it. The dark sky might hide his identity, but he was still too close to the ship to be anything but their prisoner escaping.

The shout went up, and Gilly staggered into the closest thing to a run he could approximate, a listing, limping thing that set his head and ribs to throbbing, the world shuddering like an opera curtain, whisking back and forth.

"Gilly," a low raspy voice called, "hurry." Reaching the end of the pier, he found cool, smooth fingers on his arm; the pursuing captain drew to a halt.

"Lady," he said, wary.

Lady? Gilly craned his head to look but was defeated by the dizziness. The rasping voice took on a clear sweetness that Gilly had heard before. "Why ever are you hunting my servant? Has he been brawling with the crew?"

"He's mine. Four lunas he cost me."

"Forced labor is illegal," she said. "Such a shame, too." Gilly tried to tug free; her nails slid into his skin, waking new pains, and Gilly subsided.

"Purchasing a man's services is not." But the captain's voice already faltered. Gilly, his eyes drifting, found himself staring at a sweep of tattered silk, stained dark around the hem. A ruined ballgown.

"When those services are already promised—"

Gilly moaned and she halted herself with a wild laugh. "And here I am going on as if I need to win by words. He's mine, Captain. Do not argue further. I am most unpleasant when offended." As verbose as Maledicte, he thought, teeth chattering. But far more inimical to him.

"But still, you lost coin, and I know how dearly money can be needed. I'll repay you." She threw coins at the captain. While he scrabbled for them, keeping them from rolling through the cracks between the planks, she said in a tone like exposed steel, "Any further complaints?"

"No, my lady," the captain said, still kneeling, shivering. He knew who she was now, Gilly thought. Even the sailors had heard the tales of Mad Mirabile.

Mirabile laughed, the sound not as pleasant as it once was, like a bell cracked and off tune. She walked Gilly toward her carriage like a marionette. Wordless, he sprawled on its floor, dripping salt water and blood. She tangled her fingers in his wet hair, dragging her nails across his scalp, setting the long gash from contact with the hearth to bleeding again. "So Ixion finally removed you—or was it Maledicte who cast you into the sea?"

Gilly winced, but did not reply, concentrating on regaining his equilibrium with the sway of the moving carriage.

"No answer, and I've gone to the expense and effort of saving you. I suppose that means you're not grateful either."

"Let me go," Gilly said, sick at heart. He'd followed her lure as blindly as a hound on scent, thinking only of Maledicte.

"You'll serve me now," she said.

"No," Gilly said.

"You will," she said. "In one fashion or another. I've waited for my vengeance too long. Ani's beak has grown sharp, and I would share that pain with others."

He jerked away, reaching for the door handle, hoping to tip himself out onto the cobbles. The handle writhed in his hand, supple and scaled like a serpent, coiling around to strike him, and he let go in sheer horror. She laughed and he turned toward her, spoke the words of Baxit's countercharm. She winced, then slapped him across the face, sending him to the floor again. She slid closer, put her hand beneath his chin, forced his head up. "Such a waste," she said. "A comely young man doomed because of one man's refusal to share himself with me. I'd feel sorry for you. If I could."

"Maledicte will kill you," Gilly breathed.

She leaned closer, confiding. "Black-Winged Ani granted your master a sword. She saw to it that I would never need one. Confused, my sweet Gilly? Shall I spell it out for you? She granted me power. . . ." In her eyes, red fires flared and sank back to a simmer.

Gilly turned his head away from the madness in her gaze, and she dragged it back, effortlessly. "Look at me, Gilly. Am I not more beautiful than your master? More beautiful than those foolish debutantes?" She rolled her fingers together, opened her palm, and blew dust into his face. Coughing, he tried not to breathe but the stupor in his head settled into his bones.

"You do love me, don't you, Gilly?" She touched her lips to his; he shivered all over and felt the heat scorch from her mouth to his groin. "Tell me you love me."

"Love you," Gilly said, the words dragged from his throat.

"You'll love me until the day you die. . . ."

"Yes," Gilly said, his heart pounding under the twin stresses of fear and lust.

"More than you love him," she said.

Gilly closed his eyes. Maledicte. The image, dark hair, dark eyes, soft mouth against his own, did nothing to cool his body or his fear. Her nails tightened on his face, and he said, "Yes."

"I'll let him know you said so, when I gift him with your body. Let him see what it's like to lose someone through the caprice of another."

"—loves Janus more . . ." Gilly said, as her mouth descended on his.

She drew back. "I'll have him later. But Maledicte must come first."

The carriage drew to a halt, tumbling him into her skirts. "Clumsy thing," she said. "I'll expect better of you." She pushed him from the carriage; he got his feet under him just in time, and stood there, swaying. They were deep in the heart of Sybarite Street, past the brothels, beyond even the insalubrious dens that specialized in drug dreams and poison selling. This section of Sybarite bordered on the Relicts, the buildings more fallen than run-down. Still, if he fled, he could get to Ma Desire's, maybe to safety. If he could move.

Mirabile took his hand in her cold one, tugged him into movement like a puppet. Mirabile's coachman slipped off the driver's bench in a flurry of skirts and cloak, a familiar tail of red hair and brown eyes: Livia. Betrayed rage gave Gilly momentary strength, and he pulled away.

Mirabile snarled, "Stop." His limbs locked up at her word. Livia drew her hood up about her face, and edged past him, shifting piled-up boards to reveal a low, dark opening. The ruined building looked as if no one but rats could fit within, yet with the opening revealed, Gilly saw clear rooms inside.

"Well," Mirabile said, guiding him in, "Welcome to my parlor." His shocked gaze recognized the place, even as he started to shiver. The walls were covered with Her image; Mirabile dwelled in the ruins of Ani's temple, slept in the lee of Her wings. Livia lit lamps around the room, each one revealing another depiction of Ani. Some of them smelled new, smelled as if Mirabile had painted their rough shape with blood. On the altar itself, a dark shape muttered and croaked at their return.

While he stood numb and helpless, she drew off the ruins of his shirt, his breeches, and smiled. "Don't look so frightened, lambling. I'm not going to kill you right away."

Mirabile circled Gilly, her expression as proprietary as Vornatti's had ever been, and far crueler. Gilly felt fourteen again, remembered the dread washing over him with the soapy water, the dull light in Vornatti's eyes growing brighter with each limb washed clean. But the dread then had been fear of the adult world pressing in on him; he had trusted Vornatti not to hurt him. Gilly had no such illusion with Mirabile, not with her nail marks bleeding sluggishly on his cold flesh, or the hunger he saw in her face.

Livia, after another averted glance, busied herself lighting the rest of the gas lamps, as silent as she never had been in the town house. The small flames caught and flared under her shaking hands, illuminating wet streaks on her face. Throughout her task, she twisted her head to avoid meeting Gilly's eyes.

"When you're done, Livia, you may go. Unless I am mistaken, you have no desire to watch me at my play."

Livia shook her head, so mute that Gilly imagined atrocities—that Mirabile had torn out Livia's tongue, or bespelled her to a future as a slave.

"Come back for your coins in the morning," Mirabile said. "I'll need you to do the washing up, after. But don't return too early. I intend to be about this business until the late hours."

Livia flinched; her eyes met Gilly's for a brief, scalded moment, then blurred and ran with tears. She left with a deliberate pace, as if she wanted to run, but controlled herself.

Not enough fear, Gilly thought, and Mirabile would kill her. Too much fear and the result would be the same. Like a predator, Mirabile would hunt the fleeing creature out of instinct. Weakness spilled through him, and he slumped, unable to fall while her potions and will held him upright.

"She'll go for coin tonight. Go for Maledicte," Gilly said. "Greedy little girl." Each word was an effort to push out through his stiff tongue and lips.

"I do hope so," Mirabile said. "I doubted her for a moment there—thought I might have to send a messenger less trustworthy, or one that

Maledicte might kill on sight, and then where would I be? Without my audience."

"Maledicte's in Stones," Gilly said, finding a sudden perverse pleasure in the fact that had troubled him so greatly earlier.

"Was in Stones," she said. "You used to be better at keeping abreast of the gossip, Gilly. The rooks have all moved again. They follow him, you know." She drew her hands along his flanks, trailed inward; his muscles jumped and flinched at her touch and she smiled. "They nested at Stones while he was there, and now his little birds have flown to the Grand Hotel. They darkened the sky like a whirlwind. All that power at his will, and he refuses to reach out and grasp it. He could control them, their eyes, their secrets, would he only admit complete fealty to Ani.

"But no matter," she said, "That he fails to reach his power is only of assistance to me. But think of it, Gilly, what a sight it would make, Maledicte in the ballroom with the rooks wheeling about him, calling and excreting over all the nobles." She grinned; were it not for the mad eyes, Gilly could have enjoyed the mischief in her face.

"A pity it will never happen," she said, laughing, and wrapped her hands firmly around his genitals.

He tried to force her hands off him, but she squeezed and his breath went short with unwilled pleasure. Her nails sliced into the tender flesh and he cried out, the pain lancing over his body, then settling back into steady throbbing.

"Gilly," she said. "Take up my skirts."

Chary of her grip, her touch, he knelt, breathing more easily as her hand slid away to allow his descent. He folded her draggled skirts up about her waist. Under the finery, where the noblewomen wore their slips and petticoats, their lawn chemises, where even the poorest maids wore pantaloons, she was bare. Just above her sex, above the flame of hair, feathers had burst from her skin, small and black. At first he thought she had decorated herself as an honor to Ani, but when she urged his hands to her skin, he knew it was the inverse, that Ani was decorating her.

"My bodice," she said. He reached behind her; she knelt before him, pressed her hips to his as if she was nothing but an eager lover. Her bodice fell loose in his hands; she shrugged it from her shoulders, baring more white flesh, patterned with tiny black feathers so small they seemed like scales. He gasped, his hands flying away. She grabbed them, pressed them to her breasts, sank herself onto him. He groaned.

"You love me, Gilly."

"Yes," he said, her words in his mouth. His own words drowned as she rocked herself over him.

In his head, he began whispering prayers though the only god present was Ani. Her teeth bit into the welts left by the barnacles on the pier, raised blood again; her nails dug into the deep bruises left by Janus's fists, scribed the edges of his raw wrists. She tongued the wound on his head, lapping the blood until it stopped, then biting until it bled again. His prayers dissolved into one internal plea. Maledicte.

MALEDICTE PACED THE ROOM, agitated without cause. He had the sky now, through the high windows, and yet . . . the sword throbbed in his hands, seeking blood.

A tap on the door sent him spinning around, sword bared.

"Sir, I've brought your dinner." The girl's voice, though tight with tension, was familiar.

Maledicte drew open the door; the guards stepped back, out of reach of his sword, too cautious to let him use the maid as a distraction. One guard spoke. "Are you certain you want to go in with him, miss?"

"He's my master," she said. "I brought the food from his own table, what's left of it, and he'll be hungry."

The other guard shrugged. "It's your neck."

"May I go in?" Livia asked. "You've already looked me over, peered in the bowls. You know I have nothing to aid him." She shifted the heavy tray on her hip, and the guard nodded her in, latched the door behind her.

Maledicte watched her red hair slide over the shoulders of her damp cloak like a scarf. He raised the sword and brought it winging to her nape, halting it at the very last.

She gave a stifled shriek, too frightened to move. Then the long braided tail of her hair slithered to the floor, cut. He picked it up. "Get undressed," he said. "And don't think of crying out. I've no need to hurt you but I must find Gilly."

Her skin paled white as marble; her mouth worked, soundless. Maledicte read the word on her lips. "Gilly?"

Behind his cold rage, the hunger, something as warm as baked bread rose, soothing his temper, then settled back into rage. Anything Livia knew, with her eyes like a dead woman's, was not going to please him.

Livia licked dry lips.

"If you don't find your voice, I'll hunt it with my sword," Maledicte said.

"You have to help him. Mirabile will kill him."

Maledicte put his hands around her neck, found a vicious satisfaction in making her flinch, and undid the knotted strings of her cloak. "Get undressed," he said again.

"They'll never believe it—" she said, fumbling her bodice off, her skirts.

"They don't have to for more than a moment. It's vision driven by expectation, but never mind all that," he said, tugging her skirt up over his breeches, watching her blink astonishment when the buttons closed around him. "Your bodice," he said. "Your cloak."

"If you're taking my cloak, I don't see why you need—"

"Because a cloak over breeches looks like a cloak over breeches, and a skirt is an entirely different thing," he said. "As glad as I am you found your voice, now I want you to be silent again."

She stood stripped to her chemise, shivering in the chill room.

"My dressing gown," Maledicte said, motioning to the bed and the heavy drape of quilted fabric lying across the bottom. "Put it on."

Pulling it off the bed, she pulled it on, her hands shaking as she tightened the tie around her waist. He bit back the rage swelling in him, and, unwilling to risk the guard's overhearing, said with hushed impatience, "For gods' sake, don't show off your narrow waist. Have you no sense at all? Tie it around your hips. Turn around. Stand in the window."

She did, visibly reluctant to turn her back to him. Maledicte snarled. Her hair, rough cut by his sword, stood out like flame in the dark glass. He looked at the fireplace, long cold, long cleaned, and turned to the oil lamps instead.

"Gilly," she said again. "You have to go to him."

"I am endeavoring to do so. Or would you have me call a challenge to the guards in the hall, forcing me to dally in bloodlust until dawn? Gilly would be long dead by the time I fought my way clear." He pinched out the wick, pulled off the glass, ran his hands over the residue inside; his fingers came away streaked black. He scrubbed his hands into her hair, pushing her against the window. She grabbed the frame with shaking hands, clung to it as if she feared he would push her through it and onto the cobbles below.

He blew out another lamp, dimming the room, rubbed the lampblack into her hair again, and stepped back to look at her. "Unconvincing. Stand up straight," he said. "Like you're so frightened your spine is an icicle." She stiffened, her hands on the window frame whitening.

"Better," he said. "A few lessons in comportment and you might be able to pass as a lady. Or a lord." One more thing was needed, one last piece to anchor belief, even fleetingly. The fireplace would aid him after all. He drew out the poker from its rack with a rasp that made her shudder. "Take this," he said.

She clutched it.

"Like a sword, Livia, like a sword."

He threw the food into the fireplace, tucked the loose braid of her severed hair into the neck of the cloak, and drew the hood around his face, leaving only the flare of redness hanging out, the rustle of lace and skirt.

Maledicte took the sword up by its blade, held it below the hilt, angled it so it lay under his forearm and extended only a foot past his fist. Picking up the dinner tray, he laid it over the visible blade, and then tapped on the door.

The guard opened it warily, gaze slipping over the tray, the hair, the cloak, and lit on the figure shadowed beyond. Maledicte stepped up to him, and slid the sword through his throat.

These guards were not the simple Particulars who had come with Echo to arrest him; the other guard had stayed out of easy reach, and even now turned to shout for aid. Maledicte threw the tray, caught him in the throat, and while he was reeling from that, brought the sword up and made him as mute as his thrashing friend.

"Livia," Maledicte said. "Come."

"I thought I was to stay," she said, but hustled toward him anyway. "I thought you were going to sneak out, and leave me behind so they wouldn't notice."

"They'll notice the bodies in the hall. And even had I time to dispose of them, I do not have time to scrub the carpet clean. When you came in, where were the main force of the guards? And where were the balconies? I foresee a climb in our future."

"The front," she said. "Both at the front of the hotel."

"They would be together, of course. Still, no help for it. Let's find a front-facing room," Maledicte said. Despite the fear for Gilly, Maledicte almost enjoyed having a goal at hand with the promise of bloodshed at the end of it. For this moment, Ani and he moved in rare concert.

He darted down the corridor, pulling at the skirts and cloak, trying to keep them from tangling his legs in a hindering embrace. Behind him, Livia trailed, and he reached his hand back and tugged her alongside him. "Hurry, Livia."

They turned a corner, startling a drunkard returning to his room. "Are you lovely girls come to warm my bed?"

"Of course we have," Maledicte whispered. "A noble with a room with a view. You gladden my heart." He pushed past the man as he fumbled to close the door, threw open the glass-paned windows.

"Perfect," he said. He tucked the sword into Livia's skirt, and looked down. "Livia, look, climbing roses, how lovely." He swung his leg over, settled his boots onto the thickest branch. "Livia."

She dodged away from the drunk, pushed him back outside the room, and slammed the door. Maledicte began his descent, wincing at the sharp needle kiss of the thorns.

Livia's face peered down at him. "Oh, I can't."

Maledicte called up in a hoarse whisper. "You'll be hanged for helping me, if you don't come down—"

Ashen, she clambered over the balcony rail, tearing the dressing gown on its wrought-iron finials, and reached her toes out for a foothold. She let out a little shriek as her weight settled.

"Hush," Maledicte said. Above, he could hear the drunkard coming to at least a fraction of his senses, pounding on the door. The second story was going to be full of people soon and there were two dead guards waiting to be found. Maledicte looked down; the ground, dark with distance, seemed to recede. A droplet, warmer than rain, dripped onto his cheek, rolled toward his mouth. Salt and iron. Blood. He licked it up, looked up. Livia's soft slippers were wet with blood.

Maledicte settled his hand on a wickedly large thorn, watched the blood well up and stop when he removed it, the pain vanishing. "After all," he murmured, "we can't hold a sword with damaged hands."

He dropped the last few feet, skidded on a rounded cobble, and fell hard, wrenching his ankle. "Ani," he said. "We can't fight with a bad limb." The soreness retreated, the swelling receded, and he stood.

"Drop, Livia," he said and she was either so exhausted or so frightened that her body obeyed without hesitation. He steadied her as she rocked on sore feet, muffled her cries in the cloak. "Shh."

Lights flared on the second story, bobbed from window to window; faintly he could hear a woman screeching.

"Rot them all," Maledicte said. "Does no one sleep anight anymore?"

He dragged Livia forward. "Tell me where he is." She was too slow to keep up with him, too fragile to fight.

"Her temple. Sir, it's my fault, all my fault," she moaned. "I told her—told her you loved Gilly. If he dies—I never meant—"

Behind them, the hotel doors were flung wide, disgorging the Kingsguard. Shouts rang through the night, including the one Maledicte had been dreading. "There they are! By the wall!"

Maledicte reached out, intending to shove Livia toward the shadows and dubious safety, but Ani had other thoughts. His hands pulled her before him, into the torchlight; his rumpled dressing gown, the short sooty hair— the guards fired at once. The shot sent her reeling backward, falling into the cobbles. Maledicte turned and ran, hands clenching at his side, shivering, refusing to feel guilt, not while Gilly needed him.

"Her temple," he muttered, thinking of the elaborate and twisted length of Sybarite Street between him and the ruined Relict temple, the only temple to Ani he knew. He had no doubt at all that Mirabile had made her quarters there where he had begun his own quest.

Maledicte slowed his steps as he reached Sybarite Street and the evening's crowds. He drew the cloak tighter, keeping a wary eye out. The guards would know their mistake soon enough.

Lights bloomed in the windows of pleasure houses, and slow, drugged laughter spilled like syrup on a cold day. Maledicte moved on, hand clenching around the sword, seeking the darker shadows, tracking his way back to a place he had never thought to revisit. But as if he had mapped the route, he guided himself as steadily, as surely as if he were going home.

And he gave his soul into Ani's keeping and became Her Avatar,
winged and blood-mantled, a sorcerous nightmare in human flesh, who
carved his way through the battlefields and laughed. And his words be-
came ravens, and where he walked, men died of plague. . . .

—Grayle's *Book of Vengeances*

IRABILE ROSE FROM GILLY'S BODY, shaking her skirts down, stretching her arms above her head. Along her breasts, the feathers shivered. Gilly rolled onto his side, huddled on an earthen floor warmed with his heat and blood.

"Poor Gilly, but the sea captain might have used you as roughly. I spared you that at least." Mirabile knelt, turned his chin up to peer into his face.

Gilly tried not to meet her eyes.

"Such blueness," she said. "So clear." She dropped her voice to a whisper. "Do you see the gods with those clear eyes?"

"Only Ani," Gilly said, wrenching his head away.

"Well, we can't have that. You spying on Her at all hours, watching Her, judging Her; it's the raven for you." Mirabile stood, walked away from him.

Gilly took a careful breath and rolled onto his hands and knees. Her spell, whatever it had been, cantrip or poison, had left him. His body was his again. Slow, weak as an infant, and hurting, but his.

Across the room, Mirabile tugged the weight of rotting fabric from the covered bulk on the altar. The raven in the cage beneath woke to raucous complaint.

"Easy, love, easy. Haven't I got the bluest eyes ever seen this side of the sea? And they're all for you." She freed the massive bird from the cage. It turned its head up to look at her with one glossy black eye and she dropped a kiss on its head. It clattered its beak and croaked at her.

Gilly rolled to his belly, wrapped his arms around his head. "Please," he whispered, remembering Westfall and the others, found eyeless, their faces shredded until all that identified them were their clothes.

"None of that now," she said, toeing him in the side, trying to turn him from playing turtle, but he clenched himself farther into the floor, knotted his eyes closed.

"Gilly, I could bespell you again. But wouldn't you rather die your own man?" she asked, pulling his hair until his scalp stung. When that didn't work, she slipped her hand beneath him, slashed her nails over his bare skin. He twitched; she levered him over and dropped the bird onto his chest.

Gilly recoiled as the stink of its blood-matted feathers washed over him. He tried to shove it away with leaden hands. Its talons scrabbled for purchase on his chest; its flapping wings slapped his ears, left them ringing, and its hungry beak stabbed at his defensive hands. Mirabile reached around the bird's wings and pinned Gilly's hands to his sides. He closed his eyes, waited, numb and sick.

"Go on then," she said. "Peck, bite, maim."

The feathers rustled as the bird settled again, wafting stale blood and feather molt into his face. Gilly shuddered and opened his eyes, stared at the foreshortened beak.

Mirabile slapped the ground. "Do it now, bird. I command you."

Behind her, movement. Gilly's heart gave a great leap in his chest. "Livia, please...."

Mirabile shifted her weight, silencing him. "Back already? Did you see him? Is he coming?"

Livia nodded, her disheveled braid slipping over her shoulder, her heavy cloak shielding her face from the sight.

"Your time is near, my pet," Mirabile told the raven. "It's his eyes or yours." The bird jerked forward at her pinch; Gilly felt the beak rip the skin of his face, tracing a careful, delicate line along his jaw.

Mirabile hissed, following the gash with her finger. "Maled—" The raven went wild in her grip, wings pelting them both, before it turned and clawed its way across Mirabile's face and hair. She leaped up, and slapped it down to the floor, crushed its body with her heels.

Gilly could only stare at Livia, at the braid sliding loose and limp to the floor, at the pale shine of the face beneath the hood and the black eyes. He knew those eyes, the rage within them, but not like this, not wrapped in woman's flesh. Maledicte, he thought, dizzy and worn past sense, made an almost convincing woman—if it weren't for the spare lines of his shoulder and chest, the strength in the white hands, even now pulling the sword free.

"You came," Mirabile said, brushing her disordered hair back in long-ingrained habit, playing the coquette. On her face, the weals left by the dead bird sealed flawlessly.

"With such an invitation, how could I not?" Maledicte said.

"But, my intemperate guest, you have come before the hostess is quite ready," Mirabile said. "Still, I can find something to occupy you while I finish with your pet."

Maledicte threw himself forward, the sword ripping through the cloak, the skirt, without effort; he dove toward Mirabile, sword extended, aiming at the dark blossom of feathers on her breast.

Mirabile raised her hands, cried a single word, and flew out of reach of the sword like smoke blown across the room. Maledicte's eyes widened, then grew thoughtful. The shadows in the room caressed Mirabile's ragged skirt, and she drew their darkness up her body.

"You're weak, Maledicte. You carry a remnant of conscience, and you'll never know vengeance or true power until it dies. Until you take Ani in fully. . . ."

Maledicte shrugged out of the cloak remnants. "Why all this advice— you want me? Fight me."

"I have no desire to kill you," Mirabile said. "I want to rule you. And in turn, you and I, ruling this kingdom, the sky dark with Her wings—" She stirred the shadows alongside her, her breath rasping.

"Mal," Gilly said, his warning caught in his throat, drowned by his heartbeat. The shadows shaped themselves under her command, taking familiar form. Something skinny and tall, someone holding a stick in a clenched fist.

Maledicte's eyes narrowed. "What is this?"

"You want a fight, I'll set you fighting yourself first."

The shadow snapped into flesh, corpse-pale, with wild snarled hair, a ragged stick held like a sword. Gilly knew this image: a scarecrow boy standing in a pile of broken glass and snow in an old man's library, a feral child crawling from beneath an altar in his dreams. Maledicte's own childhood.

Mirabile swayed on her feet, panting, the feathers on her skin ruffling with exhaustion. Maledicte stepped forward again, the sword gleaming; the shadow child bared his teeth and charged at the sword, stick raised and fearless.

Trying to gain his feet, Gilly stumbled, found himself clutching Mirabile's tattered skirts for support. She staggered beneath his weight and he yanked harder, wanting her to fall, wanting his hands around her neck. He brought her crashing down, and struggled to crawl up her body enough to put his hands to use.

She scrabbled at the floor and swung a piece of stinking darkness at his face; the raven's body, he realized, even as its beak scraped his neck and shoulders. Mirabile was laughing, high and wild, as she flung the bird at him again. He deflected it, and she kicked him in the stomach, sending him rolling back, giving him a surging view of the room. Of Maledicte diving at his shadow self, the sword barely missing the boy's head.

"No, Mal, no," Gilly said. "No." If Maledicte killed that child self, what would he become, freed from the child's innocence? Ani would swallow him entire.

Mirabile grabbed his hair, reminding him of his own battle, and slapped his face. "I'd wanted him for my audience, but I suppose it's going to be the other way around. You can watch if you like. A man with a sword against a boy with a stick. And when it's done . . . he'll kill you himself for all those whispered prayers, all those little warnings you dared to voice. Against *me*." Blood touched her lips for a moment as Black-Winged Ani surfaced and faded, leaving Gilly shaking in the presence of the god.

The sword flashed down, impacted on the boy's stick. Gilly winced, but the stick held firm, the stick and the sword grating against each other. The shadow boy kicked Maledicte on the shin, and Maledicte broke their clinch with a curse. Following the small advantage, the shadow boy slashed at Maledicte's head with the stick; when Maledicte reached up to block it, the boy darted the stick toward his stomach instead, and Maledicte jumped aside.

Gilly moaned, sick with dread. There could be no good end to this. For Maledicte to destroy his own conscience, or to lose Maledicte to a shadow of himself . . . Mirabile laughed, pressing herself against Gilly's side, excoriating his tender skin with her feathers. The boy wiped his face; his shoulders heaved with effort, but the stick, held out before him, never wavered. Maledicte's sword hand shook; the blade tip magnified that tremor into a palsy.

The boy danced forward and Gilly saw the confidence in his face, realized the boy's mistake: Maledicte was shamming. The boy had all of Maledicte's ferocity, the bloodthirsty desire to rush for the throat, but no idea of swordsmanship or strategy.

"No," he cried out. "No."

But the boy was extended, the stick thrust out too far, and Maledicte knocked it aside. The stick, loosed from the boy's hand, disappeared into shadow, unmaking itself before it touched the floor. The boy gritted his teeth, eyes wild with panic and rage. Maledicte's blade, unhindered now, slipped through the boy's flesh without a sound, and passed through his throat. Maledicte's hand and hilt protruded from the boy's nape, dripping shadow plasm.

Horrified, Gilly could only stare, the boy dead, trying to imagine Maledicte without even the smallest leavening of conscience or kindness.

Mirabile stood, hands outstretched, smiling. "My compatriot—"

Maledicte carried his forward momentum on, stepped through the dissolute shadow that had been himself, and took her head from her body, the blood spray splashing Gilly's skin.

Mirabile fell, her blood spreading outward in a tide. Gilly crabbed away from it, scuttling on weak limbs to avoid its touch. Maledicte stepped into it, unconcerned, and pierced her heart, then ripped her body open, spilling her guts out onto the floor. "Need I do more?" he asked, voice a wisp. "Will Ani heal that?"

"I don't know," Gilly said. The numbness of his limbs had spread to his lips; he felt as chilled as a corpse. His muscles, so long tensed in struggle, deserted him. He collapsed to the floor, sprawled out, face-to-face with Mirabile's head. He could see Mirabile's unwinking eyes staring back at him, and he retched drily.

"I quite agree," Maledicte said. He picked up the head and threw it into the raven's cage, covering it with the altar cloth.

Gilly curled up, shaking, tears scalding his cheeks. "Gilly," Maledicte said, kneeling beside him. Gilly felt the soft warmth of Livia's ragged cloak enfolding him, felt the floorboards shift as Maledicte sat beside him. "Gilly, are you—" The rasping voice cracked, resumed. "Will you be all right?"

Gilly had no words at all, nothing but the tears that streamed from him, as if anxious to wash away the spilled blood. He folded into Maledicte's lap, pressing his face against Maledicte's thighs, sobbing.

"My poor Gilly," Maledicte said, voice so soft that Gilly had to strain to hear it, stifling his tears. "Vornatti should have cast me back to the snows, never disturbed the pattern to your days." Maledicte's fingers traced soothing lines on his back, bringing slow warmth to his frozen skin. So gentle. Gilly winced. But the shadow boy—

"You killed—" Gilly said.

"Am I supposed to regret it? Woman or not, Mirabile was a monster."

"But the boy," Gilly said. "Your own shadow." He forced himself to look into those dark eyes that he feared to see soulless now.

The black eyes were dark-ringed with fatigue and worry, but they were calmer than Gilly could ever remember.

"Yes," Maledicte said. "I should have done it long ago."

"But your innocence—"

Maledicte laughed, as silent as a cat, his shoulders shaking, near hysteria. "Did you think that Relict rat was innocent? That creature who knew no kindness, only hunger, fear, and rage—whose only virtue was a love so mad that Ani could find purchase in my soul? I am not that thing anymore. How could I be, with you teaching me kindness? For all that I've corrupted you, my sweet Gilly, you've bettered me. I would not have made the same choice I did then, were I offered it now."

Gilly's breath let out on a gasp, his chest pounded. "Mal—" Maledicte gathered him close, kissed his ear, his temple, drew back when his lips touched the wound on his head.

"She used you so hard," Maledicte said. "How did you fall into her hands . . . did Livia entrap you?"

"No," Gilly said, flushing with embarrassment and revulsion at the resurgent aches of his body. For a moment, he had forgotten pain in hope.

Maledicte awkwardly rocked him in his arms, Gilly overflowing his narrow lap. "Shh, I'll take you someplace safe."

"Janus," Gilly said.

Maledicte stilled, waiting.

"He found out I let you go to Stones, instead of fighting them off; he beat me, and sold me to the sea."

"And Mirabile?" Maledicte's voice was cool, as disinterested as if these names were those of strangers.

"She was on the docks when I escaped. I think she had been watching us all," Gilly said.

Maledicte's lips thinned; absently he stroked Gilly's shoulders. "We'd best get you someplace safe, then. I've escaped the Kingsguard. Echo will be hunting me. And Janus—best not chance his temper again. Will the madam at Lizette's take you in, do you think? It's near enough."

"If we pay her," Gilly said, dismayed at Maledicte's cool abstraction, his willingness to ignore Janus's murder attempt.

"Mirabile will have coin somewhere," Maledicte said. "It only remains to find it." Gently Maledicte set Gilly from his lap, and searched the room. He riffled through a stack of papers, pausing as he found the note from the palace spy warning of Maledicte's imminent arrest. "Mirabile's been stealing our correspondence, Gilly." Gilly made no answer, and Maledicte bit his lip, turned back to searching with more urgency. He found the coin purse beneath the altar stones, and tucked it into his shirtsleeve. In another makeshift safe, he found her poisons and rummaged through, muttering to himself. Then he knelt back beside Gilly. "Drink this—it should fire your blood. I cannot carry you."

Gilly couldn't focus on the vial, only on the red-washed skin of Maledicte's hands. He flinched. "Drink it," Maledicte said.

The liquid, bitter as gall, flamed down his throat, spreading heat to cold limbs. His heart drummed for a frantic, caged moment, then settled.

"Better?" Maledicte asked, sliding his arm beneath Gilly's shoulders.

"Yes," Gilly said, kissing the frowning face bent so near his own.

Maledicte pulled away. "Not now, Gilly." He tugged, and Gilly raised himself into Maledicte's bracing arms. The temple wheeled around him; the trickle of blood on his cheek shifted direction, dripping over his collarbone and chest. "What was that?" Gilly asked.

"Sailor's Dream, I think," Maledicte said.

"You think," Gilly said, licking his lips.

"Gilly, don't fuss at me," Maledicte said, "I'm bone-tired, and doing what I can." His arms trembled around Gilly's chest, and Gilly forced himself to his own support, aware again of Maledicte's slightness.

"As slight as a girl," Gilly said, patting the embroidery on Maledicte's cuffs.

"Yes," Maledicte said. "I am. And you're as big as an ox, and about as easy to steer."

Gilly nodded, forced himself to concentrate not on the wonderful warmth seeping through his mind and body, but on the blood-damp footprints they left on the temple floor.

MALEDICTE SWORE. Gilly had stopped again, and weariness was ripping through his bones, weighing him so that he felt he might sink into the earth at any moment. "Come on, Gilly," Maledicte said, pulling.

Gilly still balked, and, overbalanced, Maledicte fell up against him, warm skin exposed by Livia's inadequate cloak. Gilly's hands wandered again, and Maledicte, trying to secure the cloak, didn't step away. Damn Mirabile, he thought with a snarl. If she'd wanted him so badly, all she had to do was give him a dose of Dream, and he would have been hers. But she chose to hurt him, instead.

He shook with a rage that was all his, without the taint of Ani at all. Where was Ani? Maledicte wondered. She'd been still and quiet since the shadow boy's death, since Mirabile's death, when he had expected Her to rise screaming from his belly, expected to have to fight Her. But She was silent; it made him nervous, like a sailor beneath a storm-clouded sky.

Gilly's hands were under his shirt now, Maledicte noticed with a sudden warmth of his own, tracing lazy circles on his back, slipping lower.

Blood touched his face, and Maledicte looked up, watched another thin rivulet sneak past the slow crust forming on Gilly's head wound. Rising to his toes, he licked at it, hoping some of Ani's healing might be found in his spit. The copper taste woke him to the urgency of moving on, of not being found near Mirabile's body, of not being found at all.

Gilly fumbled at Maledicte's breeches and frowned in drugged puzzlement. "Livia?" Gilly whispered.

"No," Maledicte said, stung. He shoved Gilly into movement again, promising himself a confessional with Gilly as soon as he was sober. He had nothing to hide anymore; the unexpected freedom of it washed over his skin. Maledicte was a dead man, on the run, ruined. And he, who had changed his identity once, was free to do so again. The sword twanged against the door-jamb as they passed it, sparking a muttered response from Ani lurking within.

Not free yet, Maledicte thought, sobered. He had his vengeance to complete, though he knew it was an empty gesture now. Last was long dead and buried, his enemies gone—Kritos, Last, Amarantha, Dantalion, all fed to the crow-bitch, leaving him never sated. If he killed the child, would Ani leave him then, their compact finished with the infant earl's death? Maledicte felt Her whispering inside his blood, murmurs of agreement and coaxing. Just one more and then he'd be free.

Free, Maledicte thought, to do what? Change his name, leave the city, leave Janus? The breath fell out of him; his heart throbbed. Janus—back-to-back, fighting the world, only each other at the last. Maledicte, swaying under Gilly's weight as they shambled up the street like two drunkards, felt clearheaded for the first time in months.

Vengeance was a cold thing, and his prize . . . he had bartered his soul for Janus, and his prize was not all he'd expected. Golden Janus, his lover, his most trusted friend, had sent Gilly to the sea. . . .

Rosy light washed over them, flushed their skin with a false health as they passed beneath the brothel windows. Maledicte dragged a protesting Gilly down the alley and hammered on the back door. When it opened, he drew his sword and levered himself and Gilly past the girls.

"A room," he said. "Now."

A butterfly flutter of silk told him one girl had run for the madam and likely for whatever protector she hired for the brothel. Maledicte intended to have Gilly ensconced before their arrival. He went toward the stairs, and Gilly, moving by muscle memory, stumbled up them, and chose a room without hesitation. Empty, thankfully, Maledicte thought. He could bribe the whores, but a customer might be another matter. And how long had it been since his escape? Had they posted guards on the streets yet?

He pressed Gilly back into the sheets, wrapped him in blankets, and sat down on the edge of the bed.

"Will you forgive him this, too? If he has killed me?" Gilly whispered.

"You're not dying, Gilly." Spoken, the fear was real in the room. Maledicte took Gilly's hand in his own, sought out the steady throb of the pulse, the warmth of his fingers, and repeated, "You're not dying. You're hurt. But you'll recover. Street urchins get beat worse than this by their parents in the Relics, and look how well they grow."

"Stop crying then," Gilly said. "If I'm not dying."

Maledicte put his hand to his face; it was wet and stinging with tears that he hadn't noticed. He sniffed them back, letting them add to the pressure within him.

"I don't forgive him," Gilly said. "Even if I'm not dying." He closed his eyes, blooming bruises and exhaustion spreading shadows under them.

"Nor do I," Maledicte whispered. "Not this. Not you." The door opened again, and the madam stood there without the protector Maledicte had expected. A sudden dismay rose in him that he wouldn't have to fight anyone. He took a slow breath, forcing Ani back again.

"The girls said it was Gilly," she spat, seeing Maledicte seated on the bed.

"It is," Maledicte said, leaning back so she could see Gilly's sprawled form.

"And you've done this to him?" she asked. "Like my Lizette?"

"No, to both," Maledicte said. "I need a safe place for him to stay. To heal." He felt as if he were talking at a distance, the room seen down a telescope.

"He can stay. You try to, and I'll summon the guards."

"I wasn't going to," Maledicte said. Gilly clutched his hand, and Maledicte returned the pressure absently. "He's hurt, though. And on Dream. He'll need stitches for his head, and balm for the rest." Maledicte dropped the pouch of coins to the floor; the madam scooped it up and disappeared through the door.

"You can't go," Gilly said. "Where are you going?"

"Away," Maledicte said. "It seems that killing Mirabile was not wise, despite my satisfaction. I had not realized how much of Ani's concentration was focused on Mirabile. And now, there's only me to see to Her whims." Bile seared the back of his throat; he coughed it back. Gilly pushed himself up to his elbows, eyes going wide, even in his drugged state.

"Mal, I can hear Her in you—"

"Yes," Maledicte said. "Ani's coming back. I can't stay near you. It's not safe." He stroked Gilly's arm, felt his other hand seize the hilt of the sword.

"Mal," Gilly said. "Let's leave Antyre. Let's go to the Explorations, please."

Yes, Maledicte thought, yes. Away from the kingdom, away from Ani's tyranny and Her never-ending vengeance. But he was gagged by the taste of Her feathers and Her searing hatred.

Gilly touched his throat, traced the god-*avert* over his flesh with trembling fingers, cooling his heated skin. The obstruction in his throat lifted.

"Yes," Maledicte said. "Yes, I'm done with this. With this fruitless vengeance, with ashes in my heart, with—" The heat scalded him, raced up his spine, his throat, scorched back into his belly, his arms; the sword jerked and quivered, demanding that Maledicte remove Gilly's offensive, charm-using hands.

Maledicte screamed under the weight of Ani's will, Her thundering voice demanding his loyalty, his promise completed, obliterating everything else in his mind. The shadows moved inward, blinding him.

Not Gilly, he thought. *Let me finish my compact instead. You are the god of love as well as vengeance; let me leave Gilly alive. Please.* Maledicte remembered Gilly saying Ani destroyed the Relicts when Her follower denied her. Maledicte shivered, trying to keep the image of the brothel slipping into the earth at bay. *Anything*, he pled. *Anyone. I'll bring them to you.* Ani bent her head to his first prayer and Her wings fluttered in triumph.

Maledicte stood, hand on sword hilt, and brushed by Ma Desire, who stood trembling in the doorway, hands full of clean bandages. Her shocked face was the last thing he saw before Ani took complete control.

GILLY STRUGGLED WITH THE CLOAK, with the sheets, hearing again that stifled raw shriek, trying to get his stubborn legs sorted out so he could rise and go after Maledicte. Ma Desire hurried over and pressed him back. "No, you let that one go to the hell he's headed for. You don't go with him."

"But—" Gilly said.

She covered his mouth with her hand. "There's nothing you can do. He's wing-bent."

"No—" he said, and she tipped a glass against his open mouth, made him sputter even as he recognized the taste of the Laudable. Behind the window, in the night sky, he could see darker clouds flowing lowly across the sky, full of the feather-rasp of flying rooks. A dark cloud in the night, moving through the heart of the city, following their master toward the palace.

ALEDICTE WOKE TO HIMSELF on the grounds of the palace, staring up at the brick wall of the residential house, with only a dreamlike idea of how he'd arrived. The sky was dark, he knew that, and the rooks were everywhere. Had he flown? He raised his arms, peeled back his sleeves, looking for feathers, but saw only smooth skin, unmarred.

The light in the window beckoned him; the bars on the frame told him it was the nursery. Maledicte sheathed the sword and reached upward. He pressed his fingers into the brick mortar and it gave, creating a fingerhold. Raising himself one handhold at a time, he climbed, the birds swooping around him, carrying shrouding darkness on their wings, delaying morning.

On the streets below he could see lamps guttering and being relit against the thick darkness. Being lit against him, loose in the night, and within those glows, the gleaming gilt of the Kingsguard, huddled close.

A shadow moved across the window, and Maledicte clung to the wall with a predator's caution and patience. He shook his head, trying to clear this dreamlike sensation from his skin, trying to feel something other than Ani's fevered determination. Mortar and brick crumbled under his fingers, spat one hand into the air, left him hanging by the other. Below him, duller uniforms mingled with gold and blue: the Particulars with their pistols close to hand. Maledicte shifted his weight gingerly, trying to ease the cramp threatening to destroy his precarious grip on the wall.

Trust Me. He heard Ani's whisper, not in his ears, or his mind, but in the tides of his blood. It strengthened him like a tonic, and he clawed another foot upward.

Sweating, gasping, Maledicte gave himself over to the simplicity of Ani's will, of climbing the wall. He crept up to the lighted square of the nursery window, braced one foot on the sill, and peered inward. A kingsguard leaned up against the glass, spreading his bulk between the light and Maledicte.

Hanging motionless, Maledicte watched, wondering why the guard never turned to look outside, then understood. This man was there to watch the inside of the room, secure in knowing that there were guards posted at every entrance, and that the window was barred and, moreover, three stories above ground.

Maledicte, clinging with one hand to the stone sill above the window and braced by his feet, his ribs pressed against the sharp corner of the sill, reached for his sword. He slid the blade through the age-bubbled glass as smoothly and as cleanly as if it had been through paper, pressed it home before the guard could turn at the tiny chime of breaking glass. The sword bit deep into the guard's heart, and he stiffened against the pane. Maledicte withdrew the sword, leaving a ring of blood on the glass as the wet sword returned.

The guard slumped, and Maledicte, clinging to the bars of the window, waited a moment, to see if anyone within the room would object—wet nurse, child, or another guard. But the minutes passed in silence, with only Ani's urging to be heard.

He measured his shoulders against the bars, measured his head; the bars were too narrowly spaced for him. Designed to keep small children within, they also kept larger predators out. But as he ran his hands against their iron length, waiting for Ani to act, he realized they didn't go all the way to the top; their pointed finials stopped before the window did, leaving a gap. Too high for a child to climb to, but for him on the outside—it was the only way in, unless he expected Ani to peel back the bars one by one.

The gap wasn't much, a space of eight inches high, and only as wide as the window. Maledicte raised himself up, slid his legs past the iron prongs and slowly, gingerly, worked his way through, the sharp tips pressing against his rib cage, ripping a line through his shirt and spilling a tuft of padding from his corset. Pressed between the bars and the glass, he used the sword hilt to work up the latch.

Dropping into the room, he landed on the dead guard, and rolled away, came up with the sword extended. He bent and pulled the guard to his feet, using the man's belt to fasten him to the bars. A brief look in the night-dim nursery would see the man dozing against the window. But he hadn't played puppetmaster with the body unseen, he realized, as he heard the steady breath catch in surprise.

Across the dimly lit playroom, Adiran stared at him. Nested in blankets, surrounded by his blocks, he hadn't slept in his bed. Ani moved Maledicte's feet toward the boy. At the end of the playroom, closed in Adiran's room, a dog barked sharply.

Adiran smiled up at him, fumbled in the blankets beside him, and held up a hand. Ani smiled and accepted the token, the little porcelain puppet with black wings. She touched Adiran's head, and said, "Sleep, wingless one." As he had in Stones, Maledicte felt something transfer through him, not the same toxic wave of sickness, but something small and sharp, a crystalline seed. Beneath his hand, Adiran's eyes fluttered. Sighing, Adiran folded back into his blankets. The dog scratched madly at the door, and Ani hissed. It whimpered and fell silent.

"Hela?" The main door started to open, and Ani fought a brief battle with Maledicte over the necessary movement. Blood or stealth? Maledicte won by a bare margin, and ducked behind the carved toy chest, sheltering in its shadowed bulk.

The guard looked in and about, saw Adiran sleeping, and shut the door again, oblivious of the scent of blood that filled Maledicte's senses.

On silent feet, Maledicte ghosted toward the other end of the room and the other bedroom door. He opened it, the sword slipping free, but the wet nurse snored in her chair, her gas light guttering.

Ani prodded her with the tip of the sword, drawing blood, but no flinch, no waking; surprise and thwarted bloodlust drove Her back again. Maledicte touched her cup; sniffed the dregs of tea. Drugged. He smiled, a lean, cold thing that had more of Maledicte in it than Ani. Janus had been here. Janus was working with him. But where was he? Maledicte turned to search and Ani showed him the crib instead.

The earl of Last. My enemy. The last death. Maledicte bit his lip at the idea. The freedom from Ani, their goal met, but the idea warred with a simpler image—Gilly's face, flushed with distress over murdering an infant. Ani snarled within him, reminded him that She had let Gilly live. "I promised,"

Maledicte said, took a step forward; the cradle linens seemed crimson with blood, the copper tang of it rich in the air. He curled cold fingers around the hilt. One more, he thought, and inched forward.

He reached into the cradle and touched warmth and wet, and pulled his hand back. The blood on his hands was not the child's murder played out of time, not Maledicte's imagination, or Ani's vengeful illusion. The blood on his hands was real. And the infant lay in a sleep from which it would never awaken.

Maledicte made a noise in his throat of utter protest, a double-throated thing, his choked cry of pity and revulsion, and Ani's harsh gasp of thwarted rage. A shadow detached itself from the wall, took his wrist. "Shh, Mal, not yet...."

"Janus," Maledicte breathed, the room shivering around him like something in a dream, like it might fly apart and show itself to be mere delusion.

Janus touched his mouth; the odor of blood washed over Maledicte with the touch. It soaked Janus's cuff. Maledicte backed away, leaned against the closed doors. "You killed—"

"Saved you the grief," Janus said, his voice low. "I saw how it distressed you. The idea of killing Auron. But it had to be done. When I heard you'd fled the hotel, I knew you'd be coming here. I thought you'd be quicker, though."

"I had to retrieve Gilly," Maledicte said, numbly. He waited to feel something, but Ani's rage, though white-hot, only dimly touched him. He wished it would wash over him, comfort him, take this cold horror from his belly, that this man with bloody hands and cold eyes was his lover, his companion for years, his beloved.

"Gilly, again," Janus said, scowling. "Timing is important, Mal. My plan—"

"To be earl, I know. You hated this child," Maledicte said.

"It was only a child, unworthy of hate. I never hated Auron. And I don't care about being earl any longer."

"What?" Maledicte whispered, startled out of his dream world, back to the solidity of this room, this moment, his breath fast in his chest, the ruined, wet texture of the baby's skin still warm against his hand. He shuddered all over, wanting out, wanting to run, but the guards were outside the doors and he couldn't imagine climbing down the way he knew he'd come.

"Janus," he breathed, seeking understanding and freedom from this room that had become a trap.

"I intend to be king," Janus said, the words cool and measured in the quiet of the room. "My blood's good enough, and why not, there've been bastards on the throne before. I can rally some support already. DeGuerre, some of Westfall's friends. But I had to make a choice. Kill Aris, that vacillating, sentimental fool, or the babe? Assassination of a king's always a chancy thing. But kill Auron, and who's left for Aris to turn to but me, when the only blood left is mine or Adiran's?"

Maledicte leaned against the wall, chilled at the pale fire in Janus's eyes. Ani surged in him, screaming so harshly that nothing of Her words was distinguishable, only the shrieking desire to kill. At this moment, Maledicte didn't know who she hungered for. The earl of Last was his promise—and the babe was dead.

"Ani still rides you," Janus said, stepping back and away, calculation in his face. "Does She know, does She understand—I am the earl of Last, now?"

Maledicte moaned, the sword leaping in his hands, darting toward Janus. Maledicte fought it, but Janus stepped closer, let the blade bite into his arm. Janus savaged his lip, but did not cry out.

Janus danced back, hand clutching his wound. Blood rose and welled between his fingers, flowing down his sleeve and mingling with Auron's spilled blood. "I knew you would understand. Perfect." His eyes widened suddenly and he rolled beneath the cradle to avoid the next swing, rose on the other side. "Once is enough, Mal. You must control Ani. Use Her abilities for our ends."

Maledicte gasped for breath, shuddering with exhaustion and dread that Janus thought to play puppets with the god. The sword burned in his grasp, the feathered hilt sinking into his skin. Janus's eyes narrowed, gas-flame blue, as the sword moved toward him like a needle on a compass. Maledicte lunged again and found Janus using the same gambit Maledicte had used in all his duels, stepping too close for the sword to be brought to bear. Janus grabbed Maledicte's wrist, holding it out like a pinned wing.

"Shh," he whispered into Maledicte's ear. "You cannot kill me. I am both your Love and your Vengeance now. The thing you wanted and the thing you hated. Ani cannot kill me without breaking your compact. We've caged Her perfectly within you. After all, Her skills are far too valuable to lose."

Maledicte dropped the sword, trembling all over, wordless. Kaleidoscope images burst behind his lids, of Last dying, of Auron's blood, of Mirabile's feather-studded skin. He whimpered, sobbing for air and reason. Janus's blood perfumed the air, the wound near his face. "Miranda, trust me. I know what I'm doing," Janus said. "Now pick up your sword. You'll need it."

Janus stepped back, and Maledicte, blank-minded, did as his lover bid. As his fingers touched the hilt, there was a sudden shatter of glass from the other room as the crack made in the window by the sword raced side to side. Rooks blew through it, and the mastiff broke into frantic barking.

Janus fell back against the cradle, bloody wound clutched in a hand, smiling. "Go."

Maledicte fled the pale, ecstatic light in Janus's eyes, the sword shivering at his side, ran through the swirling cloud of rooks, leaping over the crumpled guard. He made a leap for the barred window, but his hand, still slick with the infant's blood, slipped down its length without catching.

The guards burst into the room at Hela's barking, and Maledicte reacted, slicing into them, severing the first guard's arm from his body and driving the sword through the chest of the next one. Panting, he put his foot on the corpse, levered his sword free; it stuck on a rib, and he yanked harder. Dimly, he saw Adiran, awakened, standing beside him, blue eyes wide and worried.

Before the next guard could reach him, Maledicte freed the sword, and grabbed up Adiran. The guard faltered. Adiran clung to his neck and began to cry. Behind him, he heard Janus stumbling into the room and checking also, as if only waking from an assault.

Maledicte swallowed hard, the child's wailing in his ear. He moved toward the door, and first one guard, then the next, stepped out of his path.

Adiran pushed feebly in his grip, his wailing breaking into uncertain hiccoughs. Maledicte clutched him closer, his mind twisting ideas together, trying to think of escape and only imagining a noose. The guards would follow him to the ends of the earth as long as he held Adiran. He could set him down and flee—he had nearly the length of the room on them—could kick the door closed, delay them that second longer. But, to set Adiran down now—the guards would surge after him like hounds, leaving Aris's beloved son, Aris's heart, behind in the nursery. Alone with Janus.

Maledicte turned and raced the long hallway, found guards pelting up the main stairs nearly on him. Jasper headed them, his eyes fever-bright with anger. Seeing Adiran clutched so close, he waved the rest to a halt. They paused, piling into each other, but despite Maledicte's fervent wishes, stayed upright. The second mastiff, pushing through them, had no hesitation at all. Despite Jasper's snatch, Bane came roaring through, savaging his restraining hands.

Maledicte dropped Adiran and bolted. The child, startled again and terrified at the rage in the air, began wailing. Bane gained his side, and, frantic, began slicing the air with his teeth, keeping everyone away from his charge, and obstructing the hall. Adiran clung to Bane and howled. The guards were stymied. For the moment.

But the floor shivered beneath Maledicte's feet with the arrival of more guards. He shuddered. The palace was worse than a beehive struck unthinkingly.

Within him, Ani whispered, let Me make it better, let Me make them all suffer. Give yourself to Me.

No, Maledicte thought, pushing away from a wall, taking the corner too fast, his boots skidding on the polished wood. He saw another stairwell and raced for it. Janus had a plan; Maledicte had to trust him. There was no alternative. It was only their old game, made more risky. Miranda had done the running before, dashed away with stolen goods, or the weapons to be hidden. She had always been able to outrun the blame, and Janus—had always been able to deny it.

This was more of the same, all part of the plan. *Janus's plan*, Maledicte thought, savagely. *Not mine.* His breath tore in his chest, his heart hammered; he grabbed the railing of the stairs, saw more guards coming up them, just two, roughly woken and still addled with sleep. He shrieked and dove forward. The first man took the blade in the face and collapsed instantly, blood bubbling through the wreck of his nose. Maledicte tumbled down the stairs on top of the other, using the man's body to cushion his own bones against the risers' edges.

Panting, Maledicte slit the man's throat when he started, clumsily, to fight back at the base of the stairs.

If he could only get outside the palace, the night itself would hide him; the clouds of rooks would shelter him, as safe as any babe— In the disused dining room, Maledicte leaned against the wall and retched, wiped his bloody blade clean on the shrouded table.

Trust in Me, Ani whispered, coaxing, gentle, as compelling as Her first words to Miranda had been. Huddled beneath the altar, the salt burning her eyes, her skin, her scraped flesh, and Ani asking, What wrong has been done to you, little one? Tell Me what you want. . . .

Now Her words were gentle again, the strident, bloody harridan only a nightmare image in his heart. Why trust Janus? Everything you've done, everything you've been, you've done for him. And is he the man you thought him to be? Hasn't he lied to you? Can you trust him? There's only Me to protect you, now.

Maledicte sucked in his breath, quieting its wheeze, ignoring Ani as best he could. They had lost him, albeit briefly. Best to make the most of it. Curtains draped the far wall, and Maledicte, hoping for windows, yanked them back. Painted gardens, sunlit, even in the dark of night. Maledicte laughed wildly; he hated this court, the overwhelming falsity of it all, where not even the architecture could be relied upon to be honest.

Footsteps sounded outside the doors. He ran for the servants' entrance, yanked the door open at the expense of its hinges, and dashed into the dark corridor beyond, the door listing in the jamb, a clear pointer to his direction.

Darkness and shadows and enclosed walls struck both Maledicte and Ani nerveless—the specter of Stones again. If he were caught—to spend the last moments of his life in a cell—Maledicte ran blindly down the hall, toward a faint spark of light growing in the distance. A maid with a lantern crept out of a room to see what was happening. She opened her mouth to shriek, but Maledicte pounced, snatched the lantern, and pushed her into the center of the hall. Gasping for breath, shocked, she sprawled across the smoothed floorboards, watching as he retreated. Maledicte grinned. Let her lie there in a stupor; let the damn guards trip over her, and buy him a few precious moments.

He wanted more stairs, more windows, some hint of where he was. Why had Janus never given him a map of the palace when he had known it must come to this?

Maledicte shivered, though his skin was hot with sweat, and the lantern's heat burned his left hand. He had no answer for himself. He was bent on escape, and thinking was for later.

His feet pounded along the hall; the servants' passageway, though narrow enough to prevent the guards from surrounding him, was stripped of carpeting, and his steps echoed like pistol shots. They could track him by that alone, and he had no idea which of the doors held more stairs, winding their ways, mazelike, through the palace. There had been stairs in the dining room, but he had fled mindlessly past them, and the pursuing guards, their cries audible now, made doubling back impossible. The dining room would have needed to be connected to the kitchens, and the kitchens always opened out to the world. Maledicte pushed open the next door, slid through it, and shut the door again.

A woman repairing sheets looked up at him, the needle held in her mouth, the thread dangling. It dropped and Maledicte lunged at her. "Not a word." He blew out the lantern, slid himself under the sheltering drape of the sheet she was sewing, pressed the sword tip up against her belly. "Not a word," he said again, his voice rough with fear. Had he been in court, he would have done his best to disguise that weakness, but here his desperation could only insure her obedience.

The door swung open and guards spilled in like a piled mass of hunting dogs.

"What do you want?" she said, her voice shrill, going shriller as Maledicte leaned his weight on the blade. A thin line slid down the blade, as thin as her linen thread, but dark, and forming a slow droplet at the end. Maledicte caught the drop on his fingertips, lest somehow the guards hear that small act of violence over their searching. They yanked open all the connecting doors, threw the loose piles of sheets around the room, until the seamstress cowered, bending her face near to her waist. Maledicte could see her features, distorted by fear, through her pale linens.

The guards left, slamming the door again, and Maledicte slid away from her. "Please," she said. "Please."

Maledicte knew killing her would buy him time, prevent her from shrieking that he'd turned rabbit and bolted back the way he'd come, but her blood was already streaking his blade; the sight of it made his stomach churn. A fine time to lose the taste for it, he thought bitterly, but Ani only laughed.

If you won't come to Me, why should I help you? She asked.

Maledicte put his hand over the seamstress's mouth, put the blade to her throat; the woman paled, her tongue licked out nervously to touch dry lips.

Maledicte pulled away, the blade no more bloodied than before, and ran.

He had reached the dining room again when he heard the muffled violence of her screaming.

Fool, Ani said within him. Betrayed fool. Lose yourself in Me and I will aid you. He clattered down the stairs, burst into the kitchen, and found it overfull of guards, watching the exits.

Maledicte turned and fled back upward, aware of the upstairs contingent approaching. "Help me," he whispered.

Yes, Ani said, Go always upward, and the rooks will aid you. He kicked the stair doors shut in the guard's face as the first man reached it, and he kept going up, past the landing to the servants' quarters, past the point where the stairs were kept in good condition, and became friable, bowed with time. He stumbled, but kept going, secure in the knowledge that these stairs were blind. There were no doorways to open up at his side, disgorging guards or Particulars. No maidservants to trip over, just a straight shot to the sky.

An explosion snapped through the air in the hall; the plaster near his face puffed into dust, and Maledicte spat. Pistols.

He turned and cursed them for cowards. The Particular drew another pistol and fired again, then screamed as the pistol exploded in his hand. Ani's doing, or pure luck. It didn't seem to matter. The stairs came to an abrupt end, spilling him out into a jumbled attic.

Upward. In the shadowed ceiling, the door to the rooftop was hinted at by a darker patch, a square with a telltale latch. He climbed the pile of aristocratic refuse and forced the latch back, even as the guards swarmed in and spread out, creating a net of flesh and swords.

Maledicte levered himself up and through, and found himself on the flat roof of the palace, the night air cool and crisp in his face, and the sky alive with wings. Within him, Ani spread Her wings, stroking his fears back.

He laughed, stood over the trapdoor, and took the head of the first guardsman to climb through, pushing the body back down onto his colleagues. Maledicte kicked the head through as an afterthought and dropped the trapdoor closed.

There was nothing there to hold it closed; the latch was on the other side, but the very fact that only one man could come through at a time acted like a weight on the guards below. Maledicte left the trapdoor, ran to the edge of the roof, and looked down. Dizzyingly far, the ground seemed as unattainable as the sky as a means of escape. He leaned over the edge, testing the wall for scalability. In this part of the castle, it was old stone, not soft mortar and jutting brick. More, Ani showed no inclination to grant him preternatural skills again, and only a fool tried to descend a sheer stone wall.

Beneath his feet, the muttering panic of the guards went quiet and orderly; one voice cracked out above them all. Echo, taking charge. At least there was that at the end.

He watched the trapdoor lift, disgorging Echo, who rose like a stage demon, flung aloft by his guards, pistol in one hand, sword in the other, and a length of chain mesh guarding his throat.

Maledicte danced toward him as Echo leveled the pistol, eyes narrowing. The puff of smoke, the ricochet of sound struck Maledicte a moment after the lead did. He stumbled, but the ball had only penetrated his leg; Ani chased it out, healing its intrusive heat, absorbing the hurt. Maledicte reached out with his sword and took the pistol from Echo's hand, flung it off the roof.

"I'm glad you came," Maledicte said. "This wouldn't have been the same without you."

"I'll see you dead," Echo said. Behind him, the guards started to join them, and Maledicte pivoted, kicked the first one in the throat, and sent him backward. Echo's blade whistled in the sky, coming for his chest, and the air was suddenly full of rooks. Echo flailed his sword, trying to clear them from his face, the stabbing beaks, the snatching claws, and Maledicte screamed, "He's mine."

The space between them cleared, the rooks pulling away into the sky like a windspout, flowing upward and then falling back toward them, circling them. "All your tricks won't help you, now. Aris will see you hanged," Echo said, closing.

Maledicte took the blow on his blade, skidded under the man's weight, and stepped aside at the last, forcing Echo off his blade. Maledicte thrust, aiming for Echo's exposed side, but the man pivoted and parried.

Maledicte stepped back, trying to keep an eye on both Echo and the door to the attic. Echo was not any of the fools that Maledicte had dueled previously, buoyed by tradition and stupidity; should Maledicte be struck from behind by a guard, Echo would finish him from the front without hesitation.

Maledicte jumped the low thrust Echo aimed in an attempt to hamstring him, and swept the blade outward, pushing him back. The trapdoor started to rise, and Maledicte leaped on it, his sudden weight forcing the guards back. But only for a moment. They shoved upward; Maledicte felt the wood shift beneath his feet, saw Echo's blade coming for him, and tumbled forward, going head over heels away from the strike.

He knelt, heart pounding, blood singing in his ears, listening to Echo's approach. Not an honorable fool, Maledicte thought, not loath to strike down a fallen man, but a fool nonetheless. Maledicte dropped from his knees to his thigh, rolling and turning. Echo leaned inward just as Maledicte pushed the blade up into his chest. He worked the blade through, then worked it free, letting Echo fall as the guards gained the roof.

Suddenly leaderless, they hesitated. Echo bled out before them; the rooks swirled, filling the air with their cries and feathers, and Maledicte levered himself to his feet, panting through bared teeth. They spread out loosely, but none approached.

Maledicte leaned back against the parapet, looking over them all. What now, he wondered. Fly, Ani urged him. Fly.

"I cannot," he said, not caring that he spoke aloud. The guards flinched and one, braver than the rest, stepped forward. Maledicte shifted his grip on his sword, and said, "Don't do that. Your colleagues aren't going to support you and I'll kill you. We'll wait."

The trapdoor rose again, and Maledicte found a smile at the pale gilt hair, at the blue eyes. "Janus," he said. Now the game could continue—Janus's plan unfurl.

"Sir," the guard said. "Be careful. He killed Lord Echo."

"And so you are all waiting for someone else to stop him. How brave of you all," Janus said, his tone caustic. "Had you all rushed him, this would be done with by now."

Maledicte felt his heart jerk and flutter, as if wings were beating in it. It was an act, he knew it was, but it felt—

He's betrayed you, Ani crowed. You know he has. Thrown you over for ambition and a golden throne. Give your future to me. I'll bring their city down on them all.

Janus would not turn on him—Maledicte clung to that certainty as he had clung to the wall earlier. Janus loved him more than the world itself.

Janus took a sword from the nearest guard and paced forward, his face set, as white as the marble busts that lined the king's hall.

It was not the sword, or the implacability of his face that seeded doubt into Maledicte's heart, but the clammy remembrance that Janus had waited for Maledicte to arrive before striking the child. That he had plotted to use the gods, and one so mad as that might dare anything. More still, the simple fact that Janus had had his wound dressed and his shirt exchanged for a fresh one. While Maledicte ran, Janus had been dressing for this moment.

"Ani," Maledicte called out to the sky, his voice a croaking plea, his pain choking him. "Ani."

The sensation burst over his skin like a thousand needles stabbing; his hands shook, and the sword fell with a clatter on the stone. He could smell it, the rough scent of new feathers springing out, cloaking his skin, letting Ani free. Beneath his feet, the palace twitched, like an animal waking, like a horse shaking off a bothersome fly, like wings unfurling.

The guards rocked on their feet, their eyes wild. Two of the Particulars fled for the stairwell and disappeared into it.

"No," Janus said, stepping forward, his sword hand moving.

"Sir, the king wants him for a trial," a guard called.

"And risk the palace?" Janus countered. "Risk the ceilings crushing his son?" He struck like a snake.

Maledicte rolled away from the blow. He backed away from Janus, wishing Ani would hurry with this transformation, would hurry with his obliteration.

A faint thought crossed his mind, shocking him to stillness—Gilly, waiting for him. Gilly. Ani shrieked within his skin, the rooks flew into the ranks of guards, blinding one man, and causing chaos.

"Mal—" Janus said. "Mal—" A warning in his voice, or entreaty. Maledicte didn't know which it was, only knew that his lover came for him with a sword, that Ani raged within him, and that the small quiet space left in him was weeping for Gilly. Then there was nothing in his mind but the black arrival of Ani, holding him immobile as She sought control of his body, making it over as She wished.

The moonlight reflected off the blade as Janus pulled his arm back and thrust forward. Despair let him break Ani's grip; Maledicte's hand flashed out, pressing the blade aside as it moved, blood spattering from his palm as he pushed, trying to shift the sword, trying to shift it away from his tender flesh. He moved it a bare half inch. Not enough.

The sword sank into him as if it had always belonged there, the slick heat of it intimate within his chest, nestled inside.

Janus's eyes were wild; his mouth slack, as if he hadn't believed he could do it at all. The blade slid free despite Maledicte clutching at it, holding it to him. Blood sprayed over Janus's clean shirt, hit his face and mouth. Janus flinched, and closed his eyes. Maledicte, still standing, felt his body going numb and distant. He watched Janus wipe the blade clean with his hand, sheeting his blood from the steel to the stones of the roof. The guards' faces were stupid with shock, as if they hadn't believed Maledicte could be killed any more than Maledicte had.

"Ani," Maledicte breathed. Ani poured Herself into the wound and found it mortal.

She screamed, Her burgeoning power pushed back and redirected, fighting to stay ahead of Maledicte's death. The stones of the roof birthed ravens, and the guards stumbled, waving their swords blindly in a blizzard of black feathers.

The rooks skied away, shrieking, as the ravens rose. But as Ani's hold on the world faded, the ravens slowly became stone once more, shattering at the touch of a sword. Maledicte watched it all, sinking back against the edge of the roof, sliding down to lie on the surface.

Janus knelt, pressing his hand to the wound. "Mal—"

"I wouldn't have—" Maledicte whispered. Blood washed up and brushed his lips. "You didn't have— Why?" His breath gave out, and he saw tears standing out in Janus's eyes. They made him angry, but his blood was too thin for the old fire to catch, too thin and spreading out over his shirt, Janus's hands, the roof tiles.

"Shh," Janus said, bending forward, pressing him close. It woke pain in the wound and Maledicte moaned in the dark shelter of Janus's shoulder. "Drink this," Janus said, a small vial in his hand. "Please. It'll ease the pain."

Maledicte let the liquid trickle into his mouth, felt Janus rubbing his throat to make him swallow, and the pain receded into numbness. Ease it, he thought muzzily, when they hang him. A lover's last gift—the gift of oblivion in the face of a slower death. He closed his eyes and welcomed it.

· 4 3 ·

*D*O YOU SEE THE BIRDS?" The whisper woke Gilly from his Laudable stupor.

"Did you hear the bells?" another whore asked.

Gilly could hear it now, through senses dulled and fogged, the deep tolling of the castle bell. He choked on an indrawn breath. He forced himself to his feet; something heavy and cool slithered down his legs. He caught it absently and staggered to the window. The women squeaked as he fell into the frame beside them.

The rooks were wild, flying without pattern, without sense, over the city, flickers of a dark night lingering into the dawn. *The rooks follow him*, Mirabile had whispered. But now, they flew without purpose, without destination, and Gilly felt their panic and loss sinking into his bones. He knew, without words, without telling, that there was no one for them to follow now.

His hand clenched around the object that had been on the bed with him. He opened his palm, saw a watch engraved with sailing ships, and his breath left him, overwhelmed by despair.

JANUS STOLE THROUGH THE HALLWAYS of the palace; those who saw him backed away. He couldn't blame them. He knew his temper, knew what it was like at the best of times, and this was far from being that. Those unafraid of his rages waited to see what his position would be, now that his lover had murdered the infant earl.

Panic gripped his throat again. What if he had been wrong? What if he'd miscalculated? The threat of Aris deciding that Janus was to blame for Auron's death was nothing compared to this. Even had he calculated right, the window of safety was so narrow—they meant to hang his body from the turrets in a few hours.

The chapel was silent and dark, empty except for Maledicte. Aris had refused to let Auron lie in the same room as his murderer, had kept Auron by his side. *But such only aids me,* Janus thought, *keeps Aris stupid with grief, and Mal—*

He hesitated near the marble bier. So white that even the dried blood on his mouth seemed scarlet instead of brown. No one had cleaned him, given him the courtesies granted the dead. No one would. But in denying the rites, they aided Maledicte one last time by keeping his secret. More, their neglect kept her life . . . Janus forced a smile at the irony, forced himself to believe that he had been right, that the books thieved from Gilly's possession had been accurate.

Janus nerved himself to rest his hand on Maledicte's chest. It was cool to the touch, as still as marble. But when he pressed his fingers against the wound, they came away touched with fresh blood.

Janus dropped to his knees. Thank you, Ani—thank you. As possessive as the books stated, Ani would not relinquish Her hold while the compact remained undone. The relief unmanned him as the fear had not. It took him long moments to regain his composure.

Ani's strength would keep Maledicte from death, while the poison from the Itarusine court would mimic the symptoms of it. Janus had planned it to a nicety, all variables controlled, and still, it had gone wrong. Maledicte had moved. Had endured a far more lethal blow than the one Janus had intended, had let the blade bite into the heart itself.

Shaking, he wrapped Maledicte around with the shrouding cloth, lifted him into his arms, and headed into the hall.

He left the main halls for the servants' corridors, hurrying along, careless of noise. This deep into the old palace, the corridors were thick with dust and cobwebs. But once he reached more modern segments, he hesitated. Only one last stretch lingered between him and the stables and his waiting carriage. But a single servant now could see his plans ruined. Or a guard resting in the stables. He closed his eyes, trusting to chance and a castle steeped in mourning.

"Just a little longer, Mal," he said. "Then it'll be all over. We'll have won and we'll be together." He forced his mouth shut; a whisper where none should be might bring a servant to investigate or overhear. And there would be mayhem enough when the discovery of Maledicte's disappearance was made. Better they think him mad with grief, determined to preserve dignity for his lover, than to even suspect that Maledicte might live yet.

The passage stayed silent, and Janus brought Maledicte out into the mid-morning sunlight. Janus flinched at the brightness after the dark corridors, but Maledicte's face stayed fixed. Janus shivered.

He laid him on the seat of the carriage, and called up to the driver, "To Lastrest, and stop for nothing."

The paid driver looked back at the bundle in Janus's arms and shuddered, but snapped the reins, spurring the team into a trot.

Janus folded Maledicte's fingers about his own, but they refused to stay there, slipped away from him, limp and chill. Janus pushed panic away. Maledicte could still die. The wound was so deep, and if Ani's touch faded . . . If She forsook their bargain, Maledicte might wake only to bleed to death in his arms.

Janus compared the risks of rough travel and the virtues of speed, and yelled up at the coachman to spring them. The horses surged into a gallop. In the jolting coach, Janus held Maledicte to him more tightly, shielding his body from the worst of the rattling, and thought, *Now, if only that damn boy has done what I asked.*

His stomach clenched and roiled. When the rain started, he relaxed a little. The rain could only help. He wondered where the pursuit was now, whether Maledicte had been missed yet, and if so, if the guards had gone to Aris first, disturbing his solitude, or if they'd simply taken off after him. With Echo dead and Jasper dog-mauled, Janus assumed the Kingsguard would dither for some space of time before intruding on Aris.

The coach clattered through the gates of Lastrest, and Janus sprang out of it, carrying Maledicte into the house.

His sudden arrival startled the servants into action; Janus ignored them, headed for his bedroom. He laid Maledicte on the bed, then shut the door firmly behind him, latching it. "Mal?" he said.

But Maledicte was still white, still unresponsive, and cool to the touch. Janus winced; the serum should have worn off by now, and his control veered into panic again. What would he do if Maledicte were gone? If he had killed—

"Sir?" the boy said, the hidden door sliding open. "You've been gone a long time."

"Did anyone see you?" Janus asked, staring at the young man. Slim as a sword blade, dark-haired, and as pale as powder could make his skin—he made Janus's heart clench.

"No, you said not to come out. And I've been so bored." The boy turned his lips down in a sullen pout and Janus laughed.

"Sorry, Mal."

"My name isn't—"

"It doesn't really matter," Janus said, standing. "Does it?"

"What's that?" the young man asked, as curious as a cat, and as fickle with his attention as the whore he was.

"You," Janus said, unwrapping Maledicte with careful fingers. "Come and take a look."

"It's a wax doll," the boy said, coming closer.

"No," Janus said, laughing as Maledicte's lips tightened, his eyelashes flickered at the light shining on his face.

"I don't like it," the boy said, backing away. "I want to go back to the brothel."

Janus fought the urge to just grab the sword. Chasing the boy around the room would do no good, but he burned to have the deed done, the time spent sealing Maledicte's wounds. "Without being paid?" Janus said, letting disdain slip into his voice. "I haven't had you yet. But you've had my bed to lie in, the food and drink I gave you."

The young man came closer, licking his lips. "You won't—"

"Won't what?" Janus asked, leaning back against the bedsheets, slipping his hand onto the hilt of his sword, hidden by the shroud.

"Won't make me touch that—" The boy jerked his head toward Maledicte, still more corpse than living flesh. Janus found a hot ember of his temper left, and said, "If you touched him, I'd have to kill you. I don't share him."

"Well, that's all right, then, 'cause I ain't going to touch it," the boy said, slipping around to Janus's side. Janus drew the boy close, kissed the soft mouth, and pressed the sword home. The boy jerked and gasped, blood spilling up into Janus's mouth, hot and salty.

"I'm sorry, Mal, I'm so sorry," he whispered, licking the blood away. "I never wanted to hurt you." A footstep in the hall woke him to the reality. Not the rooftop again, not Maledicte in his arms, but a paid boy. Janus let him drop, wiped his mouth, and bent his attention to Maledicte. He picked Maledicte up again, passed through the door the boy had used, entered the secret room. Aris would know about it, of course, having grown up at Lastrest, but he might not think to look in it. Not with a body to be found elsewhere.

Janus laid Maledicte down, shoved the debris of the boy's meal away, and picked up the medical supplies he'd laid in. He stitched the wound closed, reaching in past the skin, beneath the small breast, to sew up muscle and tendon, working with shaking hands. What if it didn't work— He poured whiskey over the stitching, and Maledicte arced his back, the tendons in his throat standing out.

"Shh," Janus said, kissing his forehead, wrapping a layer of cotton gauze around the damaged hands where Maledicte had tried to stop the sword. It made him uneasy that these smaller wounds hadn't healed yet. "I'll be back. Just rest."

He shut the door behind him, and wrapped the whore in the shroud, carried it downstairs past the gaping servants and into the gardens, wet with rain.

When he returned to the house, mud-covered and shaking with exertion, wound reopened and bloody, Aris was waiting for him.

"Where is his body?" Aris said; his face was lined, wet with tears and rage. "Where is it?"

Janus knelt. "Find him yourself. Sire." Aris moved forward and struck him across the face, the blow knocking Janus back across the floor. Exhausted and in no mood to feign obedience, Janus still kept control enough not to strike back, to continue his schemes. Besides, the guards even now clustered around Aris. Instead, Janus let tears spring to his eyes, and whispered, "I loved him too well to see his body displayed, to let them bet on when the crows would take his eyes, and which bones would fall away first, to see the rabble fight over his dropped finger bones."

"You've buried him on the grounds? Here, on the family property of the child he's slain? He cannot stay here. And he will be hung high. As all traitors are." Aris paced the room, peered out through the rain-streaked glass, gestured to the guards. "Start searching. Look for turned earth."

They bowed and went out. Janus sank down to a crouch again. "Uncle, please." He made himself think of Maledicte outside, in the earth, trying not to let any trace of his triumph show.

"Did you know?" Aris said, tugging Janus's face up to meet his. A very different king, this, Janus thought. No longer passive and beaten, but charged with grief and rage. "Did you know what your lover intended?"

"No," Janus said. "No."

"The only thing sparing your neck is that he came up the wall, like some damned demon. And he didn't know how to escape; had you aided him, I would have expected him to sneak in through the doors and flee with more ease."

Janus wondered if another denial would be more or less convincing than the first. He kept silent, waiting.

"I trusted Maledicte too long, played the fool. You lived in his pocket and yet claim I should trust you— I wish I could believe you," Aris said. "Wish I could trust my own flesh and blood, but death seems overinterested in smoothing your path." Aris leaned against the table, his face older than Janus had ever seen it.

"I could have you imprisoned or executed, but there is no other left of our blood. If the line of Last is to continue, it must be through you." Aris's hands knotted and unknotted uselessly against his coat. "As for banishment, Itarus would be only too glad to take you in, to use you against Antyre. How would Adiran fare then? I have not the stomach to fight another war over my throne."

Aris held out a hand, face grim. Janus cautiously took it. Aris clenched his hand tight, drew Janus close. "This is my sin—and my guilt. That I would prefer a conspirator on my throne to the bloodshed that would follow a war or my death without a viable heir. So you have won, Janus. To a degree.

"You will continue as a member of my court. My third counselor. But the moment you approach Adiran, I will have the dogs at your throat. Without hesitation. Your life is now linked to his. If he contracts fever, should he suffer hurt of any kind, you will pay for it. Do you understand me, nephew?"

Aris's eyes were the cold blue of winter skies, and Janus found himself looking away first for once.

"I would never hurt Adiran," he said, finding his voice. There was no need. Adiran's presence could only aid him. If he were regent for the simple young man Adi would be, it would be no different from being king in name. But all those thoughts passed in a driving need to return to Maledicte, to make sure the stitches were holding as the poison wore off, to ease his pain.

"Janus, I am sick of your meaningless words. Go upstairs; you are confined to your quarters until we have recovered his body."

Janus fought a surge of angry temper, reminding himself again that it was the boy, the bait, that they hunted. Doors slammed upstairs, and he focused his eyes on the floor, dropping into a bow, though alarm shot through him. He had expected the guards to confine their seeking to the grounds of Lastrest, ignoring the house itself. Casting a final glance at Aris's ravaged face, at the guards in the drive passing out spades, he left the room as if reluctant, even while his blood whispered, *hurry hurry.*

Upstairs, he found the door to his rooms open, his armoire opened, guards looking through it. He parted his lips to object and his blood froze in his veins. The opened armoire door had blocked the wall from his sight, and the hidden room's door gaped wide.

"There's blood on the bed and the floor," the guard said.

"I was injured earlier. Defending Auron." His voice was without conscious control; the entirety of his being vibrated with the need to shut the door to the hidden room, though he knew it was too late.

The guards shrugged and left, locking him in as they did, and Janus stumbled into the hidden room, finding only shadows and darkness within its narrow confines, the candles gone out and cold.

Janus fumbled his numb, blind way toward the dusty chaise where he had laid Maledicte. Surely he had not recovered, was not playing a second, lethal game of cat and mouse even now. . . . Janus's breath caught; he bit back a sob, imagining the guards finding so much more than they expected, not a corpse but a revenant, weak but alive. Easy prey. He dropped to his knees, reaching out in entreaty, and then his hands touched clammy, sweating flesh; a whisper of a moan reached him, and when he drew his hands back, blood marked his fingers.

Ani's doing, Janus realized; this empty room not empty at all. The same weaving of shadow that had snared Last now spared Her vessel. He burst into laughter, tinged with hysteria, and startled himself silent. But such power She held, and Miranda held. What he couldn't do with it at his side. . . . He and Maledicte would rule this country as surely as they had ruled the Relicts. If Maledicte lived.

Janus pressed his body against the chaise, clutching those cool, twitching fingers in his own.

THE FLAVOR OF DUST and blood filled her mouth, and a faint tang of oiled steel, as if it had risen through her veins from the wound. Pain radiated out, central, devastating, lethal. Miranda opened her eyes with bleary effort. Dim shadows draped her, and steep walls surrounded her. Too steep to be those of a coffin, and too far away. But Maledicte was dead, she knew that; Janus had done that, chasing even Ani back down into the depths of her body, cowering.

Raising her hand took all her will, and she let it drop on her chest, tangling in the stiff linen stitching at the heart of that pain. The shadows pressed in, and her eyes closed; the room promenaded around her, spinning her in elaborations as fanciful as the dance steps Aris had taught her in the gardens. When she could open her eyes again, the walls had returned to the static stone that they were.

A pallid gleam swam toward her, a square of darkness pivoting to birth a white-shirted figure with gilded hair.

"Don't touch that. It's so close to your heart. I thought I'd lost you."

"Janus—" Miranda breathed his name out on a delicate exhalation. More than the faintest motion of her chest woke wet heat and lung-locking agony.

"Shh." He knelt beside her, took her bandaged hand in his own. It brought a new smell to her senses, the dark scent of turned, wet earth and leaves; it overwhelmed even the blood scent of her skin and the stale exertion of his. Black earth and loam, cold soil from deep beneath the surface where the sun could never reach. Miranda knew the scent, had sniffed it at Vornatti's interment. Janus had been digging graves.

"I had it all planned, Mal. Why did you move? I almost killed you."

Maledicte breathed. Tried to. Forced his mouth into a rictus movement, put his tongue to his teeth, shaped words without breath. "Ani never stops fighting. I couldn't stop fighting. Even you. Thought you meant to kill me."

He let the darkness roll over him, muffling his senses, his fingers numb on his chest, his legs as inert as lead.

"I'd never hurt you." Janus's hand, so hot against his cold flesh, seared him to wakefulness once more.

"Hurts now. . . ."

"I thought She'd heal you faster than this. That it would be a matter of minutes. Not this." Janus dropped his head; his hair trickled muddy water onto the pillow, splashing Maledicte's face, startling him with little bursts of sensation. When Janus raised his head again, Maledicte could see wet tracks coursing through the begrimed skin. Janus fumbled a bottle out of his shirt. "I brought you Laudable. Do you think you can swallow?"

Maledicte said, "Elysia—"

"I haven't any, and with Aris here, I can't send for it. I'm sorry."

Pain swept over him again, stabbing outward, throbbing, setting sweat to slicking his side. "Send Gilly," he said. The threat of continuing torment scared him as nothing else had, save being buried in Stones.

"Shh." Janus helped Maledicte raise his head, lifting gently at his nape. A bare inch from the pillow, the movement contracted tiny muscles along his neck, his rib cage, and Maledicte lost the room to an inner blackness.

"Mal?"

Parting his lips, Maledicte tried to focus. Janus trickled the Laudable in; Maledicte choked, and rolled his head, spilling most of it back out onto the pillow. Rather that than a paroxysm of coughing as it burned down his lungs. Maledicte would rather drown on the syrup than deal with that anticipated agony. A bare taste sank down his throat, scorching it, and spreading a blaze in his chest.

Maledicte breathed. The room throbbed dark and darker. Janus's hands stayed steady at Maledicte's nape. When he could see Janus's face again, Janus spoke. "Another mouthful?"

Maledicte tilted his chin a little higher, waited. "Slower," he breathed, felt the glass lip rest against his tongue, the liquid spreading thinly over his tongue, coating it. Maledicte swallowed, a deeper mouthful this time, managed another, before letting the rest trickle over his cheeks and chin.

The pinpoint heat of candlelight in Miranda's eyes brought her back to awareness. Numbness spread over her body like a shroud, and Janus, bent over her, seemed only a dream. He touched the bandaging on her chest and pain flared anew. He peeled back the bandaging, washed it with spirits and salve. Miranda shuddered, and wondered if time had passed or not. If this were her death, and it would repeat forever, Janus, the wounds, the pain, the words. But the dirt was gone from Janus's face, the hair dried in awkward waves.

"You had to move. I had it all planned, a simple stroke, a clean miss of everything vital, but you had to move. I thought you loved me more than that, Mal. Knew me better than that. You thought I meant you dead. . . .

"I don't know if you'll heal. I don't know if I can save you. . . ." Janus's voice cracked and faded away.

"Love you?" Maledicte said, his breath coming a little easier now. "I do love you, loved you for so long, my Janus. My king. But I don't know that I trust you."

Janus's hands paused in his ministrations. "You can always trust me." The quick heat in his eyes seemed brighter than the candle flames. He smoothed the bandages back down, sealing the wound closed.

The counter to that was on Maledicte's tongue, a single name, Gilly, but he swallowed it instead, let the word nourish him.

"Here," Janus said, bringing the glass back up to his mouth. "Rest."

A faint sound reached Maledicte's ears, and Janus pressed the glass to his chest. "Not a sound." He disappeared back through the door, sealing Maledicte into the shadows again. Gingerly, Maledicte tipped the bottle to his mouth, swallowed several deep drafts, before letting the bottle roll away over the sheets, soaking them.

SHE WOKE AGAIN TO HEAT and fever, stretching walls and stone. Trying to piece together even the simplest things—who was she now? Miranda was dead, had died in the Relicts, and Maledicte had met death on the palace tower. Janus had dug his grave. The wet earth smell lingered in his nose; the sheets were muddied with it where they swept the floor. Blood spattered the floor, his blood, and tear tracks on Janus's face. Maledicte must be dead; his body lay numb and mute, cold as clay. But he could think. . . . A ghost, then. Some pale half-life, not one thing or another, as dusty, as empty as this room. But the fever that burned in him made him feel alive. Death wouldn't hurt so much, surely?

"And yet, no proof either way." Rambling, muttering aloud, the room sent his raspy voice back at him like the skitterings of rats. And yet there were other voices in the air, whispers traveling through the walls, secrets overheard by stone. He got out of the bed, forcing numb legs to react, falling, swooning, stumbling until he leaned against that whispering spot in the wall. Words filtered through, meaningless to the ghost-creature, yet he stored them in his memory just the same.

"Janus, you must tell us where you've buried him. I will not have Auron's murderer lie here. We will find him. Why delay the inevitable?"

Other voices shouted outside, their voices spiraling away in clear air, creeping in through the shielded, narrow slit near the eaves. Maledicte raised his arms, gingerly. . . . Were he a ghost he would fly to that spot, peer down at the scramble of living soldiers, watch them unearth his bones from the raw earth, the spades slicing the soil as his sword had sliced him from the court.

"We've found it, sir." A new voice, closer by, respectful.

Aris sighed. "At last. Bundle it up. Take it to the palace for display."

My body, Maledicte thought, the Laudable's effects fading with the weary pain in Aris's voice, the quiet defeat in Janus's. "You will not allow him to lie here."

"He will not lie anywhere in Antyre," Aris said. "When the birds are done with him, his bones will go to the sea."

Maledicte slid down the door, unable to stand upright, but the shock that ran through him on hitting the floor stabilized reality for him, even as it washed him with waves of breath-stealing discomfort. If he were alive—

The door opened, spilling him at Janus's feet. Janus swore, lifted him into his arms. "Are you mad? That door could have opened at any time with you leaning on it. What a sight for Aris that would have been." He carried him over to the chaise, and with a grimace at the stained sheets, set him down beside it.

"Who was it?" Maledicte asked.

Janus stripped the sheet from the furniture, laid out another with the awkwardness of a man who rarely had to do such things. "Just some boy. He looked enough alike, and four days in the dirt will have helped it along."

"Some innocent who died because he looked like me," Maledicte said.

"Don't—" Janus said. "Gilly was the worst influence on you. Giving you a veneer of morality and conscience. The boy was nothing compared to you.

The moment I saw him, I knew his fate would be to spare you yours." Janus lifted him onto the cushioned seat; Maledicte bit his lip with the pain, and then relaxed into the softness.

Janus smiled at him, "You're doing so much better. For a while there, I thought I'd lost you. That Ani had left you and you were vulnerable."

"Ani," Maledicte said. "No, She's still within." But so small, so hidden; Maledicte had to search for the spark of her presence, that black well of anger buried under the weariness and ache of his bones. "Have you won, then?" he asked, drowsing. "Has Aris forgiven you for loving me? Does he believe you blameless?"

Janus sank down beside him, stroking Maledicte's matted hair. "I am not punished, but neither am I trusted."

Lacking the energy to move his head away from the stroking fingers, Maledicte tried to push him off with words. "You cannot seem to hold trust for long, can you?" The heat in his voice woke answering pain in his chest.

Janus paused in his caresses, then continued. "I'm sorry you doubted me. I'll teach you, and Aris, to trust me again."

"Doesn't matter if I do," Maledicte said. "I am a dead man after all."

"Shh," Janus said, bent close and pressed his mouth to Maledicte's. "All will be well. We'll be where we've always wanted to be. You'll see."

· 44 ·

ALEDICTE WATCHED the blank walls moodily, pacing with his eyes since his body could not. His chest burned, but with the heat of healing wounds instead of outraged flesh. He stared at the window slit, back at the door. It had been silent for hours, or days; he was still not sure how much time had passed, lost in Laudable dreams and delirium.

The blood-heavy scent and the dark tang of deep grave dirt had gone from the room. The linens that draped him carried only the aromas of starch and the iron. A confectioner's assortment lay untouched beside him, one of Janus's attempts to nourish him. Maledicte opened it, but the chocolates only raised memories of drugging Gilly and Lizette's untidy death.

A tray beside the bed was cold, despite the covering cloths, the teapot stained with tannin from the oversteeped leaves. The wine bottle was half full, the Laudable bottle near empty. A hunk of bread, still fresh enough to be tempting, lay beside the pot. He took a bite, though the effort to chew made his body ache. He dropped it back to the plate, and it rolled off, tumbling down a cliff of piled novels.

The whole room maddened him. It was like something out of one of Vornatti's mindless tales, the invalid girl beset by suitors' gifts and doomed to a tragic end.

He shifted gingerly to his side and when the pain, his most faithful attendant, stayed with him but pressed no closer, he foundered to his feet, breath whistling in his throat.

He stumbled the length of the room and rested against the door, seeking the catch. He forced it open with a whimper of exertion, letting himself out into Janus's empty chambers. The room was dark, the curtains drawn over the windows, and the door out of the room, when he tested it, resisted opening. Bending, Maledicte saw the key in the hole and sighed. A caged bird still. But where would he go—when Maledicte had been so well-known?

He made his creeping way to the window, and pulled back the curtains a small inch. Sunlight sloping over the grounds gave him his first solid time— it was early evening, with twilight closing in. A fitting time for a ghost to walk, he thought. Below, he heard carriage wheels on the oyster-shell drive, approaching without haste.

In the gardens, limned by the setting sun, servants' children, dressed neatly in patched hand-me-downs, whispered to each other and then scattered as the carriage swept by. Maledicte watched them race to their respective places, envying them their small freedoms; one boy paused and looked up at him, eyes going wide.

Maledicte dropped the drape and stepped back, heart pounding. But what could the child have seen? Only a shadowy figure in a darkened room.

The key turned behind him, and Maledicte darted for the bed curtains, vision swirling with the sudden effort. He sucked his breath in, fought to stay silent when his body ached. When Janus stepped in, Maledicte released it in a rush.

"Mal—" Janus said, in a startled whisper. "Someone might see you."

"In a locked room?" Maledicte asked, sinking down onto the bed, holding the ache in his chest.

Janus came to him, leaned over, and the chain of roses around his neck slipped free. Maledicte reached out and broke the string, sending petals and leaves over the sheets. "A betrothal charm?"

"I wed Psyke Bellane in three days, by special license and the king's decree," Janus said, biting back a grin. "I presume Aris means to use her as a spy. Poor child, and how like Aris to mistake intelligence for competence."

"You're so clever," Maledicte said, lying back against the mounded pillows, slanting his forearm over his eyes. "I always thought I was the clever one. And yet, you've gotten everything you've wanted. And I—I am a ghost."

"Too much Laudable for you, love," Janus said. "You're quite alive."

Anger, as always, restored his strength and breath. "But mewed up like a corpse. I am not your mistress, your lover, your courtier; I am your secret, kept behind stone walls, hidden from the servants and living on your stealthy leavings.

"Now you're to wed; you'll be off on your wedding tour, and tell me, my love, who will feed me? I am utterly dependent on your goodwill. Will you trust a man with your secret—and such a dangerous, treasonous secret I am—or will I creep like a rat through your home, stealing a loaf of bread here, a sausage there, and hearing the servants quarrel and split blame for their loss?"

"Mal, enough." Janus kissed his mouth, sealed the complaints with his lips.

Maledicte kissed back with teeth and protest, and tore his mouth away when he could, wishing he could stand and storm out.

"Haven't I made that room more a haven than a prison? The finest linens, the finest furniture, the newest books and treats. It won't be forever. Only until they forget."

Maledicte drew himself up, long hair spilling over white flesh, livid scars on cheek and chest, acid in his voice. "Am I so easily forgotten?"

Janus stroked the dark hair back from Maledicte's face, and Maledicte shook his head away, refusing Janus's touch.

"No glib answer for me?" Maledicte said. "I believe your son, should you have one, will still hear my name in whispers. I will be dead in truth long before they forget me. You've seen to that. I am the monster of ballads."

"There will be no wedding tour. Even could I stand to be gone from your side, Aris wants me under his eye. I will bring her here."

"Bring her here . . ." Maledicte echoed. He stood and headed back toward the hidden chamber. "Won't that be pleasant for you, dividing your time between your wife and your dead lover."

He worked the catch just as Janus approached, eyes wary, and had the satisfaction of closing the door in his face. Were Maledicte feeling stronger, he would push the table before the door and let Janus explain the noise away as best he could. As it was, he lay down on the mattress, and stared up at the bare ceiling. His hand shifted against the sheets, questing for a nearly forgotten comfort, and he sat in one quick movement, pain dismissed. Where was it?

Within him, Ani stirred for the first time since the night at the palace, hungry.

He lay back, closed his eyes, and remembered the way the hilt fit his hand, the roughness of the metal feathers caging his fingers, the easy weight of it balanced in his palm, along his arm. Maledicte closed his hand on the cold touch and opened his eyes, rolling to look at the sword. Dark with dirt and blotched with damp, it was as much a revenant as he. Maledicte wiped it off on the linens, leaving rusty trails of old blood and earth, and blew along its length. Where his breath touched, the mottled damp faded to matte black. The raven's eyes gleamed, and he curled himself around it, remembering how it had been. Miranda, under the altar, curled around her pain, and Ani's voice cresting in her mind.

MALEDICTE HEARD UNEASY LAUGHTER in the air, distant but startling in the silent house, and drew himself away from his meal. The elaborate food and spun-sugar decorations had told him what day it was, even without Janus's unusual absence. Now he rose and went to the door, levered the catch open, just enough to release him from his cage. Sword in hand, he stalked through Janus's empty room, and braved the hall.

The door immediately opposite drew him. He had heard the servants moving furniture and gossiping, knew whose room it would be. Maledicte opened the door a bare fraction, giving him a narrow view of the chamber beyond. Janus teased Psyke, soothing her, leading her toward the bed. Psyke's cheeks flushed with wine and nervousness, and Janus paused to kiss the palms of her hands, making her laugh.

Maledicte clenched the hilt of the sword as he watched Janus bed Psyke, enjoying himself, enjoying debauching her, teaching her things she hadn't imagined, until Psyke gasped and laughed and cried out. She kissed Janus's neck, and his eyes, bored, roamed the room, widening as he saw Maledicte. He pressed Psyke's face closer to his shoulder, blocking her view.

Maledicte smiled and reached out with the sword. Not to touch bare flesh, but to push the gilded frame of the marriage portrait from the wall. It crashed to the floor; Maledicte had sealed himself back in the room before Psyke's first shrieks rang out, hiding his own laughter.

WITHIN DAYS, Maledicte found himself glad of the marriage, glad to have something to occupy his time and attention. While it palled, the idea that the terror of the court was reduced to "haunting" a timid girl, it was more satisfying than watching her coo over Janus. Satisfying to wake her in the night by dropping a pillow over her face, touching her with a chilled hand, making her hate Lastrest, making her hate the husband who would not take her back to the city.

"You're driving her mad, Mal." Janus slammed the door back, burst in heedless of noise.

"Careful," Maledicte said. "Do you really want your wife to hear you yelling at a ghost?"

"Why are you doing this? I'm supposed to keep her content. Instead, she's jumping at shadows. Worse, Mal, she's beginning to ask questions. Clever ones. Little Psyke is not as foolish as she appears."

"Why don't you just kill her?" Maledicte said, daring Janus to obey. The flame in Janus's eyes sparked one in his own chest, making his breathing rapid, making the wound sting and pull.

"She is a favorite of the court. She is Aris's pet. I cannot do such a thing."

"Will not. A harmless babe gave you no trouble. Or is it just that you fear you will have no one to blame for her death?" Maledicte grinned.

"Mal! Stop."

Maledicte raised the sword, tested his endurance by taking three quick fencer's steps. The pain tugged his lips back from his teeth; he let the sword tip drop.

"Where did you get that?" Janus said, stepping away.

"It's mine," Maledicte said. "You left it in the dirt."

"It's dangerous, Mal."

"Of course it is. It's a sword. You kill people with it; enemies, babies . . . wives." Maledicte set it down with a sigh. "Unfortunately, I'm not up to strength yet. You'll have to do it yourself."

Janus flinched, and Maledicte said, "Too late to be squeamish, now. Is it fear that binds you? Or is the obstacle something else—do you care for her?"

"You're jealous. . . ."

"No," Maledicte denied, quick and hot, then, "Yes. Of her position, her freedom. And she wastes it, blindly listening to you. She's a dog, not a woman. Obedient but mindless. Should I whisper in her ear at night, tell her what trusting you can lead to?"

"I've given you everything. We have money and power, now. The safety and luxury we've always craved. What more can I do?" Janus's temper sank, left him looking strained and miserable.

Maledicte's breath caught, remembering the boy companion of the Relicts, his lover, his beloved. They had come so far, with nothing but each other. . . . But sentiment was not enough. He steeled himself and said, "I have neither money nor power. I am relegated to being your prisoner. And you say you love me. If you love me—" Maledicte paused, rawness slipping into his throat, making his words more obvious than he meant. "Find Gilly for me. Let him serve me. Be my eyes and ears while you are gone. . . ." Maledicte felt the tears start behind his eyes, blinked them back furiously; Gilly's absence worried at him like the wound, catching him at unexpected moments with pain.

"Gilly's dead," Janus said. The simple words seemed louder in the room than his previous shouting. Maledicte sucked in his breath.

"Think sense, Mal, do you really think Aris would have let him live? Your confidant, your eyes and ears. . . . His skull's up there next to yours."

Maledicte shuttered his face, unwilling to let Janus see how much that hurt, how much he hated him in that moment, for telling him, for taking that last dream. He closed his eyes against tears. "Go away."

"Mal, it's just you and me again. Only each other at the last, remember?" Janus said, reaching out and pulling Maledicte into his arms.

Weak with shock, Maledicte leaned up against Janus, rested his head on his shoulder, let him wrap his arms more securely about him. "But it's not just us," he said in a whisper. "It's you and the court and your wife and your king. I'm nothing now."

"You're everything," Janus said. "Mal, this melancholy is only lingering effects of the Laudable. You've been ill, you've been hurt— I confess, right now I see few paths to your freedom, but I found a way to dispose of Auron; I'll find a way to restore you to court. I depend on you. You'll stand at my side—"

"In your shadow—"

"—ruling Antyre yet, my dark cavalier."

Miranda let Janus press her back against the sheets, touching her gently. He peeled up her gown, kissed the slow-healing scar over her chest. "We'll have you back on your feet, a force in the world again, your blade at my command . . . even if we have to kill everyone who ever laid eyes on you as

Maledicte." He kissed her mouth, and she closed her eyes, listening to his promises, his body moving against hers. She ran her fingers through his silken hair, trying to convince herself that Janus's love, Janus's schemes would be enough. Only each other at the last, she thought, biting her lips. It was everything she had fought for.

· 4 5 ·

GILLY PASSED BY THE PALACE, his collar turned up high around his face. Despite himself he looked up, stared at the sad remnants tattered by wind and rain. He had been there when they were hung; Ma Desire hadn't been able to dose him with Laudable enough to keep him away.

Swaying on his feet, heart numb, Gilly had still found a faint surprise in him as the body was exposed. So ordinary. Just an assembly of ruined flesh and bones, the personality gone with the breath. And yet—some suspicion so small he couldn't name it had surfaced and sunk without ever coming to light. All he knew was that the body displayed was the body of his master, fed on by the rooks and ravens that had once followed him. Outrage had welled in him at that, the anger that Ani allowed Her feathered disciples to feast on one of Her own.

He had picked up stones, intending to knock them away, but Ma Desire had tugged him back to the brothel, kept him there for days, drunk and despairing. Kept him there through the outcry of Mirabile's body being found, kept him there through the state funeral for the infant earl. Gilly couldn't imagine attending anyway, couldn't stomach the idea of seeing Janus standing at the king's side.

"He was a wrong one," Ma Desire said. "You're better off without him."

Gilly had nodded in polite obedience, but inside, he rebelled. The infant—he couldn't imagine Maledicte killing the infant, no matter how hard Ani had ridden him. Especially after his triumph over the shadow boy, his baser self. That quiet belief, bitter in the face of the charges laid to Male-dicte's account, slowly woke Gilly from his stupor. Antyre held nothing for him now, and the *Virga* shipped out soon. He meant to be on it.

It had taken some time, collecting money from the banks, careful in case the Kingsguard sought him. Wasted care, Gilly realized after the first few transactions. He was only a servant, after all, in a city full of servants, invisible.

The wind shifted, bumping the ragged body against the tower with a faint rattling as of wind chimes. Some children shrieked and laughed beside him, jumped to their feet, letting their ropes reach hand to hand.

> "Maledicte lived and Maledicte died
> Only at his birth did anybody cry
> How many people did he kill?"

The young girl tripped on the third skip and they all switched places, started again.

> "Maledicte snooped and Maledicte pried
> Not a soul escaped the notice of his spies
> How many secrets did he buy?"

The boy kept the rope moving so long that Gilly, after the first flinch, tuned them out.

> "Maledicte fought with a blade so black
> Can't be beat with Ani at his back
> How many duels did he win?"

Another girl took over the chanting, her voice as sweet as Mirabile's, as sweet as poison. Gilly watched her skip, her curls flying.

> "Maledicte fled and sought the sky,
> Ended bent and broken, hung on high
> How many times can Maledicte die?
> One!"

She stopped immediately and burst out laughing.

Gilly felt the tears start in his eyes, realized that a guard was looking at the playing children, at his distressed face, and he tugged his coat closer and turned away.

One. Even with Ani's aid, he was only mortal. Gilly made his way down the main street, past Vornatti's town house, still closed and dark, waiting the pleasure of its Itarusine owners. He let himself in, forcing the lock on the kitchen door, and drifted through the empty house, thinking, *Here I told him stories, and made him supper, and here I played the spinet and watched them dance. Here he made me try on all of Vornatti's clothes, for fit. And here, I killed a man for him.*

But the house stayed cold and shadowed, refused to be peopled with his ghosts of memories. He left the door open, walked down to the docks, sat on the quay where he and Maledicte had sat once watching the *Virga* come in. Then he rose, and went to the shipyards to buy his ticket to the Explorations.

He left the harbormaster with his ticket and a tight throat, fighting the urge to return and request a second, pretending just a little longer that Maledicte might be coming with him.

A blue-lacquered carriage passed him by, and he turned to watch it go even as he stepped into a shadowed alcove. Janus, in town? Since the murder, Janus spent all his time at Lastrest, so much so that rumor whispered he'd been banished there. Gilly followed the carriage at a distance, watched Janus hand Psyke down and follow her into the DeGuerres' estate house, smiling.

"Is he visiting?" Gilly asked the driver, stopping to pet the horse's nose.

"He and his wife. Stopping for a fortnight. Though he'll hare off home soon enough. Doesn't like to leave Lastrest, he don't. But she's like all wives, wants the city life, the shops, the culture."

"I see," Gilly said, handing the man a luna. A fortnight. The *Virga* didn't leave for three days. Time enough to go to Lastrest. One final pilgrimage. The place where Maledicte had found rest, even briefly.

When he reined the horse to a halt, he saw children skipping in the courtyard, as they had outside the palace. The children of farmers and house servants took the opportunity of Janus's departure to play over the grounds unhindered.

Gilly caught only a fragment of their skipping song, enough to know it was the same one making the rounds of the city. A housemaid in a starched apron came out and slapped the eldest boy. "You know how Lord Last feels about that one," she said.

"He's not here, is he?" the boy said.

"You'll forget and sing it when he's back and then we'll be out of a job. Mind your tongue." She marched back to the house.

Gilly swung down from the horse; the boy rushed up to hold it. "The master's not here."

"That's all right," Gilly said. "I haven't come to see him."

"You're one of the Kingsguard, aren't you?" the boy asked. "They come every time he leaves, and snoop around. Don't know what you're looking for, do you?"

"No," Gilly said. "Not really." He walked up to the front door, lifted the latch.

"Hey, mister," the boy said. Gilly looked back.

"Watch out for that ghost. It's a mean one. Ripped up the master's room something awful. . . ."

"Just watch my horse," Gilly said. He went inside; with Janus and Psyke gone, the main hall was dark and silent, all the liveliness of the house behind the scenes in the servants' quarters. Gilly drifted up the stairs; the long portrait hall had a new picture now. Janus and his wife, the frame chipped at one edge. Gilly turned his face away, wandered into the study where Maledicte had first shown his talents for petty burglary.

For spite, Gilly palmed a letter opener, and then, reconsidering, put it back. If the servants decided he wasn't a kingsguard, he didn't want to be found a thief, either. He went upstairs along the central hall, and opened a door, one of two master rooms. This was a lady's chamber, Psyke's: fussy, ornate, and boring. He closed the door, opened the opposite door.

"Ripped it up something awful." The relish in the boy's voice came back. Gilly stared. The window glass was cracked, the drapes sagging down in long tatters. The decanters on the dresser had been unstoppered and tipped over, allowed to spill into opened drawers, over clothes and furbelows. A chair, its tufted back sliced open, oozed stuffing. Gilly turned at a whisper of sound, almost expecting to see Maledicte, sitting shamefaced in the midst of his wreckage, tidying after his tantrum.

But it was only the shuff of pale feathers blowing across the floor, tangling in the bed curtains like fish in nets. Gilly pulled back the bed curtains and nearly choked.

The sword. Ani's sword. Gilly found his hands shaking. The sword was driven through the mattress, feathers bleeding out of the ticking, snowing the room.

Janus kept the sword, Gilly thought, aghast. He touched the hilt, and twitched as if a spark had touched his skin. The sword was warm to the touch, and fluttered against his palm. Whispering.

Gilly could almost hear the words. Something of pain, something of loss, of love torn away—if he listened harder, maybe he would hear what had driven Maledicte. If he listened long enough, maybe Ani would hear his pain as well. The cage of the hilt warmed, shifted, making room for his fingers and palm.

Gilly smiled, imagining taking the blade to Janus, destroying the smug, golden monster with a single stroke and erasing the raw burn in his chest that cried protest that Janus survived when Maledicte did not. Slow images trickled behind his closed eyelids, a visual parade of encouragement—Janus, on his knees before him, that gas-flame blue of his eyes dulling, as Gilly pulled the sword back. In a sudden flash, the image forced itself wider, not Ani's doing, but Gilly's own, showing him more—the carcasses strewn behind him, casualties of his quest.

He jerked his hand away, scraping his knuckles and bloodying his hand. He wouldn't share his hate with Ani, or his pain, wouldn't let it twist and distort his mind the way it had Maledicte's.

He licked the blood from his hand, turning around and around in the room, tracking Maledicte's presence. It seemed so strong in the room, a scent, a warmth lingering, here in this place where his sword stood, here where he never was in life. It drove Gilly to melancholy wonderings of Janus haunted as the boy said. Janus deserved it, but Gilly wished—

His horse whickered outside and he fled the room. The boy looked up at his approach. "Did you see the ghost?"

"No," Gilly said. "I saw nothing." He hesitated. The boy holding the horse looked at the other children, a little distance away, and lowered his voice.

"I bet I know what you really want to see."

"What is that?" Gilly said.

"Where they dug up the murderer. I'll show you for two lunas."

Gilly closed his eyes. Did he want to see that? The pain in his heart said finish it, see it all, and go. But touching the sword woke an anger in him, raising the numb curtain he had been living behind. He wanted to leave a mark here, something to hurt and sting, a last message to Janus.

"One luna," Gilly said, reminded of haggling with Maledicte. "And another verse to your skipping song."

The children stepped closer. "You know the song?"

"All the verses by heart," Gilly said. "Including the real end one."

"What is it?" the boy said. "If it's good, I'll show you the grave."

The girls lowered the rope, started it spinning. A small boy jumped into it, and Gilly spoke his lines.

"Maledicte loved and so Maledicte died.
He never saw the truth behind his lover's lies.
How many lies can blue eyes hide?
One, two, three—"

The children picked it up, chanting it, skipping its measures into their memories. It would pass on, Gilly knew, from one voice to the next. Even the palace wouldn't be exempt. Faintly, Gilly smiled.

The boy holding the horse's reins watched the skipping with a thoughtful gaze. "But what does it mean?"

"It means there are two sides to every story. Even this one," Gilly said. "Show me the grave?"

The boy tied the horse to the gatepost, beckoned Gilly into the shadows. The site was not too far from the curve of the drive, within a stand of trees, and within sight of Janus's bedchamber window. Gilly drew his lips down. Even dead, Janus didn't want Maledicte out of his sight. A stone marker lay there, left in the dirt. The boy went as far as the shadow of the trees, then balked, obviously afraid to go closer. Gilly went the rest of the way alone.

Gilly touched the stone. It was plain basalt with only a name carved into it, and some wearing of the stone that looked like feathering. "I wish you were coming with me, instead of your memory," he said, voice rough. "I always hoped you would." It wasn't enough; like an altar, the gravestone expected offerings.

Fumbling in his pockets, Gilly found the receipt for his berth on the

Virga, and a stub of a pencil. He hesitated, then put the words to paper that he had never been given a chance to say. He folded the parchment and put it at the base of the marker, weighing it with a rock.

The horse, restless, pawed at the ground. Behind him, the children sang the song again, starting at the beginning. Gilly looked over and up; he caught a faint movement in the window of the bedchamber. If he pretended, it could have been a dark-eyed, pale face, but the thought of Maledicte linked to Janus even in death was bitter, and he looked away. He unfastened the horse's reins, and swung into the saddle, left the children practicing their song with careful volume, wary of adult chastisement.

GILLY RETURNED THE HORSE TO the tavernkeeper, and asked when the next coach to the city was coming through. When the answer was dawn, he chose not to take a room, not wanting to be alone. He sat in the main tavern room until the hour grew late, and then settled himself on the bench outside, sleeping among the others too poor to take a room, or too thrifty.

When he woke to the sound of the team's hooves, his coat was wet with morning dew, and stiff with chill. He stretched, watching his fellow passengers loom out of the morning dimness. They gathered slowly, drawn from inside the inn and from the nearby fields by the music made in the jingling harnesses and stamping hooves. The coachman and his assistants unharnessed the first team, changing horses for the trip to the city. The youngest assistant crept inside. Gilly saw him coaxing bread from the innkeeper and returned his attention to the coach, looking toward the future, and not the past.

A young family waited, one whining child shifting from foot to foot until his mother picked him up and held him. A young man, either tutor or clerk, stood stiff and self-conscious in a shiny new coat. Two young men waited, dressed like the nobility, and muttering about the cost of the coach. Gilly surmised a country romp, maybe a gaming hell, and their pocket money all but gone. They'd learn better, or not; Gilly couldn't find it in him to care.

A girl in a much-turned dress of bottle green, clutching a case to her side, waited near the door of the tavern, visibly nervous; her chaperone, an old woman, glared at Gilly and he looked away. The last to take shape was a maid in a heavy dark dress, coming slowly down the tree-lined path. The shadows clutched at her, only resentfully relinquishing her to the thin morning sunlight.

Her thick wool dress was too big for her; she seemed bent under it. Her face was obscured by an ugly bonnet, years out of fashion, and her dark hair spilled dully from behind it. She held herself with the fragile rigidity of sickness or hurt. Consumption, Gilly thought, or simple hunger, maybe a beating— He wondered what her story was, whether she was waiting for someone to arrive, or going somewhere, and if she would be welcome when she got there. He welcomed the curiosity, indulged it, knowing it heralded healing, to feel interest beyond the scope of pain, love, and vengeance.

Gilly was the last to get on the coach, still studying his enigma, wishing he could see her face, know if she were young or old, worn or serene. All his conclusions could be dismissed with the face. He left the little mystery with reluctance and climbed the steps into the coach. When he looked back, he saw her approach, a passenger after all. From his height he saw only the top of her bonnet. She paused at the step, and held up a thin, sinewy hand.

A faint whisper, like a voice from a dream. "Help me up, Gilly." She tilted her face to his. So thin, so pale, the scar white as bone, her eyes dark as the grave.

Is this what Janus felt, Gilly wondered, *that first night at the solstice ball?* This heart-racing immobility? This disbelief, this impossible joy?

Wordless, he stretched out his hand, jolted when her hand in his was real, and not some product of his grieving heart. She climbed up beside him, her weight mostly in his hands, managing her skirts with visible impatience. She folded herself into the space beside Gilly with a gasp and a wince. He found his voice, breathless but audible. "Mal—"

Her raised hand cut him off. The horses started, and, flinching, she rocked with their movement. He slipped off his coat and tucked it behind her back, trying to cushion her body. Run through, they'd said. Through the heart.

"What's your name?" Gilly asked, the question of years ago, new again.

"Can't you guess?" The rasping voice was an anomaly in the maid's throat. Her lips quirked downward.

Gilly shook his head. He couldn't put two rumors together at this moment. She only smiled at him, and he found he had an answer after all, a collection of pieces belatedly put together. "Miranda," he said.

"Miranda," she agreed. She wove her fingers into his, sat upright, with only that tenuous connection between them.

Gilly could only stare, wondering at his blindness all these years. It was as if a painting had been blurred and out of focus, and he had finally found his spectacles. After a cautious glance at the other passengers, she said, "I own I am surprised to find you live and hale. I had heard otherwise."

"Your surprise is nothing to mine, I assure you," Gilly said, smiling like an idiot. It hadn't been a ghost after all, peering down at him, but flesh and blood. "But how?"

"It wasn't complete," she said. "Ani would not loose me, not while my vengeance lay undone. And Janus made it impossible."

"The babe?" Gilly said, his voice a whisper. The coach seemed full of prying ears, and his happiness felt fragile.

"Not by my hand," she said.

Gilly brought her fingers to his mouth, kissed them, studied the veins standing out in such relief. "You're so thin," he said.

"I need looking after," Miranda said. "I admit as much. Maybe I can find someone to do so." She curved her mouth in a way that made him want to laugh. So falsely demure.

"Where are you journeying, Miranda?" Gilly asked, teasing in return. "Only the city? Or farther still—" The question, asked in amusement, ended in uncertainty. He was afraid to hope, though sense told him otherwise.

"I thought to seek the Explorations," she said. "I want to see some savages. Did you know they wear feathers instead of leather?"

"I told you that," he said.

"Ah, that's why I believe it then, but Gilly, I hope you have money. The pawnbrokers took ruthless advantage of me; I wasn't in any fit mood for haggling. All I've got are the clothes on my back, and I'd rather not have them."

"Anything you want. Just tell me, will it be breeches or skirts?"

"Skirts until we reach the Explorations. I cannot chance recognition. After that," she said, smiling up at Gilly, "breeches, I think. I had forgotten how unwieldy these things can be."

Gilly's smile grew wider as another thought touched his giddy mind. "Ship captains are notoriously choosy about female passengers. Shall I claim you as sister—?"

Miranda smiled back. "I think not. Perhaps you'd best reassure the captain. Prevail on him to marry us. What's more common than that? A wedded pair seeking a new life in a new land."

"I will speak to the captain as soon as we step aboard," Gilly vowed, laughing. Then he sobered. A question burned in his mind, one he was loath to ask, loath even to mention. But it had to be asked. "What about Janus?"

"Janus—" She turned her head as if she could see her past behind her along the road. "He was taken from me and I fought to reclaim him. I would have died for him without hesitation, were it not that he was not as I remembered. Were it not for my vow. Ani knows, Ani told me, but I didn't want to listen. Where there's love, there must be vengeance. But I'm done with vengeance now."

"You sated Ani?" Gilly asked.

"Ani cannot be sated. I will bear Her company for the rest of my life. Janus, clever creature that he is, saw to that. I cannot wreak vengeance on the one I vowed to love. On the one I vowed to hate, when they are one and the same. Still," Miranda said, sighing, "I can leave him, and find some small measure of satisfaction there. But be warned, you take a perilous creature to wife. . . ."

"I'd have no other kind," Gilly said. He kissed her closed eyes, tasting salt in the soft tangles of her lashes, and dreamed of the sea waves ahead of them.

About the Author

LANE ROBINS was born in Miami, Florida, the daughter of two scientists, and grew up as the first human member of their menagerie. When it came time for a career, it was a hard choice between veterinarian and writer. It turned out to be far more fun to write about blood than to work with it. She received her B.A. in Creative Writing from Beloit College, and currently lives in Lawrence, Kansas.

About the Type

Jenson is one of the earliest print typefaces. After hearing of the invention of printing in 1458, Charles VII of France sent coin engraver Nicolas Jenson to study this new art. Not long after, Jenson started a new career in Venice in letter-founding and printing. In 1471, Jenson was the first to present the form and proportion of this roman font that bears his name.

More than five centuries later, Robert Slimbach, developing fonts for the Adobe Originals program, created Adobe Jenson based on Nicolas Jenson's Venetian Renaissance typeface. It is a dignified font with graceful and balanced strokes.